About th

Maureen Child is the autho novels and novellas that routinely appear on bestseller lists and have won numerous awards, including the National Reader's Choice Award. A seven-time nominee for the prestigious *RITA®* award from Romance Writers of America, one of her books was made into a CBS-TV movie called *The Soul Collector.* Maureen recently moved from California to the mountains of Utah and is trying to get used to snow.

Essence bestselling author **Donna Hill** began her career in 1987 with short stories and her first novel was published in 1990. She now has more than seventy published titles to her credit, and three of her novels have been adapted for television. Donna has been featured in *Essence, the New York Daily News, USA Today, Black Enterprise* and other publications. Donna lives in Brooklyn, NY with her family.

Kate Hardy has been a bookworm since she was a toddler. When she isn't writing, Kate enjoys reading, theatre, live music, ballet and the gym. She lives with her husband, student children and their spaniel in Norwich, England. You can contact her via her website: katehardy.com

Once Upon a Time

June 2023
Beauty

July 2023
The Beast

August 2023
Cinderella

September 2023
A Perfect Fit

January 2024
Charmed

February 2024
Heartbreaker

Once Upon a Time:
Cinderella

MAUREEN CHILD

DONNA HILL

KATE HARDY

MILLS & BOON

First Published in Great Britain 2023
by Mills & Boon, an imprint of HarperCollins*Publishers* Ltd,
1 London Bridge Street, London, SE1 9GF

www.harpercollins.co.uk

HarperCollins*Publishers*
Macken House, 39/40 Mayor Street Upper,
Dublin 1, D01 C9W8, Ireland

Once Upon a Time: Cinderella © 2023 Harlequin Enterprises ULC.

The Lone Star Cinderella © 2013 Harlequin Enterprises ULC.
The Way You Love Me © 2015 Donna Hill
Dr Cinderella's Midnight Fling © 2012 Pamela Brooks

Special thanks and acknowledgement to Maureen Child for her contribution to
Texas Cattleman's Club: The Missing Mogul series.

ISBN: 978-0-263-31964-4

This book is produced from independently certified FSC™ paper
to ensure responsible forest management.

For more information visit: www.harpercollins.co.uk/green

Printed and Bound in the UK using 100% Renewable Electricity
at CPI Group (UK) Ltd, Croydon, CR0 4YY

THE LONE STAR CINDERELLA

MAUREEN CHILD

To Kate Carlisle and Jennifer Apodaca – great friends
and wonderful writers who helped keep me sane
during the writing of this book!

One

Dave Firestone was a man on a mission.

The future of his ranch was at stake and damned if he was going to let scandal or whispered rumors ruin what he'd spent years building. It had been months now since Alex Santiago had disappeared and Dave *still* felt a cloud of suspicion hanging around his head. Time to find out one way or the other what the law in town thought of the situation.

He climbed out of his 4x4, tugged the collar of his brown leather jacket up around his neck and squinted into the East Texas wind. October was rolling in cold, signaling what would be an even colder winter. Nothing he could do about that, but Dave had driven to the border of his ranch to get at least one part of his life straightened out.

A tall man wearing a worn, black leather coat and a tan, wide-brimmed hat was patching the barbed-wire fence that separated Dave's ranch, the Royal Round Up, from the neighboring ranch, the Battlelands. Behind the man in black, another man, Bill Hardesty, a Battle ranch hand, unloaded wire from a battered truck. Dave nodded a greeting to Bill, then focused his attention on Nathan Battle.

Nathan looked up as Dave approached. "Hey, Dave, how's it going?"

"Going fine," he said, because Dave Firestone never admitted to having a problem he couldn't solve. "I went by the main ranch house and Jake told me where I could find you. Didn't think I'd find the town sheriff out fixing fence line."

Nathan shrugged and glanced out over the surrounding land before shifting his gaze back to Dave. "I like getting out on the ranch. Gives me a chance to think. Clear my head. My brother does most of the heavy lifting on the Battlelands, but I'm a full partner and it feels good to get back to basics, you know?" Then he grinned. "Besides, Amanda's on a remodeling binge, getting ready for the baby. So we've got one of Sam Gordon's construction crews at the house all the time. Being out here..." he said, then sighed in pleasure. "Quiet."

From his spot on the truck, Bill snorted. "Enjoy it while it lasts, boss. Once that baby comes you can kiss 'quiet' goodbye forever."

Nathan chuckled, then said, "Just unload the wire, will ya?"

Dave ignored the byplay. He wished he'd found Nathan alone out here, but he was going to have his say whether Bill was listening in or not.

Things had changed a lot around Royal in the past few months, Dave thought. Nathan and Amanda were married and expecting a baby. Sam and Lila were expecting twins. And then there was the reason Dave had come to see Nathan on his day off.

The disappearance of Alex Santiago.

He wouldn't claim to have been friends with Alex, but he'd never wished the man harm, either. This vanishing act of his was weird enough to keep the people in town talking—and most of them were talking about how Dave and Alex had been business rivals and wondering if maybe Alex hadn't had some help in disappearing.

Dave had never been one to give a flying damn what people had to say about him. He ran his life and his business the way he saw fit, and if people didn't like it, screw them. But like he'd just been thinking, things had changed. Irritating to admit that gossip and the threat of scandal had chased him out here to talk to the town sheriff, but there it was.

"Yeah, I get that. My foreman's the best there is, but I like doing ranch work on my own, too. Always have," Dave said, snatching his hat off to stab his fingers through his hair. "And I hate to ruin your peace and quiet…"

Nathan hooked his pair of wire cutters into the tool belt at his waist and looked at Dave. "But?"

"But," Dave said, with the briefest of glances toward Bill, who wasn't even bothering to hide his interest in the conversation, "I need to know if you've got anything new on Alex's disappearance."

Scowling, Nathan admitted, "I've got nothing. It's like he dropped off the face of the earth. No action on his credit or debit cards, either. Haven't got a clue what happened to him and, to tell you the truth, it's making me nuts."

"I can imagine," Dave said and tipped the brim of his hat back a bit. "It's not doing much for me, either."

Nathan nodded grimly. "Yeah, I've heard the whispers."

"Great." Just what he wanted. The town sheriff listening to rumors about him.

"Relax." Nathan waved one hand at him and shook his head. "I know what the gossips in this town are like, Dave. Hell, they almost cost me Amanda." He paused for a second as if considering what might have been. Then he shook his head again and said, "If it helps any, you're officially *not* a suspect."

He hadn't really thought he was, but it was good to hear anyway. It didn't solve his problem, but knowing that Nathan believed in his innocence was one less thing to worry about. Dave knew how it must have looked to everyone in town. He was among the last people to have seen Alex before he went missing. And the argument they'd had on Main Street had been witnessed by at least a dozen people.

Plus, it was pretty much common knowledge around Royal that Alex had snapped up the investment property that Dave had had his eye on. So yeah, Dave had been furious. But he hadn't wanted anything to happen to Alex.

"Glad to hear you say that," Dave finally said. "In fact, it's what I came out here to ask you. Feels good knowing I'm not a suspect, I'll admit. But it doesn't change how people in this town are looking at me."

He'd been in Royal three years, and he would have thought people would know him by now. But apparently, one whisper of juicy gossip was all it took to have people looking at him with a jaundiced eye.

Nathan dropped one hand to the top of the fence post and said, "People talk, you can't stop it. God knows I've tried. And in a town the size of Royal, that's about all they've got to do to fill the time, you know? Doesn't mean anything."

"Not to you, maybe—and I'm grateful, don't get me wrong," Dave told him. "But I'm trying to land a contract with TexCat and—"

Nathan chuckled and stopped him. "No need to say more. Hell, Texas Cattle is legendary. Everyone in the state knows about Thomas Buckley and how he runs his company. The old man is such a straight arrow…" He broke off. "That's why the concern over the gossip."

"Yeah, if Buckley hears those rumors, I'll never get the contract with him to sell my beef." Scandal could sour the deal before it was made, and damned if Dave would let that happen.

TexCat was the biggest beef buyer in the country. But it was a family-run company and Buckley himself ran it along the narrowest lines possible. No scandal had ever touched his company, and he was determined to keep it that way. So if he got wind of rumors about Dave now, it would only make all of this more difficult.

"Ol' Buckley is so worried about what people think," Bill pointed out from his spot on the truck, "I hear he *sleeps* in a three-piece suit."

Dave frowned and Nathan shot Bill a look. "Is that wire unloaded?"

"Almost," Bill said and ducked his head as he went back to work.

"Sorry," Nathan said unnecessarily, then grinned. "Everybody's got something to say about everything around here. But you already know that, don't you?"

"You could say so," Dave muttered.

Still smiling, Nathan added, "Where Buckley's concerned, it's not just the rumors you've got to be worried about."

Dave frowned. "Yeah, I know."

Nathan's smile widened. "Buckley only deals with married family men. Last time I looked, you were single. I figure the rumors and whispering should be the least of your problems. How're you planning on coming up with a wife?"

Dave huffed out a disgusted breath. "Haven't figured that part out yet. We're just at the beginning of negotiations with TexCat. I've still got some time." He jammed his hat back on his head and hunched deeper into his jacket as a sharp, cold wind slapped at them. "I'll think of something."

Nathan nodded. "If not, TexCat isn't the only beef buyer in the world."

"No," Dave agreed. "But they're the best."

He wanted that contract. And what Dave Firestone wanted, he got. Period. He'd clawed and fought and earned his success the hard way. Not a chance in hell he'd stop before he was finished.

Mia Hughes opened the pantry door and stared inside at the nearly empty shelves as if expecting more food to suddenly appear. Naturally, that didn't happen. So, with a sigh, she grabbed another package of Top Ramen and headed for the stove.

"Honestly, if I have to eat noodles much longer..." She filled a pan with a cup of water, turned on the fire underneath and watched it, waiting for it to boil. She glanced at the package in her hand. "At least this one is beef flavor. Maybe if I close my eyes while I eat it I can pretend it's a burger."

Well, that image made her stomach growl. She slapped one hand to her belly as if to appease it somehow. It didn't work. She was on the ragged edge and had been for a few weeks now.

As Alex Santiago's housekeeper, she'd had access to the household account at the bank. But she'd been using that money to pay utility bills and the hundreds of other things that had come up since Alex had disappeared. She hadn't had any extra to waste on trivial things like her salary or *food*. So she'd made do with the staples that had been in the pantry and freezer. But the cupboards were practically bare now and only ice cubes were left in the freezer. And it wasn't as if she had money coming in. Even her intern position at Royal Junior High was ending soon. She couldn't go out and get a job, either. What if Alex called the house while she was gone?

"Of course," she reassured herself aloud, "the upside is you've lost five pounds in the past couple of weeks. Downside? I'm ready to chew on a table leg."

Her voice echoed in the cavernous kitchen. The room was spotless, but that was due more to the fact that it hadn't seen much action in the past few months than to Mia's cleaning abilities. Though she took her duties as housekeeper seriously and kept the palatial mansion sparkling throughout. Still, since Alex went missing a few months ago, there hadn't been much for Mia to do in the big house.

The water came to a boil and she stirred in the dried noodles and flavor packet before putting the lid on the pan again then moving it off the heat to steep. While she waited for her lunch, she wandered to the wide windows overlooking the stone patio and the backyard beyond.

From this vantage point, she could also see the rooflines of Alex's neighbors, though the homes in the luxurious subdivision known as Pine Valley weren't crowded together. Each home was different, custom designed and built by the owners, and each sat on a wide, wooded lot so there was plenty of privacy.

Right now though, Mia had too much privacy. She'd been alone in the house since Alex's disappearance. Alone with a phone that hadn't stopped ringing in weeks. Reporters hounded her anytime she left the house, so she rarely left anymore. Since Pine Valley was a gated community, only a few reporters had managed to sneak past the gate guard to annoy her. But she knew that wouldn't last. The longer Alex was gone, the more brazen reporters would become.

A wealthy man going missing was big news. Especially in a town the size of Royal.

She tapped her short, neat fingernails against the cold, smooth, black granite countertop. Mia's stomach did a slow turn and she swallowed hard. Alex had been good to her. He'd given her a job when she'd most needed one. He'd allowed her the space to continue her education and because of that, she was close to getting her counseling degree.

Not only did Mia really owe Alex, she liked him, too. He'd become a good friend as well as her employer, and Mia didn't have many friends. She stared blankly out the window and absently noted the treetops whipping in the cold October wind. She shivered involuntarily and turned her back on the view. She didn't want to think about winter coming and Alex still being gone. She hated not knowing if her friend was safe. Or hurt. But she had to keep positive and believe that Alex would come home.

She also couldn't help worrying about what she was going to do next. The bills had been paid, true. But her tuition was due soon and if Alex wasn't there to pay her...

When the phone rang, she jumped and instinctively reached for it before stopping herself and letting it go to the answering machine. Weeks ago, she'd decided to let the machine pick up so she could screen her calls, in an attempt to avoid reporters and the unceasing questions she couldn't answer.

Still, she was always hoping that somehow the caller might be Alex, telling her he was fine, and sorry he'd worried her and oh, that he was wiring more money into the household accounts. Not very realistic, but Mia's innate optimism was hard to discourage.

The machine kicked on and after the beep, a female voice asked, "Mia? You there? If you're listening, pick up."

Smiling, she snatched up the receiver. "Sophie, hi."

"Still dodging reporters?"

"Every day," she said and leaned back against the counter. Her gaze slid to the backyard again and the trees waving and dancing in the wind. "They don't give up."

"At least they can't get past the gate guard there to bother you in person."

"A few of them have managed, but one call to security and that's taken care of." Though she hated feeling as though she was living through a medieval siege. And she had to admit that living alone in this big house made her a little nervous at night. Yes, Royal was a safe place, and a gated community should have made her feel even more secure. But with Alex gone and the world wondering *why,* Mia was always worried that someone might come sneaking around the house at night, looking for clues or a story. But Mia didn't want her thoughts to go to the dark side. Alex was missing, yes. But she couldn't allow herself to think he was gone forever.

"My offer to come and stay with me for a while still holds, you know."

Sophie Beldon was a good friend. She was also Alex's

assistant, and since his disappearance, the two women had become even closer friends. Together, they'd done all they could to search for Alex, and still had come up empty. But they had another plan now. One that had Mia looking for more information on Dave Firestone, a business rival of Alex's. Of course, she hadn't actually *started* on that plan yet, since she had no idea how to go about it.

"Really, thank you. It's tempting, believe me," Mia confessed. But she couldn't very well move in with her friend and leave Alex's house unguarded. Not to mention that Mia hated the idea of mooching meals from Sophie. She didn't like asking people for anything. She was far too used to doing things herself and she didn't see that changing anytime soon. "It's really nice of you to offer, Sophie. But I really want to be here. In case Alex calls or comes back. Besides, I wouldn't feel right leaving his house vacant."

"Okay. I can understand all of that," Sophie said. "But if you change your mind, the offer stands. So how's everything else going? Is there anything I can do?"

"No, but thanks." Mia cringed a little, hating that her friend knew just how bad off Mia was. The two of them had gone out to lunch just a couple weeks ago and when she'd tried to pay the bill, as a thank-you to Sophie for being so nice, Mia's debit card had been denied. Her bank account hadn't had enough in it to pay for a simple *lunch*. Mortified, Mia had been forced to let Sophie pay for their meals.

She hated this. Hated worrying about money. Hated worrying about Alex. She just wanted her nice, safe, comfortable life back. Was that really so much to ask?

"We're friends, Mia." Sophie's voice was soft and low. "I know you need money. Why won't you let me help you out temporarily? It would just be a loan. When Alex comes home, you can pay me back."

Again, so very tempting. But she didn't know how or when she could pay her friend back, so she couldn't accept the loan. Mia Hughes paid her own way. Always. Heck, she didn't even have a credit card because she paid cash or she didn't buy.

"Sophie," she said on a sigh, "I *really* appreciate the offer. But we've been looking for Alex for months and it's like he vanished off the face of the earth. We don't know when he'll come back." *If ever,* her mind added, but she didn't say it aloud, not wanting to tempt whatever gods might be listening in on them. "I'm fine. Honest. The thing with my debit card was just a bank mistake." Okay, a small lie, but one she would cling to. She didn't want her friend worried about her and she simply could not accept a loan. Mia had been making her own way in the world since she was eighteen, and she wouldn't start looking for handouts now. No matter how hungry she was.

"You have the hardest head," Sophie murmured.

Mia smiled. "Thank you."

"Wasn't a compliment," her friend assured her on a laugh. "But okay. I'll let it go. For *now.*"

"I appreciate it."

"That's not why I called, anyway," Sophie said.

Instantly, Mia's friend radar started humming. Sophie had only recently become engaged to Zach Lassiter, Alex's business partner. After a shaky start, the two were so happy together, Mia was afraid that something had gone wrong between them. "Are you and Zach okay?"

"We're fine. He's great. This isn't about us."

"Okay, then," Mia said as she carried the phone across the kitchen, lifted the lid on her lunch and sighed before setting the lid back in place. "What is it about?"

"Remember how we talked about you going out to gather more information on Dave Firestone?"

"Yeah," Mia said. "I don't have anything yet, though. I'm not exactly a private investigator." She'd tried internet searches, but so far all she had found were the sanitized information blurbs you found about *any* wealthy, successful man. And she wasn't sure where to dig up anything else.

"Well," Sophie told her, "I have something. I just got off the phone with Carrie Hardesty."

Mia frowned, trying to place the name. Before she could say she didn't know the woman, Sophie was continuing.

"Carrie's husband, Bill, is a ranch hand on the Battlelands."

"Uh-huh." She still didn't see what this had to do with her or Dave Firestone or why she might be interested. And now she was hungry enough that she was even anxious for her beef-flavored noodle lunch.

"So Bill called Carrie to tell her he'd be home early today because he and Nathan had finished work faster than they'd thought despite an interruption."

"Okay…" Mia had to smile. She still had no idea why this should interest her, but Sophie's voice had taken on that storytelling tone, so she didn't stop her.

"Bill told Carrie that Dave Firestone had shown up to talk to Nathan."

Mia stiffened. Dave had been one of the last people to see her employer before he disappeared. She'd heard the talk around town. She knew that people were wondering if Dave had had something to do with Alex going missing. But she also knew that gossip was the fuel that kept small towns going, so she didn't really put a lot of stock in it.

Still, though, Dave Firestone was wealthy, determined

and too gorgeous to be trusted. Plus, she and Sophie had decided to check the man out.

"What was he talking to Nathan about?"

"Apparently, he went there to find out if he was a suspect in Alex's disappearance."

Mia sucked in a gulp of air. "He did?"

"Yep," Sophie said, then added, "but Bill says Nathan assured Dave that he was officially *not* a suspect."

Disappointment curled in the pit of her stomach. Not that she wished Dave Firestone arrested or anything, but she wanted answers. Soon.

"It's not surprising," Mia said, chewing at her bottom lip. "Dave Firestone is an important man around here. There would have to be *serious* evidence against him for Nathan to keep him as a suspect."

"I know." Sophie sounded as dejected as Mia felt.

"Tell the truth, Soph," Mia said. "Do you really think Dave is involved in Alex's disappearance?"

"Probably not." Her friend sighed.

"Me, either," Mia agreed.

"But he's the only link we have, Mia. I think we should stick to our plan and you should find out anything you can about him. Even if Dave is innocent, he might still know something that he doesn't even know he knows, you know?"

Mia laughed a little. "Sadly, I understood that completely."

Sophie added, "And according to what Bill told Carrie, Nathan admitted that he doesn't have a clue what happened to Alex."

Her heart sank a little further at that news. Of course, she'd thought as much. Nathan Battle had been working this case for months and he'd kept her apprised of his lack of progress. The sheriff and Alex were good friends, so

Mia knew that Nathan was just as much personally involved in the search as he was professionally.

And none of that had helped them find Alex.

In the time Mia had worked for Alex Santiago, she'd known him to be warm, generous and kind. But he also had secrets. No one was allowed in his home office, for example. He had only allowed Mia in to clean once a month and then only if he was present. And when she and Sophie had started comparing notes, Sophie had told her about the secret phone calls Alex had been getting.

Since Alex had been gone, Mia had searched his home office top to bottom and Sophie had gone through his emails and phone records, but they hadn't discovered a thing.

Which told her that either Alex had taken whatever he'd been safeguarding with him—or whoever had taken Alex had also gone through that office and taken what they'd found.

There was that now familiar twist of worry inside. Where was Alex? Was he hurt? Was he...

"He'll show up," Mia said, cutting short a disturbing train of thought. "There's a reasonable explanation for all of this and when Alex comes back, it will all make sense."

"You really believe that, don't you?"

"Absolutely." *Almost,* she added silently. But Mia had spent so much of her life searching for the silver lining in dark skies that it was instinctive now. She wouldn't give up on Alex and, until he was home, she would do whatever she could to help find him.

Even if it meant eating enough flavored noodles to sink a battleship.

"Oops," Sophie said suddenly, "Zach's at the door. He's taking me to lunch at the diner. I'll talk to you later, okay?"

Mia said goodbye, wishing she were at the diner right now, too. What she wouldn't give for a hamburger, fries and a shake. Sighing, she let the wish go and dumped her noodles into a bowl. Grabbing a fork, she took a bite and tried to swallow her disappointment along with the noodles.

A knock sounded at the front door and Mia took it as a reprieve from her boring lunch. She set the bowl down on the counter and headed through the house. Whoever it was knocked again, faster and louder this time, and she frowned. Did another reporter get past the gate?

At the doorway, she glanced through the glass panes on one side of the heavy door and gaped at the man standing on the porch. Before she could think about it, she yanked the door open and faced Dave Firestone.

He wore black jeans, a dark red collared shirt, a battered brown bomber jacket and scarred boots. He held his hat in one fist, and his dark blond hair ruffled in the wind. His gray eyes locked onto her and Mia felt a jolt of something unexpected sizzle inside her.

"Mia," he said, his voice deep enough to rumble along her spine, "I think we should talk."

Two

"What're you doing here?"

Dave took a good long look at the woman standing there glaring at him. Her long, dark brown hair was, as usual, pulled back from her face and twisted into a messy knot at the back of her neck. She wore faded blue jeans and a long-sleeved, navy blue T-shirt. Her feet were bare and he was surprised to see her toes were painted fire-engine red. Mia Hughes had never seemed like the red nail polish type to him. She was more of a pastel woman, seemingly determined to fade into the background. Or so he'd thought.

Something inside him stirred whether he'd wanted it to or not. He lifted his gaze to hers and the strength of her even stare punched out at him. Her wide blue eyes were unenhanced, yet they still seemed to captivate him.

He didn't want to be captivated.

"I think we should talk. About Alex."

"How did you get in here? The gate guard should have called me."

"I asked him not to." He shrugged. "He knows me, so it wasn't a problem."

"Well, it should have been. He never should have let you in here without contacting me." She folded her arms across her chest.

Dave scowled. He wasn't used to being kept cooling his heels outside. But Mia Hughes was guarding Alex Santiago's front door like a trained pit bull. "I think it'd be better if we went inside to talk."

"First, tell me what this is about." She cocked her head and the toes of one foot began to tap impatiently.

"I'm not your enemy." He took a step closer and noticed that she didn't move back but held her ground. He could admire that even as she frustrated him.

He'd come here to compare notes. To see if she knew anything that might shed a light on Alex's disappearance. But damned if he was going to have this conversation on the porch.

"No," she conceded. "You're not." Her stance relaxed just a fraction. "And I was going to call you later anyway…"

"Is that right?" Surprised, he took another slow look at her and he noted that her eyes were gleaming with something he could only call interest. "About what?"

"About Alex, of course," she told him with a shake of her head.

"Well, it's good that I showed up today, isn't it? Because that's just what I want to talk to you about." He glanced over his shoulder at the empty, meticulously kept grounds before looking back at her. "I want to know if there's anything you know about Alex that you haven't told Nathan Battle."

"Of course there isn't," she said, clearly insulted. "Do you really think I haven't been helping the police? I've done everything I can think of to find Alex."

"That's not what I meant," he said, cutting her off before she could erupt into a full-on rant. Hell, Mia Hughes was usually so quiet he hardly noticed her. But apparently on her own turf she wasn't so reticent.

"It better not be," she countered, and those blue eyes of hers flashed dangerously.

"Look, you don't have to be so defensive. Alex and I weren't exactly friends…"

She laughed shortly.

He frowned and continued, "But that doesn't mean I wish him harm. Hell, right now I want to find him more than anybody in this town."

A second or two passed in tense silence before she sighed and her stance relaxed. "Okay, I can understand that."

"Thanks," he muttered. "So can I come in and talk to you about this now?"

"I guess—" She stopped, looked over his shoulder at the yard and said, "Don't!"

Instantly on alert, Dave whirled around and saw a young man, somewhere in his early twenties, aiming a digital camera at them and clicking away.

"Hey," Dave said, stepping off the porch toward the man.

The guy jumped backward, shaking his head and grinning. He held out a digital recorder and shouted, "Great pictures! Chester Devon from All The News blog. Care to comment?"

"The only comment I have is one you can't print, Chester," Dave told him as he stalked toward the reporter, who had somehow slipped past the Pine Valley gate guard. "And no pictures, either."

"Free country, man," Chester countered, still grinning. "I think my readers will be interested to see Santiago's housekeeper and a suspect in his disappearance looking so cozy…"

His readers, Dave thought. All ten of 'em. Still, if this guy posted pictures to his blog, they would eventually get around and make for more of the kind of scandal he was trying to avoid.

"Cozy? Oh, for—" Mia broke off, then spoke up again, louder. "I'm calling security."

Just what he needed, Dave thought grimly. Not only a reporter but security coming over, too. More food for the local gossips. He couldn't do anything about Mia's call to security, but maybe he could head the reporter off at the pass.

"I'll give you a thousand dollars for your camera."

"Are you serious?" the kid asked with a laugh. "No way, man."

Great. A budding reporter with morals. Or maybe Dave just hadn't hit the guy's price yet. "Five thousand."

Chester wavered.

Dave could see it in the kid's eyes. He was thinking that with five grand in his pocket he could buy a better camera, maybe get a job at a real newspaper.

"I don't know…" Chester ran one hand across the chin sprouting a few stray whiskers. "With this kind of shot, I could maybe get a job at a paper in Houston."

Dave understood the kid's dreams. He'd had a hell of a lot of them himself once. And he'd worked his ass off to make sure they all came true. Didn't mean he was going to be the rung on the ladder beneath Chester's feet, though.

"Haven't you heard, kid? Newspapers are dinosaurs."

"True…"

Dave had the kid now. This guy wasn't enough of a poker player to hide the avarice in his eyes. Everyone had his price, Dave reminded himself. All he had to do was find the right number and this guy would cave. "Call it ten thousand and I want your recorder, too."

"Seriously?" Chester's eyes lit up. "You got a deal, man."

The kid followed while Dave went to his car, grabbed a checkbook from the glove compartment and wrote out a check. He signed it, then held one hand out.

"Let's have 'em," Dave said. The kid laid his camera and the recorder on Dave's palm, then snatched the check. He stared at it for a couple seconds, a slow smile spreading on his face.

"This is seriously cool, man. With this, I can get out of Royal and move to Houston."

"Good." The farther away the better, as far as Dave was concerned. "You should get moving before security gets here and starts asking you uncomfortable questions."

The kid looked up and grinned. "I'm practically gone."

A second later, Chester was sprinting off across the yard, and then lost in the scrub oaks and pines defining the edge of Alex's lot. Probably scaled the fence to get in here, Dave thought and had to give the kid points. He approved of determination. He also approved of getting rid of the kid as easily as possible.

Ten thousand was nothing. He'd have paid twice that to keep Chester quiet. As that thought moved through his mind, Dave realized that his problem might not be completely solved. Just because Chester didn't have photographic proof didn't mean he'd be quiet about Dave's visit to Mia.

So it was time to put a different spin on this. His mind raced with possible solutions and almost instantly, he came up with a workable plan. And if he worked it right, this could actually solve all of his problems. He glanced toward the house, where Mia was again standing in the open front doorway.

A Pine Valley security car pulled up to the curb and a uniformed guard stepped out. Before he could speak, Dave pointed and called out, "He ran toward the ravine."

The security guard hopped back into his car and went in pursuit, but Dave knew that kid was going to evade the guard. He'd gotten *in* to the gated community without being caught, hadn't he?

"What's going on?" Mia stepped out onto the wide, brick porch. "How'd you get him to leave?"

"Made him an offer," Dave said as he walked toward her.

She blinked at him. "You paid him off?"

"I did." Dave took the porch steps and stood directly opposite her. "Bought his camera and recorder."

She looked up at him and he could see disdain in her eyes. "It's easy for you, isn't it? Just buy people if you have to."

"I didn't buy *him,*" Dave corrected with a smile. "I bought his stuff."

"And his silence," she added.

"In theory," Dave agreed. "But there's nothing to stop him from spreading this around, despite his lack of evidence."

She wrapped her arms around her middle. "Then paying him off accomplished nothing?"

"It bought me some time," he said, mind still racing.

"Time for what?"

"That's something we should talk about." The more he considered his idea, the better he liked it.

When Alex had disappeared, Dave had hired an investigator. He'd seen the writing on the wall and had known that sooner or later, people would start suspecting *him*. As always, he'd figured it was better to be prepared. The investigator hadn't turned up much information on Alex, but Dave now knew enough about Mia to convince him he could get her to go along with his plan.

"But first," he said, meeting her eyes, "tell me. Do you think I should be a suspect?"

She looked at him for a long, silent minute. He knew she was thinking that over and it irritated him more than a little that it was taking her so long to make a judgment call. "Well?"

She slumped one shoulder against the doorjamb. "Probably not."

His mouth quirked. "A resounding testimonial."

"I don't know you well enough for that."

"Right. Well. That's something else we should talk about." He glanced over his shoulder at the empty yard and scanned the tree line looking for another sneaky reporter. He'd learned over the years that reporters were like ants at a picnic. First you saw one. Then two. Then the picnic was over.

"Can I come in?"

"All right." She stepped back, allowing him to pass by. Dave caught the faintest whiff of a light, floral scent that reminded him of summer.

Once in the house, Dave headed for the living room. He'd been here before, to meet with Alex. It was a nice house. Plush but tasteful. Cream-colored walls, bold, dark red-leather sofas and chairs and heavy dark tables. The windows looked out across the yard and were tinted, making it easy to see out but almost impossible to see in.

"What's this about?" Mia asked.

Dave turned to look at her. "I'll come right to the point. Alex being missing is hard on both of us."

"Is that right?" she asked. "How are you suffering?"

"Gossip." He tossed his hat onto the nearest couch, then shoved both hands into his jeans pockets. "The whispers and rumors about me might screw up a deal I'm working on."

"A deal?" Her eyes widened. "Alex is missing and you're worried about a deal?"

"Life goes on." He said it flatly. Cold and hard. He saw reaction glitter in her eyes and he could appreciate that. He admired loyalty. "I didn't have anything to do with Alex's disappearance and I don't think you did, either."

She laughed shortly. "Well, thanks very much. I didn't know I was a suspect."

"Why wouldn't you be? You're his housekeeper."

"You can't be serious."

"Why not?"

The look on her face was pure astonishment. And no, he wasn't serious. No one would ever suspect Mia Hughes of anything illegal. She was quiet, shy—or at least she had always seemed so until this morning—and she didn't exactly come off as a femme fatale. First, she was too skittish to be involved in any kind of plot. She'd blow the whole thing in minutes if it came down to it. And secondly, she was just too all-American-girl-next-door.

Shiny red toenails notwithstanding.

But throwing her off balance was just what Dave needed. Because he needed her. In fact, she was damn near perfect. The plan that had occurred to him while he was dealing with the would-be reporter actually depended on her. If she agreed—and she *would*—then he had a way to explain him being here—should the kid decide to go ahead and post to his blog anyway. And it might also appease Thomas Buckley and his narrow view of life. What Dave needed was a wife. Not a real wife, mind you. But something temporary. Something that would buy him the time he needed to clinch the deal he wanted. But the women he normally went out with would never convince Thomas Buckley they were the home-and-hearth type.

Mia Hughes, on the other hand, was just the woman for the job.

"I've got a proposition for you."

"And why should I listen?"

"Because it benefits both of us," he said simply. "And you're too smart to say no before you've heard me out."

Her lips pressed together and her eyes narrowed. "Flattery?"

"Truth."

She took a breath and blew it out again in a huff. "Okay, I'm listening."

He rubbed one hand across his face, then waved at the big red-leather sofa. "Have a seat."

Obviously still on guard, she walked to the couch and perched on the edge, clearly ready to bolt the moment he said the wrong thing. Well, Dave wasn't about to blow this. He had never once gone into a negotiation blind and today was no different. Didn't matter that he hadn't come here with this plan in mind. He was flexible enough that he could turn any situation around to his favor.

Dave stood in front of the couch, looking down at Mia. "I need a wife."

"*Excuse* me?" She started to rise but he waved her back down.

"Relax," he said. "I'm talking more of a fantasy wife than the real thing."

Fantasy? It was laughable, really. In what parallel universe would Mia Hughes be *anyone's,* let alone Dave Firestone's, fantasy? This was either some bizarre joke or he really was nuts.

"Relax?" Mia jumped to her feet, unable to sit still a moment longer. She and Sophie had wanted to check Dave out, which was the main reason Mia had allowed him into the house in the first place. But if she'd known what he was going to say she'd have left him on the porch and thrown the deadbolt to keep him out. "I really think you should go."

He shook his head and stood his ground. He was so tall that even with Mia on her feet, he was looking down at her.

"Not until you've heard me out."

"Oh, I think I've heard enough," Mia assured him. She tried to move past him to lead him to the door, but he laid one hand on her arm and stopped her.

She felt the burn of his hand on her skin and told herself to get over it. To pay no attention. But inside, her hormones were concentrating on that rush of heat. This was so not good. He was too tall. Too gorgeous. Too sure of himself.

He smiled as if he knew what she was thinking, feeling. Well, she'd wanted to know more about Dave Firestone. Now she knew just how formidable he was. And she was worried he was just a little crazy.

His hand fell from her arm and, despite her best intentions, Mia missed that blast of heat from his fingertips. Okay, maybe he wasn't nuts. But he was…distracting.

Then he was talking again. "I'm working on a deal with Texas Cattle—the best company in the state for beef buying—but the head of the company is a pretty conservative guy. He only deals with family men. Thinks they're more stable or something. Anyway, the upshot is, I need a temporary wife—or at the very least a fiancée. Just long enough for me to seal this deal. Once that's done, we'll 'break up' and it's over."

"You're crazy."

"Just determined," he assured her. "I know money's got to be tight with Alex gone."

She stiffened and lifted her chin.

"With him wherever the hell he is, you're not being paid and," he paused to let that sink in, then added, "the household account you have access to is almost dry."

Stunned, she whispered, "How do you know that?"

"Same way I know you've got school loans to pay off, tuition due in a month and that your debit card was declined at the diner last month."

Embarrassment roared to life inside her and she felt heat crawl up her cheeks to flood her face. Bad enough that her friend Sophie knew how little money she had. Having Dave Firestone know it was almost too much to take.

The question was, *how* did he know it?

"Are you spying on me?"

He laughed. "Hardly. I had an investigator looking for Alex and, since you're the man's housekeeper, you got checked out, too."

A wave of outrage crested over the embarrassment, smothering it completely. "You had no right."

"Whether I did or not, it's done," he said easily, as if

invading her privacy meant nothing to him. And, it probably didn't. "The point is, you need money. I need a wife."

"What?"

"I think you heard me."

"You can't be serious." This was, hands down, the most bizarre conversation she'd ever had. A *wife?* He wanted to *pay* her to marry him?

"I don't joke when I'm making a deal."

He stood there, tall and gorgeous and completely at ease, as if he owned the world—and from what she knew of him, he *did* own a good chunk of it. But his attitude was so confident, so…superior. As if he knew absolutely that she would agree. Well, he had a surprise coming.

"No deal," she said and instantly felt a sense of righteous satisfaction. Sure she was out of money and eating Top Ramen and daydreaming about hamburgers. But she wasn't so desperate that she was willing to sell herself to a man who already thought far too highly of himself. "I'm not interested in being your wife…real, temporary *or* fantasy."

"Sure you are," he said easily and gave her a half smile that tipped up one corner of his mouth and flashed a dimple at her. "You don't want to be interested but you are. Why wouldn't you be? Mia, this is a good deal for both of us."

She hated that he was right. She didn't want to be interested but she was. The whole situation was too strange. His offer was crazy. And yet…she looked around the empty living room. This place had been her first real home in too many years to count. She had cared for it and watched over it in Alex's absence. But the truth was, if he didn't come home soon, she didn't know what she would do.

The money was almost gone. Soon, she wouldn't be

able to pay the monthly bills. She had no idea what she'd do then.

People in town were already speculating about Alex's disappearance. This couldn't possibly help the situation.

"What about the local gossips?" She shook her head. "Don't you think they'll be a little suspicious of your sudden engagement plan?"

He frowned. "Hadn't considered that," he mumbled. "But it doesn't matter. In this town, the gossips love a good romantic story better than anything else. They'll glom on to our whirlwind romance and let go of suspicion."

He was probably right, she told herself. The main gossip chain in Royal was female and they were more interested in fairy-tale romantic stories than anything else. This might actually take the heat off them where Alex's disappearance was concerned.

Oh, God, she didn't know what to do.

"Think about it, Mia," he said and she could only imagine the snake in the Garden of Eden had sounded just as convincing. "This would solve both of our problems."

"I don't think so," she said, though her grumbling stomach disagreed. Still, she wasn't starving. She had a roof over her head and noodles in the pantry. And she had her pride, right?

Oh, God. Her pride was already shattered. Dave Firestone knew she was out of money. Knew how desperate she was. And he knew just what kind of temptation to use against her.

"You're considering it."

"I'm considering lots of things," she told him. "Like throwing you out, finishing my lunch and then maybe polishing the kitchen floor. Lots of options."

"So I see," he said, a slow, knowing smile curving his mouth. "Any idea which one you're going to go with?"

"I haven't decided yet," she said on a sigh.

"Let me make it easy for you, then." He moved in closer and Mia felt caught in the steady gaze of his eyes. "I'll pay you ten thousand dollars to pretend to be my fiancée until I get that deal with TexCat."

"Ten thousand—" She broke off, stunned at the offer. Just the thought of that much money made her head swim. She could pay the bills. Take care of Alex's house until he got back. She could make a payment on her tuition and finish her counseling degree.

She could buy *meat*.

"And," he said.

"There's more?"

"Yeah. Along with the ten thousand," he said, voice dropping to a low, seductive level, "I'll pay off your college loans. You could start your career out fresh. No debt."

Staggered, Mia actually swayed on her feet. That was a tremendous offer. If she didn't have to pay back school loans, she could build a life for herself much more quickly. Glaring at him, she said, "You're really evil, aren't you?"

He grinned, fast and wicked. "Just a master negotiator."

He was that, she told herself.

"Still want to polish the kitchen floor?"

She frowned at him. "Ten thousand dollars."

"That's right."

"And my loans paid off."

"You got it."

"How long would we have to pretend?"

He shrugged. "Shouldn't take more than a month."

Nodding, she tried to think clearly despite the racing, churning thoughts in her brain. "A month as your fiancée."

"Yeah."

Her eyes narrowed on him. "And what does this 'pretending' entail?"

It took a second for him to get what she meant and then he laughed shortly. "Trust me, your virtue is safe. When I want sex, I don't have to pay for it."

She could believe that. Heck, just standing next to him had her skin buzzing. He probably had women throwing themselves in his path all the time. Which made her wonder why he hadn't asked one of the no doubt *legions* of women littering his bed to be his pretend fiancée.

Maybe, she thought, none of them needed money as much as she did. Well, that was depressing.

Just to be sure of where she stood, Mia said, "Then we agree. No sex."

"Agreed."

She kept talking. "No touching of any kind. No kissing—"

"Hold on," he stopped her in midstream. "We have to convince this guy we're a real couple. So there *will* be touching. And kissing. And there will be you looking at me with adoration."

She laughed.

He frowned.

"Fine, fine," she said, waving a hand at him. "I'll be a good fiancée and the occasional touch or kiss—in public—is okay."

"Then we have a deal." He held out one hand to her and waited for her to take it. "You should come to the ranch for dinner tonight. We can work out the details there."

Nodding, Mia slid her hand into his and couldn't help feeling that just maybe she was swimming in waters *way* too deep for her.

Three

Dave pulled the collar of his dark brown leather jacket up higher on his neck and squinted as he climbed out of his 4x4. He took a deep breath, dragging the cold air into his lungs with a smile. Just being on his ranch settled him like nothing else could.

Land swept out to the horizon. He took a long look around, taking in the wooded area crowded with wild oaks. The stock watering pond shimmered a dark blue beneath the lowering sun and the grassland was dotted with Black Angus cattle. He tossed a glance at the dark, cloud-studded Texas sky. October was rolling in cold, signaling a rough winter to come.

But he was prepared. No matter what Mother Nature threw at him, Dave was ready. He had the ranch he'd always wanted, more money than he knew what to do with and the future was looking good—except for one small fly in his proverbial ointment. But, he reminded himself, he'd found a way to take care of that, too. Who would have guessed that Mia Hughes would be the solution to his problem?

One thing he'd learned over the years, though, was that sometimes answers came when you least expected them. And he was quick enough to take advantage of opportunities when they presented themselves.

He'd worked for years to get this ranch. He'd sacrificed, wheeled and dealed and risked more than he cared to remember. But he'd finally done it. He'd reclaimed the life that should have been his from the beginning. And he'd done it in style.

Damned if he'd be defeated now.

His ranch would be a success without TexCat and he knew it. But the bottom line was they were the best, and he wanted that contract to prove his ranch was the best. It was a milestone of sorts for Dave and he wouldn't rest until he'd reached it.

Walking away from his 4x4, he tugged his hat down lower over his eyes, stuffed his hands into his jacket pockets and headed for his ranch foreman, Mike Carter. Somewhere in his late fifties, Mike was tall and lean and the best ranch manager in Texas.

"Hey, boss," he said as Dave approached. "We found those ten yearling calves we were missing huddled together in Dove canyon."

With this much open land, cattle tended to wander, following the grass. And the young ones were always straying from the safety of the herd, going where they were easy prey for wolves and coyotes. It was inevitable to lose a few head to predators every year, but Dave was glad to hear they'd recovered the stock safely this time. "Good news. You got all of 'em?"

"All but one." Mike pulled his hat off and tipped his face into the wind. "Wolves got that one. Found the signs."

Nodding, Dave frowned. The one thing he did *not* have control over was nature. If wolves wanted to pick off a calf, there wasn't much he could do about it. Losing one was hard, but they'd saved nine, so he'd have to accept that and be grateful for it.

"Fine. But I don't want to lose anymore. Let's move the herd farther from the canyons, make it harder for the young ones to wander off."

Mike grinned. "Already done. Got a couple of the boys moving cattle to the west pasture."

"Good." Dave glanced around, his gaze sweeping across his land, and he knew he'd never tire of the view. Acres of good Texas earth stretched out for miles in all directions. There were rolling hills, meadows that ran so thick with sweet grass the herd couldn't manage to eat it all. There were wooded acres of oaks, a dozen stock ponds and a couple of lakes with the best damn trout in Texas. It was everything he'd planned for, and now Dave just needed to seal the ranch's success.

"I bought some first-calf heifers this morning," Dave said, remembering the phone call he'd made before setting out to talk to Nathan and Mia. "They'll be here by Friday and should start calving in the next couple of weeks."

"Good deal," Mike said. "We can always use new stock. But what about that new beef contract with Tex-Cat?"

Frowning, Dave said, "I'm working on it. Should know something soon. Meanwhile, start culling the herd, separating out the stays from the gos."

"We'll do it."

When Mike went back to work, Dave told himself he should do the same. Ranch work wasn't all done outside.

There were papers to go over, bills to pay, calls to make. Plus, he had a "fiancée" coming over for dinner and he'd better let his housekeeper, Delores, know.

He drove back to the main house, but rather than go inside, he walked to his favorite spot on the Royal Round Up ranch. He skirted the flagstone decking that ran the length of the sprawling ranch house, walked around the massive free-form pool and took the rough-hewn stairs to the rooftop, wraparound deck.

From that vantage point, he could see for miles. His gaze slid across the beautifully maintained grounds, the stocked trout lake that lay just beyond the pool and then to the massive guesthouse he'd had built two years before.

The guesthouse was an exact replica of the ranch house that had been his family's until he was ten years old. Until his father had lost the ranch and then took off, leaving Dave and his mother on their own. He'd built the damn guesthouse as a trophy. A way of reclaiming the past. And as a way of giving his mom a place to call her own. A place where she could take it easy for a change. But the hardheaded woman refused to leave her small apartment in Galveston. So the completely furnished, three bedroom, three bath guesthouse stood empty.

Until Dave could change his mom's mind. Which he would manage to do eventually. Hell, he'd gotten Mia Hughes to agree to his proposition, hadn't he?

The wind pushed at him as it raced across the open prairie, carrying the scent of grass and water and *land*. His land. He felt like a damn king when he stood up here surveying the stronghold he'd built.

He slapped both hands onto the thick, polished wood rail and leaned forward, letting his gaze move over the view. His hands tightened on the railing in front of him as he eased the jagged edges inside him by staring out at his property. Good Texas pastureland stretched to the horizon and it was all *his*. He'd come a hell of a long way in the past several years and there was more to do yet.

Landing that deal for his cattle was paramount for the rest of his plans. He wanted his ranch supplying the beef to the best restaurants and organic grocers in the state of Texas. And TexCat would help him accomplish that. Without that contract, Dave's plans would take a lot longer to come together. And if this bargain with Mia worked as he thought it would, the deal was as good as done.

Smiling to himself, he gave the railing a slap, took one last look at the vista rolling out into the distance and then took the stairs down. He'd head back to the main house and get some work done before it was time to meet with his fiancée.

Scowling, he realized it might take some time to get used to even *thinking* the word *fiancée*.

He ducked his head into the wind and muttered, "A hell of a thing to need a *wife* to make a deal."

Mia didn't know what to wear.

Was there a protocol for having dinner with a pretend fiancé who was *paying* you to pretend to love him so he could sell cattle? She laughed a little. It sounded bizarre even to her, and she was living it.

"Oh, God. I'm letting him *pay* me."

Her chin hit her chest and she took a long, deep breath to try to steady the nerves jumping in the pit of her stomach. It didn't help. Sighing, she flipped through the tops hanging in her closet and listened to the clatter of the hangers sliding on the wooden rod. She wasn't finding anything. It had been so long since she'd been on an actual *date*—she stopped short at that thought.

This wasn't a date. This was…

"I don't even know what this is," she muttered and grabbed a dark blue cable-knit sweater from the closet. Why she was worried about this was beyond her. What did it matter what she looked like? It wasn't as if she was trying to impress Dave Firestone, for heaven's sake.

"Exactly," she told herself. "This is business. Pure and simple. He didn't ask you to dinner because you swept him off his feet."

Mia laughed at the very idea. She was so not the type of woman to catch Dave's eye. No doubt he went for the shiny, polished women with nice hair, beautiful clothes and the IQ of a baked potato.

Potato.

"Oh, God, I hope he has potatoes at dinner." She sighed again. "And steak. I bet there's going to be steak. He's a rancher, right, so he's bound to like beef."

Her mouth watered and her stomach rumbled so loudly it took her mind off the nerves still bouncing around in the pit of her belly. Shaking her head, she carried the sweater out of the closet and tossed it onto the edge of her bed.

Since taking the job with Alex Santiago as his house-keeper, Mia had been living in the private suite of rooms off the kitchen of the big house. Living room, bedroom and bath, her quarters were lavishly furnished and completely impersonal but for the few personal touches she had scattered around the place.

Mia had been travelling light most of her life, so she didn't have a lot of *things*. There were a few photographs and a ratty stuffed bear she'd had since she was a child. But mostly, there were books. Textbooks, paperback thrillers and romances, biographies and sci-fi novels. Mia loved them all and hated to get rid of a book. She'd recently treated herself to an ebook reader, but as much as she loved the convenience, she preferred the feel of a book in her hands.

"And you're stalling," she told herself as she walked to the bathroom. Staring into the mirror, she looked into her own eyes and gave herself a stern talking-to. "You're the one who agreed to this, so you're going to suck it up and do what you have to do. It's only temporary. One month and you'll have enough money to pay the regular household bills and no school loans hanging over your head. Of course, if Alex isn't found by the end of the month, then you're right back where you started...." She stopped that thought as soon as it popped into her head. Alex would be found. And with the money from Dave she could pay pesky things like the water and gas and electric bills. Thank heaven Alex didn't have a mortgage on the place because she didn't know how she would have made the payment.

One month. She could do this. And get her life back on track.

Sounded good, she thought as she picked up the hair dryer and turned it on. She ran her fingers through her long, dark brown hair as the hot air pushed at it. Okay, she was nervous. But she could do this. How hard could it be to pretend to be crazy about Dave Firestone?

At that thought, she remembered the buzz of something...interesting she'd felt when he'd laid his hand on her arm. Thoughtful, she set the dryer down onto the pale cream granite counter and stared at her own image in the mirror. "Probably didn't mean anything," she assured her reflection. "I was probably just weak from hunger. Any man would have brought on the same reaction. It just happened to be Dave."

The woman in the mirror looked like she didn't believe her and Mia couldn't blame her. It had sounded lame to her, too.

Shaking her head, she walked back to the bedroom, grabbed a pair of dark wash jeans from her dresser drawer and tugged them on over a pair of pale pink bikinis. When she had them zipped and snapped, she pulled on a white silk tank top, then covered it with the dark blue sweater. She stepped into a pair of black half boots, then walked back to the bathroom.

Her hair was still damp, so instead of the tight knot she usually wore it in, Mia quickly did up a single, thick braid that hung to the middle of her back. She didn't bother with makeup. Why pretend to be something she wasn't? There was going to be enough pretending for her over the next few weeks. Might as well hold on to *some* form of reality.

With that thought in mind, she flipped off the light and walked through her apartment. She stopped long enough to snatch up her black leather shoulder bag, then she was out the door and into her car before she could talk herself out of the craziest thing she'd ever done in her life.

An hour later, she was so grateful she hadn't changed her mind about coming.

"Steak done the way you like it?" Dave asked from across the table.

"It was perfect," Mia answered, though the truth was, she had been so hungry, if they had trotted a cow through the living room, she might have gnawed on it raw. At the moment though, she was comfortably full of steak, a luscious baked potato swimming in butter and sour cream and the best fresh green beans she'd ever eaten.

She sighed and lifted her coffee cup for a sip.

Dave was watching her, and she noted one corner of his mouth quirk.

"What's so amusing?" she asked.

"You," he admitted. "I've never seen a woman enjoy a meal so much."

She flushed a little, then shrugged. No point in pretending she hadn't been hungry. He had already checked her out, so he probably knew just how many packages of Top Ramen were left in the pantry. "Maybe you should broaden your horizons a little. Date a woman who eats more than half a leaf of lettuce."

He grinned. "Might have a point."

Her eyes met his and in the soft light of the dining room, his gray eyes looked as deep and mysterious as fog on a cold winter night. He wore a black sweater, black jeans and his familiar, scarred boots and he looked, Mia thought, dangerously good.

"I like your house," she blurted when his steady stare was beginning to make her twitch.

"Thanks," he said and glanced around the dining room. Mia did the same, taking another long look at her surroundings. Sadly, between her still unsteady nerves and the fact that she'd been so seduced by the scent of the meal, she hadn't taken the time to really get a good look at the room.

One thing Mia had noticed was that every doorway in the house was arched. There was a lot of wood and a lot of stone throughout—definitely a man's house. Even the dining room was oversized, and somehow so...male. The table could easily seat twenty. Heavy oak, the table's thick edges were covered with intricately carved vines and flowers. Each chair boasted the same carvings and the seats were upholstered in dark red leather.

A black wrought iron chandelier provided the lighting, and framed paintings of the Texas landscape dotted the walls. Her gaze slid back to meet Dave's and she felt that jump of nerves again. Well, she was going to have to get over that.

"Come on," he said, pushing up from the table and holding out one hand to her. "I'll show you around. You'll have to know the place if you're going to be my fiancée."

"Okay..." She turned her head toward the closed door leading to the kitchen.

"What is it?" he asked.

Mia looked at him. "No dessert?"

Surprised, Dave laughed and this time it was real laughter, not the sardonic smirk or the condescending chuckle Mia was more familiar with. Amazing how real emotion could completely change Dave's features from gorgeous to heart-stopping.

Oh, Mia hadn't counted on this. Okay, yes, she'd felt that mild sizzle earlier today when Dave had touched her. But that could've been static electricity, too. In fact, she hadn't felt any interest in a man in so long, she'd begun to think she was immune.

Now was not a good time to find out she wasn't.

"Come on," Dave said again, "I'll take you on a tour, then we'll have dessert in the great room."

"All right," she said, and stood, putting her hand in his. She determinedly ignored the fresh sizzle she felt when his hand met hers. Instead, she focused on the promise of sugar in her near future.

He kept a firm grip on her hand as they walked from the dining room and Mia idly listened to the sounds of their boot heels on the tile floor. When she'd first moved in as Alex's housekeeper, she had been so impressed with the flawless beauty of his home. It was elegant and lovely in an understated way that she'd come to admire over the past couple years. But now, seeing Dave's house, she was bowled over by the sheer scope of the place.

It was lovely in a completely different way from Alex's home. This was rustic, and as she'd already thought, completely *male* in an unapologetic, straightforward manner. The floor tiles were beige and brown with splashes of cream to lighten the feel. The walls were a mix of stone and wood and textured, cream-colored plaster. Dark beams bracketed the high ceilings and arched windows boasted leaded glass. Every door was a curved slab of heavy, dark wood that made Mia think of centuries-old English estates.

"You've seen the dining room and the great room," Dave was saying as he led her down a long hallway. "This is the main living room." He kept walking, then paused to open another door. "My office."

She caught a quick glimpse before he was moving on again and saw more dark wood, a large desk and a stone fireplace that looked as wide as her living room at home.

"This is the game room." He stopped again, swung a door open and Mia saw a huge flat-screen TV hanging on the wall, a pool table, a couple of vintage video games and a well-stocked bar.

"You've got PAC-MAN."

"Yeah." He looked at her. "I'm surprised you know the game."

"I spent a lot of time in arcades as a kid," she said and let it go at that. No reason to tell him that while her father was earning a living playing poker in bars and casinos, she was left to her own devices and had become a champion at video games.

A flicker of admiration shone in his eyes. "We'll have to have a match sometime."

They passed through the foyer and Mia glanced at the

clear panes of glass arranged in a wide arch around the double front door. It was dark out, naturally, but there were solar lights lining the walkway to the circular drive-way. When she'd arrived, she had noticed the number of outbuildings. There was a barn, a paddock and several smaller houses all at a distance from the main house. The Royal Round Up was a prosperous, working ranch that no doubt required dozens of employees.

The whole place was huge. Dave was even more wealthy than she had guessed him to be. Which explained how he could offer to pay off her school loans without so much as blinking. She had no idea how to live like this. Not even how to *pretend* to live like this. Yes, she worked for Alex and he was wealthy, too, but in his house, she was the housekeeper. She wasn't expected to act as though it was her own home. To act as though living like this was second nature to her. The more she saw, the more anxious Mia became. What had she gotten herself into?

"This hall takes you back around to the kitchen," Dave said, and she glanced where he pointed. More art on the walls. More miles of gleaming tiles. She would never be able to find her way around this house. Plus, she didn't even have the kind of wardrobe the fiancée of a wealthy man would wear. She didn't fit into this world and she knew it. How could she possibly pull this off and con-vince anyone? Maybe, she told herself, it would be best if she just backed out of this deal right now. It wouldn't be a complete waste; she *had* gotten a terrific steak din-ner out of it.

An inner voice complained that without Dave, she'd be paying back college loans for the rest of her life. But surely that was the saner approach to take. Nodding, she braced herself to tell Dave that she simply couldn't do it.

She'd thank him and get out fast before she could change her mind.

Just then, he stopped in front of another door and threw it open. "This is the library."

If he continued speaking, she didn't hear him. All she could think was *books*. Acres of *books*. Floor to ceiling shelves lined with thousands of *books* ringed the cavernous room. There were couches, chairs, tables and reading lamps. There was a fireplace and giant windows overlooking the front lawn. With sunlight streaming through that glass, the room would be beautiful. The spines of the books lining the shelves must shine like rainbows, she thought, moving into the room and turning in a slow circle to take it all in.

"Finally found something to impress you, huh?"

"Hmm? What?" She glanced at him and smiled. A man who had a room like *this* couldn't possibly be a bad guy. Maybe she should rethink her earlier decision. "Oh. It's wonderful. Are you in here all the time?"

He leaned one shoulder against the doorjamb and shrugged. "Not as much as I'd like. Usually I'm in my office or out on the property."

But he loved the room, she could tell. And this one, beautiful library was enough to convince Mia that she might be able to handle this, after all. They at least had books in common.

"Oh, if I had this room, I'd never leave it."

"Not even for dessert?" he teased.

She gave him another smile. "Okay, maybe I'd have to leave once in a while, but," she added, looking around her again at the thousands of books, "I'd always come back."

"Steak, dessert, video games and books." Dave looked at her for a long minute. "You're an interesting woman, Mia."

Weird, he probably meant, she assured herself. But that was all right. She could live with that.

She met his gaze squarely. "Well, you're a surprise, too."

"Yeah? In what way?"

"I never would have thought *you* would have a room like this."

He gave her a sardonic smile. "I should probably be insulted."

She shook her head. "Not really. I guess it's just the impression you give off."

"Which is?"

"A man who only cares about the next deal."

"That's not far wrong."

"No," she said, "I've seen this room now. So I know there's more to you than that."

He frowned a little as if he didn't enjoy her delving into his psyche, no matter how shallowly she went.

"Maybe this room is just for show," he said.

"No, again," she said and leaned out to run the tips of her fingers along the richly detailed leather spines of the closest books. "That table alongside the chair by the fire has a book on it. With a bookmark at the midpoint."

He nodded thoughtfully. "Okay, good eye."

"You can't fool me now," she told him. "Any man who can appreciate a room like this is more than he appears to be."

"Don't count on that," he said softly. Then, shaking his head, he added, "You know, I always thought you were the shy, quiet type."

"I'm surprised you thought about me at all."

"Well, then, we're both surprised tonight," he said,

and stood back to allow her to pass him into the hallway. "Should be an interesting month."

"Or," she muttered as she slipped past him, her shoulder brushing across his chest, "a train wreck."

Four

"My bedroom and four guest rooms are upstairs," he said, and waited a moment before adding, "Shall we continue the tour?"

"Oh, I think I've seen enough," Mia assured him. Not only was she feeling uncomfortable about this whole thing, there was something else going on, as well. Some weird flashes of heat kept shooting through her and every time he touched her hand, she felt a buzz all the way down to her bones. No, seeing his bedroom probably wasn't a good idea.

"Your call," he said as he reached for her hand again. "But you should be familiar with the whole house. Be comfortable here. Learn your way around so you can convince anyone that you're used to being here."

"I don't know that I'm that good an actress."

Mia was really trying not to feel the heat between

them, but his hand over hers was strong and warm and hard to ignore.

He was talking again, his deep voice seeming to echo off the high ceilings. "Good actress or not, you're motivated to make this happen."

"True," she said, because why deny it? They both knew the only reason she was here with him right now was because he'd made her an offer impossible to refuse. Which, really, Mia told herself, she should always keep at the front of her mind.

Anytime she was tempted to think of Dave as charming or when he seemed to really like her...she had to remember that he was simply playing a role. Getting into the whole act of pretending to be crazy about her. That, and the fact that he was clearly a master manipulator.

"So does this house come with a map?"

"You'll get used to it," he said.

"Highly doubtful," Mia countered as he led her toward the great room.

"You haven't even seen the outside yet."

"Why such a big house?" she asked. "I mean, you live here alone." She looked around. The place was gorgeous but massive. "What's the point of having so much room for one man?"

He stopped walking and studied her for a long moment. "Did you ask Alex the same question about his place?"

She laughed. "This is easily twice as big as Alex's house."

He gave her a quick grin filled with satisfaction. "It is, isn't it?"

Were men *always* competing? she wondered idly. Were they always striving to keep one pace ahead of whoever they saw as their rival?

"So there is no point to this giant house."

"It was the best," he said simply. "I always get the best."

Until now, Mia thought, wondering again why he'd chosen *her* for this subterfuge. Of course, maybe he didn't know any other really desperate women. Another wave of depression swamped her but she pushed through it to keep her mind on what was happening.

"Still think you should see my bedroom," he said.

"I don't see why."

He glanced back at her and gave her a half smile. "Because you're my loving fiancée who would be completely at ease there."

"Right." Not at ease. Not even close. Her stomach started jumping again and lower portions of her body heated to a slow boil.

In a house this size, she told herself, you could have five or six kids running around and still find acres of room to have some space to yourself. When she was a child, she would have loved a house like this. Especially that library. She would have camped out in that room and been deliriously happy.

Of course, when she was a kid, she would have been ecstatic with any house to call her own. A place where she could belong, bring friends. A room of her own to do homework in or daydream. Instead, she'd moved from hotel to motel back and forth across the country as her father followed the next poker game.

Watching Dave, she had to wonder if he was actually happy here. Or if the house was more a *trophy.* A tangible sign of success.

When they walked into the massive great room, Mia paused a moment to look around. The fire had been lit in the hearth and the snap and hiss of flames devouring wood whispered in the air. A few of the table lamps had been turned on, and pools of golden light fell across the furniture. Tan leather couches and chairs sprawled alongside light oak tables. Wide windows at the front of the house would, in daylight, afford an amazing view of the yard. Now, though, night crouched on the other side of the glass and the sea of blackness was broken only by the soft glow of the solar lights placed along the walkway.

Dave took a seat on one of the couches and reached for the white thermal coffeepot sitting on the low table in front of him.

Mia's gaze fell to the plate of brownies and cupcakes beside the coffeepot, and she walked over to take a seat within reach of the dessert tray. She picked up a napkin and a brownie and took a bite. Chocolate melted on her tongue and she closed her eyes and sighed a little in appreciation. When she opened her eyes again, Mia found Dave watching her. His gray eyes looked smokier than ever and his lips were tight. Tension radiated from him. "Is everything okay?"

Dave took a breath and blew it out again. He was suddenly rock hard and in pain. Who would have thought it? Mia Hughes wasn't exactly the kind of woman he usually went for. There was no cleavage displayed. No short skirt to afford him a view of silky skin. No lipsticked mouth to tempt him. Not even a damn seductive smile.

And yet when she'd taken a bite of that damned brownie and made that soft groan of pleasure, his body had lit up like a lightning strike.

"Yeah," he said shortly as he fought to get a grip. "Fine." He poured them each a cup of coffee, then reached for a manila envelope lying on the table. Back to business, he told himself. Keep focused.

He pulled out a single sheet of paper, glanced at it then handed it to her along with a pen.

"What's this?" She took the paper but kept her gaze on his.

"Our agreement in writing. We'll both sign it so there won't be any questions later."

"A contract?"

"Easier all the way around to have everything laid out in black-and-white." Dave wasn't the kind of man to leave anything to chance. If there was one thing he'd learned over the years, it was that most people couldn't be trusted.

He took a sip of coffee and watched her as she skimmed the document.

Dave knew what it said. He would pay her ten thousand dollars up-front. All school loans to be paid off at the end of the month or the closure of his deal with Tex-Cat, whichever came first. In return, she would feign love for him and do everything necessary to make sure this game worked.

She read it through and he saw her wince once or twice. He wondered what had brought on the reaction, then reminded himself that it didn't matter. They had a deal and he'd hold her to it.

"Questions?"

"One." She looked at him. "How do we explain to people in town that all of a sudden we're engaged? I mean, the whole point of this is to avoid gossip and scandal, right?"

He'd considered that, of course. Dave always thought through any proposition. "We'll say it's a whirlwind kind of thing. Unexpected. Passionate."

She laughed and he frowned. Not the reaction he'd expected. Outrage, maybe, or even embarrassment. But not outright laughter. "What's so funny?"

"You," she said as she shook her head and took another

bite of brownie. She sighed a little and his groin tightened even more. If she had more than the one brownie, he might explode.

"No one's going to believe that," Mia told him. "I'm so not the type of woman a man like you would go nuts for."

He studied her for a long minute and had to admit that she had a point. If he'd noticed her at all over the past couple of years, it was only as Alex's housekeeper. He'd never looked beyond her quiet demeanor or the plain way she dressed and fixed her hair. His mistake, he thought now, looking into blue eyes that were the color of a Texas summer sky. He'd never noticed her full lower lip, the dimple in her right cheek or her quick wit. Mainly because he'd never bothered.

He was bothering now, though, and he sort of wished he wasn't.

"Okay, you have a point."

"Thanks very much."

He ignored the sting in her words and said, "Mainly it's the clothes. You need to go shopping."

She laughed again and that dimple winked at him. "With what? If you think I'm going to spend my ten thousand dollars on dressy clothes I won't need when the month is over, you're crazy."

"Fine." He nodded sharply. He could see her side of this. He took the paper from her, made a quick note and initialed it. "We'll make it ten thousand for you, five thousand for shopping expenses—"

"Five—"

"And your school loans. Deal?"

"Of course not! I'm not letting you buy me clothes."

"It's an act, Mia," he told her, voice firm and unyielding. "I'm paying you to play a part. I'm only giving you the props you need to make it real."

She shook her head and he sensed her pulling away. She might be sitting right beside him, but mentally she was out on the road, driving home and putting all of this behind her. So he put a stop to it.

"We agreed on this deal. This is just another facet of it. Nothing's changed but your wardrobe." He looked her over again and said, "You should go into Houston. They'll have more to offer."

"Any suggestions on what you'd like me to wear?"

He heard the sarcasm and again, he ignored it. "Tailored clothes would be best, I think. Get a couple of cocktail dresses while you're at it."

She huffed out a breath and stared at the agreement in her hand. "I don't know."

"Sign it, Mia," he said, holding out a pen. "One month and your loans are paid off and you and I go our separate ways. You know you want to, so just do it and get it over with."

She nibbled at her lower lip long enough to have Dave want to squirm just to relieve the pressure in his jeans. He'd thought the coming month would be a breeze. Now he had to wonder if maybe he wasn't signing up for a month of misery.

Although, he thought, maybe not.

Yeah, he'd told her that sex wasn't part of their deal, and it wasn't. But that didn't mean it had to stay that way. They were going to be spending a lot of time together. Giving him plenty of opportunities to seduce her and get her into his bed.

Damn, the thought of *that* had him getting even harder. Odd that Mia Hughes was hitting him so hard. Probably because she wasn't even trying. Had made a point of saying she didn't want to have sex with him.

Nothing more intriguing than a challenge.

"I really hate doing this," she muttered, then signed her name on the dotted line.

They were both committed to this path now, and there was no turning back.

Mia had no idea where to shop for the kind of clothes she needed. She'd never had enough money to worry about it before and even if she had, she didn't think she'd be comfortable paying several hundred dollars for *one dress*. Jeans, T-shirts and sweatshirts were her usual wardrobe, along with sneakers and sandals. The thought of her joining, even briefly, the kind of society that only the rich experienced would have been laughable if it wasn't so terrifying.

She was so not a part of the world Dave Firestone belonged to. How was she supposed to fool anyone into thinking any different? Not only did she not have the clothes for the part, she didn't have the attitude. She needed help and, thankfully, she knew just the place to find it.

Which was why Mia had come here, to the Royal Diner.

In June, Amanda Altman—now Battle—had come home to Royal and taken over the day-to-day running of the family diner with her sister, Pam. It hadn't been easy for the Altman sisters to get over their past and build a bridge to the future, but they'd managed it. And it hadn't taken Amanda and Nathan Battle long to rekindle their romance. Now they were married and Amanda was pregnant and driving everyone in town crazy with her decorating and shopping plans.

Mia smiled just thinking about her friend. She and Amanda had connected almost immediately when they'd met, and over the past few months they'd become friends.

Since Mia didn't have many, she treasured the friends she did have.

Mia claimed one of the booths along the wide front windows that offered a view of Main Street. But instead of watching the people passing by, Mia looked around the familiar diner. It was old-fashioned, she supposed. When Amanda had come home she had upgraded a few things, though not enough to change the feel of the place.

The walls had been painted. Once a bright white, they were now a soft, cool green and dotted with framed photos of Royal through the years. The old chipped and scarred red counter was now a shining sweep of a deeper, richer red. The black-and-white-checked floors had been polished and the red vinyl booth seats had all been revamped. There were new chairs pulled up to the scattering of tables and sunshine streamed through the windows lining Main Street.

There was an old-style jukebox in the corner, though thankfully it was quiet at the moment. It was still morning, too late for breakfast and too early for the lunch crowd that would stream in by noon. At the moment, there were just a few customers, huddled over their coffees or chatting softly in small groups. The clink of silverware on plates was its own kind of music and settled the nerves that seemed to have taken up permanent residence in Mia's stomach.

This was all Dave's fault, she told herself. Waving money in front of a desperate woman was just…she frowned. Very, very smart. He'd known just how to reel her in. And now that she was in, she had to stop worrying over it. Too late to back out, Mia told herself, as she silently admitted that she probably wouldn't quit now even if she could. Just a few minutes ago, she had deposited the fifteen-thousand-dollar check from Dave that she had needed so badly. The deed was done. She could pay bills, buy groceries and find a way to hang on until Alex returned.

He *would* return, she assured herself. And now that she would be spending lots of time with Dave, maybe she would be able to discover information that would help locate Alex. Not that she believed Dave had had anything to do with Alex going missing. But he might know something and not even realize what he knew.

And… She was rationalizing her involvement in this crazy plan of his.

It was one month—and maybe not even that long, if he could land that contract for his cattle sooner. When the time was up she'd be free and clear to start her own future unencumbered by massive debt. A good thing. The heat she felt around Dave? A bad thing. That swirl of nerves erupted in the pit of her belly again and she had to fight them into submission. Not easy.

Somehow, she had to find a way to keep her hormones in check and remember that none of what would be happening between her and Dave was real.

She spotted Amanda and waved when her friend smiled in greeting. Pam was running the cash register, and beyond the pass-through into the kitchen, Mia spotted their chef putting a plate together.

Morning in Royal, Mia thought. There was comfort here. Familiarity. Things she'd longed for most of her life, she had found here. And she would do whatever she had to to keep them. Even entering a deal with a man who was dangerously attractive.

"Brought your usual iced tea." Amanda walked up to the booth and set a glass down in front of Mia.

"Thanks." Her usual. Wasn't that a gift, Mia thought,

to be so well-known in a place that she had a "usual" order.

"I'm so glad you came in this morning," Amanda said. "I've got a few pictures I want to show you."

"More baby room ideas?" Mia asked.

Amanda laughed and lovingly patted her slightly rounded belly. Mia caught the gesture and felt one sharp, swift tug of envy. Amanda had a man who loved her. While Mia, on the other hand, was going to pretend to be in love for a hefty paycheck.

"I know," Amanda said with a grimace. "I've become an HGTV zombie. I swear, Nathan's afraid to come home after work because he never knows what new project I'm going to hit him with."

"Nathan's nuts about you."

"Yeah," Amanda said with a private smile. "He really is. Which is why he didn't even flinch when I had Sam Gordon's crew break out the wall in the baby's room so they could add a connecting door to our room."

Amanda and Nathan lived on the Battlelands ranch in a house Nathan had had built a few years ago. It looked like a Victorian but it had all the modern conveniences.

"A connecting door makes perfect sense."

"It really does," Amanda agreed as she slid into the bench seat opposite Mia. "Of course, I'm also having Sam add on a balcony to our room, and Nathan was a little surprised to find gaping holes in *two* of our walls when he came home yesterday."

This is another reason why Mia had come to Amanda for help. Their lives were so different. Not only did Amanda have a home and a family to call her own, but she was a part of the very society that Mia would be pretending to belong to. The Battle family was every bit as wealthy as Dave Firestone and Amanda had found a way to not only fit in, but thrive.

Hopefully, she could help Mia do the same, however temporarily.

She took a quick drink of her tea and swallowed, pushing down the huge knot lodged in her throat. "I'd love to see the pictures of the baby's room," she said, looking up into Amanda's smiling face. "And I've got a favor to ask."

Instantly, Amanda's smile faltered and she reached out one hand across the table to lay it on Mia's arm. "A favor? Is everything okay?"

"Everything's fine, why?"

"Because you never ask for anything," Amanda pointed out. "I swear, if you were on fire, you wouldn't ask for water."

Mia blinked at the apt analogy. She hadn't realized that her friends knew her so well. But she'd learned long ago to stand on her own two feet. To not count on anyone or anything. And to never ask for help—because invariably people would see that as a sign of weakness.

Wow. Childhood issues, she told herself. Amazing how much she had held on to from when she was a girl. It was never easy to be objective about your own past and your life choices, but even Mia could see how her childhood had affected her as an adult. Heck, until the past few years, her past had kept her from even attempting to make friends. Thankfully, she'd at least been able to overcome that hurdle.

Smiling, she said, "I promise, Amanda. If I ever need water that badly, I'll *ask*."

"Deal." Amanda waved to her sister, indicating she was taking a short break. "Okay, now, before I run to the back and get my three-ring binder with all of my decorating pictures to show you…you first. Whatever you need, I'll do it."

"Without even knowing what's going on?"

Amanda shrugged. "We're friends."

A rush of warmth spilled through Mia at those two simple words. Having a friend to count on was such a gift, she didn't think she would ever take it for granted.

"Thank you. I really appreciate it."

"I know you do, sweetie. So what's going on, Mia?"

God, she hardly knew where to begin. Cupping her hands around the tall glass in front of her, Mia started talking. She started at the beginning and told Amanda all about the reporter and Dave and the offer he'd made and why she needed to go shopping. When she finally wound down, she took a long drink of her tea and waited for Amanda to tell her she was crazy.

Instead, her friend grinned. "That is so fabulous."

"You really think so?"

"Well, come on," Amanda said, lowering her voice. "Honey, I know you hate to admit it, but you really *do* need the money."

Instantly, Mia flushed, remembering how her debit card had been refused right here at the diner just a few weeks ago. Amanda was right. She *did* need the money. And she *did* hate to admit it.

"I know things will be better when Alex comes back…" Amanda paused and both of them were silent for a moment, thinking about their missing friend. "But for now, it's perfect. You each need something, and with this one little deal, you'll be setting up your future. How much better can it get? Plus," she added with a wide smile, *"shopping."*

Mia was still laughing when Abby Price entered the

diner and walked up to the booth smiling. "What's so funny?"

"Nothing," Amanda said with a wink for Mia. "What can I do for you, Abby?"

Abigail Price was taller than Mia, with long, wavy red hair and an air of elegance about her. She also had a ready smile, a loving husband and an adorable, adopted three-year-old daughter, Julia.

"Well," Abby was saying, "you know the day-care center at the TCC is almost ready to open for business."

The day care had been at the center of a contentious battle in town for months. The Texas Cattleman's Club had been around for generations and they were pretty much stuck in the mud when it came to changes. It had only been a couple of years since they'd allowed women to become members. And now those women were spear-heading the move to provide a safe, comfortable place for children to stay when their parents needed to be some-where else.

Most people in Royal were all for it, but there were a few who were still fighting it even though it was a done deal. Before Alex disappeared, he had told Mia all about the TCC meeting in which the decision had been made to go ahead with the facility. Naturally, it had been Beau Hacket and his cronies, like the Gordon brothers, who had argued against it. Mia thought if Beau and his bunch had their way, everyone would still be driving wagons hitched up to horses. The man hated change of any kind and didn't care who knew it.

But bullies hadn't been able to stop progress, and the day-care center was nearly ready to open.

"Since everyone in town is talking about nothing else these days," Amanda said, "yeah. I know."

"Well, I was thinking," Abby said, "that we should

have a launch party, so to speak. You know, sort of an open house, to let everyone come in to see what we've done."

"That's a great idea," Mia said. "I know I'd love to see it."

"Thanks!" Abby smiled at Mia, then turned back to Amanda. "But we'll need food and that's where the diner comes in. I know you and Pam do catering and I'm thinking small sandwiches, potato salad, some vegetable platters…"

"We can do that, absolutely," Amanda told her. "Do you want to go over the menu and what you'll need now?"

"Oh, no. I've got a million things to do," Abby told her with a quick glance at her watch. "But I'd love it if we could talk it all over tomorrow sometime."

"That's perfect. Pam and I will be here all day, so come whenever it's convenient for you."

Abby bent to give Amanda a quick hug. "Thanks. Now, I've really gotta run. See you, Mia!"

And she was gone.

"Abby's pretty much a force of nature, isn't she?"

Amanda agreed. "She's always in high gear, that's for sure. Now," she said, "let's get back to the fun stuff. *Shopping.*"

Mia laughed and took a sip of her tea. "I'm glad you think it sounds fun. I have no idea where to go or what to buy."

Amanda clapped her hands together, then scrubbed her palms. "I, on the other hand, know *just* where to go."

"Dave suggested Houston."

"Of course he did." Amanda waved that suggestion aside. "Men don't know anything. We don't have to go into the city. All we have to do is head down the street to Monica's shop."

"Monica?"

Amanda laughed a little. "Monica Burns. She's on the outskirts of town and she has this darling dress shop. Monica carries great stuff you won't find in department stores. Really different, really gorgeous."

"Why have I never heard of her before?"

Amanda cocked her head to one side. "Shop often, do you?"

Mia laughed. "Okay, no."

"Have to warn you, though," Amanda added, "she's pricey."

Pricey. Well, that's the kind of stuff she had to have and, thanks to Dave, she could afford it.

"Oh!" Amanda leaned over the table and lowered her voice. "You know what else we should do?"

"I'm almost afraid to ask. You look way too eager."

"That's because this is a brilliant idea," Amanda told her. "We should go to the day spa. Get the works."

"The spa?" Mia's voice defined the hesitation she felt over that plan. Saint Tropez was a local, upscale hair salon and day spa. Mia had never actually been inside— frankly, even if she could have afforded it, she would have been too intimidated to go in. She wasn't exactly the mani-pedi kind of girl, after all, and she hadn't gone for a haircut in years.

"You don't have to sound so horrified. I didn't suggest a trip to a torture chamber." Amanda shook her head and smiled.

"You might as well have," Mia admitted.

Her friend sat back and gave her a long look. "You said yourself you have to look the part of Dave's fiancée."

"Yes…"

"Well, sweetie," Amanda said gently, "that's going to take more than new clothes."

Mia laughed. How could she help it? "Thanks very much."

"Oh, I didn't mean it the way it sounded. I just... Okay, take your hair, for example."

She lifted one hand to the knot at the back of her neck. Her hair was neat and tidy. What else did she need, really? "What's wrong with my hair?"

"Nothing that a trim and some highlights and throwing away your rubber bands wouldn't fix."

Mia frowned thoughtfully. She kept her hair twisted and off her neck because it was easy. And, she silently admitted, because she was used to being...invisible. It was comfortable. Safe. No one noticed a woman who did everything she could to *avoid* being noticed.

But she'd been working for years to build a new life, hadn't she? Why else had she gone back to school? Worked as an intern at Royal Junior High? And if she was building a new life, did it make sense to hold on to the past? To cling to her old ways of doing things? To continue to hide when what she really wanted was to embrace the life she'd always dreamed of having?

She took a deep breath and asked, "How much do you think I should have trimmed?"

Amanda grinned. "Trust me."

Five

That afternoon at the Royal Round Up, the ranch hands were moving the herd to winter grass and Dave was happy to be on horseback joining them. Yeah, he could have stayed back at the main house and just issued orders, but running a ranch was in his blood. Nothing felt better to him than being on a horse, doing the work necessary to keep a ranch this size operating.

Every month of the year had different demands when you worked and lived off the land. In October, there was plenty to get accomplished while getting ready for winter.

Dave tugged his hat brim lower over his eyes and guided his horse after a steer wandering off on its own. He turned the animal back toward the herd, then mentally reviewed the list of chores still to be done.

After they had the cows, bulls and steers moved to their winter field, the six-month-old calves would be separated from their mothers and weaned. Then the vet would have to come out and vaccinate them before they were turned out to the pasture along with the rest of the herd. Dave knew that a lot of the ranchers in the area turned the calves into feedlots, where they spent their days caged up in small pens with hundreds of other animals. Nothing wrong with the system, Dave supposed, but he preferred keeping his cattle free-range even if it did mean more work for the ranch hands.

His gloved hands tugged at the reins and sent his horse off to the right, where one or two of the heifers were beginning to stray. A cloud of dust hovered over the moving herd and swirled around the cowboys moving in and out of the steers with calm deliberation.

"Hey, boss."

Dave looked over as Mike Carter rode up, then drew his horse alongside. "Herd looks good."

"It does," Mike agreed, squinting into the late afternoon sunlight. "I sent a couple of the guys ahead to set up the temporary weaning pens for the calves."

"Good. If we can finish separating the calves from the cows by tomorrow, I'll have the vet come out the day after to take care of their inoculations."

"That'll work," Mike told him. "We can get the identification ear tags on them at the same time and have the work done, I figure, by the end of the week." He grinned. "Just in time for the first-calf heifers to arrive."

Dave smiled, too. "Always something, isn't it?"

"If you're lucky," Mike agreed. "By the time the doc's finished inoculating the calves, the first year heifers should be here. He can check them over at the same time. Save himself another trip to the ranch."

"Good idea," Dave said, watching as a couple of the cowboys swooped around the edge of the herd, guiding them toward the winter grasses.

There hadn't been much rain this year and the grasses were sparse. He'd already cut back on the number of head of cattle they were running, in spite of the fact the stock ponds were still full and water wasn't really an issue for the herd. The point was, the grasses had dried out and without enough rain, they wouldn't be coming back.

Ranching was always a series of strategic maneuvers. Paring down the herd, moving calves and saving breeding stock. You had to plan for weather you had no way to predict and try to outthink Mother Nature from month to month. It wasn't easy, but it was all Dave had ever wanted.

Right now, his concern was the land. Making sure it stayed healthy. Dave was thinking they needed to thin the herd again. With the first-year heifers arriving, and their calves born come spring, the ranch would be carrying more beef than the land could support if they didn't act soon. Now was the time to make that beef sale.

"We've got to get that deal with TexCat, Mike." He shook his head as the dust cloud rose even higher as if to highlight exactly what Dave had been thinking. "The grass can't support too big a herd for long."

"You heard anything from Buckley?"

"Not in a few days," Dave told him, and felt a flash of irritation. He wasn't used to not being in charge on a deal. Now he was in the position of having to wait on someone else, and Dave didn't *do* waiting. When he wanted something, he went out and got it. Hell, he thought with an inner smile, he'd gotten a fiancée when he needed one, hadn't he?

"When are you meeting him next?"

Dave frowned. "I'll set something up with him in the next week or so. Want to give him time to have our operation checked out."

"Buckley's not an easy man to deal with, but he's fair,"

Mike said. "He'll figure out we've got the best beef in Texas soon enough."

Dave did have the best beef around, and everyone knew it. Hell, his cowhands did everything short of singing the steers to sleep at night. The herd was free-range Black Angus. Organic, too—no antibiotics, no feedlots. He'd put his heart and soul into building this ranch, and now he had a fiancée who would convince Buckley that Dave Firestone was a settled, trustworthy man. Everything was moving as it should.

So why was he still feeling…off balance?

It was Mia.

The woman kept slipping into his thoughts. Ever since their meeting the night before, he hadn't been able to keep her completely out of his mind. And he knew why. She hadn't been what he'd expected and Dave wasn't used to being surprised. When he made a move—in business or his personal life—he went in knowing exactly what would happen. Knowing ahead of time how his adversary would react.

Mia had thrown him. Without even trying, she'd aroused him. Intrigued him. And set him up for more surprises. Which he didn't want.

"So, is your mom coming out to stay over Christmas again?"

Dave came up out of his thoughts and shot a look at his foreman. Mike's expression was hard to read, as if he were trying to be deliberately casual.

"Yeah," Dave said. "She'll be here in November, like always. Stay through the first of the year."

Mike nodded. "Sounds good."

Frowning, Dave briefly wondered why his foreman was so interested in his mother's upcoming visit. Then he shrugged it off. Bigger things to think about.

"Looks like you've got company, boss."

Mike jerked his head off to the west, and when Dave looked in that direction he saw a man on horseback headed their way. Even at a distance, Dave recognized him.

Chance McDaniel. Chance owned a thriving guest ranch and hotel on the other side of Royal. He made millions by hosting city people who wanted to pretend to be cowboys for a week at a time. Then there was the four-star hotel on the property that was a popular spot for weddings, conferences and all kinds of gatherings.

But McDaniel's Acres was a working ranch as well as a dude ranch. Chance ran some beef and horses on his land, too. The two of them often shared the work at busy times of the year, lending out cowhands and doing whatever was needed. He was a good friend and like Dave, preferred, when possible, to be out riding a horse to doing just about anything else.

When he was close enough, Dave held up a hand in greeting. "What are you out doing?"

"Heard you were moving your beef to winter pasture," Chance said with a shrug. "Thought I'd ride over and lend a hand if you need it."

"Hell, yes, we can always use another cowboy," Dave said. "Appreciate it."

Chance grinned. "Beats being at McDaniel's Acres today. My guys are helping tourists try their hand at roping. Set up a plywood steer and they're taking turns using a lasso." Laughing, he added, "There's gonna be more than a few of them looking for aspirin tonight."

Laughing, Mike said, "It ain't easy being a cowboy." Then he nodded and moved off to join the other hands circling the slow-moving herd.

The two friends rode in silence for a few minutes until

Dave finally said, "You usually enjoy watching city guys try to ride and rope. So why are you really here?"

Chance glanced at him. "Thought I'd let you know that the state investigator's staying at my hotel."

"She is?" Dave felt like he'd just taken a hard punch to the gut. He'd heard about the FBI-trained investigator, of course. Nothing stayed secret for long in Royal, and it wasn't as if Bailey Collins was trying to keep a low profile, either.

She was working out of the Dallas office and had been looking for Alex for weeks. Dave had spoken to her once himself and he knew that she'd worked with Nathan to discover that Alex Santiago had a few secrets of his own. In fact, Santiago might not even be his real name. Questions brought more questions and there simply weren't any answers to be had. But knowing that Bailey Collins was staying at McDaniel's Acres told Dave that she wasn't going anywhere. Which meant that she wasn't finished looking into Alex's disappearance. Frowning to himself, Dave realized that though Nathan Battle might not consider him a suspect, Bailey might feel differently.

Dave looked at his friend, waiting. It didn't take long for Chance to continue.

"I'll say, the woman's gorgeous, really." He gave a fast smile. "If you can get past what she does for a living."

"Why's she staying on?" Dave asked it, but he knew damn well why the woman was still here. A wealthy man didn't just drop off the face of the earth and not leave a ripple.

There were people asking questions. Reporters hadn't let go of the story at all. If anything, they kept digging deeper. Asking more questions, raising suspicions. Naturally, the state would want its investigator to stay put and keep gathering information.

Hell, when Alex did finally turn back up, Dave wanted to punch him dead in the face for causing all this.

"She's talking to people," Chance was saying. "She's been all over my ranch already, chatting up the cowboys, looking for any piece of information she can turn up."

"Great."

"Yeah." Chance snorted. "She questioned me once and I think she's looking for another shot at me. So far, I've managed to avoid her."

"By coming over to help your friends ride herd?"

"Doesn't hurt," he admitted.

Dave didn't blame him. He was sick and tired of talking about Alex Santiago. Hell, he and Alex hadn't exactly been friends before the man took off or whatever. Yet, ever since he'd been gone, Alex had become a huge part of Dave's life. Gossip, innuendo and scandal kept hanging over him like a black cloud threatening a storm.

And Chance had had it just as bad for a while. He'd been dating Cara Windsor until Alex had moved in on him. Then Cara and Alex had become an item and Chance was left on the sidelines. Naturally the gossips in town had run with that, painting Chance as a pissed-off lover wanting revenge. Which was laughable. Chance had liked Cara, but not enough to make Alex disappear.

"Looks to me like she plans on talking to everyone who knows Alex." He glanced at Dave. "Which would surely include *you*. I'm thinking you're going to look real interesting to her seeing as how you and Alex were rivals, so to speak."

"Great." Snatching off his hat, Dave pushed one hand through his hair, then settled the hat into place again. "Nathan just officially cleared me of suspicion and now I've got someone else coming in to set the town gossips raging again."

"Yeah, and they'll be all over it."

Disgusted and frustrated, Dave muttered, "Gonna go over real big with Thomas Buckley, too."

"That pompous old goat? He hates everything."

"Yeah, but I can't afford to have him hating me at the moment."

"The contract for your beef?"

"Exactly."

Chance nodded grimly. "Maybe this woman Bailey will be discreet."

"Won't matter," Dave said. "Once folks in town realize she's looking at me, the gossip will start up and it will reach Buckley."

"You can get Nathan to vouch for you there," Chance pointed out. "How're you going to handle the whole have-to-be-a-family-man-to-sell-to-TexCat thing though?"

"That part I've got covered," Dave said, with just a touch of smug satisfaction in his voice. Quickly, he outlined his plan and his agreement with Mia.

Chance gave a long, low whistle. "You're clever, I give you that. But Alex's housekeeper?" He shook his head slowly. "To some—including Bailey—that might look like you're trying to buy her silence."

"What?" Dave hadn't looked at it like that at all. Now that Chance had brought it up, though, it made a horrible kind of sense.

"Hey," Chance said, "not to me! I know you didn't do anything to Alex. I'm just saying that suddenly turning up engaged to the housekeeper of a man who's disappeared might start even more tongues wagging."

He was right and Dave knew it. But the plan was set and damned if he'd back out now.

"They're gonna wag no matter what I do," Dave told

him. "At least this way, they're all talking about what I *want* them to talk about. The engagement."

"It ain't easy living in a small town, is it?"

"Not by a long shot," Dave agreed. "Still, you want to give it up and move to Houston or Dallas?"

Chance grinned. "Hell, no. Where would I ride my horse in the city? Besides, when you're *not* the center of gossip, it can be downright entertaining."

"Yeah," Dave countered, "but when the gossip's about *you,* it's a damn sight less fun."

"True."

Dave frowned. "Think I'll be spending as much time as I can out here with the cattle." He couldn't see a woman from the city hopping a horse to chase him down for an interview.

"Can't say it's a bad idea," Chance admitted. "Let's face it, Dave. You and I were the top suspects when Alex took off, and they haven't found anyone else to take our places, have they?"

"No," Dave said thoughtfully.

Nodding, Chance continued. "Y'know, when Alex *does* get back, he's got a lot to answer for."

"Damn straight, he does." Dave kneed his horse into a hard run and Chance was right behind him. A couple hours of hard work should be enough to clear their heads for a while.

Amanda didn't waste time once she'd made up her mind. Before Mia even knew what was happening, she and Amanda were at Saint Tropez being pampered.

Just walking into the day spa, you could feel tension slide from your body on a sigh. There was soft, ethereal music piped in from discreetly hidden speakers high on the pale pastel walls. There were fresh flowers scenting the air and frosty pitchers of lemon water sitting on silver trays alongside crystal goblets. The colors in the place were designed to soothe tattered nerves. Soft blue, sea-foam green and varying shades of cream covered every surface. Chairs were plush and overstuffed, lamps were dim and the aestheticians were warm and welcoming.

Since Mia had never done anything like this before, she was completely out of her element and grateful to have Amanda as her guide to the world of "girlie."

She should probably feel guilty for spending this kind of money, Mia told herself. But somehow, she just couldn't seem to drum up the guilt. She was way too busy feeling…relaxed. For the first time in months, her mind was blissfully blank and her body was free of tension.

"You're sighing," Amanda said.

Mia did it again, then smiled. "I'm lucky I'm not just a puddle of goo on the floor. You know, I've never had a massage before and—"

"You poor, deprived girl," Amanda interrupted.

"I know, right?" Mia looked over at her friend with a smile. "It was amazing. Every muscle in my body is taking a nap."

"Oh, mine, too. Of course, since I've been pregnant, I can take a nap anywhere." She laughed a little. "Nathan swears I fell asleep standing up in the kitchen the other night."

Mia smiled to herself as Amanda continued talking about Nathan and the coming baby and their plans for the future. She was happy for her friend. Really. Amanda and Nathan had had to get past a lot of old hurts and mistrust to find their happiness now. But at least silently, Mia could admit to feeling more than a twinge of envy.

After growing up as a wanderer, she'd finally found the place that was home. But she was still looking for the family she wanted to be a part of so badly. For the love that had eluded her all of her life.

"Mia?" Amanda's voice cut into her thoughts. "You okay?"

"What?" She jolted in her chair. "Sure. Why?"

"Because Natalie's asked you three times if you like the shade of nail polish on your fingers and toes."

"Oh!" She winced, looked at the woman sitting at her feet and said, "I'm sorry. I zoned out."

"Happens all the time here, believe me," the woman said with a knowing smile. "So, the dark rose works for you?"

Mia checked out her fingers and toes, wiggled them for effect and said, "Yes, thanks, it's great."

Another first, she thought. Mia had never treated herself to a mani-pedi before. But she wouldn't confess that to Amanda.

"Good. Now I'll get you some wine while you dry and then we'll escort you into the salon for your color and trim."

She winced at the thought of facing a haircut and highlights. A small thread of fear slid through the relaxation that held her in its grip. Before she could think about it too much, though, Natalie was back, handing Mia a glass of white wine. She'd also brought a glass of ice-cold lemon water for Amanda.

"Wine," Amanda said wistfully as she looked at her own goblet of water. "I miss wine. And caffeine."

"Yes, but when nine months are up, you'll have a baby in exchange for your sacrifice. That seems fair."

"It does," she agreed. "Though I've already told Nathan to bring a bottle of chardonnay to the hospital. I'm going to want a glass or three right after delivery."

An hour or so later, Mia was sitting in a salon chair

staring into the mirror at a stranger. She smiled and the reflected woman smiled back.

Okay, there had been some nerves when Tiffany had come at Mia's head with a pair of shears. But the panic had dissolved when she'd realized that the beautiful Tiffany was only trimming and shaping Mia's long-ignored hair. But before she could admire herself, Tiffany had mixed up some color and affixed it to Mia's head with small sheets of aluminum foil.

While she sat under a hot dryer, wondering what she'd gotten herself into, Amanda had been right there, chatting and laughing with the other women in the salon. Even though Mia wasn't part of the conversation, she felt as though she were.

There was that tantalizing sense of belonging that she'd yearned for most of her life. This was her home. She had friends. She had purpose. And now…she had a fiancé. Who, she told herself as Tiffany blew her hair dry, was going to be very surprised the next time she saw him.

"You're being really quiet," Amanda said.

"Just thinking."

"About?"

"About today, mostly," Mia said with a half smile. "This was a great idea, Amanda."

"Wasn't it?" A short, delighted laugh spilled from her as she walked up behind Mia's chair and met her gaze in the mirror. "Honestly, sometimes I'm just brilliant. Of course, I'll seriously owe Pam for taking diner duty herself until our extra waitress comes in. But it was worth it."

"It was." Mia swiveled around in her chair and stood up. "I feel more relaxed than I ever have."

"Well, you look great, too." Amanda did a slow circle around Mia. "I love what she did with your hair. It's still long and it's so thick I could hate you for it…"

Mia laughed and gave her head a shake, watching in the mirror how the long, layered waves swirled out, then shifted right back into place. It was amazing. She hadn't even known her hair could *do* this.

"...and the layers. I love the highlights, too. It's still dark brown, but there's warmth mixed in there now, too."

Mia lifted one hand to slide her fingers through her hair. "It feels softer, too."

"Mia?"

A voice spoke up from the side and both women turned to look at the speaker. Piper Kindred was standing in the open doorway. "Is that you, Mia?"

"It is," she said and grinned like a fool. How fun it was to see the surprise on her friend's face and to imagine how much greater Dave's shock was going to be. "Amanda talked me into a spa day."

"And doesn't she look fabulous?" Amanda said. "Well, except for the faded jeans and the long-sleeved T-shirt. Shopping is next on our list."

Piper's curly red hair was drawn back into her usual ponytail. She wore dark blue jeans and an oversized black sweatshirt covering up a curvy figure. Her green eyes were shining and her lips were curved in a wide smile.

"Good luck with that, Mia. Amanda's always loved shopping, but I don't envy you at all."

"Exactly how I feel about it," Mia admitted.

Amanda shook her head at both of them. "And you call yourselves women. Where's your gender pride?"

"Women do more than shop," Piper pointed out with a chuckle. "Like say...work as paramedics?"

"Yes, yes," Amanda retorted with a grin. "We all know you're a paramedic and that's wonderful. But there's no reason you can't be female while you do it."

Piper winked at Mia. "I'm always female, Amanda. I'm actually here for a haircut and a pedicure."

Amanda waved one hand in front of her face. "Hold me up, Mia. I think I might faint."

Mia laughed, delighted with the banter between the two old friends.

"Very funny," Piper drawled, then turned her gaze back to Mia. "Seriously, though, you look terrific."

"Thanks," Mia said. "The terror was well worth it, I think."

"Since she just got engaged to Dave Firestone," Amanda was saying despite Mia's look of stunned shock, "I thought it was time she knocked his socks off."

"Really?" Piper's eyes widened. "Well, congratulations. Kind of sudden, isn't it?"

"Yes," Mia said, throwing a quick frown at Amanda. "We were sort of swept off our feet."

"And now she's almost set to do even more sweeping," Amanda interrupted. "When Dave gets a look at her, it's going to blow him away."

"Hmm…" Piper glanced into the mirror at her own reflection. "Maybe I could use a makeover myself."

"Any particular reason why?" Mia asked.

Piper shrugged and shook her head. "It's just, the work I do, the men I work with all look at me like 'one of the guys.' I think even Ryan Grant—my best friend, mind you—forgets I'm a woman most of the time."

Mia could understand that. She'd been ignored or overlooked for most of her life. At least Piper had her coworkers' respect. She wasn't invisible. But now, after experiencing the past few hours, Mia knew what the Saint Tropez salon and day spa could do for Piper.

"We could fix that," Amanda said in a tempting, singsongy voice. "Just let me know when you're ready and we'll have you buffed and polished and I would *love* to get you out of those sweatshirts you wear."

Piper laughed and stepped behind Mia as if to use her as a shield. "Down girl," she said, still laughing. "You've already got your 'project,' so stay away."

"Fine, fine," Amanda said. "But you'll be sorry. Mia is going to be the talk of the town when I'm finished with her. You just wait and see."

"Oh, man…" Mia murmured, as nerves rose up inside her again. *The talk of the town?* She didn't know if she'd be able to handle that.

"Yep," Piper whispered. "You're toast now. Once Amanda gets going, nobody can slow her down. Good luck!"

Amanda took Mia's hand and dragged her from the room, already talking about what they would be buying at Monica's. Mia threw one last look back at Piper and was not reassured to see the other woman laughing.

Six

Mia sipped her glass of sauvignon blanc and willed the wine to soothe the nerves jittering in the pit of her stomach. Apparently, though, it was going to take a lot more than a sip or two.

She had a seat at the bar in the lounge at Claire's restaurant. The bar was as elegant as the restaurant itself. Small, round tables, candles flickering in the center of each of them. The polished mahogany bar shone under the soft glow of overhead lighting. Smooth jazz sighed from speakers tucked against the ceiling, and a long mirror backed the bar itself, reflecting the patrons seated in the room. Some, like Mia, were waiting to meet their parties and have dinner. Some were there for a quiet drink with friends.

She gave her own reflection a wry smile and still hardly recognized herself. In the deep scarlet, long-sleeved silk blouse and black slacks, she was out of her comfort zone and into foreign territory. It wasn't just the new clothes or the hair, or even the makeup she'd taken the trouble to apply, though. It was the whole situation. The subterfuge. The lies that would dominate her life for the next month.

And, she was forced to admit, if only to herself, that being around Dave constantly wasn't going to be easy, either. He was too gorgeous. Too sure of himself and far too touchable.

In just a couple of days, her life had been turned upside down. Now, instead of being curled up in her suite at Alex's house, watching TV, she was here, wearing silk, drinking wine and fighting the urge to bolt.

Being in the bar wasn't helping the situation any, either. She felt out of place, alone on her barstool. She'd never been comfortable in places like this, despite the elegance. Mia had spent too much of her childhood in the back rooms or kitchens of bars and restaurants and casinos. The clink of glasses, the murmured conversations and the smell of alcohol awakened a memory, and for just a moment or two, she was ten years old again.

The back room of the bar was small and so well lit Mia didn't need the pocket flashlight she always carried so she could read wherever she happened to be. Tonight, she sat in a corner, a glass of root beer at her side, and tried to concentrate on the magical world of Narnia.

But the poker game going on across the room from her made it really hard. Men argued and grumbled and the laughter from the women sounded sharp and brittle.

She looked around the group of men and caught her father's eye. He winked at her and Mia smiled. This was just one more poker game in a never-ending chain of them. This bar was in St. Louis, but winter was coming and her father had promised they were headed West after he got a stake from tonight's game. Vegas, he'd said. With maybe a side trip to California and Disneyland.

Mia smiled to herself and shifted her gaze back to her library book. Her father always made wonderful promises. But she had learned when she was just a little kid that she couldn't always count on them.

"How you doing, Princess?"

She looked up from her book into her father's big blue eyes. She had his eyes, he always told her. And her beautiful mother's nose and mouth. Every night before bed, her father showed her pictures of the mother she couldn't remember. The pretty woman had died when Mia was still a baby. It was sad, but she still had her daddy and that was enough.

"I'm fine, Daddy."

"Hungry?"

"Nope, I'm just reading."

"Just like your mom," he said and kissed her forehead. "Always have your pretty nose in a book." He smiled and smoothed one hand over her hair. "One of these days, sweet girl, we're gonna hit the jackpot. We'll buy us a house with a library just like the Beast's in that cartoon movie you love. You'll have your own room you can decorate any way you want and you can go to school."

That was her favorite dream. She couldn't even imagine going to sleep and waking up in the same room every day. A house to call her own. On a nice street, maybe with trees and a swing in the backyard. And she could have a puppy, too. And the puppy would love her so much it would sleep in her bed with her. And she could go to school and have friends and every day when she came home on the bus her dog and her father would be waiting for her, so happy to be together again.

But it wasn't going to happen. Her daddy was a pro-

fessional gambler and she already knew that they had to go where the games were.

So they did.

"Hey, Jack," someone called out. "You playin' or what?"

"Right there," her father answered, then leaned in and kissed the tip of Mia's nose. Whispering, he said, "Another hour or so, Princess, and we'll head back to the hotel. Tomorrow morning, we'll get on the road early and head for Vegas. You good with that?"

"Yes, Daddy." Her father never left her alone in a motel room. Too afraid of losing her, he always said. But the truth was, Mia wouldn't have stayed even if she could have. She wanted to be where her father was. They were a team and he was all she had. They might not have a puppy or a house, but that was okay because wherever Jack Hughes was, that was home.

"That's my little good-luck charm," he said and kissed her again. "Another hour, tops."

She would have waited for him forever.

Dave grabbed the cell phone when it rang and said, "Hello?"

"Dave, did you buy me a new car?"

He smiled at the familiar voice and the note of outrage in it. "Who is this?"

"Very funny," his mother retorted. "Now explain the new Lexus that was just delivered."

"What's to explain?" he asked as he checked for traffic then loped across the street. He was headed for Claire's to meet Mia for dinner. He hadn't wanted to bother scouring the parking lot for a space, so he'd parked on the street and walked over. "You needed a new car, now you've got one."

"My old car was fine," his mother said with a sigh of exasperation.

"Key word there being *old*," Dave told her. Then he stopped outside the restaurant, leaned against the edge of the building and let his gaze sweep the small town while his mother talked in his ear. After a long day on the ranch, he was tired and hungry and eager to get his deal with Mia started.

He'd already stopped at McKay's jewelers for a ring. Which, he knew, thanks to Erma McKay, owner and one of the top links on the Royal gossip food chain, would be all over town before he got to the restaurant. Dave smiled to himself as he remembered Erma's nose practically twitching as she'd sniffed out his story of a whirlwind romance and a surprise engagement.

He glanced up and down Main Street. It was dusk, so streetlights were blinking to life. Cars were pulled into the parking slots that lined the street in front of the shops. A kid raced down the sidewalk on his skateboard, wheels growling in his wake.

The jeweler's box in his jacket pocket felt as if it was burning through the fabric. He had never considered getting married. Or if he had, it was in a "someday maybe" sort of context. Now, even knowing the engagement was a farce and all his own idea, he felt a proverbial noose tightening around his neck. Dave hadn't exactly grown up with the best example of a working marriage, so why in hell would he be interested in tying himself down to risk the same sort of misery?

"David, this has to stop. You can't keep buying me things," his mother said flatly, and that caught his attention.

"Why not?"

"Oh, for heaven's sake, enjoy your money. Go buy something fun for yourself."

He had, he thought. He'd bought himself a fiancée, but not being an idiot, he didn't say that out loud. "Mom…"

"I'm serious, David. If you want to give me something, make it grandchildren."

Dave shook his head as a woman with two kids, one of them howling as if he was being tortured, went past. Kids? No, thank you. "Cars are easier. Just enjoy the Lexus, Mom."

"How can I when I know you're spending your money on *me?*"

"I'm doing it for myself," he said, knowing just how to get gifts past his too-proud-for-her-own-good mom. "I worry about you and if you're in a safe, new car, that's at least one thing I don't have to worry about."

She sighed on the other end of the phone and Dave knew he'd won this round. His mother had worked her ass off taking care of him and seeing that he got all of the opportunities she could manage. And if he had his way, she'd be treated like a damn queen now. Even if he had to fight her to make it happen.

"I don't know where you got that hard head of yours," she said in a huff. "But I'm out of time to argue with you. I'm meeting Cora for dinner, so I've got to run."

"Me, too. I've got a dinner date."

"Ooh." His mother's radar instantly went on alert. "Who is she?"

Dave grinned. "Have a good time, Mom."

"Fine, fine." Exasperation coloring her voice, she said, "You're an evil son to not tell me about this woman, but you have fun, too."

Still smiling, he hung up, stepped into Claire's and headed directly to the bar, knowing that Mia would be there waiting for him, since he was late. That thought wiped the smile from his face. Dave didn't do late. He was always on time, always in control, and the fact that that control had started slipping the minute he got involved with Mia hadn't escaped him.

He scanned the bar quickly, thoroughly, and didn't see her. Had she stood him up? Changed her mind about the whole thing? Well, damned if he'd let her back out now, he told himself. They had a plan and they were going to stick to it, even if she...

He caught a woman's gaze in the wide bar mirror and his breath left him in a rush. It was her. Mia. And she looked...amazing.

Mia was, quite unexpectedly, Dave told himself, the most beautiful woman he'd ever seen. How could this stylish, sophisticated brunette sitting alone at the bar possibly be Mia? Where was the tidy bun at the back of her neck? The unadorned eyes and the naked lips? Admiration mingled with desire inside him and frothed into a dangerous mix. He took a moment to catch his breath, and to enjoy the view. Her legs looked impossibly long in her sleek black slacks and he found himself wishing she'd worn a damn dress so he could get a good look at those legs.

He had to wonder if that glance they'd shared in the mirror had displayed the hunger in his eyes. Damn, he hadn't had a rush of pure, unadulterated lust like this in— Hell, he couldn't even remember the last time he'd *wanted* anyone this badly.

If he hadn't already decided to seduce her into his bed, seeing her tonight would have made the decision for him. He was hard and eager and ready to say screw dinner and just whisk her back to the ranch. Unfortunately, he thought, she was going to take some convincing. Still, there was nothing he liked better than a challenge.

"Mia?"

She blinked, and her eyes lost that faraway look and focused on him in the mirror. Her lips curved and his groin tightened.

Damn, it felt like a fist to his chest. Amazing what a woman could do to a man with a single look and a knowing smile. Were her eyes always that big? he wondered. Were they really so deep it seemed he could dive into their depths and drown?

"Dave?" Her voice shook him. It was deep, filled with concern. "Are you okay?"

Get a grip. "Yeah. Fine. Just…" His gaze swept her up and down. "Stunned. You look beautiful, Mia."

She actually flushed, and until that moment, Dave would have bet cold hard cash there wasn't a woman alive who could still do that.

Something fisted in his chest and breath was hard to find. He had to regain the upper hand here. Fast.

"Hope you didn't wait long." Not an apology, he assured himself. Just a statement.

"No." She gave him a curious look, as if she was wondering why his voice had suddenly shifted to cool and businesslike.

Well, hell, if she knew how he'd had to fight for that dispassionate tone, she'd have all the power here, wouldn't she?

"Are you ready for dinner?"

"Yes, but they haven't called our table yet and—"

"My table's ready when I am," he told her.

Both of her perfectly arched eyebrows lifted on her forehead. "Well, I hope you use your power for good instead of evil."

He laughed shortly. He hadn't expected to actually *enjoy* Mia's company. She was just full of surprises. So, to continue her comic book theme, he said, "With great power comes great responsibility."

She gave him a wide smile as a reward and lust roared up inside him, hotter than before. Shaking his head, he told her, "Leave your drink. We'll have champagne at the table."

"Champagne?" she asked as she took his hand and slid off the bar stool. "Are we celebrating?"

"Shouldn't we be?" he asked, catching her soft, floral scent as she moved closer. "We're engaged, right?"

"Yes," she said after a moment or two, "I guess we are."

Her fingers curled around his and Dave felt heat slide through him so fast it was like a sudden fever.

But fevers burned themselves out fast; he'd do well to remember that.

He led her through the bar to the restaurant, where the hostess recognized him instantly and picked up two menus. "Welcome back, Mr. Firestone. If you and your guest will follow me…"

The young woman headed into the interior of Claire's, where the lights were dim and the pristine, white linen tablecloths shone like snow in the darkness. Candles flickered madly, sending shadows dancing across the walls. Couples and larger groups sat at the tables and booths, their low-pitched voices no more than white noise. The same smooth jazz from the bar sighed into this room as well and gave the whole place a sense of intimacy.

Dave had brought a few dates here before, but mainly he used Claire's as a place to talk business. The waitstaff was attentive but not cloying, so you had plenty of time to talk without being interrupted constantly.

Tonight, though, was a different kind of business.

And damn if he'd risk his future because his rock-hard body was screaming at him.

With his hand at Mia's back, he steered her through the maze of tables and chairs. The cool silk of her shirt and the heat of her body mingled together to twist his guts into a knot that tightened with every breath.

The hostess showed them to Dave's usual table, a secluded booth at the back of the restaurant, and once they were seated she moved off, leaving them alone. Mia picked up her menu immediately and Dave smiled. It was actually nice to be out with a woman who liked to eat. Most of the women he spent time with never ate more than a salad and, even with the dressing on the side, they seldom finished their meal. A little irritating to pay for food that ended up being tossed.

She looked at him over the top edge of her menu. "I've never been here before. It's lovely."

"Yeah," he said, glancing around. "I suppose it is."

He'd become so accustomed to Claire's that he hadn't bothered to even notice his surroundings in longer than he could remember. Now, seeing it through Mia's eyes, he saw that it was more than a handy meeting spot. It was refined, yet casual enough to be comfortable.

In the candlelight, Mia's skin looked like fine porcelain, her eyes reflected the dancing flame in the center of the table and her hair fell in long, soft waves over her shoulders. The top two buttons on her silk blouse were undone, giving him a peek at smooth skin that only made him want to see more.

Sure, he'd been attracted before, but this Mia was at a whole new level. She'd surprised him, and that wasn't easy to do. He wondered what she was thinking as she stared back at him and realized that it was the first time he'd even cared what a woman was thinking. She was hitting him on so many different levels, it was almost impossible to keep up.

To get his mind off what his body was clamoring for, he said, "When I walked in tonight, you looked a million miles away."

"What?" she frowned. "Oh." Shrugging a bit, she said, "I was just remembering."

Curiosity pinged inside him. "Remembering what?"

"My father," she said simply.

He hadn't expected that, either. Her voice was soft, filled with fond affection that he couldn't identify with. He laid the menu down since he didn't need to read it anyway. Dave knew what he was going to order. Same thing he always got. Steak. Potatoes.

Instead, he focused on Mia. Her eyes drew him in and he tried to figure out what exactly she'd done differently. Makeup, sure. Eyeliner and a soft brown shadow on her lids. But it was the emotion in her eyes that grabbed at him. "Where is he now?"

"He died about ten years ago."

"Sorry," he said and meant it because he could see what the man's loss meant to her.

"What about you? Is your father still alive?"

He stiffened. See? He told himself. This was why he rarely took notice of someone else's life. It inevitably turned around on him. "No idea."

"What do you mean?"

"He walked out on my mom and me when I was ten. Never saw him again."

Her eyes instantly went soft. "Oh, Dave, I'm sorry."

He didn't want sympathy. Didn't need it. He'd long ago left behind the boy who'd missed his father. Dave had done just fine without the man who'd walked out on his responsibility. His *family*.

"I don't know what to say," Mia murmured.

"Nothing to say," Dave assured her, and wished the waiter would bring the champagne he'd ordered ahead of time. "Long time ago. He left. We lost our ranch and my mother became a cook for the family who bought the place."

His voice was clipped, cool, giving away nothing of the still-hot bubble of rage that these memories brought to him. Even after all these years, Dave could feel the helplessness that had gripped him as a boy.

Watching his mother work herself to the bone as an employee in what used to be her home. Hearing her cry at night and knowing there was nothing he could do. Hating his father for walking away, and yet at the same time, praying every night that he would come back.

But he didn't. And Dave had grown up quickly. He'd made a vow to become so rich no one would ever be able to take away what was his again. He would take care of his mom and make sure she never had to work for someone else.

And he'd done it.

Made good on his promise to himself. Made himself into a man others envied. And he wouldn't stop now.

Mia was still staring at him, and he could see hesitation in her eyes. As if she was arguing with herself internally about whether to offer sympathy or congratulations on what he'd become. He'd save her the question.

"The past doesn't matter."

"You really believe that?" she asked.

"I do. All that counts is now and the future you build."

"But it's the past that made us who we are."

"You're right. But you can't change the past, so why think about it?" he asked.

"To learn from it? To remember the good things?"

Their waiter showed up at their table, ending their conversation as he carried a silver ice bucket with a chilled bottle of champagne inside. They were silent as the waiter popped the cork and poured a small amount into a wineglass for Dave to try. When he approved it, both glasses were filled and the waiter took their orders.

Dave smiled to himself as Mia ordered the same thing he had. Steak and a baked potato.

"Still hungry?" he asked, before she could return to the conversation about the past. He was done looking backward.

She shrugged. "No point in pretending not to have an appetite. This isn't exactly a date, is it?"

He laughed a little. "So women only pretend to not be hungry when they go out?"

"Sure," she said. "I bet every skinny woman in the world goes home after a date and dives into her fridge when no one's looking."

"Speaking from experience?"

"Not really," she admitted with a shrug. "It's been a *long* time since I was on a date."

"I don't get that." She was gorgeous, funny and smart enough to know a good deal when it was presented to her. Why wouldn't men be interested?

She picked up her champagne and sipped at it. A slow smile curved her mouth when she swallowed and a twist of need tightened Dave's guts. Damn, she was a dangerous female.

"I haven't had time for dating, really," she was saying. "Getting my degree has taken up all my time, and then there's taking care of Alex's house to be able to pay for school. Not to mention the interning at Royal Junior High. So, dating? Not really a priority."

"I can understand that," he said, impressed with her work ethic and determination to carve out her life on her terms. "You have a goal, you do what you need to do to make it happen. I did the same thing."

"How do you mean?"

The restaurant was quiet, just the hum of low-pitched conversations and the background music that drifted in and out of notice. The candlelight created an air of intimacy, so Dave could have believed that he and Mia were the only two people in the room. Maybe that was why he'd told her what he'd never discussed with anyone else before.

He took a sip of champagne and thought how different his life was now than it had been just ten years before. Back then, it was cheap beer and big plans. He started talking, his voice hardly more than a hush.

"I worked my way through college, like you." His fingers, curled around the stem of the wineglass, tightened slightly as memories rushed through his mind. He never looked back, so when he did, it jolted him. "Took whatever job I could. Paid for school, and saved whatever else I could. In my geology class, I met a guy, Tobin Myer."

"Interesting name," Mia said.

"Interesting guy," Dave countered. "He didn't have many friends. Spent most of his free time exploring, doing tests on vacant land."

"What kind of tests?"

He chuckled and relaxed into the telling. He wasn't sure why talking to Mia was so damn easy and didn't think he should delve too deeply into that. "Y'know, even now, I couldn't tell you. Tobin could, of course. He could

talk for hours about mineral deposits, shale, oil traces...
the man was born with dirt in his blood, I swear."

"You liked him."

Dave glanced at her. "Yeah. I did. We were both lon-
ers. I didn't have time for friends and parties. Tobin was
too far out there for anyone else to give a damn about
him so... Different reasons, but we were both still alone.
Maybe that's why we connected. Anyway..." Enough of
the psychological B.S. "Tobin found a piece of land that
had him excited. Said the signs of mineral deposits were
through the roof. But he needed a backer. Someone with
enough money to buy the land and be his partner in de-
veloping it."

"You."

He nodded. "Me." Hell, even he found it hard to believe
that he'd taken the risk, spent the money it had taken so
long to put together. "I took my savings and invested it
in Tobin and that parcel of land."

"I'm guessing," she said, lifting her wineglass, "that
since we're sitting here drinking this lovely champagne
and you're paying me an extraordinary amount of money
for a few weeks' time, Tobin was right."

"Oh, he was better than right," Dave told her. "That
piece of land was worth a fortune."

"So you sold it?"

"No, we leased it to a huge oil and gas company outside of Dallas," he said. "They wanted to buy, of course,
but instead we kept the title, and in exchange they paid
us a boatload upfront and a hefty royalty every quarter."

"Your idea?"

"Absolutely." He grinned, remembering his first big
deal. He'd stood his ground with the big company, kept
Tobin from having a stroke due to anxiety and he'd pulled

it off. "Tobin would have taken their first offer, he was so excited to be right about the land."

Dave could still feel the rush of satisfaction that had filled him when he and Tobin had made the deal. They'd each received a small fortune on signing and the royalty checks over the years had only gotten bigger. That was what had given him the means to buy his ranch and build his house, and was the seed money for everything that had come to him since.

"Do you still see Tobin?"

He looked at her. "Yeah, I do. He's based out of Dallas now, but spends most of his time in his jet, checking out land all over the country. Still following that love of dirt."

"And you're still partners."

"Ever hear of MyerStone Development?"

"Actually, yes. They're in the business section of the paper a lot and—" She stopped and smiled. "You and Tobin."

"Me and Tobin," he said, and lifted his glass in a salute to his partner.

"So the past can be nice to look back on."

He caught her eye and nodded. "Touché."

They ordered their meal, and throughout dinner, they talked of everyday things. What was new in Royal. The fact that there was no news about Alex, and then, finally, just how they would convince Thomas Buckley that they were a couple.

The longer he was with her, the more Dave figured he had the answer to a lot of problems. Over cake and coffee, he made his move.

"I think you should move into the ranch with me."

Seven

Mia froze with the last forkful of cake halfway to her lips. "What?"

She looked like a deer caught in headlights. Good. He preferred her off balance. This would all work much better if he could keep Mia dancing in place just to keep up with him.

"Finish your cake," he urged. "You know you want to."

She popped the piece of double-chocolate lava cake into her mouth and chewed frantically. While she was quiet, Dave went on.

"Think about it for a minute. We're engaged. We'll be meeting with Buckley out at the ranch anyway. It'll be handier with you there."

She swallowed, waved her fork at him and argued, "But you told me that Buckley is really conservative. He probably wouldn't approve of us, well, living together."

"We're engaged."

She took a breath, blew it out and reluctantly set her fork down.

"Which reminds me," Dave said, reaching into his pocket for the jeweler's box.

When she saw the dark red velvet, her eyes went wide and she dropped both hands into her lap. "What did you do?"

"Mia, no one's going to believe that a man like me proposed without a ring."

Her eyes met his and he could see nerves shining back at him. Again, good. If her mind was whirring in high gear, she wouldn't be thinking clearly about much of anything.

"I don't know…"

"We're already in this. The ring is just a symbol of our bargain."

"A symbol." She took another long, deep breath, then grabbed her fork again and scraped it across the dessert plate, catching every last drop of the chocolate sauce. She licked the fork clean and had zero idea what watching her tongue move across the tines was doing to Dave.

"It's just a piece of jewelry," he said and flipped the box lid open.

She gasped and he smiled. Eyes wide, she stared at the ring and slapped one hand to her chest as if to hold her heart in place. "You can't be serious."

Pleasure filled him. Her expressions were so easy to read that he could see that she both wanted the ring and wanted to run. When she reached out a hesitant finger to touch the five-carat diamond, he knew he had her.

Her fingertip slid across the wide surface of the diamond, then dropped to follow the smaller, channel-set diamonds that surrounded it. After a long minute or two, she lifted her gaze to his.

"It's gigantic."

"It sends a message."

"Yeah. 'Here I am, robber! Take me!'"

"In Royal?" He laughed, shook his head and plucked the ring from the box. Sliding it onto her ring finger before she could pull her hand back, he said, "What it will say to everyone here is, Mia belongs to Dave."

"Belongs."

She whispered the word, but he heard it. And just for a second, that imaginary noose tightened. He ignored the feeling and focused on the plan.

Her gaze fixed on the ring for a long moment before meeting his eyes again. "I'll wear the ring—"

"Good."

"But as for moving in with you—"

"It makes the most sense."

"But I have to take care of Alex's house."

"Alex isn't there," he reminded her quietly.

"I know but—"

"And the longer he's gone, the more intrusive the reporters are going to get," he went on. "Right now, most of them are being stopped at the gate. But a few have gotten through to harass you."

"True."

"More will come. Especially once word about us gets out. They'll start speculating about us getting together. Why not be at my place? No reporter will be able to reach you there, and you can check on Alex's house whenever you want."

"I don't like leaving Alex's house," she admitted. "What if he calls? What if he needs help?"

Frowning, Dave paused and thought about it before saying, "We'll have the phone company forward calls to my place. Good enough?"

She was thinking about it. He could see her working through internal arguments, trying to decide what she should do. But he'd have his way in this.

Having her at the ranch would cement their "engagement" for everyone in town and Thomas Buckley. More than that, having her in his house would speed up the seduction—which he was really interested in. Just sitting across the table from her was making him crazy.

Every time she chewed at her lip or took a deep breath, Dave felt a slam to his center. Mia Hughes was going to be his. On his terms. Soon.

"Mia, you're living alone in that big empty house, and there's no reason for it," he reminded her. "For the next few weeks, move in with me. Take a break."

She laughed. "A break?"

"Yeah. No house to clean, no worries."

"*You'll* worry me," she admitted.

"Me? I'm harmless."

She laughed again, and he liked the sound of it. "You are many things," she said, "but harmless isn't one of them."

"Not afraid of me, are you?"

"Said the big bad wolf," she murmured, then shook her head. "No. I'm not afraid of you, Dave. I'm just…"

"…going to agree."

"Do you always get your way?"

"Always," he said.

She looked at the ring, then him and finally said, "Then I guess you win again. Okay. I'll move in."

"That wasn't so hard, was it?"

"You have no idea."

"Here," Dave said, sliding his untouched chocolate cake across the table toward her. "You look like you could use this."

She picked up her fork and dug in. "Thanks."

* * *

After a week at the Royal Round Up Ranch, Mia was no more at ease than she had been the day she'd arrived. If anything, her nerves were stretched a little tighter. Royal had been buzzing about their engagement for days. Whenever she went into town, she was stopped a half dozen times on Main Street with people wanting to talk about her "romantic, whirlwind engagement." Which only made her feel like a cheat. And if there's one thing her father had taught her, it was that "cheating is the coward's way."

She hated lying. Hated playing a part. And really hated thinking about what everyone in town would be saying when her engagement ended.

But that was a worry for further down the road. Right now, even though it wasn't easy, she was grateful to be at the ranch because Dave had been right. The reporters were even more intrusive than before, though none of them could get to her here at the Royal Round Up.

She steered her old Volkswagen Bug through the gates of the ranch and waved at the guard Dave had posted there. No reporter could get past that guard, and if anyone tried to just hop a fence and cross the ranch, they'd get lost long before they made it to the main house.

Smiling to herself, Mia drove down the winding road toward the ranch house, her mind wandering as she traveled the now-familiar route.

It had been a weird week. Oh, she was used to his house now, had even learned her way around. And in spite of its size and innate elegance, it was a homey place. Warm and welcoming. Her bedroom, directly across from Dave's, was bigger than her entire suite of rooms at Alex's house. And she was getting very used to waking up to a spectacular view of Dave's ranch. The land stretched out forever, marked by stands of wild oaks and stock ponds. It was quiet, as it could only be in the country, and at night, the sky was velvet, covered by a blanket of stars so thick it took her breath away.

It wasn't her surroundings making her nervous.

It was Dave.

And it wasn't as if he'd gone out of his way to make her jumpy. On the contrary, he'd done nothing but be very nice. Thoughtful, even. They had dinner together every night and spent hours in the library she had loved from the moment she first saw it. He took her on rides around the ranch and introduced her to his mare, due to deliver her foal any day.

Every time she turned around, there he was. Gorgeous. Warm. Sexy. He was turning her inside out and she had the distinct feeling he was doing it on purpose. That he knew by his constant attention he was wearing down her resistance. Seducing her.

And damn if she wasn't enjoying it.

It was a bad idea, though. Mia knew that. This wasn't going to be her home. He wasn't going to be hers for any longer than it took to make the deal he wanted so badly. Nothing about their relationship was real. Except the wanting. And the desire that thrummed inside her all the time was as insistent as a heartbeat.

But if this was seduction, it was the long way around. He hadn't even tried to kiss her.

"Why not?" she muttered, then glared at herself in the rearview mirror.

When this whole deal had begun, she'd made a point of saying that sex wouldn't be a part of it, so why was she...disappointed that he was keeping to their bargain?

"Because you can't stop thinking about him, that's

why," she told herself and gritted her teeth as her car hit a bump on the gravel road.

That was the simple truth. She thought about him all the time. And the fact that he was so determined to keep his distance was driving her a little crazy.

"Which is just wrong and I know it," she said aloud. It wasn't as if she was a highly sexual woman, after all. She'd been with exactly two men in her life, and neither one of those occasions had been worthy of mention. There hadn't been fireworks. The angels hadn't sung.

So why was she so hot and bothered by the thought of Dave?

"Oh, for heaven's sake." The spectacular house rose up in front of her and she drove on, past the circular drive-way that curved around the house. Instead, she parked her car closer to the barn. Mia just couldn't bring herself to park her beater car in front of that gorgeous house. It would be like seeing a pimple on the face of the Mona Lisa.

She looked through the windshield and saw a couple of the ranch hands at the paddock, where Mike Carter was putting a young horse through its paces. Dave was there, too, arms hooked over the top rail of the fence and one booted foot propped on the lower rail. Over the past week or so, she'd discovered that the Dave who lived and worked at the ranch was a wildly different man than the cool, focused businessman she'd first known. It was as if he kept his soul here at the ranch and without it, he was a different man.

Unfortunately for her, she'd been attracted to the hard, distant businessman...but the rancher was unbelievably hard to resist.

Mia sighed, stepped out of the car then reached back in for her bags and the small blue glass vase that held three daisies and a red carnation. She looked at the bedraggled flowers and smiled. A grocery store special, they couldn't have cost more than five dollars and they meant more to her than two dozen roses would have.

"Mia!"

She turned at the sound of her name and saw Dave striding toward her. Late afternoon sun was behind him, and her breath caught in her chest as she watched him approach. His hat was pulled low on his forehead. He wore a blue work shirt, the sleeves pushed up to his elbows, and faded jeans that clung to his long legs and stacked on the tops of his scarred brown boots.

Dave Firestone was the kind of cowboy that would make any woman's heart beat just a little faster than normal. So she really couldn't be blamed for enjoying the view, right?

When he was close enough to reach out and touch her, he stopped, glanced at the flowers she held and smiled. "You want to tell me who's giving my girl flowers?"

His girl. Something warm curled in the pit of her stomach and she was forced to remind herself that he didn't mean it. Just part of the game they were playing. The ranch hands were close by and no doubt watching them, so he was playing to his audience.

"I told you today was the last day of my internship at Royal Junior High…"

"Not even the end of the semester, was it?"

"No. The school board makes fall internships short and then does follow-ups come spring. Gives us more time to devote to schoolwork."

"Okay…"

"Well, two of my kids bought me these," she said, glancing down at the flowers that meant so much to her.

"Nice kids," he said.

She looked up at him. "They really are. I'm going to miss them."

He moved in closer. Close enough that she caught the scent of his aftershave still clinging to his skin. Her heartbeat sped up in response.

"You'll see them all again in the spring. And then again after you get your degree and start working there full time."

Since she still had a few months of school left and there was no guarantee of a job when she was finished, Mia could only hope he was right.

"You were late getting home," he said. "I was worried. Thought maybe this...*car* of yours finally gave up the ghost."

She frowned at him. Okay, her old VW wasn't exactly a luxury ride, but it was loyal, she knew all of its quirks and as long as she added a quart of oil a week, it kept running. It fired right up every morning, and it got her where she needed to go and that was enough for her. Mia didn't have enough money to think about making a new-car payment every month. "Don't make fun of my baby."

He shook his head. "Nothing funny about this car. It should have been junked years ago."

As if he could hear her thoughts, he changed the subject. "Leave your bags here," he said and scooped everything but the flowers from her arms, then stacked them on the hood of the car. "There's something I want to show you."

Excitement shone in his eyes and that half smile of his that she loved so much was tipping up one corner of his mouth. He was irresistible. She set the vase of flowers down on the hood. "What is it?"

"You'll see." He caught her hand in his and headed for the barn.

Mia had to hurry her steps to keep up with his long-legged stride. The warmth of his hand against hers simmered in a slow heat that slid through her system to settle around her heart.

The men gathered at the paddock called hello to her as they passed and she smiled, enjoying the sensation of being part of ranch life—even if it only was temporary. With that sobering thought in mind, she followed Dave into the shadow-filled barn.

It smelled like hay and horses and she heard a shuffling sound from animals shifting position in their stalls. Dave led her to the far stall, then pulled her close to look over the edge of the door.

"Oh, my…" Mia's heart twisted in her chest. Dave's mare, Dancer, was nuzzling a brand-new foal, still shaky on its impossibly long, thin legs.

"Happened just a couple hours ago," Dave whispered, his breath warm against her ear. "Dancer came through like she'd done this a hundred times before."

"I'm so glad," Mia said, wrapping her arms around him for an instinctive hug. She knew how much the horse meant to him. He'd even been planning to have a vet attend the birth because he didn't want to take chances with the mare's life.

And that endeared him to her. He might pretend to be cold and shut off, but the truth was, he had a big heart. He was just careful whom he showed it to.

"Yeah," he answered, looking down into her eyes as his arms closed around her, drawing her even closer. "Me, too. I raised Dancer, so she means a lot to me."

"I know." She couldn't look away from his fog-gray eyes. She held her breath, afraid to speak, afraid to shatter this sudden shift into intimacy.

His gaze moved over her face like a caress. "It's weird,

but I was anxious for you to get home, so I could share this with you."

"Really?"

"Yeah." He lifted one hand to cup her cheek. "Wonder what that's about?"

"I don't know," she said, "but I'm glad."

"Me, too," he said, and bent his head to hers.

She was dazzled with the first brush of his lips against hers. Sighing, she leaned into him and he held her tighter, pressing her body along the length of his.

Mia was lost, spiraling away into the heat and desire burning inside her. She forgot all about where they were. The barn and the horses faded away. The voices from the cowboys outside silenced and it was just her and Dave, locked in a moment that filled her with pleasure despite a tiny, tiny touch of worry.

When he parted her lips with his tongue and the kiss deepened into something amazing, the worry dissolved under an onslaught of emotion so thick and rich that Mia's mind shut down completely. She leaned into him, her arms tightening around him, her tongue tangling with his in a wild dance of a passion she'd never felt before.

Their breath mingled, their bodies pressed together and Mia heard Dave groan as he claimed her again and again. His hands swept down to the hem of her shirt and slid underneath it. The touch of his hands against her bare back was magic and she suddenly wanted more. Needed more.

But he tore his mouth from hers and left her struggling to catch her breath, fighting to find her balance. She leaned her forehead against his chest and shivered. "Why did you stop?"

He chuckled and his voice sounded raw and strained when he answered, "Because we're in a damn barn, Mia.

With my ranch hands right outside that door. If we're gonna do this, then we're gonna do it right."

He paused, lifted her chin until he could look into her eyes and asked, "We *are* gonna do this, right?"

There was her out. Time to snap out of this sexual haze and remember what she was doing here. Who she was with. And why. He'd just handed her the chance she needed to reach for calm, cool logic and call off whatever it was that was happening between them. She should be grateful. Should be smart. Should tell him, "No, we're not."

"Absolutely," she said. "When?"

"I'm thinking *now.*"

"Oh, good idea." Mia was still trembling. Still shaking from needs awakened and screaming inside her. "Where?"

"Your room. Fifteen minutes."

"Right. Fifteen minutes." She took a breath and blew it out. "Why so long?"

He laughed and she did, too. This was ridiculous. She was acting crazy. She'd never done anything like this before. It was so out of character for her. And she liked it a lot.

"Because," he said, letting her go long enough to adjust his jeans, "I'm not going to be able to walk across that yard for at least ten minutes."

She flushed, then grinned. Wow. She'd never done that to a man before. Had him so hard he wasn't able to walk. It felt…great.

"Okay, then," she said, taking another breath, which only succeeded in fanning the flames licking at her insides. "I'll be waiting."

His gray eyes burned with an intensity that was new to her as he promised, "I'll get there as fast as I can."

Nodding, Mia scuttled out of the barn, waved to the guys in the paddock and hurried toward the house. She stopped at her car long enough to pick up her things, then she practically ran to the ranch house and the staircase that led to her bedroom.

Mia didn't have much time. She raced up the stairs, praying she wouldn't run into Dave's housekeeper as she went. She hit her bedroom at a dead run and pulled her clothes off as she hurried across the room to the attached bath. She hopped into the shower and thanked heaven she'd shaved her legs the day before. When she was finished, she dried off and slipped into the heavy, white robe hanging on the back of her door, tying the belt with shaking hands.

She was taking a step here. A big one. She hadn't meant for her relationship with Dave to go this far, but now that it had she wouldn't regret it. Instead, she was going to grab at the chance fate had handed her. For years, she'd been locked away in schools, libraries, tucked up in her suite of rooms at Alex's house. *Life* had been passing her by and she'd hardly noticed.

Mia took a deep breath and slapped one hand to her belly in a futile attempt to quell the butterflies swarming inside. She hadn't once, in the past few years, had so much as a date. She'd been too focused on her future to enjoy her present.

Well, today that stopped. Today, Mia Hughes was going to take the time to live a little. To be with a man who *wanted* her. Whatever happened tomorrow, she'd simply have to deal with it, because she wasn't going to back away.

Mia sat down on the edge of her four-poster bed and, to distract herself from the nerves of waiting, glanced around the room that had become so familiar over the past week. The whole house was golden oak and rough-hewn stone, and her room was no different. There was a deeply cushioned window seat below the arched bay windows that overlooked the backyard. The view was of rolling green grass, stands of live oaks and ponds for the Black Angus cattle that wandered the fields. A stone fireplace, cold now, stood against one wall, and on the opposite wall was a dresser beside a walk-in closet. It was perfect. Just like the rest of this house.

And right now, all it was lacking was Dave.

A knock on her door startled her out of her thoughts. She opened the door, looked up at Dave and knew that somehow this was meant to be. She wasn't going to question it. She was just going to *live.*

"You look like you're silently arguing with yourself," he said, his voice a low rumble of sound that seemed to reverberate in the big room.

"Nope," she said, shaking her head. "No arguing."

"No second-guessing?"

"No."

"No changing your mind?"

"No."

"Thank God." He stepped into the room and used one bare foot to kick the door shut behind him. "If you had changed your mind…"

"What?" she asked, excitement jolting to life inside her. "What would you have done?"

"Left," he admitted, then added, "and would have sat in my room, moaning in pain."

"That would have been a shame."

"Tell me about it," he said with a grin as he closed in on her. "You've been making me crazy, Mia."

"I have?" Oh, that was lovely to hear. She hadn't known she was capable of driving a man crazy.

"Oh, yeah." His gaze swept up and down her body and then met her eyes. "What's under the robe?"

"Me." She lifted her hands to the belt at her waist, but he stopped her.

"Let me."

She stood perfectly still while he untied the belt and pushed her robe open. The cool air in the room brushed her skin, raising goose bumps that were dissolved in the heat of Dave's touch.

His hands smoothed over her hips and up to cup her breasts. She swayed, but kept her eyes open, determined to see him, to experience every moment of this time with him.

He'd taken a shower, too, before coming to her. His dark blond hair was still damp. He wore a black T-shirt, jeans and he was barefoot. He looked sexier than she'd ever seen him and that was saying something.

He bent to kiss her and she moved into him, relishing the buzz of sensation as his mouth met hers. Once, twice and then he straightened up, looking down at her again. "Gotta have you, Mia."

"Yes, Dave." She reached up, wound her arms around his neck and whooshed out a surprised gasp when he scooped her up into his arms.

She laughed, delighted. It was all so romantic, she could hardly believe it was happening to her.

He took a step and stopped. "I surprised you," he said, grinning.

"You did."

"I like your smile."

She liked a lot about him. Staring into his eyes, Mia knew she should call a halt to this and knew just as well that she wouldn't. Sighing, she said, "Oh, this is really going to complicate things."

Dave shook his head. "Doesn't have to."

"Of course it does. Sex always complicates things."

"Complications aren't necessarily a bad thing."

"I hope you're right."

His grin widened briefly. "I'm always right."

He laid her down on the bed and she pushed herself up onto her elbows to watch as Dave stripped out of his clothes. In seconds, he was on the bed with her, gathering her up in his arms and rolling them across the mattress until she was breathless. Legs tangled, hands explored, mouths tasted, teased. Breath came fast and short and whispered moans and murmurs filled the room.

Mia arched into him when his mouth closed over her nipple. Lips, tongue and teeth worked her already sensitive skin until she was twisting and writhing beneath him, chasing the feeling that was growing inside her.

Mia had never felt like this. Never even come close. Dave was stroking her, dipping his fingers into her heat, touching her inside and out. And with every caress the fire engulfing her grew brighter, hotter. Her hips lifted into his hand, as she instinctively moved toward the release waiting for her.

"I've wanted to touch you like this for days," Dave murmured, then closed his mouth around one of her nipples.

"Oh…" She held his head to her breast and her eyes closed with the sheer bliss of the moment.

"I love the little sighs and moans you make," he said, lifting his head to look down into her eyes. "I love the way you feel. I love the scent of you."

Love. Love.

But not the Big L. A corner of her mind realized that

and made sure she didn't cling to any false hopes. He didn't *love* her. He loved what they were *doing.* And so did she. *Don't think,* she ordered her mind and deliberately turned off everything but the sensations cresting inside her.

Again and again, he stroked, delved, caressed and nibbled. Foreplay became forever-play. She wanted him inside her and he kept making her wait. He was pushing her so high, so fast, she could hardly breathe with the wanting.

No one had ever touched her like this. No one had ever made her *feel* so much. He kissed her, using his tongue to steal the last of her breath. Mia didn't care. At that moment, all she cared about was finally, finally reaching the climax he was promising her with every stroke of his fingers.

When he broke the kiss and she reached for him, he grinned. "Hold that thought."

Then he eased off the bed, grabbed up his jeans from the floor and reached into one of the pockets. He tossed a handful of condoms onto the bedside table, then opened one of the foil packets.

A buzz of expectation sped through Mia as she shot a glance at the condoms, then at Dave. "Planning a long night?"

"Good to be prepared," he countered, and sheathed himself before joining her on the bed. "Now that I've got you where I want you, I may not let you go again."

"Who says I'm going to let *you* go?" Mia teased.

He grinned at her again. "That's what I like to hear." He dropped a kiss at the base of her throat. "You're so warm."

"Getting warmer every second," she said.

Smiling, he parted her thighs and knelt between them,

pausing long enough to slide the tip of one finger along her folds, making her shiver.

She planted her feet on the bed and lifted her hips into his touch. Licking her lips, she murmured, "Please, Dave. No more waiting."

"No more waiting," he agreed and entered her in one long stroke.

Mia gasped, looked up into his eyes and sighed as she reveled in the sensation of him filling her. He was part of her. His body and hers locked together. She wrapped her arms around his neck and didn't take her gaze from his as he moved within her. Over and over again, he rocked his hips against hers, setting a rhythm that she eagerly matched. They moved as one, their bodies each straining toward a shattering climax.

Their sighs and groans filled the room like music. Sunlight speared through the windows and spotlighted them on the wide bed as they came together in a need that swamped everything else.

Mia held on to him as tension gripped her, coiling tighter and tighter. She moved with him, met him stroke for stroke. She slid her hands up and down his back and felt his muscles bunch.

This moment was all. Nothing beyond this room— this time—mattered.

She stared into his fog-gray eyes and watched her own reflection there as her body erupted. Mia called out his name and clung desperately to him as a shock wave thundered through her.

She was still trembling when Dave reached the same peak she had. And together, they slid down the other side into completion.

Eight

Dave was shaken, but damn if he'd admit it—even to himself.

Lying there on Mia's bed, with her curled up to his side, he stared at the ceiling and tried to understand just what the hell had happened.

He'd put her in this guest room on purpose. So she'd be close enough to make seduction that much easier. Problem was, *he* was the one who had been seduced. And that hadn't been part of the plan at all.

"That was so good," Mia murmured, her warm breath brushing across his chest.

"Yeah, it was." Better than good, he thought, frowning a little as his brain began to click again now that the burn in his body had eased some. He'd figured from the beginning that getting Mia naked would take care of the desire that pumped through him every time he was near her. Instead, his body was stirring already at the feel of her hand stroking slowly across his chest.

Until today, he hadn't had a woman in more than six months. Just hadn't had the time or the inclination. Now it made sense, he thought. He'd needed a woman *badly,* so it was no wonder he'd been so frantic to get his hands on Mia.

The question was, why had the sex been so off-the-charts great? His mind was sluggish but still trying to find a way to save his ass. He'd spent more time with Mia than he had with any of the other women in his life. He *knew* her—had seen her at Alex's house. Talked with her in town. It was a connection that he'd always avoided with women before now, so of course the sex would be more…personal. More… Hell. Just *more.*

"I wonder if Delores has any chocolate cake left?" she murmured.

Dave laughed and looked down at her. Here he was, thinking about taking another bite out of her and she had already moved on to chocolate. Humbling to know your woman was more interested in your housekeeper's home-baked desserts than she was in taking another ride.

Changing her mind about *that* was just the kind of challenge Dave liked best.

He went up on one elbow and looked down at her. "Chocolate cake's got nothing on what I'm about to give you."

"Really?" She lifted one hand to stroke her fingers along his chest.

Dave hissed in a breath. "Oh, yeah. When I'm done, you won't even remember what chocolate *is.*"

As he slid down along her body, he felt her shiver and heard her whisper, "I can't wait…"

* * *

A few days later, Dave sipped his coffee and looked out the diner's window at the town of Royal, going about its day. He was tired. Hadn't been getting much sleep lately. He smiled to himself. Hell, once he and Mia had gotten started, there'd been no stopping either of them.

After their first night together, Mia had moved her things into the master bedroom and, Dave had to say, he was liking having her there. Strange because until Mia, he had never spent the night with a woman. It had always been get some, get gone. Easy. Uncomplicated. No expectations. No strings.

There weren't supposed to be strings now, either. But sometimes, Dave could swear he felt silky threads wrapping themselves around him, and he wasn't sure how to slip out of the knot that would only get tighter. Mia had been right, he told himself.

Sex had complicated the situation.

But he couldn't regret it. Hell, he'd have to be crazy to do that.

In fact, the only thing he was regretting was the fact that he had to leave her alone for a few days. Tonight, Dave was riding out with some of the ranch hands to where the herd was being held. The vet had already been out to inoculate the yearling calves and check out the rest of the cattle. He'd already taken care of the new beef that had arrived; now it was time for his regular herd to be checked over. Rather than ride in and out to the ranch, Dave and his employees would be camping out.

So he'd come to Royal to ask Nathan Battle to keep an eye on the ranch while Dave was gone. Not that he was worried about reporters getting to Mia. He was leaving enough of the ranch hands behind to see to her safety. But it never hurt to have a backup plan.

The Royal Diner was, as always, a morning hub of activity. He heard Amanda and Pam laughing at something, and the buzz of conversation from the other customers rose and fell like waves. Sunlight slanted through the windows, and outside an impatient driver hit the car horn.

From the corner of his eye, he saw someone approach, and expecting it to be Nathan, Dave turned his head and smiled a welcome. That smile froze in place when a lovely woman slid into the booth seat opposite him.

"Good morning," she said, shaking her hair back from her face and holding one hand out to him. "Remember me? I'm Bailey Collins. I work for the state investigator's office."

Dave shook her hand and released her. "I remember. We've 'talked' before."

He studied her for a second or two. She had shoulder-length dark brown hair with reddish highlights. Her chocolate-colored eyes were locked with his as if daring him to look away. If she was waiting for him to cower, she had a long wait coming.

His good mood drained away as if it had never been. Dave had already talked to cops and private investigators about Alex's disappearance and nothing had changed. He still knew nothing. Couldn't help in their search. Didn't have a clue what had happened to the man and was fast coming to the point where he didn't care, either. Sure, if Dave had a choice in it, he'd like to see Alex come back safely. But more than that, he'd like to see people leaving *him* the hell alone.

"What do you want?" he asked, though he already knew the answer to that question.

She gave him a wide smile and shook her head. "Well, aren't you charming?"

"I didn't realize charm would make a difference with you."

"It wouldn't," she admitted with a shrug.

"There you go, then." He wasn't going to play a game. Pretend to be understanding about all of this when his patience was long since shot to hell. So she could say her piece and get out of his life.

"All right," she said, "we're on the same page. I'm here in Royal to do my job, not make friends. I realize we've already spoken and that you're probably tired of answering questions, but I promise you, this will go much easier for both of us if you cooperate."

"Heard that before," he muttered.

She gave him a smile. "Look, why don't you tell me everything you know about Alex Santiago's disappearance."

"I'm sure you've read all the reports. I've told you already what I know and I can tell you now I haven't remembered anything new," he said, reaching for patience and just managing to grab hold of the tail end of it. "I've discussed it all with Nathan. With the feds. With you."

"And now," she said simply, "with *me* again."

Amanda walked up to the table, carrying a coffeepot. She looked from Dave to Bailey and back again. "More coffee?"

"Sure, thanks," Dave said.

"Me, too. Thanks." Bailey pushed the extra cup toward Amanda.

Once the cups were filled, Amanda gave Dave's shoulder a pat in solidarity, then moved off again.

"You've got friends in town."

"Guess I do," he said, nodding. Funny, he'd never really thought about it before, but in the years that he'd been in Royal, he *had* made some good friends. He was grateful for them. Especially now.

Bailey doctored her perfectly good black coffee with cream and sugar, took a sip and said, "Why don't you tell me one more time what you know about Alex's disappearance."

"It won't take long," Dave assured her. He launched into the story he'd already told too many times to count, and when he was finished, Bailey just looked at him for a long minute or two. They probably taught that move in investigator school. How to Make Potential Suspects Squirm 101.

But Dave had played with the big boys for a lot of years. He'd made deals, negotiated contracts and the one thing he'd learned had been "he who speaks first loses power." So he kept his mouth shut and waited her out.

It didn't take much longer.

"All right, thank you. I appreciate your time," she said and scooted out of the booth.

"That's it?" he asked, hardly daring to believe she wasn't going to pepper him with even more questions.

"You were expecting rubber hoses?" Her smile was friendly, but her eyes were still too sharp for comfort. "Oh. Just one more thing. I hear you're engaged to Alex's housekeeper Mia Hughes."

Dave went stone still. "And?"

"Nothing." She shrugged a little too casually. "It was sudden though, wasn't it?"

"I suppose. Is there a problem?"

She paused for a moment as if considering her answer before finally saying, "No. Look, I happen to agree with Sheriff Battle. You're not a suspect. But I have to talk to everyone who knew Alex. I'm hoping that someone knows something they don't even realize they know."

Nodding, Dave said, "Okay, I get that."

"Good." She stood up and bumped into Nathan Battle as he walked up to the booth. "Sorry, Sheriff, didn't see you there."

"It's okay." Nathan glanced at Dave, then looked at Bailey. "Am I interrupting?"

"No," she said with a last glance at Dave. "We're done here. Again, thanks for your time, Mr. Firestone."

When she walked away, Nathan took her seat, signaled to his wife, Amanda, for a cup of coffee then asked, "So what was that about?"

"The usual." Dave watched Bailey leave the diner and shook his head ruefully. "That was me, being officially ruled out by everyone."

"About time," Nathan said, wrapping one arm around his wife's expanding waist when she brought him coffee.

"Damn straight," Dave agreed and lifted his own coffee for a long, satisfying drink.

The next day, Mia was feeling Dave's absence. He'd ridden out early that morning with Mike Carter and several of the other ranch hands, and watching him ride off had torn at her. She hadn't even noticed over the past two weeks just how much she'd come to depend on having him around. They'd had a nice little routine going.

He worked outside and she studied in the library, preparing for her final exams. Yes, she still had time, but Mia wasn't taking chances with her future. They still managed to spend time with each other every day. They shared lunch, sometimes taking a picnic out to the lakeside. She helped him with the ranch ledgers and he'd showed her how to ride a horse. And one spectacular weekend, he'd arranged for his company plane to fly them to San Antonio. They'd had dinner on the River Walk and then went dancing. It had been the most romantic time in her life and it had ended all too soon. There had been warmth and laughter and an ease between them that she'd never felt with anyone else.

And now he was gone. Without him, the house felt bigger and far less warm. She could still smell him in the room they shared and caught herself listening for the sound of his boot heels on the floors.

But he would be gone at least two days, so Mia was just going to have to deal with it. Actually, being without him would be good practice for when this month with him was over. When she moved back to her suite of rooms at Alex's house, she wouldn't be seeing Dave again. Wouldn't go to sleep in his arms or wake up to his kisses every morning. Her heart ached at the thought of that and she realized just how deeply she'd allowed herself to fall in the past couple of weeks.

Oh, Mia knew that she had been ripe for the kind of acceptance and belonging she'd found at the Royal Round Up. The ranch hands were wonderful. Delores, Dave's housekeeper, had practically adopted her. And the big house felt like home.

She'd hungered for *home* for so long, it was no wonder Mia had embraced what she'd found here. But it was so much more than that. She didn't want to think about it. Didn't want to even consider it. But the sad, hard truth was that she was falling in love with Dave. Oh, she knew that road led only to misery, but she didn't know what she could do about it now. And maybe she wouldn't change it even if she could. Yes, there would be pain coming her way, but the only way to avoid that pain was to not feel the way Dave made her feel. And she wouldn't give that up for anything.

Strange how everything, your whole world, could change so quickly. Just a few weeks ago, she'd been half convinced that Dave wasn't to be trusted. That he might have had something to do with Alex's disappearance.

Now she knew that the only thing he was guilty of was making her love him.

"Oh, this is not good," she muttered, closing the book on her lap.

She was curled up in a wide, leather chair in the library. There was a fire burning in the hearth and outside, gray clouds scuttled across the sky while a cold October wind rattled the trees and buffeted the windows.

The room was cozy and comforting but without Dave, it was empty.

She glanced at the sofa where they usually sat, wrapped up together, talking, laughing, *kissing.* A sigh slipped from her as she thought about how little time she had left with Dave. He'd set up a meeting with the owner of TexCat for next week. Once he got the cattle deal he wanted, their time together would be over. And oh, how she would miss being here. Miss *him.*

When the phone beside her rang, Mia grabbed it, grateful for a reprieve from her own thoughts. "Hello?"

A woman's voice, quick and friendly. "Hello, may I speak to Dave?"

"No, he's out with the herd for a few days," Mia said, wondering who the woman was and why she wanted to speak to Dave. But in the next second she told herself that she had no right to wonder. She and Dave weren't a *real* couple, after all. But playing her role, she added, "I'm Mia, Dave's fiancée. Can I take a message?"

"His *fiancée?*" the woman repeated, her voice hitching a bit higher. "Isn't that *wonderful!* No, there's no message, thank you. I'll catch him another day. And, oh, congratulations!"

"Thank you," Mia said, but the woman had already

hung up. Okay, she thought, setting the receiver back into its cradle, that was odd. But since the mystery woman seemed more excited than angry to hear Dave was engaged, Mia felt better about her. Sure, she didn't have the right to feel jealous, but that didn't stop the sharp sting of it.

Jealous. She had to get past that, because once their time together was over, Dave would be dating other women. Women who would come here, to this house. Be with him in his bed. Stare into those fog-gray eyes as his body claimed theirs.

And after a while, she thought dismally, Dave probably wouldn't even remember her.

By the time Dave got back to the house two days later, he was dusty, tired and damned crabby. Of course, he knew the reason for his bad mood.

It was Mia.

Or rather, the *lack* of Mia.

Spending those long nights out on the ranch used to be something he looked forward to. Getting away from the house, from the business side of things and getting back to the heart of ranching. Working the cattle, sleeping under the stars with nothing but a few cowboys and the crackle of a campfire for company. It kept him connected to his land and to the men who worked for him.

Now, thoughts of Mia, hunger for Mia, had ruined the whole damn experience for him. What the hell did that make him? What had happened when he wasn't looking? She was slipping under his skin. Getting to him in ways that he hadn't thought possible. Her laugh. Her scent. The feel of her long, supple fingers sliding over his body.

Everything about the woman was more than he'd expected. Who would have thought that a shy, quiet housekeeper would be so multilayered? So easy to talk to? Hell, she even liked playing video games and had damn near kicked his ass at one of his favorites.

She was only in his life temporarily. Their bargain was a business deal, that was all. Didn't matter if he had a good time with her. Didn't matter that he wanted her more than his next breath. When the deal was over, they'd go their separate ways. That was the point of a signed contract, he reminded himself. Rules were laid out, plain and simple, so there were no mistakes and no recriminations. If he wanted to keep the relationship with Mia going after the terms of the contract had played out—then that left him open to all sorts of trouble. He'd learned long ago that the only way to have a woman in his life was to keep it simple. Hence, the rules. Without them... Even wanting Mia as he did, he didn't think he could continue to see her when this was over. It would get...complicated.

Promises made were too easily broken. He wouldn't set himself up for that kind of misery. Better to have the "rules" laid out in black and white.

Yeah, the deal had become a little more than he had planned. After all, he'd expected that one night of sex with Mia would ease the craving for her. Instead, it had only grown until she was all he could think about. So yeah, a flaw or two in the plan.

But he'd find a way to get his equilibrium back. And when he did, he'd discover a way to keep Mia at a distance even while he was inside her.

Nodding, he told himself to get right on that.

But not tonight.

Tonight, he wanted a shower, and then Mia.

He opened the front door and stepped into the golden lamplight of home. Then he tore his hat off and tossed it onto a nearby chair. "Mia! I'm home!"

His gaze scanned the foyer, the wide, curving staircase and the hallway beyond. Where the hell was she? Then he heard it. Quick, light footsteps. He grinned, turned in anticipation and felt the air *whoosh* from his lungs in surprise.

A short, trim woman with chin-length blond hair and fog-gray eyes threw herself at him with a delighted grin. Dave wrapped his arms around her, returned her bear hug and said, "Mom? What're you doing here?"

Behind his mother, at a slower pace, came Mia. Her gaze met his and he read the worry in her usually sparkling blue eyes. But before he could figure out what was going on, his mother started talking. And once Alice Firestone got going, there was no stopping her.

"I can't believe you didn't tell me about Mia," she was saying, and reached up to pat his cheek just a little harder than necessary. "You should have told me. I'd have come sooner."

He finally found his voice. "Sooner than what? How long have you been here, Mom?"

Alice patted her son's chest as she stepped back and beamed at first him, then Mia. "I called to talk to you and when Mia answered and told me the good news, I came right away!"

"She arrived later the same day you left," Mia said, flashing him a silent "don't say anything" signal with her eyes.

"Naturally, I had to rush out here and meet my new almost daughter," Alice was saying. "So I called Tobin and he sent his plane for me. I was here in just a couple of hours."

Tobin. Damn. Dave hadn't thought about explaining the situation to either his partner or his mother and now he was paying the price. His mom had been after him for so long to get married and give her grandchildren that she wasn't going to take it well when she found out the engagement wasn't real. Perfect. And God knew whom Tobin was telling the news to. Dave shot a look at Mia and could see that her thoughts were running along the same lines.

"Oh, and Tobin said to tell you that he and his wife are so excited for you. They're planning a trip here to meet Mia as soon as they get back from North Dakota."

Great, he thought. More explanations to come. That's perfect.

"David, Mia and I have had so much fun these past two days," his mother said. "She's just a delight! Did you know that she'd like to have four children? Oh," she said, waving a hand in the air, "of course you know. The two of you probably have names all picked out."

Four children? He fired a look at Mia and she shrugged helplessly, turning both palms up. Marriage. Kids. Hell, this was getting out of control fast.

"Just so you know, I'm okay with whatever names you choose. I'll just be so pleased to have grandchildren!" Alice gave him a wide smile. "This is so exciting, David."

Before he could speak, Alice turned to Mia. "You know, sweetie, I've been so worried about him. I hated to think of him living his life alone. And then there was the guilt of course, for not exactly providing a good example of a happy marriage—"

"Hardly your fault, Mom," Dave interrupted. Damned if he'd let her feel guilty because Dave's no-good father had walked out on them.

"That's nice of you to say, honey, but a parent worries about their child *always*." She reached up and brushed his hair off his forehead. "It doesn't matter if that child is an adult, the worry doesn't stop. Neither does the love. But you two will find that out for yourselves soon."

That noose he'd once felt locking around his throat was back again, tightening incrementally until Dave felt his breathing being choked off. Another glance at Mia and he read her expression easily. Misery and guilt. Well, hell, he knew how she felt, didn't he?

Damn, all he'd wanted was a shower and some hot, steamy sex with Mia. Now his brain was cluttered with his mother and imaginary children clambering all over his house. Talk about a mood killer.

Mia looked as if she wanted to crawl into a hole, and Dave understood. He should clear this up now, and he knew it. No point in waiting, because if he didn't cut his mother off at the pass, so to speak, she'd have a judge out at the ranch that weekend, performing a ceremony.

As if she read his thoughts, his mother said, "Mia and I were talking wedding plans, of course, *so* exciting. Mia insists you wouldn't want a large wedding...." She paused and watched him for confirmation.

"Yeah. I mean no, I don't."

"She knows you so well already," Alice said, eyes bright. "Isn't that lovely? So, we think it would be best if you hold the wedding right here on the ranch. There's plenty of room," she continued before he could say a word. "And Delores is full of wonderful ideas for a buffet menu. Mia and I can go shopping for her wedding dress—" She broke off and looked at Mia sheepishly.

"I'm sorry, honey. I'm just including myself, but of course if you don't want me to go with you..."

"It would be great, Alice," Mia said, her voice thick with emotion. "I'd love your opinion."

"Isn't that wonderful?" Alice turned back to Dave and gave him another hard hug before slapping one hand to her chest, overcome with emotion. "I always wanted a daughter, you know, and Mia and I already get along famously!"

Dave hugged his mom and regretted that he was going to have to burst her bubble. But that bubble would only get bigger and the hurt deeper, if he waited.

"Mom…" He looked over his mother's head to Mia who was shaking her head wildly and waving her hands. Narrowing her eyes, she glared at him and mouthed the word, *don't*.

Why the hell not? He scowled at her and she frowned right back, shaking her head again, even more firmly this time.

Fine, fine, he wouldn't say anything until he and Mia had had a chance to talk. Talking hadn't been on his agenda for tonight, but it looked like that was going to change.

Damn, he was too tired for all of this. He hugged his mother and let her go.

"Mom, I'm glad you're here, but after nearly three days on the range, I really need a shower."

His mother stepped back and sniffed delicately through her wrinkled nose. "I didn't want to say anything."

Wryly, he said, "Thanks."

Then his gaze shifted to Mia again and his mother noticed.

"Oh, you two must have a lot to 'talk' about." A smile flitted across her mouth. "Why don't you and Mia go on upstairs and I'll just head over to the guesthouse."

Dave was nodding. He was glad to see his mother, sure. But at the moment, he had other ideas on how to spend his time. At least he *had,* until this latest wrench had been tossed into his carefully laid-out strategy. Now he had the distinct feeling that Mia would want to talk before they did anything else.

When he just kept staring at Mia, his mother chuckled. "Okay, then, I'm going. You two enjoy your reunion and I'll see you both in the morning, all right?"

"That'd be good, Mom, thanks," Dave said, still staring at the woman who haunted his every thought. She chewed at her bottom lip and the action tugged at something inside him. Hell, maybe talking could wait after all.

He hardly noticed when his mother left until the front door closed behind her. In the silence, he and Mia stared at each other for a long minute. Then she rushed at him and he opened his arms to her.

Holding on to her tightly, Dave buried his face in the curve of her neck and lifted her clean off the floor. Mia wrapped her legs around his waist, then pulled back and looked at him. "I really missed you."

Danger signs fluttered to life inside him, but it was way too late to pay attention to them. "Yeah," he admitted. "Me, too. And *damn* you smell good."

She gave him a smile and shook her hair back from her face. "I'm sorry you got blindsided by your mom, but I didn't know how to tell you she was here. I tried reaching you by cell, but..."

"It's okay," he said. "Not much coverage at the far corners of the ranch. Gotta get a satellite phone. I'm guessing her showing up out of the blue was a bigger surprise for you than for me anyway."

"You could say that." Her arms were linked around his neck, her ankles crossed at the small of his back. "She's so great, Dave. You're really lucky to have her."

"Yeah, but this is kind of a mess."

"More than you know," she said and unwound her legs from his waist to drop to the floor. Her eyes were shadowed and he knew she was feeling badly about deceiving his mother. Well, hell, so was he.

"She brought me a present."

Warily, he asked, "What?"

"I'll show you," she said on a sigh. "It's upstairs in your room."

"Just where I wanted to go, anyway." He dropped one arm around her shoulder and, pulling her in close to his side, headed for the staircase.

He didn't want to think about the fact that being with Mia made him feel…complete. Didn't want to acknowledge that the cold, hard spots inside him had been eased into warmth just by seeing her.

Because once he acknowledged any of that, there would be no going back.

Nine

Dave's room held more oversized furniture, just like the rest of the house. The bed was massive. A light oak four-poster was positioned against one wall. A flat-screen TV hung on the wall opposite and a bank of windows, drapes open to the night, took up another wall. There were scatter rugs in dark colors spread across the gleaming wood floor, a fireplace crackling with heat and two comfy chairs pulled up in front of the carefully laid blaze.

When Mia had first moved her things into this room, she'd felt a little awkward, out of place. Now it was cozy, filled with amazing memories of nights spent in Dave's arms and the promise of more to come.

He stood in the middle of the room and stripped out of his shirt. Tossing her a quick look, he said, "I'm going to jump into the shower, then we'll talk."

"Okay." Was it cowardly to prefer to put off the conversation she knew they had to have? If it was, she was fine with it. A few more minutes to gather her thoughts couldn't be a bad idea.

She heard the water when he turned it on and instantly pictured him in the shower. His long, rangy body covered in soap suds, hot water streaming across the hard planes and lines of the muscles carved into his skin by years of physical work. She pictured him tipping his head back under the rain showerhead, letting the water stream through his hair and down his back.

Swallowing hard, Mia edged off the bed. She didn't want to think. She just *wanted*. Dave had been gone for days and she'd missed him. Missed his touch. His taste. His scent. She'd missed what he could do to her body and she knew that conversation could wait.

She didn't want to waste a moment of her time with Dave. She loved him and all too soon, she'd be living without him. That thought made her heart ache as she walked across the room. So she put it aside for now. There would be plenty of time later for sorrow, for misery. Right now, there was only love.

She slipped out of her clothes as she crossed the bedroom and was naked by the time she walked into the adjoining bath. It looked like a spa in here. As big as her own living room at Alex's place, the bath was done in shades of green and cream tiles. There was a giant Jacuzzi tub sitting below an arched window that offered a wide view of the front of the ranch. A double vanity stretched the length of one wall, and on the opposite side of the room was a shower that could comfortably hold six people. There was no door, and because the area was so huge, no water from either the overhead rain nozzle or the five side sprays could reach the floor.

Dave had his back to her as he washed his hair and for just a minute, Mia simply enjoyed the view. He had the best butt in the world. And the rest of him was just as good.

Quietly, she slipped into the shower behind him and the hot water sluiced across her skin as she wrapped her arms around his waist and pressed her breasts against his back.

He groaned, turned around and cupped her face in his palms. "This kind of surprise I could use every day," he whispered and dipped his head to kiss her, hard and long and deep.

Her mind fuzzed out, but her body leaped to life. Every inch of her skin was buzzing. Her insides lit up like a fireworks factory on fire and the sensation of the water coursing over them only added to the sexual heat stirring between them.

"I decided I'd rather not talk right away," she said when he came up for air.

"My kind of girl," he murmured, smiling into her eyes.

Mia wished it was true. Wished that what they had was more than a signed contract and a promise to lie to an entire town. She wished that what they felt when they came together would be enough to *keep* them together when the month was over, but she couldn't fool herself. Couldn't hang on to false hope. Couldn't set herself up for more pain than was already headed her way.

So, instead, she told her suddenly active mind to go to sleep. She didn't need to think. She only needed to *feel*. For now, that would have to be enough.

Still smiling, Dave used the soap dispenser on the wall of the shower and pumped some of the clear green gel into the palm of his hand. Then, scrubbing his palms together, he worked up a lather before cupping her breasts and smoothing the luxurious soap over her skin.

Mia sighed and swayed unsteadily. His thumbs worked

her nipples into hard peaks and a burning ache set up shop between her legs. She moved into him, and ran her hands up and down his back and over his butt. She grazed him lightly with her fingernails and heard him hiss in a ragged breath. She smiled, knowing that he was as wildly needy as she was.

"God, you feel good," he told her, bending to kiss the curve of her neck and trail his lips and teeth back up the column of her throat to her mouth. "Taste good, too."

She shivered as he turned her until her back was against the smooth, gleaming tiles.

"Bet you taste good all over," he whispered and slid down the length of her body, taking his time about it, kissing her, stroking her until Mia was a quivering mass of sensation, pinned to the wall.

"Dave…"

The hot water rose up in steam all around them, blossoming like fog in the big bathroom. Mia opened her eyes and looked down to where he knelt in front of her and she swallowed past the knot of need and anticipation clogging her throat.

Dave nudged her thighs apart with his fingertips, and still meeting her gaze, rubbed the core of her with the pad of his thumb. Electrical jolts shattered her and she gasped in response, instinctively widening her stance for him, silently inviting more of his attentions. Again and again, he stroked her until Mia was whimpering with need.

She reached for him blindly, threaded her fingers through his hair and said, "Dave, please. I can't…"

"Yeah, you can," he murmured, then leaned in and took her with his mouth. Lips, tongue, teeth all worked her already sensitized flesh. He licked and tasted and nibbled until Mia's nerve endings were strung so tightly she thought she might simply explode into millions of tiny, needy pieces.

She braced one hand on the shower wall and with the other, she cupped the back of Dave's head, holding him to her. Her hips rocked in the rhythm he set and her breath came in short, hard gasps. Tipping her head back against the shower wall, she opened her eyes, stared into the steamy fog and felt lost. As if she'd been swallowed by sensation. There was no up. No down. There was only Dave and what he was doing to her.

"Dave… Oh…my…" Every word was a victory. Every breath a triumph.

When he pushed her closer and closer to the edge of completion, Mia looked down at him, wanting to see it all. Wanting to have this picture in her mind. So when she remembered this time with him she'd have something specific to torture herself with.

Then his tongue did a slow swirl over one particular spot and the moment ended with Mia shouting his name as her body splintered all around him.

She couldn't stand, so Dave lowered her to the long, wide seat carved into the wall of the shower itself. Then he turned, adjusted a few of the shower jets, aiming them directly at the bench where Mia lay sensually sprawled.

"We're not done, you know," he said.

She fixed her eyes on him and gave him a slow satisfied smile. "I'm so happy to hear that."

Damn, this was some kind of woman, he told himself as he leaned over her, bracing his hands on either side of her head. She was beautiful and sexy and always ready for him. She was a match for him in a lot of ways, and if he were a man looking for a permanent woman, Mia Hughes would be the one he'd chase down and hog-tie.

But he didn't do permanent because there was no such thing. People made promises to each other all the damn time and broke them just as often. He wouldn't be part of that. Wouldn't make a promise only to let it shatter. Wouldn't walk out on his responsibilities. And the one way to make sure that didn't happen was to avoid making those "forever" kind of promises in the first damn place.

That's why he insisted on contracts for even the most minor deals. Harder to break a signed promise.

So he would have Mia as often as he could. He would give her all he had.

For the time they had together.

Then it would end.

She reached up and pushed his wet hair back from his face. Frowning slightly, she asked, "What're you thinking? You look so...sad, all of a sudden."

"It's nothing," he lied, and lowered his head to hers for a kiss. "Nothing."

She didn't look convinced, but he'd change her mind about that. His body was hard and hot and so damn eager he had to force himself out of the shower long enough to cross to the top drawer in the vanity. He yanked out a condom, tore the package open then worked the sheath down over his straining erection.

When he turned back to the shower, he saw that she was waiting, gaze fixed on him, and it wasn't worry he saw in her eyes now, it was need. Fresh. Raw. Powerful. He'd never been with a woman so in tune with his own desires. Mia was more than a match for him in so many damn ways he couldn't even count them all. But at the moment, it was their identical cravings that pulled at him.

He went back to her, and as the shower jets pummeled at their bodies, he levered himself over her and pushed himself into her depths.

Like every time with Mia, that first slide into her heat was a welcome into heaven. He felt surrounded by her, his body cradled within hers. She wrapped her arms around his neck, pulled his face down for a kiss, and he let himself drown in her. The heat of her. The sexual draw between them was overpowering, all consuming. And yet it wasn't just sex that simmered between them.

It was the connection he still feared and couldn't trust.

He moved inside her, pushing them both toward the climax he knew would crush him. Dave felt her shiver. Felt the first of the tremulous quakes racking her body and when she surrendered to them, he went with her. Giving himself up to what he had only found with Mia. The completion. The rush of pleasure, excitement and peace that existed only when he was in her arms.

A half hour later, they were dried off and in his bedroom. As she took a pair of jeans from a dresser drawer and tugged them on, he asked, "Sure you wouldn't rather just wrap up in robes? Be easier than getting out of all these clothes again later."

She whipped her hair back from her face and gave him a wicked smile that set his insides on fire. "A few clothes won't slow you down. Think of it as a challenge. Plus, I'm not cooking naked and I'm hungry."

He laughed. "Of course you are."

"Besides," she said as she tugged a long-sleeved, dark red sweater on over her head, "we still have to talk."

"Right." He grabbed a pair of his own jeans and pulled them on. He didn't bother with underwear, since his plan was to get her naked again as soon as he'd fed her. "Can't forget the talk. So. Before we head to the kitchen, you want to show me what my mom brought for you?"

She pointed. "It's in that box by the fire."

He spotted it on the table between the two armchairs. Barefoot and shirtless, he walked over and pulled the lid off. Beneath a layer of tissue paper was a white, lacy baby dress slightly yellowed from age. "What the—"

"It was your christening gown."

"Gown?" He turned around and stared at her, horrified. "I wore a dress?"

Mia laughed shortly and shook her head. "*That's* what's bothering you about this?"

"Hell, yes. Boys don't wear dresses."

"Not a dress. A gown."

"Same damn thing if you ask me." He dropped the offending item back into the box and set the lid in place again. "Why would she bring it to—" He broke off, tipped his head back and stared at the ceiling. "Oh, crap."

"Exactly." Mia sat on the edge of the bed, her bare feet dangling inches above the floor. "She brought it to me so we could use it for our baby's christening."

Mia wants four children. He could hear the glee in his mother's voice still. Four kids. And here's the dress they get to wear, poor things. Kids weren't in his plans, Dave reminded himself sternly even while a weird feeling crept over him. His mind provided an image to match that weird feeling and suddenly he had the mental picture of Mia, pregnant with his child. Even through the wave of terror the image projected, he could admit to himself that she looked lovely pregnant.

But there weren't going to be any babies.

He gave the closed box another glare and rubbed at the ache in the center of his chest. "This has gotten out of hand."

"I know."

Fixing his gaze on hers, he said, "You should have let me tell her the truth."

"I couldn't. She was so happy, Dave. So excited. So pleased for you and happy for *us*." Shaking her head, Mia sighed. "Alice has spent the past two days telling me all about you, showing me pictures of you as a child. She's..." Mia shrugged helplessly again. "I just couldn't tell her. And I couldn't let you, either."

"Mia, she's got to know." He wasn't looking forward to breaking that news, but he knew it had to be done.

Her voice was soft, but there was steel in her words when she said, "Please don't make me a liar to your mother."

"What? You're not a liar."

"Of course I am," she argued miserably. "While she was going on and on about how happy she was to have me for a daughter all I did was sit there, *basking* in it. She thinks we're really engaged and I *let* her think it. That makes me a liar and I can't stand the thought of her knowing."

"Mia..." He headed across the room to her, drawn to the slump of her shoulders and the distress in her voice.

She scooted off the bed and wrapped her arms around her middle in a classic self-protection stance. "I just don't want her to think badly of me, okay?" Looking up at him, she tried to explain. "I never had a mother, you know? I mean, she died when I was a baby and I always wondered what it would have been like if she had lived." She was talking faster now, as if words were gathering in the back of her throat waiting for their chance to be spoken. "How different would our lives have been? Having a mom teach you to cook. Going shopping for prom dresses. All the little things that I missed. I can't help but wonder what it would have been like to experience it all."

She took a deep breath and blew it out again. "I know how dumb that all sounds, but I swear, Dave, when Alice was talking to me and being so nice, I just…couldn't give that up by announcing that what you and I have is just role-playing. I couldn't do it."

He laid both hands on her shoulders and stared down into her eyes. "I get it," he said. "And trust me when I say I know how hard it is to get a word in edgewise when Alice Firestone is on a roll. She's like this gentle, sweet-natured steamroller. There's just no stopping her, so in your defense, she probably wouldn't have given you a chance to confess even if you'd wanted to."

Mia smiled up at him. "Steamroller, huh? She's a sweetie and you're lucky to have her."

"I know it," he said, "but she's flattened me a few times, too."

"Did you deserve it?"

"Probably," he admitted.

"Like I deserve it now," she muttered. Shaking her head, Mia shoved both hands through her hair, then let her hands drop to her sides. "But I'm asking you not to say anything to her, Dave. She's so nice and she loves you so much and she's so excited…. I'm a terrible person."

He chuckled and was rewarded with a frosty glare. "No, you're not. You're the exact opposite because you're worried about my mom's feelings in this."

"Yeah. I don't want her to think I'm a liar." Her head hit his chest. "Just don't tell her, all right? The month is almost up. You've got the meeting with TexCat arranged for next week. So just wait. When the deal is done, we'll break up as planned, and then she'll never have to know the real reason behind any of this. And she won't hate me." She tipped her head back to look up at him. "I really don't want her to hate me, Dave."

In that moment, he would have given her anything, promised her whatever she wanted. Her blue eyes were drenched with emotion and the subtle sheen of tears she refused to let fall. She hadn't asked him for a thing since this whole bargain had started, so this request seemed reasonable. Besides, he was in no hurry to tell his mother her dreams of grandchildren weren't going to happen.

"Okay," he said, wrapping his arms around her. "We won't say anything until we have to."

She snaked her arms around his waist and held on. "Thanks."

"Sure." He kissed the top of her head. "Still hungry?"

"Am I breathing?"

Dave laughed, released her and gave her bottom a swift swat.

"Hey!" She grinned at him. "What was that for?"

"I just couldn't resist that cute little butt of yours, I guess."

"Maybe you could not resist me again after we eat?"

He grabbed a shirt, yanked it on and snatched her hand, tugging her out and down the hall to the stairs. "This is going to be the fastest meal in history."

Her laughter bubbled out around them and just for a second, Dave didn't worry about how happy Mia made him.

Mia reheated the stew Delores had made earlier and Dave managed to throw together some garlic bread. It was…*cozy,* being alone with her in the huge kitchen. Just the two of them, with the night outside the wide bay windows and lamplight casting a soft glow over the room. That ache in his chest was back, but Dave ignored it.

After they'd eaten, Mia put together a plate filled with cake and cookies for Dave to take to his mother in the guesthouse.

"She's probably getting ready for bed," he argued,

since he'd rather take Mia back to their bedroom than take a walk.

"She's not ninety, Dave," Mia said with a laugh. "And she left before she got any of the cake."

Mia was polishing off a slice of Delores's famous mocha fudge cake as Dave picked up the plate with a resigned sigh. "I'll be right back."

Mia smiled at him and licked her fork lovingly. "Take your time...."

He watched her tongue make short work of the frosting on that fork and could only mutter, "Five minutes, tops."

Outside, it was cold, but Texas cold—so his bare feet on the flagstones didn't bother him a bit. He glanced around the ranch yard as he walked silently through the darkness. Dave noted lights on in the houses set aside for the ranch hands and frowned when he noticed the foreman's house was dark. Well, hell, on the ride home, all Mike had talked about was taking a shower and going to bed. Guess he meant it.

Shaking his head, Dave skirted the pool, walked past the line of Adirondack chairs and headed for the guesthouse. He'd built the damn place especially for his mother—he'd wanted her to live here, but to have her own space, too. Still, it had never been more than a way station for his mother, who refused to "be a wet blanket on her son's party." This time, though, he told himself, maybe he could get her to stay.

Once Mia was gone, the ranch was going to be... lonely. He frowned as that thought registered. Alone wasn't lonely, he insisted, but that argument was ringing false, even with him. He couldn't even imagine sleeping in his own bed without Mia beside him. Which told him that this whole situation was taking a turn he hadn't expected.

Dave was still frowning when he gave a perfunctory knock to his mother's door, then opened it. He stopped dead on the threshold and was pretty sure he'd been struck blind.

Mike Carter, wearing only a pair of white boxers, was *kissing* Dave's *mother*. Worse, she was kissing him back. And since when did mothers wear short nightgowns with spaghetti straps?

"What the hell?"

The couple broke apart at his shout and Mike whirled around to face Dave while at the same time shoving Alice behind him, standing in front of her like a human shield. "Dave—"

"What's going on here?" he demanded, then held up a hand. "Don't answer that!" He knew exactly what was going on and really didn't need any more details.

Dave set the covered plate down on the nearest table and took a step toward Mike. His friend. His foreman. The man he trusted more than anyone else in his life besides Tobin. "Mom, leave."

"I will not."

"Alice—" Mike said.

"Don't you start, either," Alice said and jumped out from behind Mike to face her furious son. "I will not run and hide as if I were a teenager being reprimanded by her parents. David Trahern Firestone, you just remember who the parent is here and who's the child."

"I'm no child," he ground out, hardly glancing at his mother. "And I want to know what the hell Mike is doing here like...*that*."

Alice bristled again. "You watch your tone, David, do you understand?"

"No!" he shouted, throwing both hands into the air. "I *don't* understand. In fact, I think I'm having a stroke!"

"Oh, for heaven's sake!" Alice folded her arms across her chest and tapped the bare toes of one foot against the floor.

He couldn't think. Couldn't rationalize what he'd just seen, and then he heard himself babble, "What? How? When?"

"Dave, if we could talk..." Mike said, reaching for his jeans and pulling them on.

Fury was crouched at the base of his throat and betrayal was tightly wrapped around it like a fist. He could hardly talk, but he managed to say, "The only thing I'm saying to you is, you're fired."

His mother walked right up and slapped him. Dave just looked at her. She hadn't laid a hand on him since the year he was fifteen and took a ranch truck out for a joyride. "What was that for?"

"For being a boob," Alice told him, frowning. "You can't fire the man I love because you're embarrassed."

"I'm embarrassed?" He wasn't dealing with hearing his mother say she loved a man. That was just too much for any son to have to take.

"Alice—"

Dave and his mother both said, "Butt out, Mike."

"Yes, you're embarrassed," she continued, looking at him now with less anger and more understanding. "Do you think I don't know the signs? You intruded here and now there's no way out but anger."

"Intruded." Okay, maybe he had, but in his defense, he hadn't expected to find his mother with— Don't go there.

"Honey," she said, "I'm a grown woman, and now that you yourself have found someone to love, I'm sure you can understand—"

Hysterical deafness set in. It was the only answer. Dave saw his mother's mouth moving, but he couldn't hear her over the roaring in his own ears. Mike and his mother? How long had that been going on? And what was he supposed to do about it? What *could* he do about it? Scrubbing both hands over his face, he took a breath and muttered, "Mom, stop. I beg you."

"Huh." She sniffed and picked up the plate of cake and cookies. "Oh, these look wonderful. Thank Mia for me since I'm sure you didn't think of this."

How had he come out to be the bad guy here? Dave gave up trying to talk to his mother and instead focused on Mike, who was watching him with a steady stare. The older man's chin was high, his shoulders squared as if he were expecting a firing squad. Well, hell. Now Dave felt like an idiot.

They were all adults here and he had barged in without thinking. And he had to admit, if his mom was going to fall for a man, at least she'd picked a good one. Still, there were a few things that had to be said.

"I want to talk to you," he muttered and turned to go outside.

"I think—" Alice said.

"Alice, honey, it'll be all right." Mike kissed her forehead and walked outside.

Dave sighed as his mother warned, "If you fire him, I will personally make you sorry, David."

He blew out a breath, stepped into the cool night and stopped opposite his foreman. Mike still looked pugnacious, as if he were ready for anything. So just because, Dave punched him.

One swing and his fist slammed into the other man's jaw. Mike's head snapped back and his eyes flashed with fury. But he didn't lift a finger to defend himself.

"I figure you had that one coming, seeing as it's your mother and all. But hit me again and I'll hit back."

"How long has this been going on?" Dave demanded.

"I've been in love with your mother for years," Mike admitted on a sigh. "She wanted to tell you but I wouldn't let her."

"Are you using her?"

Mike glared at him. "I might just hit you anyway. I love her. And now that you've got Mia in your life, I figure you can understand how that feels. If you can't, I'll leave the ranch. You won't have to fire me. But know this. I won't give Alice up."

Everybody figured now that he had Mia he could understand love. Well, they were wrong. He didn't understand it, didn't trust it and didn't see that changing any time soon. Need was different. It was clean. Uncomplicated.

Dave's mind was racing. Everything was changing around him so fast he could hardly keep up. His world used to be so neat and tidy. He'd had complete control over his universe and he couldn't figure out where it had all gone wrong.

"Oh, relax," Dave told his old friend. "You're not fired and I'm not hitting you again— Unless," he added quickly, "you make her cry. Then all bets are off."

"Agreed," Mike said.

"Sorry I barged in," Dave said. "*Really* sorry. There are just some things sons shouldn't see."

Mike snorted a laugh. "Guess that's so. If it makes you feel better, I've about convinced Alice to move into the guesthouse permanently."

"Yeah?" He smiled, then frowned and jabbed a finger at his foreman. "If you're thinking you're living there with her—not unless you're married."

Mike grinned. "My pleasure. Now…I've got a reunion of my own to get back to."

Dave watched him go and shuddered. "No, some things a son should never even know about."

Back at the house, Mia watched as Dave stalked around the perimeter of the lamp-lit kitchen, talking more to himself than to her.

"I don't get it," he muttered. "Love? How the hell could she be in love? She loved my father and that didn't stop him from abandoning us."

"Mike's a good guy," she argued.

"Yeah," he agreed, never slowing his pace. "But that doesn't guarantee anything, either."

"There are no guarantees," Mia pointed out, turning in her seat to keep her gaze locked on him. He was shaking his head, muttering, and that frown carved into his features looked as if it was there to stay.

"That's the whole point," he told her. "Without a guarantee, why take the risk? Love is just a word. It doesn't *mean* anything."

"It means everything," she said softly and felt a hitch in her chest when he stopped pacing to stare at her.

She couldn't tell what he was thinking, and maybe that was just as well, she thought.

"No," he said quietly, "what you and I have is more. Desire is straightforward. Uncomplicated. It doesn't screw with your life and you don't get flattened when it ends."

Mia heard every word and felt them like a direct slap to the heart. He believed everything he was saying. She knew that. And she realized finally and at last that he would never allow himself to love her. Never risk his heart.

Which meant that though she was still here and with him, what they had was already over.

Ten

Thomas Buckley was an ass.

The owner of TexCat was short, balding and very well fed. His cheeks were red, his blue eyes were sharp and his ideas were straight out of the 1950s.

"A family man is a man to be trusted," Buckley was saying, smiling benevolently from behind his wide, ostentatious desk. "I always say if a man can't make a commitment to a woman, then he can't keep his word on a deal."

Dave had already sat through more than an hour of listening to the older man pontificate about morality and family values. It felt like a week. He could only imagine what Mia or his mother would say about Buckley's take on women being "the gentle sex, God bless 'em" and how they "don't understand men's business, but they keep our homes and raise our children and that's enough."

Seriously, Buckley was dancing on Dave's last nerve.

When he finally wound down, Dave asked, "So, we have a deal?"

"I've had my man go and check out your herd and he tells me it's some of the best beef he's seen in years." Buckley threaded his fingers together and laid them across his corpulent belly as he leaned back in his desk chair.

"Not surprised," Dave said quickly. "My ranch is completely organic. No feedlots, either. The land is managed so that the herd has free range and we don't take on more cattle than we can comfortably support."

Buckley nodded. "That was in the report, as well. And you say you're engaged to be married?"

Briefly, he gritted his teeth. "Yes. Mia's studying to be a school psychologist."

"Well, that'll be fine I'm sure, until your first child is born. Then she'll want to stay home."

If he gritted his teeth for much longer, Dave thought, he'd leave this office with nothing more than a mouth full of powder. "Plenty of time to think about that."

"You're right, you're right." Buckley sat up straight, held out his right hand and when Dave shook it, the older man smiled. "We've got a deal. Let's get the paperwork signed."

An hour later, Dave was back in Royal, glad to be back from Midland and the TexCat offices. He'd done it. His ranch's reputation was set now that he had that all-important deal. His plans for the future were looking good and the bargain he'd struck with Mia was now completed.

All that was left was to tell her the good news and end their faux engagement. Odd how that thought didn't fill him with pleasure. So instead of heading back to his own place, Dave drove into town to see Nathan Battle. He needed a friend to talk to.

"I don't see the problem." Nathan poured two cups of coffee and handed one to Dave. Carrying his own coffee, Nathan walked around his desk and propped his booted feet up on one corner.

The Royal jailhouse was small, but it boasted up-to-date equipment and a casual feel. Nathan had one deputy, and between the two men, the small town's citizens were taken care of.

"The problem is," Dave said, after a sip of the strong, hot coffee, "I don't need a fiancée anymore, but I don't want to end this with Mia, either."

"Ah." Nathan nodded sagely. "So, basically, you're screwed?"

"To sum it up, yeah."

"You don't have to end things, you know," Nathan mused.

Dave fired a hard look at his friend. "I've considered that…"

"And?"

"Don't know." He stood up, set his coffee on the edge of the desk and started pacing. The wood floors held plenty of scuff marks from generations of boots stomping across them, and the wide front window overlooked Main Street. Dave shoved his hands into his back pockets, stopped at the window and stared, not seeing the town beyond the glass.

His mind raced with more questions than answers. For the first time in years, Dave was unsure what move to make. All he knew was that he didn't want to lose Mia. Not yet, anyway.

Of course, he didn't plan to *keep* her in his life. They'd

made a deal after all. Signed a contract. Their engagement would end and they'd each go back to their own lives.

But he wasn't ready for that.

"Stop thinking about what you should do and tell me what you *want* to do," Nathan suggested.

Dave glanced at him over his shoulder. "What I want is to go home and see Mia."

"So do that and forget about the rest for now."

"Just like that?"

"What's the hurry? You said yourself the deal you made with Mia goes to the end of the month."

"Or until I get the contract, whichever comes first."

"There's no saying you can't renegotiate, though, right?"

"True." Great sex must have clogged his brain. Otherwise he would have thought of this solution himself. There was no reason he and Mia couldn't strike a new deal. They were good together. Maybe this was worth looking into.

"Give yourself some time to figure out what you want to do. The TCC's big Halloween party is in a few days. At least wait until after that."

He thought about it and realized that Nathan was right about something at least. Renegotiation could work. He wasn't ready to give Mia up.

"Dave, you don't have to have every answer to every question at all times."

He laughed and shoved one hand through his hair. "You know, until now, I always have."

"Things change," Nathan said with a shrug. "Trust me, no one knows that better than I do."

"Things are changing too damn much lately," Dave muttered.

Nathan chuckled. "Yeah, I heard about your mom and Mike Carter."

"Don't remind me," Dave said. It had been almost a week since the night he'd blundered into the middle of his mother's—whatever. He was almost used to the fact that his mom was in love. He wasn't used to Mike Carter living in the guesthouse with her.

Alice was happy like Dave hadn't seen since he was a kid, before his father left them. He was glad for his mom, but he couldn't understand how she could have faith again. Trust again, after how Dave's father had let her down. Abandoned them.

How did she let go of the past and risk taking another chance on love? Shaking his head, Dave told himself that Thomas Buckley had it all wrong.

Women were much stronger than men.

"Congratulations," Mia said and hoped she sounded more sincere than she felt.

"Thanks." Dave poured them each a glass of wine and handed one to her. They took their usual spots on the sofa in the library as he told her about the deal with TexCat.

She listened and tried to look happy for him, but inside she was a mess. Her heart felt twisted into a knot and breathing was so difficult, she didn't even sip at her wine, half-afraid she'd choke to death. That was it. It was done. She and Dave were over. The signed contract with TexCat signaled the end of their bargain.

Now she could move back to Alex's place and get on with her life. The only problem? She wasn't sure she *had* a life without Dave.

"I'd like you to stay," he said suddenly, grabbing her attention.

Mia's heart clenched. Her gaze locked on his. "What?"

He took her wine and set both glasses on the polished wood table in front of them before turning back to her. Dropping both hands on her shoulders, he pulled her in close, looked into her eyes and said, "I'd like you to stay—"

Hope roared to life inside her.

"—until the end of the month," he finished.

And hope drained away again, leaving her feeling surprisingly empty. He didn't want her forever. She'd been fooling herself thinking that maybe because *she* loved, that he did, too. Well, here was the eye-opener, the back-to-reality talk she'd been dreading for weeks.

"Why?"

"Why not?" he countered and gave her shoulders a squeeze.

Amazing, even though the heat of his hands was sliding through the fabric of her shirt to seep into her body, she still felt cold.

"Look, Mia," he said softly, "we've had a good time, right?"

A good time. She sighed. "Yes."

"So why let it end before either of us is ready?"

Because if she stayed much longer, she didn't know how she would leave at all. And she had to leave, she told herself firmly. She couldn't stay with a man who didn't love her. It would kill her by inches.

Shaking her head, she said, "I don't think that's a good idea."

"Why the hell not?"

She smiled. He really had a hard time when people didn't fall in with his plans. "Because we both have lives we have to get back to. I take my final exams soon and then I'll have to get busy looking for a job—"

"Royal School District is going to hire you," he said, brushing that concern aside.

"Maybe," she said. "But there's no guarantee. So I'll

have to apply to school districts in Midland and Houston, too."

He scowled at her. "You didn't tell me."

No, she hadn't. Because she hadn't wanted to think about it herself. The thought of moving away from Royal made her heartsick. She hated the thought of leaving before Alex came back and she was really hoping that Royal would hire her. And if they didn't, maybe she'd end up looking for a job here in town until everything was back to normal. Leaving without having the mystery of Alex's disappearance settled seemed impossible.

Besides, she didn't want to move from Royal, the only home she'd ever known. If she did, that would mean she wouldn't even be able to catch the occasional glimpse of Dave around town. Maybe that would be better, but at the moment, she didn't think so.

"The point is," she said, trying not to think about moving, "our time together's over."

He was still frowning when he said, "At least stay through the TCC Halloween party. That's only a few days away."

"Why?" she asked, suddenly so tired she wanted to go lay down with a pillow over her head.

"Because I'm asking you to," he whispered.

He never asked, she told herself silently. He ordered. Or growled. Or dictated. But he was asking her, and as she looked into his fog-gray eyes, she knew she wasn't ready to leave. Not yet. "I'll stay."

Three days later, Mia stepped out of the ranch house in time to see her VW being towed away. She took an instinctive step or two to chase after it, even knowing there was no way she could catch it.

She glanced around the ranch yard, hoping to find

someone to tell her she'd just had a hallucination. Instead, she saw Dave, standing beside a brand-new, shiny, luxury SUV.

For the past several days, he'd been…different. Ever since their talk in the library the night he'd gotten the deal with TexCat, things had changed between them. Oh, they were still together every night, but even their lovemaking had a different feel to it. Like a prolonged goodbye that was tearing Mia apart, piece by piece.

Now, as he watched her, she saw the same expression on his face that had been there the past few days. Not cold, exactly. But more…distant than she was used to. It was as if every time he saw her, he was letting go. She felt as though there were a giant clock inside her ticking off the minutes, and when that clock hit zero, there would be nothing left between her and Dave.

So instead of enjoying their last week together, they were each of them holding back, protecting themselves and their hearts. If she had any sense, she'd leave. But she just couldn't. Even though being here was painful, being away from Dave would be worse.

He walked toward her, every step long and determined. His features looked carved from granite and his gray eyes gave nothing away.

When he was close enough, she asked, "Who took my car? And *why?*"

"That's not a car," he countered. "It's a disaster waiting to happen. Just yesterday you got stuck on the side of the road coming home from Alex's."

"I just needed some gas." Fine, she probably needed a new gas gauge, too.

"No, you needed a new car and now you've got one." He pointed at the silver beauty.

"You did *not* buy me a car," she whispered.

"Yeah, I did. Deal with it." His voice was clipped, his eyes fierce, as if he was preparing for battle.

Well, he was going to get one. Dave Firestone was used to rolling over people to get his own way, but she wouldn't go down without a fight. Even though there was a part of her insisting that she just shut up and accept that pretty, brand-new, worry-free car.

"This wasn't part of our deal," she argued, silencing her internal voice.

"Yeah, well, I renegotiated it on my own." He grabbed her shoulders and yanked her in close. "You told me you've applied for jobs in Midland and Houston. You think I'm going to worry about you off somewhere alone in that crappy car? Not gonna happen." Shaking his head, he let her go and turned for the barn.

"This isn't over!" she called after him, even though she knew it was. Her car was gone. She shifted her gaze to the new beast shining in the sunlight.

Mia moved closer and did a slow walk around the simply gorgeous luxury SUV. She opened the driver's side door and looked inside. The interior was navy blue leather and the smell... She took a deep breath and sighed it out. Mia had never in her life owned a *new* car. All of her cars had been new to her, but considerably aged by the time she'd gotten hold of them.

She reached out one hand and smoothed her palm over the baby-soft leather seat, and for one long second, she experienced pure avarice. What would it be like, she wondered, to drive a car and not have to worry about the engine falling out? To not have to carry a case of oil with you everywhere you went? To turn the key and have the engine fire right up without the help of prayers and desperate pleas?

Frowning, Mia forced herself to step back and close the

door. Her hand might have lingered on the door handle, but who could blame her? It was beautiful. And extravagant and she absolutely couldn't keep it. She and Dave had a deal. A signed contract. And a new car wasn't part of it.

"Isn't that lovely?" Alice came up behind her and Mia turned to smile a welcome.

"It is."

"Yet you don't look happy with it."

"It's great, Alice," Mia told her with a sigh. "But I can't keep it."

"Why ever not?"

"It's complicated," Mia said, hoping the other woman would accept that and let it go.

"Mia, I know David can be impulsive. Heck, he bought me a new car just a few weeks ago and didn't bother to tell me about it beforehand."

"But you're his mom."

"And you're his fiancée." She laid one hand on Mia's forearm. "Did he surprise you with this? Are you angry that he didn't talk to you about it? Is it that you don't like the color?"

Mia laughed. Imagine saying no to a new car because you didn't like the color. "No, the color's just right. And I like surprises…"

"Then why shouldn't he buy you a car?"

"Because we're not getting married," she blurted. Oh, God. The words had just jumped from her mouth before she had a chance to stop them. She slapped one hand to her mouth, but it was too late. The truth was out and now Alice would hate her and Dave would be furious that she'd told his mother.

"I know."

"What?"

Alice smiled, put her arm around Mia's shoulder and

gave her a squeeze. "Honey, I know my son better than anyone. He doesn't go from 'never getting married' to 'I'm engaged' overnight. I knew something was up, I just didn't know what."

"Alice, I'm so sorry…" This wasn't fair. She was so nice. So understanding. So…mom-like. "I didn't want to lie to you, but I didn't want you to hate me and I asked Dave not to tell you, so it's not even all his fault. It's just so complicated."

Alice gave her another hug. "Good stories always are," she said and started walking toward the house. "Now, why don't we get some tea and some of Delores's cookies and you can tell me everything."

Too late to do anything else, Mia nodded, and allowed herself to be mothered for the very first time.

Over two pots of tea and enough cookies to make even Mia a little sick, she told Alice the whole story. When she finally wound down, she was spent. Tears still dampened her cheeks, but her breathing was easier than it had been since she'd started living a lie.

"You love my son, don't you?"

"Yes," Mia said, "but it doesn't matter."

"It's all that matters." Alice poured more tea for each of them and said, "David loves you, too."

Mia had to laugh. He wanted her, she knew that. Heck, they couldn't be in the same room together for more than five minutes without leaping at each other. But desire wasn't love and want wasn't need.

"You're wrong."

Alice shook her head. "There's a shiny new SUV parked out front that says different."

"The car?"

"It's more than a car, honey." Alice sat up, reached out

and took Mia's hands in hers. "Remember, a few weeks ago, David had a new car delivered to my house."

"Yes, but you're his mother."

"And he loves me. Worries about me driving a car he doesn't think is safe."

"He hates my car," Mia murmured.

"So he replaced it with a much safer one. And if he didn't love you, why would your safety matter to him?"

"I don't know...." She'd like to believe that. But how could she?

"It's David's way, Mia," Alice was saying. "Ever since he was a child, he's had trouble with the word *love*. But that doesn't mean he doesn't *feel* it."

A tiny kernel of hope settled in the pit of her stomach, but Mia couldn't put too much faith in it. Because if she did and Alice was wrong, her heart would be crushed beyond repair.

Loud music pumped out of speakers. Orange and black streamers and balloons hung from the ceiling, drifting with the movements of the crowd. Dry ice near the punchbowl sent clouds of vapor into the air. Vampires danced with angels, zombies loitered near the buffet table and a princess stole a kiss from a troll.

All in all, the TCC costume party was a rousing success. The club wasn't just celebrating Halloween this year, but also the opening of the new day-care center. So much fuss had been made about the center over the past few months, it was a wonder anything had gotten done.

But Mia had already taken a tour of the new day-care center and she was impressed with the place. Glancing into the large, well-appointed room, she saw lots of tiny tables and chairs for the kids. Bookshelves were stocked with row after row of wonderful stories. There were cribs for infants and on one side of the room small easels were set up, ready for little artists to paint their masterpieces.

"Isn't it wonderful?" A woman's voice spoke up from right beside her and Mia jumped. She hadn't noticed anyone approach.

The woman was a few inches shorter than Mia, with jaw-length blond hair and brown eyes that were sparkling with excitement.

"I'm sorry," she said. "I didn't mean to sneak up on you. But I saw you looking in at the day care and couldn't resist coming over." She held out one hand. "I'm Kiley Roberts, and I'll be running the center."

"Mia Hughes. It's nice to meet you." Mia shook her hand and said, "I was just thinking how impressive it is that the center has come together so nicely despite all the battles."

"Oh, I know." Kiley sighed a little. "I'm glad it's all settled and over. My little girl, Emmie, can't wait to start coming here."

"How old is she?"

"Two," Kiley said, "and she's the light of my life." She paused, spotted someone walking into the center and said, "Excuse me, I should go direct another tour."

Mia nodded as the woman moved off, practically dancing with excitement for the opening of the center. She envied Kiley Roberts, Mia realized. Kiley had a plan. A future stretched out ahead of her, and she had a child. A family.

Smiling wistfully, Mia turned away from the center, walked over to the open doorway into the main room and looked out over the gathered crowd. She spotted Dave across the room at the bar, standing beside Nathan Battle. The two men laughed at something and Mia's heart twisted in her chest. Dave looked wonderful as an Old

West outlaw. Dressed almost entirely in black, he looked dangerous and sexy. A lethal combination, as Mia knew only too well.

As if he could feel her gaze on him, he turned, met her eyes and gave her the half smile that never failed to tug at her heart. God, how she would miss him.

He left Nathan, made his way over to her through the crowd and when he stopped directly in front of her, he said, "Did I mention that you make the most beautiful saloon girl I've ever seen?"

Her costume deliberately went along with his. Her dark blue satin dress was trimmed with black lace at the bodice and the hem of her full skirt. She wore fishnet stockings, black pumps and her upswept hair had blue feathers tucked into the mass.

"I think you might have said something along those lines," she said.

"It's worth repeating." He took her hand and led her toward the dance floor. "Dance with me, Mia."

She couldn't have resisted him even if she'd wanted to.

He pulled her into the circle of his arms and began to sway in time with the music. All around her, the citizens of Royal were celebrating. There was laughter and shouts and conversations pitched at a level to be heard over the music.

Mia laid her head on his chest and followed his lead around the dance floor. It was magical and sad and special all at once. She'd have loved for the music to spin on for years, keeping them here, locked together. But she knew that couldn't happen; all too soon, the night would end and, like Cinderella, her magic would be over.

"Marry me, Mia," he whispered.

And the whole world stopped.

Eleven

"What?"

Dave grinned. He'd caught her off guard. Good. Just how he wanted her. If she was off balance, she wouldn't be so eager to argue with him. He'd never met a more hardheaded woman.

"Marry me." Hell, even he couldn't believe he was serious. But the thought of losing Mia was driving him nuts.

She went limp in his arms and he took that as a good sign. The noise level inside the club was near deafening and to make his case he'd need to get where he could talk to her loud enough to be heard.

"You want to get married?"

"Absolutely," he told her, bending his head so he wouldn't have to shout and so that no one else could hear him. "I've thought it all out and it's the best solution to the situation."

The past few days had been crazed, him knowing that

she would be leaving and not having a way to keep her there, short of tying her to his bed—which didn't sound like a bad plan to him at all.

But since that would be a temporary solution, he'd come up with something better. A marriage based not on love but logic.

She shook her head as if to clear it, then looked into his eyes and asked, "You love me?"

Something fisted tight around his heart, but Dave ignored it. This wasn't about something as ephemeral as *feelings*. This was about— Hell.

"Who said anything about love?" He frowned a little and danced them over to a corner of the floor where they would be more alone. When they were far enough away from the crowd, he backed her into a corner and stared down at her. "I'm not talking about love. I'm talking about a contract."

"A what? You mean a prenup?"

"No." He smiled at her. "I mean a contract where we promise each other we'll stay together. No divorce. No leaving. And we both sign it."

"You're kidding, right?" She blinked up at him and he had the distinct impression he was losing her.

He couldn't lose her. That was the one thing he'd figured out over the past few days. The thought of her moving to Midland or Houston was enough to drive a spike through his heart. So, yeah, he could admit that he cared for her. A lot. But he wouldn't offer a promise that was too easily broken. Love was too iffy. Too…dangerous.

"A signed contract is better than some lame promise to love and cherish. It's a legal document," he insisted. "One you can count on."

"Dave…a contract isn't a guarantee against failure."

All around them, Royal was in party mode. The music continued to pump into the room and wild laughter and shouts rose up behind them. Dave had come here convinced that he'd found a way to keep Mia with him. Now, though, here in this darkened corner in the middle of a celebration, Dave felt as though he were losing a war.

"No, it's not. But it's a start. Running your life on emotion is asking for trouble," he told her flatly. "I know because I've seen it up close and personal. I want you with me, Mia. But I can't promise love."

She reached up, cupped his cheek in the palm of her hand and said, "And that's the only thing I want from you."

Her hand dropped from his face, but he caught it in his and dragged it back up, holding her there, feeling the heat of her even as he saw a chill creep into her eyes. He had to keep trying, though, because he'd never once given up on something he wanted.

"We're good together, Mia," he said and saw a flash of hurt dart across her eyes. "You know it. We've been happy this past month."

"Yes, we have," she said, pulling her hand free of his. "But it's not enough for me. Not anymore."

"Why *not?*"

"Because I love you, Dave." She took a deep breath, blew it out again and gave him a sad smile. "I didn't mean to, it just happened."

A quick flash of something bright and amazing shot through Dave in a split second before his brain kicked into gear and rejected the emotion. He'd learned long ago that "love" was just a word. He stiffened. Looking down into her face, he read the truth in her eyes and took an emotional step back. "Love wasn't part of the agreement."

"No," she said sadly, "it wasn't."

He glanced over her head at the crowd in the room behind them, away from her eyes, giving himself a chance to take a mental breath. To get a grip. It didn't help much. "I'm not interested in love, Mia. I told you that from the beginning."

"Yeah, you did." Mia shook her head so hard, one of the feathers in her hair came free and floated to the floor. "I should have listened. But I love you anyway."

He scraped one hand across the back of his neck, then looked into those eyes of hers again. "Stop saying that," he muttered darkly. "People say that damn word so easily."

"I don't," she told him flatly. "I've never said 'I love you' to a man before. Ever."

He gritted his teeth. "Love wasn't part of our deal."

"And the deal is all-important?" she asked. "Rules? Contracts?"

"Without them, you've got nothing," he countered, his voice harsh and deep. "Love is a setup for the letdown, that's all. Throw that word out and you're supposed to forget common sense. You're supposed to believe—" he broke off and caught himself before saying "—you believe promises and one by one they're broken."

"What're you talking about?"

"Love," he snapped and wondered when this whole thing had gone to hell. "My mother believed. My father said he loved her. Us." He laughed shortly and heard the sharp, ragged edges of it. "Didn't stop him from leaving. Walking away, leaving Mom to survive however she could. We lost our home. We lost everything. I became the man of the house when he took off. I was eleven.

I stopped being a kid and watched my mother's world crumble around her. Because we believed in *love*."

"Dave…" She reached out to him but he stepped back. "That's awful and I'm so sorry…"

"Didn't ask for your pity."

"Sympathy, not pity," she corrected. "And your mom is in love again. Do you think Mike will break her heart?"

"He better damn well not."

Shaking her head, Mia said, "He won't. He's a good man and he loves her. Your mom is willing to take a chance again, so why can't you?"

God, it was hot in there. He felt like he couldn't breathe. He'd spilled his guts and she was picking them up and handing them to him. And Dave didn't have a damn answer for her. He didn't understand how his mother could trust again. Believe again. He only knew that he couldn't. He wanted Mia. Cared for her more than anyone he'd ever known. But if he used the word "love," he'd lose control.

"I won't give you promises, Mia," he told her, gathering the threads of his control. "I'll give you a contract. My word. In writing."

"Without the promise, the contract means nothing, Dave. Don't you see that?"

"Why are you doing this?" he demanded, reaching for her, grabbing hold of her shoulders and dragging her close. "We had a deal. You weren't supposed to bring emotions into this."

She laughed a little, but it was a broken sound. "Pesky humans, you just can't trust them to keep their hearts out of things."

"Damn it, Mia, I don't want to lose you. We can still have something good together."

"No. But we could have had something *great*."

"You're wrong."

"Looks like I was wrong about a lot of things," she whispered. Slowly, she pulled the huge diamond ring from her finger and held it out to him. He stiffened, gritted his teeth against the unfamiliar swell of helplessness filling him and took the ring from her, closing his fingers over the cold, hard stone.

She walked past him then, without another word. He wanted to reach for her, pull her into his arms and never let go. But he knew it wouldn't do any good. She was already gone.

He'd lost.

Amanda and Nathan gave Mia a ride to Alex's house. Thankfully, her friends didn't ask any questions. The gate guard at Pine Valley let Mia into the house and when she was alone in what had once been her home, she gave in to the tears strangling her.

All the silly, foolish hope she'd been hanging on to for weeks dissolved in that flood of sorrow. By the following morning, Mia was still miserable, and looked every inch of it.

She forced herself to get up and on with her life, because even though her heart hurt and her eyes were still red and swollen from crying, she had to keep moving. If she surrendered to her misery, she'd never leave Alex's house again.

A glance out the front window let her know that Dave had had her new car delivered. Had he brought it himself and left without seeing her? Had he had one of the ranch hands deliver it instead so he wouldn't have to risk seeing her? Did it matter?

She looked at the shiny new car in the driveway and Alice's words came back to her. *He gave you a car because he loves you.* Mia would like to believe that, but unless he actually said the words, she couldn't.

Her purse and clothes were all in the SUV, carefully packed in her suitcases. She carted everything inside and once she'd unpacked, she realized that she had better go grocery shopping. Delores wasn't around to spoil her anymore. She was on her own again and she better get used to it.

In town, she stopped in at the diner to thank Amanda for the ride home and found the whole coffee shop buzzing. People seemed angry, confused, as they gathered in groups to talk. Mia took a seat at the counter and when Amanda poured her a cup of coffee, she asked, "What's going on?"

"You haven't heard yet? The whole town's talking about it. I got the story from Nathan, of course, and I just could hardly believe it." Amanda bit her lip, shook her head and said, "It's the day-care center at the TCC."

Mia had a bad feeling about this. "What happened?"

"Someone broke in last night and vandalized it."

This wasn't the first time someone had tampered with the day-care center, Mia knew. But this sounded far worse than before.

"Oh, no! But it was so beautiful. And ready to open." She hated thinking about the loving care that had been brought to that space only to be destroyed.

"They broke all the tables and chairs and spray painted the walls with some really ugly graffiti." Amanda set the coffeepot down and placed both hands protectively on her rounded belly. "They even went in and destroyed Kiley's office. Ruined her computer, broke the printer. It's just a mess. The whole place."

"But who would've done such a terrible thing?"

Amanda looked around the diner, her gaze flicking across all of the familiar faces there before coming back to meet Mia's eyes. "To tell you the truth, I don't have a clue."

Mia winced. "Beau Hacket?"

Amanda nodded. "I'm sure he and his friends, like the Gordon brothers or Paul Windsor, are right at the top of the list. I know lots of people in town were against this, but I just can't picture someone I've known my whole life being so vicious."

"They'll still open the day care though, won't they?" Mia asked, hating to think that the wonderful place would never welcome children.

"You bet they will," Amanda told her. "Those of us who support the center are going to make sure of it." She took a breath and said, "Anyway, how're you doing this morning?"

"Not good," Mia admitted.

"Yeah. I, um, noticed you're not wearing your ring...."

She looked at her own naked finger, then dropped her left hand into her lap. "No, I gave it back to Dave last night."

"Aw, sweetie, I'm sorry."

"Thanks," Mia said with a tight grimace she hoped would pass as a smile. "Me, too."

"You need sugar. Cinnamon roll. On the house."

Mia didn't think she could eat anything, since for the first time in forever, food held no appeal. But she appreciated the gesture. "Thanks, Amanda."

Her friend patted Mia's hand and gave her a supportive smile. "It'll get better, sweetie."

"It has to," Mia said. Because she was so far down, there was nowhere to go but up.

The next couple of days were hard.

Dave worked himself into exhaustion all day and then lay awake all night. He couldn't stop his brain from racing. Couldn't stop the leapfrogging of thought to thought to thought.

There was Alex Santiago—still missing and no one had a clue where to look for him next. There was the destruction of the day-care center at the TCC. As far as he knew, there were no clues to the perpetrators there, either. He hadn't had a chance to talk to Nathan, so he knew nothing more than what was reported in the local paper, and judging by that, there were no suspects yet.

Then there was TexCat—and the deal for his beef that was at the heart of everything that had happened over the past month. He'd gotten that deal and had lost Mia. He'd secured his ranch's future—his organic beef would now have the stamp of excellence recognized all over Texas. With that contract in hand, he could grow his herd and expand his contacts. It was all good. But his personal future looked pretty damn grim.

His room still smelled of her. Her scent clung to her pillow, and when he reached across the cool sheets in the middle of the night blindly searching for her, he came up empty.

Hell, he couldn't even take a shower anymore without remembering the two of them on that wide bench seat. How Mia had looked with water streaming down her beautiful body. How she'd clutched at him and called his name. How she'd made him feel...whole.

Delores made his favorite foods, hoping to cheer him up, but how the hell could he choke down that mocha fudge cake when all he could think about was how much Mia had loved it?

Mike worked the ranch alongside Dave, but the foreman was so damn happy with Dave's mother he was hard to be around. And as for Alice Firestone, the woman was bound and determined to make sure that her son knew he was the instigator of his own misery.

"You've been many things in your lifetime, David," she said now over a glass of wine. "But I've never known you to be a coward."

His head snapped up and he looked at her through narrowed eyes. He was too tired for this. Tired down to his bones. He'd spent the day on his horse, riding over the acreage that meant so much to him. Losing himself in the land because that was all he had left. Now it was night again and he wasn't looking forward to trying to sleep in that big, empty bed upstairs.

She waved away his furious look. "Don't think you worry me with that lord-of-the-range glare. You can't fool me. I know you're hurting."

"You're wrong," he said flatly, and tossed his glass of sixty-year-old scotch down his throat as if it were foul-tasting medicine. The burn through his system was the only warmth he'd felt in days.

He wondered idly where the hell Mike was. Once the foreman arrived, they could sit down to dinner and this interrogation of his mother's would end.

"I'm not wrong, and that's what's bothering you," she said. Like a pit bull with a bone, his mother never let go once she'd clamped onto something. "You and I both know you miss Mia."

He poured more scotch. "I never said I didn't."

"Never said you did, either, but we'll let that go for the moment." Alice took a sip of her wine, set the glass down on a side table and crossed the wide great room to her son's side.

Heat from the fire in the hearth reached out to them and the crackle and hiss as flames devoured wood were the only sounds for a moment or two. Dave poured himself another drink, thinking he was going to need it.

Alice had been at him for two days, demanding that he do the right thing for himself—and for Mia. But he'd tried to do the right thing and Mia had shot him down. He'd offered her marriage and had that offer tossed back into his face.

Of course, his mind taunted him, you didn't offer her what she *needed* to hear....

Scowling down at his scotch, he tossed that one back, too. But when he reached for the bottle to pour another, his mother's hand on his arm stopped him. "David, that's not the answer."

"Not looking for an answer, Mom."

"You should be," she told him. "But since you won't, I'll just give it to you."

He groaned and shook his head. "Could you just leave this alone, Mom?"

"No."

"Didn't think so."

"Your problem is, you love Mia and you're afraid to admit it."

"I'm not afraid," he said tightly, though a part of him wondered if she wasn't right.

"Of course you are," she told him, taking one of his hands into hers and squeezing it. "When your father left us, you closed in on yourself."

He frowned. Yeah, he knew that, but for some reason, he'd always thought he'd been successful at hiding it from his mom. He should have known better.

"I saw it happening, but I didn't know how to fix it," she said softly.

He didn't want her feeling guilty about any of this. She'd done her best by him when his own damn father hadn't cared enough to stick it out and try. "Mom—"

"No, listen to me, David." She turned her face up to his and met his gaze squarely. "You were protecting yourself. A little boy who was so hurt he didn't know what to do with himself. But, David, you can't stay locked away your whole life."

"I'm not," he insisted, though his argument sounded hollow even to himself.

"Your father made mistakes. But he wasn't afraid to say the words *I love you.*"

"No," Dave said wryly. "He just was too much of a coward to stay and see to his family."

"Maybe it was cowardly, maybe it was something else. We'll never know," Alice said, her voice nearly lost in the crackle of the fire. "But if you let what he did inform the decisions you make now, don't you understand that you're cheating yourself?"

"Hey," Mike called from the doorway. "Sorry I'm late."

Alice gave her son's hand one last pat, then turned to greet her fiancé. The older man bent his head for a kiss and Dave watched as his mother threw her arms around Mike for a big hug.

He smiled to himself, grateful now that the first shock of seeing his mother with a man was over, that she'd found happiness again. That she'd found love.

And maybe she was right to call him a damn coward. Hadn't his mother suffered more than he had? Losing her husband, her home, her livelihood? She'd become a single mother overnight and Dave had never once heard her complain or even bad-mouth his father.

Instead, she'd gone on. Built a life for herself and her son. She hadn't wasted time worrying over a past that was dead and gone.

How could he do less?

"Dave?" Mike asked from across the room. "You okay?"

He looked at his foreman. "Yeah. I think I am. Or anyway," he added as his mind started clicking, "I think I will be."

The following night when the doorbell rang, Mia left the email she'd just received and went to answer it. She grabbed the bowl of Halloween candy, ready to greet yet another group of kids shouting, "Trick or treat!" With a smile she didn't feel plastered to her face, she opened the door and looked into familiar, fog-gray eyes.

"Dave? What're you doing here?" She looked past him and saw ghosts and vampires and one tiny Chewbacca running up to the house across the street. "How did you get past the gate guard? I told him not to let you in."

He frowned. "Explains why it took fifty bucks instead of twenty this time."

"Oh, for—" Of course he'd bribed the gate guard. Why wouldn't he? Dave Firestone did whatever he had to do to get what he wanted. She grabbed the edge of the door and tried to shut it, but he was too fast for her.

He slapped one hand to the heavy oak panel and said, "Let me in, Mia. Please."

Surprised that he even knew that word, she could only nod and step back.

"What do you want, Dave?"

He snatched his hat off and tossed it to the couch behind him. "That's gonna take some time."

God, he looked so good. Lamplight played over his features and pooled around the two of them as if locking them into a golden bubble of light. It had been three days since she'd seen him and it felt like forever. Mia's every instinct screamed at her to throw herself at him. To lose herself in the heat of him. To kiss him again and feel the electrical charge sizzle between them.

Heck, she'd been so lonely, there was part of her ready to tell him she'd accept his stupid contract. That she didn't need him to love her. All she needed was *him*. But if she did that, gave in to her own urges, then she would be cheating them both out of what they could have had.

"Trick or treat!"

Mia jolted and clutched the bowl of candy to her chest. "I'm sorry. Kids."

She forced herself to smile as she turned to the ballerina and the soldier standing on her front porch.

"Don't you guys look great?" she said, holding the bowl out to them. She felt Dave standing right behind her and it made her so nervous she had to grip the bowl to keep from dropping it. "Take two each."

"Thank you!" they answered, then ran off the porch and down the steps to their parents, who were waiting on the sidewalk.

Mia waved the family off, fought down the pang of realization that she would never have children with the man she loved then closed the door and turned to face the man who held her heart even though she couldn't have him. Steeling herself against whatever might be coming, she said, "Okay, Dave, what is it?"

"I want you to marry me."

"I can't believe you came all the way over here to offer me the same empty proposal." Regret and disappointment twisted together in the pit of her stomach. She shook her head and said, "I'm not interested in a contract, Dave. I already told you that."

"I didn't say anything about a contract."

Then what did he mean? And why was he here? That blasted bit of hope that was still lying buried in the bottom of her heart began to warm. Mia looked up at him and waited.

Dave stared into her deep blue eyes and started talking. Words rushed from him in a torrent. Didn't seem to matter that he'd been practicing a perfectly good speech all the way over here. Because it was gone and all he was left with was what was in his heart. He hoped to hell it would be enough.

"Mia, these past few days without you..." He scraped both hands through his hair, then let them drop to his sides again. "I know now what it feels like to walk around with a gaping hole in your chest where your heart used to be."

He reached for her, but she stepped back and he couldn't blame her. He hadn't given her a reason yet to come *to* him. But he was finally ready. Talking to his mother had helped. But the bottom line was that over the past few empty, lonely days, he'd finally realized that life without Mia wasn't worth living. He loved her. Whether he admitted it or not, he loved her. So why shouldn't she know it?

Reaching into his shirt pocket, he pulled out a ring box.

She shook her head and said, "I'm not taking that ring back, Dave."

"And I wouldn't expect you to." He grimaced tightly. "That other ring was big and gaudy and bought for all the wrong reasons. I was making a statement. Showing off. For this proposal, for the *real* proposal, I needed a ring that meant something." He opened the jeweler's box and showed her the new ring he'd purchased just that afternoon.

It was smaller than the other one. Three carats instead of five. The setting was different, too. No more modern, coldly elegant cut. This ring reminded him of Mia. Warm. Traditional. Steady.

She gasped when she looked at it and one hand crept up to the base of her throat as she lifted her gaze to his. "It's beautiful."

"The minute I saw it, I knew it was yours."

"Dave—"

"Do you remember," he asked, cutting her off neatly, "when I gave you that other ring, I said that it would tell everyone that Mia belongs to Dave?"

She chewed at her bottom lip, swiped at a stray tear trailing from her eye and nodded, clearly unable to speak.

"Well, this one's different," he told her quietly. "This one says Dave's heart belongs to Mia."

Her hand covered her mouth now and tears were

streaming down her cheeks. Every tear tore at him and Dave made a mental vow to never make her cry again.

"I don't know what to say." Her voice was choked, raw with emotion.

"Nothing yet," he said, stepping in closer, pleased when she didn't move back and away from him. "I'm not near finished talking."

She snorted a short laugh. "Always in charge…"

He gave her a half smile. "Always. Well, until tonight."

"Trick or treat!"

Dave laughed. Most important moment of his life being interrupted by groups of kids out for candy.

"Oh, God, I can't answer the door crying, I'll scare the kids." She swiped at her face, but Dave just picked up the candy bowl, opened the door and took care of things. When he stepped back inside, he set the bowl down and turned back to her.

"I've got a few more things to say and I'd like to get 'em said before the next crew of trolls and princesses shows up."

She laughed a little and nodded. "Go ahead."

"I've done some thinking and I finally realized that a contract is just as easy for some people to break as a promise is." He frowned to himself and took a breath before saying, "I was so busy getting everything on the dotted line, it didn't occur to me that if someone wants to lie or cheat…or leave, a contract won't stop 'em."

"No, it wouldn't," Mia whispered.

"But a promise made by someone who keeps their promises is as good as gold, right?"

She nodded. "Absolutely."

"Well, I keep my promises. And I want to make you one right now, Mia," Dave said, choosing every word carefully now because the next few minutes would decide his future and he for damn sure wanted to get it right. "I promise that I will always love you—"

Mia gasped, clapped a hand to her heart and started crying again. Made a man weak in the knees to see a strong woman cry—especially if he knew he was the cause. "Don't cry anymore, Mia, you're killing me."

"Dave..."

"I'm not afraid to say it now," he told her, reaching out to wipe away her tears with a gentle swipe of his thumbs. "I always thought if I never said the words, then I wasn't risking anything. But by not saying them, I was losing everything." He smiled at her. "And you know I don't like to lose."

"I know."

"So I'm promising you a lifetime of being loved. I want to marry you, Mia. I want our kids to wear that christening gown my mom gave you," he said, then paused and winced. "But not the boys, okay?"

She laughed and nodded. "Okay. We'll find manly outfits for our sons."

He grinned. "That's a deal. *Our sons and daughters.* Sounds good, doesn't it?"

"It sounds wonderful, Dave," she said, stepping up close to him. "It sounds perfect."

"Then marry me, Mia. Wear my ring. Tell the whole world that you hold my heart."

"Oh, Dave, of course I'll marry you." She watched as he plucked the ring from its velvet liner and slid it on her finger. He kissed it as if to seal it into place, then looked into her eyes.

"And you'll come home with me."

"As soon as I'm out of candy."

He grinned. "Tell me you love me."

"I love you so much," she said.

"Promise me forever," Dave whispered.

"I promise I will love you forever, Dave Firestone," she said, her heart in her eyes.

"That's all I'll ever need." He kissed her then, sealing their promises to each other.

As her arms came around him and he pulled her in close, Dave felt his world come back into balance. With Mia, with love, he had the world.

Then the doorbell rang and laughing, they handed out candy together.

* * * * *

THE WAY YOU LOVE ME

DONNA HILL

Chapter 1

The stack of overdue notices glared accusingly up at Bailey from the backdrop of her wobbly kitchen table. Credit cards. Car payment. Student loans. Overdraft fees. They all read the same: "Dear Ms. Sinclair: Overdue. Demand for payment. Respond in ten days." One after the other. What was not in the pile was what she needed most—the scholarship letter that would pave the way for her to return to law school in the fall.

She'd applied for every scholarship that she could conceivably be eligible for but had yet to receive a positive response. For years she'd put her life on hold for her family. This was her time, but now with the fall semester beginning in just over four months, her goal of completing her law degree was becoming more of a dream than a reality.

Bailey stuck the notices back in their envelopes and stared out of her third-floor apartment window at the approaching dusk that had turned the horizon into a soft rosey hue. She drew in a long breath. Sitting there wishing things were different wasn't going to get the bills paid. She had a job to get to, and her shift at the Mercury Lounge would not wait for her. She pushed back from the table, and it rocked in response.

The Mercury Lounge was the hub for the who's who of Baton Rouge, Louisiana. On any given night the patrons ranged from the average customer to politicians, business entrepreneurs, and entertainment and sports figures. She enjoyed her job. Meeting new people, listening to their stories and their problems fed her legal mind, and, of course, there were the regulars who came in to simply get free advice. Too bad that enjoying what she did for a living wasn't enough to keep her afloat.

Fortunately, she had her side hustle with her best friend, Addison Matthews, whose business was catering parties for the rich and fabulous. The extra income certainly helped, but it was no longer enough.

Addison swore that if Bailey would loosen up and give a play to one of those sexy, wealthy men that were always hitting on her, she could put an end to the demand notices and collection calls and return to school. Not to mention the perks of having a man to warm that big empty bed of hers at night. Bailey had stopped listening to Addison. She knew all too well what running after money could do. It destroyed lives, and the trait ran in her family like a string of corrupted DNA, and she vowed to break the chain. That meant doing it on her own no matter how difficult that might be.

Bailey grabbed her purse, a light jacket and her keys then headed out, hoping on her way downstairs that her ten-year-old Honda—that was five years old when she bought it—would start, just as the ringing of her cell phone slowed her steps. She glanced at the name on the face of the phone. *Her sister Tory.* Her stomach knotted.

"Hey, sis." She threw up a silent prayer. "What's up?"

"Hi, Bailey. I know you're probably getting ready for work."

"I'm on my way out the door."

"Um, you know I hate to ask…"

"What is it, Tory? What do you need?"

"You don't have to say it like that," she whined petulantly.

Bailey silently counted to ten. "What do you need, sis?"

"I'm behind on my rent."

"Again? Tory…"

"I just had more expenses than I thought this month."

"More shopping and partying."

"That's not fair!"

"How much, Tory?"

"Twelve-hundred dollars."

Bailey's jaw tightened. She did a quick calculation in her head. Giving her sister twelve hundred dollars would dig deep into her savings, set her back on her own plans. But Tory was her younger sister, and she swore when their mother died that she would take care of her sisters, no matter what. "Fine. I'll put a check in the mail."

"Thank you, Bailey. I really appreciate it. I swear I'm going to do better, sis."

"Sure. Listen, I gotta go."

"Okay. Thanks again. Love you."

"Bye, Tory." She disconnected the call, and her shoulders slumped.

Bailey arrived at the Mercury Lounge, and the instant that she stepped through the doors she felt the energy and knew that it would be a busy night. Busy was good. Busy meant plenty of customers and lots of tips. She finger-waved and lifted her chin in salute to several of her co-workers as she strolled through the lowest level of the tri-level venue. She still had about an hour before her shift started and plenty to do until then.

Although she was originally hired as a mixologist three years earlier, the owner, Vincent Mercury, "saw something" in Bailey, and when an opportunity presented itself, he offered her the assistant manager spot with a nice bump in her salary. Combined with her duties of running the bars, things started looking up for her financially. That all changed, with one thing after the other.

"Vince in back?" Bailey asked Kim, the Friday night hostess.

"He went upstairs to check on the setup in the private dining room. We have that party tonight."

Bailey squeezed her eyes shut for an instant. She'd totally forgotten. "Right." She should have come in earlier. "Guess I'd better get busy." She continued on toward the back offices tucked along a narrow corridor. She dug her keys out of her purse and unlocked her makeshift office that had been transformed from a storage room that was about a half inch bigger than a walk-in closet. The tight space was big enough for a desk the size of a small kitchen table, two chairs and a six-drawer file cabinet. She'd had the room painted white and hung a floor-to-ceiling mirror on one wall to give the illusion of space. A couple of potted plants, two wall paintings and a framed photo of her and her siblings made the space cozy without feeling overcrowded.

Bailey unlocked her desk drawer, put her purse in and locked it again. She opened the cover of her laptop and powered it up. The first thing that she needed to check was that all the staff that was scheduled for the night shift was accounted for and had not called out. Then she had to plan the scheduling for the week, verify the details for an upcoming local company luncheon and approve an order for linens that was requested by the floor manager. By the time she was done, it was about fifteen minutes before her shift at the bar was to begin, but she wanted to make a quick stop up to the private dining room and make sure that Vince didn't need her for anything before she got behind the bar.

The private dining room was on the third level. One wall was glass and looked out over the city's horizon. The space seated fifty comfortably, and for bigger events one wall retracted to join the next room that could accommodate another one hundred guests.

When Bailey got off the escalator the waitstaff was

fully engaged in preparation. She spotted Vince on the far side of the room, giving directions while checking his clipboard.

"Hey, looks like you have everything under control," she said, sidling up to him.

He barely glanced up at her over the rim of his glasses. "There's always something that doesn't get done," he said, and his tone clearly relayed his annoyance.

"What happened?"

"The centerpieces were supposed to be crystal goblets with white orchids floating in water." His brow cinched as he ran his hand through his golden-blond hair.

Bailey looked at the centerpieces, which were lovely but clearly not what Vincent requested. Instead, they were long-stemmed calla lilies in slender vases. And she realized immediately what the issue was. Even though the centerpieces were beautiful to look at, the size and type of flower obstructed the diners' views of each other at the table. Bailey folded her arms and tried to think of an option.

"I have an idea." She didn't wait for Vincent to respond. She began giving instructions to the staff to take the centerpieces off the tables, load them onto a cart and two of them were to come with her to the basement storage room. She pulled out her cell phone and called Addison.

"Hey, Addie, listen, we're in a bind. Remember those goblets that you used for your last catering job?"

"Yep. What's up?"

"I need to use them for tonight. We still have them in our storage room here at the Mercury Lounge."

"Sure. Not a problem. You didn't need to call me for that."

"I wanted to make sure it was okay."

"Listen, I appreciate you being able to hold on to my stuff for me. With the catering jobs getting bigger and bigger, I'm running out of space in my apartment. Even though it's been more cost-effective to purchase what I need instead of renting, it's taking a toll on my square footage." She laughed.

"I hear that. Anyway, thanks, girl. Gotta run."

"Talk to you later."

Once they reached the storage room in the basement, Bailey instructed the staff to box up the vases after removing the calla lilies. She laid the plants out on a long table, found a pair of scissors and started cutting the lilies down to size. Shortly after, the lilies were floating in the goblets and were being placed back on the tables.

"I don't know what I'd do without you," Vincent said, his gray eyes crinkling at the corners with his smile. He gave her quick kiss on the cheek.

Bailey blinked in surprise. "Drive yourself crazy." She patted his shoulder. "I have to get downstairs. My shift has already started."

"Thanks again," he called out.

She waved away his thanks and hurried off, pushing the impromptu cheek kiss to the back of her mind.

By the time Bailey returned to the ground level, the line for the early diners to be seated had grown. Every stool at the bar was taken, and the two bartenders were working their magic.

Bailey came around to the entrance of the bar. "Hey, Mellie, hectic already, I see," she said and took her black apron from the hook and tied it around her waist.

"Girl, you would think this was the last stop in town," she joked. She poured a splash of top-shelf rum over ice, dropped in a slice of lime and spun away toward her customer.

Bailey took a quick inventory of supplies and made sure that the snack bowls on the counter were freshened and full. Then she went to work, mixing and joking with the customers. She loved the teasing games she played with them, especially her regulars. It was all harmless fun, and it made the evenings fly by. And, of course, there were the more serious-minded conversations on politics, religion, cheating spouses and significant others and the customary legal questions. It all came with the territory.

She'd been going nonstop for about an hour when two seats in her section opened. One was quickly occupied. She took a cloth from beneath the bar counter and walked over to her new customer. She did what she always did: wiped down the counter, placed a bowl of snacks on the bar, shot him with her best smile and took his order.

"Welcome to the Mercury Lounge. What can I get for you?"

Carl Hurley scooped up a handful of nuts and tossed them in his mouth. He chewed slowly. "I'm actually waiting on my buddy until our table is ready. But how 'bout a Corona while I wait?"

"Not a problem."

She turned away and went to get the beer and a glass. When she returned, the empty seat was occupied, and the two men were in an animated conversation. She was all ready to get into her routine when he turned and looked at her. Something hit her, like a flash or a shock or something; she couldn't be sure. And for a moment she didn't breathe when the light caught in his eyes, and he smiled. Not a full smile but halfway, just the corner of his mouth. She blinked and placed the bottle of beer and glass in front of her customer and forced herself to concentrate.

"Good evening. And what can I get you?"

The dark of his eyes moved really slowly over her face, and every inch that was exposed to his perusal heated. The pulse in her throat tripled its beat.

"Hmm, bourbon. Neat. Four Roses."

"Coming right up." She spun away, and her knees were gelatin-shaky. She drew in a breath and scanned the shelf for the bottles of bourbon, missing them twice before she recognized them for what they were. At least the glasses were right in front of her. She brought the glass and the bottle of Four Roses bourbon and placed the glass in front of him. "Say when."

The warm brown liquid slid from the mouth of the bottle into the wide opening of the glass with a bare splash. The heady aroma aroused the senses.

"When…"

Bailey took her eyes away from what she was doing, and her gaze bumped right against his. She lightly ran her tongue across her bottom lip as she watched him bring the glass to his nose. Inhaled. Nodded. Took a sip. "Perfect."

"Let me know if you gentlemen need anything else." She managed to tug herself away from his magnetic pull.

"You okay?" Mellie asked as she dumped glasses in the sudsy water.

"Yeah, why?"

"You seem distracted. Not your usual bouncy self."

"I'm good. A few things on my mind, that's all."

Mellie studied Bailey for a moment then shrugged. "Cool. I'm going to take my break as soon as things slow down."

"Sure."

"Wow, that guy down on the end is hot," she said under her breath.

"Who?"

"Your customer. The one with the open-collar white shirt, no tie. Don't tell me you didn't notice."

Bailey's heart thumped. "I try not to."

"Girl, you must be angling for sainthood. Give me a minute with him." She slid her eyes in his direction.

Bailey sputtered a laugh. "You need to stop."

"And why would I do that?" she teased, emphasizing every word.

Bailey shook her head in amusement and went back to work.

* * *

Justin Lawson took a sip of his drink. His gaze kept drifting back to the woman who'd served him, subtly following her every move. "How long did they say we'd have to wait for a table?"

"At least a half hour. Didn't think we needed a reservation."

Justin glanced around. The lounge was pretty full with more patrons waiting to be seated. This was the first time he'd been to the Mercury Lounge. He'd heard good things about it, but he wanted to check it out before he brought Jasmine here.

"How is that case coming that you were working on?"

Carl sucked up a laugh. "It's a mess." He tossed back the rest of his beer straight from the bottle. "The usual corporate back room dirty deals, everyone trying to outmaneuver the other." He shook his head.

Justin, like Carl, was an attorney. Both of them worked for one of the biggest law firms in Louisiana, and they both were working hard on the side to launch Justin's nonprofit—The Justice Project—something that his father, Senator Branford Lawson, wasn't pleased about.

What is it about my sons, Branford had boomed at the last family gathering. *I build a legacy for them, pave the way for them and they go off and do what the hell they want anyway.* If their father had his way, both he and his older brother, Rafe, would be embroiled in the political quagmire of Washington, DC. Rafe preferred the life of a jazz musician and womanizer. Justin always believed it was just Rafe's way to piss their father off. But at least Justin, to appease his father, had agreed to take the position at the law firm Lake, Martin and Dubois, which is where he'd met Jasmine Dubois.

"Are you finished with the depositions?" Justin asked. He was almost done with his drink. He peered down the length of the bar to get Bailey's attention.

"Should be completed by the end of the next week. I tell you, man, it's been a nightmare."

"Once we get The Justice Project off the ground, we can finally start doing the kind of work that we want to do—that needs to be done."

"Not soon enough for me," Carl said.

"Refills, gentlemen?" Bailey looked from one to the other, refusing to settle on Justin's face.

"Another Corona for me."

"And you?"

Justin studied the lines of her face, the way the tips of her eyes lifted ever so slightly, the soft rise of her breasts beneath the stiff black shirt, and the warm caramel of her skin. "I'll take another." He lifted his glass. The path of his gaze led to hers.

That spark popped between them again. Bailey sucked in a breath when Justin ran his finger around the rim of his glass.

"Coming right up." She strode down the bar to retrieve the Corona from the icebox and filled a clean glass with bourbon.

"If you two get any hotter, you'll set the joint on fire," Carl teased.

Justin rolled his head toward Carl. "What are you talking about?"

"You know damn well what I'm talking about. You haven't stopped checking her out since you sat down."

"A man can look, can't he?" He reached for a handful of cocktail peanuts.

"Yeah, but Jasmine's doing her best to claim you."

Justin heaved a sigh. "Yeah, Jasmine," he murmured.

"Trouble in paradise?"

"Let's just say she would like us to be in a relationship, but I don't think it's a good idea." He slowly shook his head.

"Hmm, makes it kind of tough with her being the boss's daughter."

"Yeah...exactly."

"Here you go, gentlemen." She placed the beer and glass in front of Carl and the bourbon in front of Justin. "Is there anything else I can get you?"

"A table," Carl groused.

Bailey smiled, and Justin's insides shifted. He lifted his glass and let his gaze drop into the depth of his drink instead of the dark pools that were her eyes.

"We're always busy on Friday nights. I take it this is your first time here." She wiped down the space in front of them and refilled the snack bowl.

"It is," Justin said.

"I wouldn't want this to be your last time." She was talking to them both, but her eyes were fixed on Justin. "Let me see what I can do about getting you a table."

"We'd appreciate that..." Justin waited for her to fill the blank.

"Bailey."

"Justin."

"I'll see what I can do, Justin."

"Oh, and I'm Carl," he said, feigning offense at being ignored.

Bailey laughed lightly. "Carl."

Bailey and Justin shared a look of amusement before she walked off.

Carl's cell phone chirped. He pulled it out of his pocket, checked the face of the phone and frowned. "Matthew..." He listened, and his expression grew tighter. "Okay. Give me a half hour. Thanks." He disconnected the call and turned to Justin.

"What's up?"

"I have to go back to the office. Matthew got a call from Judge Graham's clerk. He wants us in chambers at nine tomorrow morning. You know how anal he is. I need to pull everything we have together on the obstruction case."

"Need some help?"

"Naw." Carl stood, finished off his beer and clapped Justin on the shoulder. "You stay. That's why we have first-year associates for times like this. I'll supervise, and they'll work." He lifted his chin. "Anyway, I'm sure you'll have much more fun here than back at the office." He set his beer bottle down. "Tab is on you. Later."

Justin chuckled and lifted his drink to his lips just as Bailey returned.

"I got you a table. Where's Carl?"

Justin's brow flicked. "He had to leave. Problem at the office."

"Oh, well, if you still want the table…"

He halfway shrugged. "Can I uh, order some food and sit at the bar?"

Her heart bumped in her chest. She felt slightly giddy. "Sure. I'll get you a menu. Be right back."

Justin watched her walk away and was immensely grateful for the anal Judge Graham.

Chapter 2

Justin looked over the menu. He was pleased at the extensive selections and finally settled on a porterhouse steak, grilled asparagus and risotto.

"I'll put this in right away," Bailey said. "It might be a while. Would you like an appetizer in the meantime?"

"I'm a patient man." He slowly turned his glass. "I can wait."

Bailey tried to swallow, but her throat was so dry that she choked.

Justin leaned forward and reached for her. "You okay?"

She blinked away the water that filled her eyes. Coughed. Coughed again and wished that the floor would open. She cleared her throat. Her vision cleared, and she realized that the fire on her hand was Justin's.

Bailey took a step back, slid her hand away. "I'm sorry. I'm fine. Guess something caught in my throat."

Justin sat back down. "Well, I would have been happy to resuscitate you had the need arisen."

Bailey's stomach danced. There was that half grin again as if he knew something that no one else did.

"I'll keep that in mind."

She walked down the aisle to the other end of the bar to check on the customers and refills and could barely concentrate. What in the world was her problem? She was all twisted over some guy who could be a gorgeous serial killer for all she knew.

"Bailey, can you check the couple on the end while I fix these martinis?" Mellie asked.

"Sure." That's what she needed to be doing—paying attention to her customers, making sure that the bar was running at optimum efficiency, not getting all hot and bothered over some guy.

"What's the deal with the two you were serving?"

"Oh, one of them had to leave. Business or something," she added noncommitally while she prepared the drinks.

"The one who stayed is yummy. And you know he has his eye on you. You gonna talk to him or what?"

"Mellie...I talk to all of my customers."

"You know what I mean. He's hot. I know you have some 'policy' about interacting with the customers, but come on, girl..."

Hot. That he was. Her hand still tingled from his touch. But she'd never taken bar talk beyond the bar. To her it was the doorway to trouble, and she didn't intend to open it. She talked, she joked, she provided drinks and that was all.

"There's a first time for everything," Mellie said as if reading her mind.

Bailey shook her head, returned the bottles to their place on the shelf and walked off to serve the customers.

Justin nursed his drink while keeping Bailey on his radar. Although he'd looked forward to an evening with his friend, he was actually glad that Carl got called back to work. It would give him some space to maybe get to know Bailey a little better. He sipped his drink. *Jasmine.*

When they'd met more than a year ago and went out a few times, he thought that she might be the one. Both of their fathers encouraged the relationship. Their friends thought that they were the perfect couple, but his brother, Rafe, of all people, was the only one who threw shade on the relationship. Rafe told him in no uncertain terms that Jasmine was the one "for the moment," but not forever, and that he'd know forever when it hit him. He'd laughed off his big brother's warning. Rafe was a notorious ladies' man, and Justin was hard-pressed to take what Rafe said seriously. But as the months progressed, and Jasmine grew more clingy, more demanding and more of what he was *not* looking or ready for, he was forced to tell Jasmine where they stood.

"Dinner is served." Bailey placed his meal in front of him.

Justin glanced up from the warm amber liquid of his glass only to swim in the depths of her chocolate-brown eyes. A slow heat flowed through his limbs. "Looks good. Thank you."

"Can I get you anything else?"

"Not at the moment."

"Enjoy." She started to walk away.

"Hey, uh, Bailey..."

She stopped and turned back to him. Her brows rose in question.

"How long does this place stay open?"

"Last call is at one. We close at two."

He nodded. "Is that when you get off? Two?"

"Yes. Late shift."

"Then what?"

She tilted her head. "Then what?"

"What do you do after you get off?"

"I'm usually too tired to do much more than go home... and go to bed." She swallowed.

He forked some risotto.

The smooth crooning sound of Kem's "A Matter of Time," moved languidly through the sound system. "Do you get a break in between?"

"Usually...when things slow down."

He nodded again without taking his eyes off her. "Stop by and check on me when you do."

"I can do that."

He lifted the fork to his mouth. "Looking forward."

Justin put the food in his mouth, chewed slowly, and unthinkable images of his mouth on her body ran havoc through her head.

Bailey inhaled deeply. "Enjoy your meal." She hurried away and told Mellie that she needed to run to the ladies' room.

Once in the privacy of the employee restroom, Bailey closed her eyes. She was actually shaking inside. It was obvious that Justin was making a play for her. She knew the signs and normally she was able to fend them off with a joke or another drink or deflect it with banal conversation. All of her tactics escaped her. She felt as if she'd been sucked in quicksand and couldn't grab on to anything to pull herself free. The music floated into the restroom.

Damn, damn, damn. She turned on the faucets and splashed cold water on her face and neck, snatched up a paper towel and dabbed the water away. She stared at her reflection. *Get it together, girl.* She sucked in a breath of determination and returned to her station.

Justin tried to concentrate on his meal, but his thoughts kept drifting back to Bailey. He could have been eating cardboard because he was only going through the motions. He wasn't sure what it was about her that had him thinking things he shouldn't be thinking. She was pretty. No doubt about that. But he'd seen and been with plenty of pretty women. That wasn't it. It was something that seeped from her pores and wrapped around him like a longed-for hug. It held him, soothed him and yes, excited him. She wasn't working him like so many of the women that he ran across. She had no idea who he was, who his family was. He wanted to keep it that way. He wanted— no *needed*—to find out what she was about, and maybe that discovery would answer the question that was hovering on the edge of his consciousness. Was she *the one*?

* * *

The evening moved on. The dance floor filled and emptied. The soft lighting tucked away in hidden places in the floor and pillars offered a seductive ambiance that was not lost on the patrons. Heads and bodies leaned close. Bubbles of laughter mixed with the music. Drinks flowed. Food satisfied the hungry palates. And Justin and Bailey teased and talked.

"So how long have you been working here?"

Bailey leaned her hip against the bar. "Going on three years."

"You must like it."

She smiled. His belly stirred.

"I do. You meet a lot of interesting people."

"Rumor has it that bartenders and hairdressers are like going to a confessional." His eyes caught the light and gleamed.

Bailey tossed her head back and laughed. Justin memorized the long curve of her throat.

"So I've heard. What about you? What do you do?"

He gauged his answer. "Attorney."

Her brows rose. "Really?"

"Is that a bad thing?"

"Not at all. Actually, I'm working on getting back into law school."

He rested his forearms on the counter. "Getting back?"

She lowered her gaze. "I had to drop out for a while."

"Oh." He nodded his head. "It can be hard." He paused. "Do you know what kind of law you want to practice?"

"I know that I don't want to work for a big corporate firm. My passion is to work with those wrongly accused and that don't have the means for high-priced attorneys. I'm thinking the nonprofit sector." She watched his expression and was pleased that he didn't seem turned off by her altruistic vision.

"The business can certainly use more lawyers like you will be one day." He reached for his drink.

"I hope so. What about you? What kind of law do you practice?"

He smiled. "The kind that you don't want to be involved with, unfortunately."

"Why do you say *unfortunately*?"

"I'll put it this way. Sometimes we have to do things we don't necessarily want to in order to get where we want to go."

Bailey nodded.

"Tell me about law school Where did you go?"

"LSU."

He hummed approval deep in his throat. He sipped his drink. "Good school. Is that where you'll be in the fall?"

Bailey averted her gaze. "That's the plan."

Justin tried to reconcile her upbeat voice with her troubled expression—and couldn't. He wanted to ask her what was really going on, but he had experience with reluctant clients. It was clear that she was hesitant and could have been for any number of reasons. What he also knew was that if asked the right questions and given enough space, a client would tell you everything you wanted to know.

"Law school, even under the best circumstances, is rough, especially if you have to take a semester off." He casually glanced at her.

Bailey's lips moved as if she would respond, but she didn't. He tried again.

"My second year my best friend Carl had to drop out—family issues. In solidarity I took off a semester, too. My family had a fit. But Carl and I made a pact when we started that we would enter together and leave together."

Her expression softened. "A man of your word."

"I try to be."

She offered a tight smile. "I better get back to work. Can I get you anything else?"

"No. I'm good. Just the check."

She nodded. "Be right back." Once he had his check there would be no reason for him to stay. She could only stall for so long. What if she didn't see him again? Why was it even important if she did? She punched in the information for his bill. There was a solidness about Justin, a confidence and warmth that couldn't be manufactured. She stole a look in his direction. She wanted to get to know him, and she knew deep in her soul that he was feeling the same vibe.

"Here's your check." She placed the bill in front of him.

He took a look at the bill. If he paid with his credit card, she'd know who he was. He wasn't ready to cross that line yet. He wanted to get to know her on his terms without the distraction of the Lawson name. Bailey seemed down to earth, a regular woman with a good head on her shoulders, but they all did in the beginning. He needed to give this some time. He plucked his wallet from his inside jacket pocket and took out a fifty and a twenty.

"I'll bring your change."

"Keep it."

Her brows flicked. "Thanks."

"Sure," he said quietly.

Justin pushed back and stood. "How many nights are you here?" he asked.

She blinked. "Oh, um, most nights, except Sunday and one Saturday a month."

"In that case, I'll see you again. If that's okay."

"Sure. I'd like that."

He gave her the full benefit of his smile that caused the lights to dance in her eyes. "See you soon, Bailey."

"Take care." He walked around the tables to the front and out the door. And for whatever crazy reason, he already missed her smile.

Chapter 3

Bailey chopped a bushel of collard greens while Addison seasoned a tub of crawfish. Addison had a bachelor party that she was catering for on the weekend, and there was still fish to fry and sticky rice to make.

"So, he was cute, huh?" Addison asked.

"More than cute."

"Did you give him your number?"

"Of course not." She paused. "He didn't ask, but he did say he wanted to see me again."

"That's a start. What does he do?"

"Lawyer."

"Jackpot!"

Bailey laughed. "You would say that."

"Well, it's true, but what's more important is that you actually took an interest in somebody." She glanced at Bailey from the corner of her eye. "It's been a long time since Adam. All you do is work and take care of your selfish family. When is it going to be your time?"

"Addy, don't start."

Addison stopped with her seasoning and propped her hand on her hip. "You know it's true, B. Your sisters drain the life out of you. You have bills up the you know what and no daylight in sight. You need someone—for you. Maybe this guy is it."

"I'm not looking for some man to take care of me, Addy. I *won't* be my mother." Her features tightened.

Addison flinched. Men. Money. Mom. The three *M*s

that remained a bone of contention for Bailey, and no amount of prodding or coaxing had changed any of it. She pushed out a breath of apology. "Sorry. I don't mean to… I just know how hard things can be for you. How hard they are." She reached out and touched Bailey's arm. "I'm your girl, Bailey. I only want you to be happy. That's all."

Bailey lowered her gaze. "I know," she murmured. She slowly shook her head. "Did I tell you that Tory called?"

"How much did she want this time?"

"Twelve hundred."

"What! Bailey…"

Bailey held up her hand. "Don't say it, okay? I know."

"Tory has got to stand on her own two feet, and she never will if you keep bailing her out."

Bailey spun toward Addison. "She's my sister. I can't just…" She covered her face with her hands.

Addison came to her side and put her arm around her shoulder. "Sweetie, when it's not Tory it's Apryl with her man-crazy self. You can't continue to carry them on your shoulders. They're living their lives. When are you going to live yours? What about going back to law school? How are you going to manage that if you keep…" She blew out a breath of utter frustration.

"I made a promise to myself when my mother died. I promised that I would look after my sisters."

"And that's what you've been doing. You put your entire life on hold, dropped out of school, worked like a field hand to take care of them and pick up their broken pieces over and over. It's your time, damn it!" She slapped down the towel on the counter.

"I don't want to talk about this anymore." She focused on the sink full of greens, wishing that it would turn into dollars and make all her troubles go away. But money wasn't the answer. Her mother was proof of that. But what Addison said was true. She knew that, as well. She *did* want someone in her life, someone to take care of her for a change, make her feel wanted, needed and loved. If she was waiting on that from her family, she knew she'd be waiting a very long time.

"What's next?" Bailey asked, shaking the water off the greens and putting them in a giant pot of seasoned steaming water.

Addison looked at her friend and saw the resolute expression in the tight line of her mouth and knew that the subject of Bailey and her family drama was closed.

"The fish needs to be dredged in the seasoning."

"Got it."

They worked in silence for a while; the only sound was the boiling water and busy hands.

"I hope he comes back again," Bailey said in a near whisper. She slid a glance in Addison's direction.

Addison grinned. "She lives!"

Every night for the next two weeks Bailey went to work with the hopes of seeing Justin again. Each night ended in disappointment.

He wasn't coming back. He talked a good game and that was it. What would a high-priced lawyer want with a bartender/would-be law student? This was why she didn't get involved, didn't hope for anything more than light conversation to pass the time. If you didn't expect anything, you couldn't be fooled or disappointed. But he'd seemed genuinely interested in her. It was probably her own need that she thought she saw reflected in him. Nothing more. He was no different from Adam. She pressed her hand to her stomach. No different.

"Hey, Bailey, it's Addy."

Bailey smiled. "Like you really have to tell me who you are. How long have we known each other—third grade?" She curved her body into the contours of her armchair and draped her leg across the arm.

"Must I remind you *not* to remind me how long we've known each other? It's much too long, and we couldn't possibly be as old as that third grade friendship would make us."

Bailey snickered. "Whatever, girl." She rested the novel that she'd been reading on her lap, and actually turned it facedown as if Addison could see that she was reading the steamy scene of a romance novel. "Whats up?"

"I'm in a jam."

Bailey shifted her position. Her senses went on alert. Addison was the most together person she knew. If Addy was in a jam, what hope did she have? "A jam. What's wrong? Are you okay?"

"Yes. I'm fine. Relax. I'm in a jam because I have a mega big party to cater this weekend, and I'm short staffed. One of my bartenders has the flu, and a hostess is preggers. So I'm crossing my eyes, my fingers and toes that you're free this weekend to help out. Pretty please."

"Addy, you don't have to ask twice. As strapped as I am for cash—I'll be there. What day, time and where?"

"Saturday night. I need you at least by seven. Can you swing that with Vince?"

"I'll make it work. I'll do the early shift. Where is this shindig?"

"At the Lawson mansion. They are throwing an 85th birthday party for the family patriarch. The guest list is loaded with Louisiana's who's who, athletes, television and movie stars, the works. So I know tips are going to be off the charts."

"*The* Lawsons...the father is Senator Lawson, right?"

"Yes."

"You done made it to the big time, girl. Count me in."

Addison breathed a sigh of relief. "Thanks. I'll text you the address. Maybe if we get lucky we'll land us a rich ballplayer or something."

"Whatever," she chuckled. "See you Saturday. And don't forget to text me the info."

"Will do. Thanks again."

"Not a problem." Bailey disconnected the call, feeling a bit brighter in spirit. She could use every extra penny, so this job could not have come along at a better time. She picked up her novel and dived in with gusto. At least she could live vicariously through the love lives of the characters.

Surprisingly, Vincent had given her a bit of a hard time when she told him she would be switching shifts. They'd actually had a real back and forth until he finally conceded. It was so unlike him, at least with her. She knew he was overworked, but she carried her end and more. It had to be something else. Their little verbal sparring was days earlier and even though he'd said everything was fine, he remained distant with her, barely looking at her when he did speak, and then his conversation was minimal at best.

Well, whatever mood he was in, he would get over it, she thought as she hustled out of the Mercury Lounge to run home and change. The Lawson mansion was at the edge of the parish where the plantations once dominated the landscape. It would take her at least a half hour to get there from her house barring any Saturday night traffic.

When she finally pulled onto the street where the mansion was located, her eyes widened in awe. The sprawling lawn that had to be several acres in size was dotted with white tents that protected circular tables covered in white linen and topped with purple orchids. Red-vested valets were busy parking the cars that had already begun to arrive. Twinkling lights were strung through the overhanging trees that gave the entire space a fairy-tale feel. Soft music came from some unseen source and wafted across the warm night air.

Wow was all she could manage as a valet came to park

her car after asking if she had an invitation. She could not imagine herself being invited to a place like this. Working here, maybe, but invited… It was so out of touch with her reality.

She turned over her keys, gathered her belongings and walked up the slight incline to the main entrance. If she thought only the outside was fabulous, she was sadly mistaken. The interior of the Lawson mansion was clearly out of some designer's dream. It had the influence of the antebellum age with all of the modern twists. Stunning chandeliers spewed diamond-like light across the gleaming wood floors. The winding staircase looked as if it could lead to heaven and beyond. Long tables lined the walls on three sides, covered from end to end with silver-covered platters. There was a small raised landing set up for a band that was tuning up their instruments. Two bars were on either side of the room with an additional bar on the patio. The wide-open layout added to the feeling of spaciousness that allowed for a magnificent view of the entire ground floor. The back wall was all glass and opened onto an amazing deck and more acreage, a pool and additional outside seating.

The house was buzzing with staff, and the heady aroma of food momentarily made her dizzy when she realized that she hadn't eaten since lunchtime.

"There you are! I was getting worried." Addison grabbed Bailey by the arm. "They're keeping the guests outside for the time being. Girl, I might be in over my head."

Bailey glanced at Addison and actually saw panic in her eyes. "Why, what's wrong?"

She lowered her voice. "I've never done anything this big or this important before. Suppose something goes wrong?"

Bailey squeezed Addison's hand and looked her straight in the eye. "They're just people who want to have a good time. You are a kick-ass caterer with an amazing staff and...you got me." She grinned, and the tight line between Addison's eyes softened.

Addison released a breath. "That's what I needed to hear."

"Good. Now, where do you want me?"

Within the hour, the front doors were opened for the guests, and the party was in full swing.

Bailey mixed a martini and handed it to the quarterback for the New Orleans Saints, followed by a gin and tonic for the morning show host for the NBC affiliate. Addison was right about the guest list. In the short time since the doors opened, Bailey had spotted several familiar faces from reality television, not to mention two Oscar winners. Addison was also right about the amount of work. They could barely keep up at the bar. She shifted her duties from one side of the room to the other and also supervised the bar outside. That didn't include keeping up with refilling the flutes of champagne that the waiters carried on trays. Rich folks sure could drink.

She had yet to spot the guest of honor, but she did get a glimpse at a few of the Lawson clan that was pointed out to her by one of the other bartenders. They were certainly a good-looking family. What did it take to be this wealthy, to be on a first-name basis with people that she only read about? This was so not her world.

The steady hum of voices and trilling laughter mixed with the four-piece combo that had taken the stage. Couples bejeweled and bedecked made their way to the dance floor while others continued to mingle and network, eat and drink.

She looked up to take yet another order and stopped cold. *It was Justin.* He was heart-stopping in his tailored black tie ensemble. She couldn't breathe. He was walking right in her direction with a stunning woman glued to his arm. What was he doing here? Her heart hammered, and she accidentally splashed vodka on the counter instead of in the glass. She quickly got a damp cloth to clean up the spill just as Justin and his date approached.

"Bailey?"

She shoved the rag under the bar. Her gaze jumped from his surprised expression to the cover model face of his date that looked more annoyed than anything else.

"What can I get you?"

"I had no idea…"

"I'll have a cosmopolitan," his date said, cutting him off.

Justin shot her a sharp look. Her brows arched as if to ask *what*?

Bailey got busy making the drink. Her hands shook.

"How have you been?"

"Fine," she murmured. She finished the drink and placed it in front of his date.

"You're chummy with the help now? That's so like you, Justin." She lifted her drink to her polished, plump lips.

"Jasmine!" he snapped.

Bailey was mortified.

He was about to say something to Bailey when a richly accented Louisiana drawl voice came over the microphone.

"Can I have everyone's attention?"

By degrees the room quieted.

"I want to welcome each of you to my home to celebrate the 85th birthday of my father, Clive Lawson."

There was a rousing round of applause.

Branford Lawson gazed out at the throng, clearly comfortable addressing a crowd. "Before we continue with the festivities, I want the members of the family to come on up."

Jasmine tugged on Justin's arm. Justin threw a look at Bailey from over his shoulder and mouthed, "I'm sorry," before walking away.

"First I want to introduce the family of Clive Lawson,"

Branford announced. "My sister, Jacqueline, my uncles Paul and Jake Lawson, their offspring Craig, Miles, Alyse, Sydni, Devon and Conner and my brother David's son, Maurice."

One by one they each stepped up onto the platform, one more gorgeous than the next.

"And my brood—my eldest Rafe, my daughters Lee Ann, Desiree and Dominique and last but surely not least, my youngest son, Justin."

Bailey's mouth dropped open. *Justin was a Lawson.* Her temples began to pound.

"My father and my mother, Sylvia, God rest her soul, made all of this possible. He set the foundation for the Lawson family, and I hope that we have made and will continue to make him proud by carrying on the great tradition of the Lawson family. Happy birthday, Dad." Branford raised his glass as did all of the guests as Clive Lawson slowly made his way to the front of his family.

Clive Lawson, even at eighty-five, was a powerfully built man. He still had a head full of snow-white hair, and the hard lines etched in his deep brown face told of his years of intense work and struggle, but the sparkle in his eyes told the real story. Pride.

Branford handed the microphone to Jacqueline, who passed it to her father.

Clive took in the eager faces. "Thank ya'll for coming. I 'preciate it." He nodded his head while he formed the words. "A man's family is his legacy, and I couldn't be more proud of mine." He glanced behind him and smiled at his assembled family. "I know I can't be here forever, but when I do leave, I know that I've done all I could. All I've ever asked is that my children and their children be true to themselves and make things better for the next. Thank ya'll again. Now, let's party!"

The room erupted in cheers and applause as the family stepped away from the stage, and the guests swarmed around Clive to wish him congratulations.

Addison appeared next to Bailey. "Big family, huh?"

Bailey was still in stunned silence.

Addison nudged her with her elbow. "Hey, you okay?"

"It's him."

"Him who?"

"Justin. The Justin that I told you about."

Addison's eyes widened. "Say what? *Your* Justin is *the* Justin Lawson?"

Bailey numbly nodded her head. "Yeah, *the* Justin Lawson."

Chapter 4

For the rest of the evening Bailey performed by rote, going through the motions and keeping a painted smile on her face, but her mind was elsewhere. She periodically scanned the room for a glimpse of Justin, but at the same time she didn't want to see him. His date's comment about talking to the help still stung, and it certainly made her question his choice of companions. What was clear was that this was not her life. It was so far removed from her reality. The rooms reeked of money and power. And Justin was part of it.

It was nearing 2:00 a.m., and the crowd had finally wound down. Addison was still in nonstop motion, checking on every detail that was under her supervision. She worked with drill-sergeant efficiency in getting her staff to wrap up the festivities, clean up, pack supplies and load them onto the rented vans.

"Whew, what a night," Addison huffed as she leaned against the counter. "We did it, and thank you so much for pitching in."

"No problem," Bailey murmured as she stacked glasses in boxes.

"You okay?"

"Fine. Just tired, that's all."

Addison studied her friend's contemplative profile. "It's more than being tired. What's up? Is it about Justin Lawson and that *woman*?"

Inside she flinched. "No. Of course not. I was surprised to see him here, that's all."

"And...?"

"And nothing." She kept her gaze averted.

"Did you talk to him?"

"No. Why would I?"

"Because the few times that I did get a glimpse of him, he was looking in your direction, but his date was holding on to him like he was pumping air into her lungs."

Bailey couldn't help but snicker. "That she was. It doesn't matter. If I even thought for a minute that there was any possibility for us to see each other, that went out the window tonight."

"Why, because of that chick?"

"Mainly...and...just look at this place, the people who were here tonight. They come from a completely different place than me."

Addison pushed out a sigh. "Girl, you don't give yourself enough credit. Take off the diamonds and that designer gown, and you have the woman beat hands down."

Bailey turned to Addison with a slight smirk. "You have to say that because you love me."

"Yeah, but it doesn't make what I said any less true."

By the time Bailey pulled into her parking spot, it was almost four in the morning. She was bone tired. All she wanted to do was take a hot bath, get into her bed and sleep for two days. Thankfully, she wasn't on duty until seven that evening, and she intended to spend every minute of it off her feet.

The Mercury Lounge was already busy by the time Bailey arrived. Although there wasn't a waiting list for tables, she knew that wouldn't last long. She waved hello to her coworkers and walked through the space to her back office. She quickly reviewed the roster for the evening and verified the schedule. Satisfied that the lounge was fully staffed for the current shift and the following day, she changed clothes to her standard black blouse and slacks and headed out front. Vincent was off tonight, so she had double duty to manage the bar as well as run the restaurant. She did a quick walk-through on each of the levels, chatted briefly with the staff and floor managers and visited the kitchen to check in with the chef. Thankfully, there were no private parties going on tonight that she had to worry about. All systems go.

Addison had promised to drop in later on and hang out for a while to chat. She was looking forward to seeing her friend. They hadn't had a chance to catch up and gossip since the party. *The party.* A twinge tightened her stomach. She still had a hard time believing how it all went down with Justin. First to find out that the man she'd been fantasizing about was a member of one of the most wealthy and powerful families in the state of Louisiana. Second, he was clearly involved with someone else. She shook her head in resignation. It was a nice fantasy while it lasted. She tied the apron around her waist and went to work. Soon she was fully involved in chatting up the customers and mixing drinks. And then there he was, coming through the front door, and she wanted to go through the floor.

Justin spotted Bailey right away and strode purposefully in her direction. Her feet felt glued to the ground.

"Hey." He slid onto the bar stool.

"Hi. What can I get you?" She refused to engage in eye contact.

"Jim Beam. No ice."

She gave a brief nod and turned to the row of bottles behind her.

"Ohhh, I see Mr. Fine is back," Mellie said, sidling up to Bailey.

"Yep," she said noncommittally. She reached for the bottle and nearly dropped it because her hands were shaking so badly. She managed to fix the drink and place it in front of him.

"Here you go. Anything else, let me know." She started to turn away, and Justin grabbed her hand.

"Wait."

She glanced down at his hand covering hers. Electricity skidded up her arm. Her lips parted slightly so that she could breathe.

"I want to apologize about the other night."

"Nothing to apologize for."

"Yes, there is. Jasmine was rude, and her comment was uncalled for. I don't want you to think that's how I think or what I feel."

She blinked. Her thoughts scrambled. She swallowed. "Whatever."

"It's true."

Her heart was beating a mile a minute. If he didn't let go of her hand, she would self-combust. She pulled her hand away. "Thanks for the apology. I've got to get back to work."

"And I'll be right here until you talk to me."

She threw him a look, and he stared right back at her. On shaky legs she turned away and walked to the end of the bar.

"What's the deal with Mr. Handsome?" Mellie asked. "I saw him grab your hand. Girl, you need to stop playing so hard to get. Even Stevie Wonder could see he has a thing for you."

"Mellie, would you please stop? He does not."

"Hmm, okay. If you say so."

Bailey dared to glance down the length of the bar, and Justin raised his glass to her. She quickly looked away. Was he really going to sit there all night? And where in the hell was Addison?

Bailey's cell phone chirped in her pocket. She pulled it

out and saw Addy's name on the screen. "Girl, where are you?" she asked under her breath.

"I'm running a little late. What's wrong?"

"He's here."

"Who?"

"Him. Justin."

"Oh, damn. Well, what happened?"

"Nothing. He said he came to apologize."

"Okay, and…"

"And, I can't talk to that man, and he said he's staying until I do."

"Don't be ridiculous. Obviously, he's interested. He didn't have to come to see you."

"He also is obviously involved."

"Maybe, maybe not. You'll never find out talking to me. See you soon."

Bailey heaved a sigh and stuck the phone back into her pocket. She glanced at Justin, who was nursing his drink. She straightened her shoulders and walked back down the length of the bar and stood in front of him.

"I accept your apology."

He looked at her from beneath those incredible lashes. He set his drink down. "Good. That's a start."

"A start to what?"

"To us getting to know each other."

"What about…your friend…Jasmine?"

"It's not what you think."

"How do you know what I'm thinking?"

"You're thinking that she and I have a real thing going on. That she's my woman and therefore there is no room for an us."

Her stomach fluttered at the tone of his word *us*. "There isn't an us."

"There can be. If you give me a chance to show you."

"You still haven't answered my question about you and Jasmine."

"Ask. What do you want to know? I have nothing to hide."

Her gaze darted around then finally settled on him. "What…how serious is it between you?" She ran her tongue across her bottom lip.

Justin angled his head to the side. "She is the daughter of one of the partners at the firm where I work. Her father and mine think that the two of us would make a perfect partnership." He paused, looked beyond her defenses and seeped down into her center. "I don't." He slowly turned his glass on the bar top, studying the remnants of the amber liquid. He lifted his dark eyes. "I want to get to know you."

Her heart thudded, and her flesh heated. The sound of his voice, the look of raw hunger in his eyes, had her wanting to believe whatever those luscious lips said.

She rested her weight on her right leg. "You used to getting what you want, Mr. Lawson?"

"Most of the time. But I do go after what I want…all the time."

Her nipples tightened. She tore her gaze away. "We come from two different worlds. I'm not the kind of woman you're used to."

"How can you be so sure that you know what I'm used to…better, what I want?"

"I was at the party, remember? I saw the kind of circles you travel in."

"And you think that's all I am?"

"Aren't you?" she challenged.

"No. And I want to prove that to you."

"Why? Why me?"

He hesitated. "Because I can't stop thinking about you. Day and night. I want to know what it's like to kiss those lips of yours, to hold you, touch you, to whisper in your ear, to make love to you." He ran the tip of his finger along her knuckles.

Her skin sizzled, and her clit twitched in response.

"I've got to get back to work," she managed to eek out.

"I'll be here when you get a break."

And he was true to his word. Justin ordered dinner at the bar. And each time that she came in his direction, he made a joke, or shared something about himself, like how he painted in his spare time, that one of his favorite vacation spots was Sag Harbor in the summer, and that his older brother, Rafe, was one of his best friends. And Bailey laughed at his corny jokes and told him about her best friend, Addison, and how she helped her out from time to time. She told him that she really enjoyed her job and how much she wanted to get back to law school.

"You mentioned that the last time we talked. Law school. Maybe I could help."

She stopped short. "What do you mean *help*?" she said a bit more harsh than necessary.

He held up his hands in surrender. "Whoa. All I meant was that maybe I could make a few calls."

"No! If I get in, it will be on my own, not because some big shot pulled some strings." She spun away, fuming on the inside. How dare he? But what could she expect? Clearly he saw her as some poor waif who needed rescuing by a knight in shining armor.

"Hey, girl!"

Bailey turned around. "It's about time," she groused.

"What is wrong with you?"

"Nothing."

Addison looked around and noticed Justin at the end of the bar. "Something go wrong?"

"Yeah, plenty. Be right back. We need some clean glasses." She stormed off.

Addison eased down the bar and took a seat that became vacant next to Justin.

"Justin Lawson, right?"

"Yes." He offered her a heart-stopping smile. His eyes cinched as he stared at her. "You're the caterer."

She grinned. "Good memory, especially with all the people there that night."

He chuckled. "I try to remember faces."

She extended her hand. "Addison Matthews."

"Pleasure." He reached for his drink and took a sip. "So you're Bailey's friend."

"Best friend."

"Hmm. Best friend." He glanced in Bailey's direction, and she was trying hard not to look interested.

"She's hard to get to know."

"Not really. She's cautious, that's all."

He nodded. "Any suggestions?"

"About?"

"About how to get past all of her caution signs."

Addison rested her forearms on the counter. She faced him. "Be honest. Bailey is a wonderful woman who puts everyone and everything ahead of herself. She could use someone in her life that puts her first for a change." She offered a tight smile and slid off the stool. "Nice to meet you, Mr. Lawson."

"Justin."

Addison glanced over her shoulder. "Justin."

By the time Bailey returned with the rack of clean glasses, Addison was already in deep conversation with a guy who'd taken a seat next to her.

Bailey unloaded the glasses. Things were always so easy for Addison when it came to men. She was fearless. She didn't care what anyone thought, and she went after who and what she wanted. There were times when she wished that she could be as cavalier about relationships; just get in them for the good times and move on. But she couldn't. She wanted more than the momentary excitement. She wanted something that would last and someone that would make *her* a priority—for once. If there was one thing that Addy was right about, it was that she did need someone to take care of her for a change. Some days she simply wanted to get in her car and drive and keep on going. But she couldn't. Her family depended on her. She finished stacking the glasses on the shelf and hanging them from the overhead rack, and when she turned around, Justin was standing in front of her.

"Wanted to say good night and pay my tab."

A knot formed in her stomach. *He was leaving.* What if he didn't come back? "Sure. I'll put your bill together." She swung toward the register. Her heart thumped, and her hands shook. The register spewed out his bill. She handed it to him.

Justin barely glanced at it. He reached in his jacket pocket and took out his wallet and handed her his black American Express card.

Bailey numbly processed the payment and returned his card. "Have a good evening," she managed to say.

Justin stared at her for a moment. A slow smile moved his mouth. "Hope to see you again when I come back."

She smiled in return. "I'd like that."

Justin took a step back. "Night."

"Night."

He was coming back, and he wanted to see her. Bailey held on to that promise.

Chapter 5

For the next two weeks, Justin, true to his word, showed up at the Mercury Lounge at least three nights a week. Bailey quietly looked forward to seeing him, although she never told him as much. When he walked through the doors and took what had become his usual seat, all the lights came on in her world, and she sailed through the night.

On the evenings that Justin didn't show up, Bailey experienced an incredible emptiness, a malaise almost as if she was lifting her feet in and out of mud.

Tonight was one of those nights. Every time the door swung open, her heart leaped only to stutter in her chest when it wasn't him.

Bailey wiped down the bar top and began putting away bottles and stacking glasses for washing. Tonight made two nights in a row that Justin had not made an appearance.

He had probably gone back to his fancy life, which was fine with her. She was crazy to think that he was really interested in her beyond some casual conversation to pass the time.

Justin was in the thick of preparing a case for one of the partners where he would serve as second chair, but his thoughts kept drifting back to the night of the party and seeing Bailey. He'd wanted to see her again, but the past couple of weeks had been grueling with him clocking in twelve-hour days. But he knew that when he saw her again, he had to come right. And coming right meant dealing with the futility of his relationship with Jasmine DuBois. As if he'd talked her up, his phone rang and it was Jasmine.

"Justin Lawson."

"Hey, sweetie."

Justin put down his pen. "Hey, Jasmine. I'm really busy right now—"

"I know. That's why I'm calling. You've been working nonstop, and don't think for a moment that Daddy hasn't noticed."

Justin's jaw tightened.

"Anyway, sweetie, I made reservations for dinner tonight. You deserve it, and it will give us a chance to talk about us."

Justin ran his hand across his face. "Jazz, I told you before, we can only be friends…a serious relationship won't work for us."

"If you're worried about what Daddy is going to say, I can handle him," she said, oblivious to what was really being said to her.

If he ever doubted for a minute before that this relationship with Jasmine was a disaster in the making, all of his doubts vanished. Jasmine's selfish single-mindedness was impenetrable. All she saw and all she wanted was whatever it took to satisfy her desires. The needs and aspirations of others never entered her radar. In the beginning, he felt that her superficiality was all for show, and that once they got to know each other, she would allow him to see the real her—a woman with some substance. He was still waiting. He wouldn't wait any longer.

"What time are the reservations and where?"

Jasmine giddily gave him the information.

"I'll meet you there."

"Sure. See you at seven…" She giggled.

"I've got to go, Jazz."

"Sure, sweetie. See you tonight."

Justin arrived home and was surprised to see his eldest sister, LeeAnn, tinkering around in the kitchen.

"Lee!" He dropped his briefcase at the entrance to the kitchen. "What are you doing here?"

LeeAnn turned from peering into the fridge and beamed a smile of delight in seeing her brother. She shut the door and crossed the room. "Hi, baby bro." She reached up and kissed his cheek. He held her hand.

"Long way from your new home in DC. Preston here, too?"

"He should be soon."

Justin frowned. "Everything okay?"

"Actually, everything's great. Desi and Dominique are going to come by also."

"Desi and Dom? Okay, spill it. What's really going on?" He leaned against the island counter.

LeeAnn drew in a breath. "Well, I wanted everyone here so that we'd only have to say it once, but I guess I can tell you if you swear you won't say anything until the rest of the family gets here."

He ran his finger across his lips in a zipper motion.

But before LeeAnn could say a word they heard the front door and the near identical voices of Desiree and Dominique in animated conversation.

"Hello, good people," Dominique greeted as she entered the archway. She kissed her brother and sister.

"What's all the secrecy, sis?" Desiree asked. She placed her purse on the counter and hugged LeeAnn then Justin.

"Yeah, spill the tea, girl," Dominique said.

LeeAnn grinned. "Can we wait for my husband to get here?"

"Well, I don't know about y'all, but I'm starving," Dominique groused. She headed to the fridge and pulled the door open then plucked out an apple. "Are you at least fixing dinner, Lee, since you got us all over here?"

LeeAnn had always been the great cook of the family, and they'd all come to expect her to whip up one of her special dishes whenever she was home. Being the eldest girl, she'd all but taken over caring for her siblings after they'd lost their mother, Louisa, and they all still looked to her for all the things that a mother would do.

"I hadn't planned to, but I suppose I could put something together."

Justin checked his watch. Jasmine was expecting him in an hour. The evening was going to be tough enough. He didn't want to add being late to the mix. But, family first. Jasmine would have to understand. "I need to make a call." He excused himself and walked into the front room. He pulled out his phone and called Jasmine.

The phone barely rang before Jasmine picked up.

"Hello, Justin," she said.

"Hi. Listen, something came up here at the house. I'm going to be late getting to you."

Silence.

"Jazz?"

"Fine. What's late?"

"I don't know, but I'll call you when I'm done here."

"We have reservations," she whined.

Justin's jaw tightened. "I know that."

He heard her blow an exasperated breath into the phone. "Well, we can cancel, and you can come here."

That was the last thing he wanted to do, but he also had no intention of dragging out the inevitable. "Sure. I'll see you as soon as I can."

"I'll make it worth your while," she cooed.

"See you later." He disconnected the call, stuck his phone back into his pocket and returned to the family gathered in the kitchen.

"Everything okay?" Dominique quietly asked while she sipped on a glass of wine.

"Yeah." He reached for the bottle of wine and filled his own glass. Of his three sisters, it was Dominique that could always read him. There was a closeness between them that often rivaled the relationship between her and her twin, Desiree. Dominique was the wild one, or so most people thought. But underneath her diva exterior, she was insightful, caring and wise beyond her years. Meanwhile, it was Desi that had a passion for the dangerous world of race-car driving. When that little tidbit of information got to their father, he nearly imploded.

LeeAnn and Desiree were busy catching up and preparing dinner for the clan. Dominique slid her arm around her brother's waist and peeked up at him above the rim of her glass. "What's really going on?"

"With LeeAnn? I know what you know. Nada." He gave a half grin.

"You know that's not what I mean." She gently nudged him in the side with her elbow. "What's going on with you? I know that look."

"You mean my strong jaw and charismatic smile." He chuckled lightly and stroked his smooth chin.

"Don't play with me."

He blew out a breath. "Making some moves, that's all."

She arched a questioning brow. "That's your final answer?"

He angled his body away from LeeAnn and Desiree to face Dominique. "Working out some things with Jasmine. She needs to understand where we stand."

"How is that going to affect things at the office?"

He gave a half shrug. "We'll see."

"If it helps, I think you're making the right decision. Jasmine is a woman for someone else. She's all about Jasmine and getting ahead and latching on to name and money." She clasped his upper biceps. "You have a vision, ambition and a commitment to society. I can't see Jasmine ever being a part of that."

Justin slowly nodded. "I agree. Don't get me wrong. I care about her. Beneath all of the shine of her exterior, she's trying to find her way. But she has been so spoiled by the life her parents have provided for her that she has no empathy for anyone who she believes has less than her. That's a big problem for me. I tried to ignore it and hoped that it was just a facade, but it's at the heart of who she is." He slowly shook his head. "I know I'm not the one for her."

"It'll be fine. Was that who you were calling?"

"Yeah. We had reservations for dinner. I'd planned to talk to her at the restaurant. Unfortunately, I didn't anticipate this…" He gave a slight tilt of his head toward his sisters.

"Hmm. So what *are* you going to do?"

"Meet at her place when we're done here."

"You know I got you covered if you need a ride-along," she teased.

Justin chuckled. "Thanks, but no need. I'm good."

"Well, I'm just a cell phone call away." She winked and sauntered over to her sisters just as the doorbell rang.

LeeAnn wiped her hands on a paper towel. "That should be Preston." She walked out and went to the front door.

"I hope so. Then we can get this party started," Dominique said and refilled her glass of wine.

Moments later LeeAnn and Preston walked in arm in arm, with LeeAnn beaming at her husband like the day she married him.

"The gang's all here," Preston greeted, kissing the cheeks of his sisters-in-law and shaking Justin's hand.

"Everyone but Rafe," Desiree added.

"I'd hoped that he would be able to make it, but he has a gig in South Beach tonight at the Versace mansion," LeeAnn said.

"He does get around," Preston said with an air of admiration.

"All this small talk is nice, but will somebody please tell me what the hell is going on so we can eat?" Dominique said.

LeeAnn looked up at her husband, and he shared a "go ahead" nod.

"Well...we have news on a couple of fronts." She drew in a breath and pushed out what they were waiting to hear. "We're pregnant."

"I knew it!" Desiree screeched.

"Congratulations, y'all," Dominique added.

"Congrats, sis and you, too, Preston," Justin joked.

They all shared hugs and kisses, and when the excitement died down to murmurs of happiness for the couple, LeeAnn took Preston's hand. "There's more."

The room quieted.

"I was offered a position with the Department of State as Deputy Director of Environmental Policy Implementation," Preston said.

A chorus of congratulations filled the air.

"Thanks. It's something that I've always wanted to do, and serving in the Senate on the environmental committee paved the way." He paused. "The position is in Kenya."

"Kenya...as in Africa, Kenya?" Desiree asked, her voice rising in pitch.

"We leave in three weeks," LeeAnn added.

Dominique put down her glass. "What? You're moving to Kenya?"

"That's a big move, brah," Justin said. "You both ready for that?" He looked from one to the other.

"We are," LeeAnn said.

"Hey, you have to do what you can to make a difference, and I know you will," Justin said. He stepped to his brother-in-law and gave him a hearty hug. "Proud of you, man."

"Thanks."

"How long will you be gone?" Desiree asked, her voice cracking.

"At least a year. It could be extended. But for now, it's a year."

"What about the baby? You're going to have the baby in Kenya?" Dominique asked, her dismay finally kicking in.

LeeAnn offered a tight smile. "Looks that way."

"Dad is going to have a natural fit," Desiree said.

"That's why we wanted to tell you all first, get your support," LeeAnn said. "You know Dad. He wants things his way, and he has Preston's entire career mapped out."

"You don't really think that Dad doesn't know, do you?" Justin said. "Nothing gets past him, and he's right there in the mix in DC."

"True. I'm sure he's heard the rumors, but he hasn't approached me, and I didn't want to say anything until LeeAnn and I had thoroughly talked about it. It's what we both want."

"You have my support," Justin said.

Desiree and Dominique added their words of support, as well, albeit a bit halfhearted.

"Damn, how in the world am I going to arrange a baby shower way the hell in Kenya?" Dominique said, and whatever thread of tension that was in the air was broken.

"I say this calls for a Lawson family toast," Desiree said then made sure everyone had a glass of wine except for LeeAnn, who had iced tea.

"To LeeAnn and Preston and the safe arrival of the newest Lawson-Graham," Justin said and raised his glass.

LeeAnn turned to Preston. "Think we should tell them the rest?"

"You do the honors, babe."

"Make that *two* little Lawson-Grahams. Doctor said it's twins." LeeAnn's eyes gleamed with joy.

Squeals and deep rumbles of shock and happy congratulations rippled through the expansive kitchen.

Justin was still smiling when he pulled out of the driveway en route to Jasmine's home on the far end of the parish. It takes real courage to make a major move like that,
especially being a relative newlywed and expecting twins,
he thought. Toss Branford Lawson into the mix, and it
could be a real mess. None of that was stopping Preston
from pushing ahead in the direction that he needed to go,
and LeeAnn was right there by his side. At a time when
most women would need to be around their family and
close friends, his sister was willing to forgo all of that to
support her husband. That was love.

He was more determined than ever to pursue his own
dream, and if he could be as lucky as Preston was in finding a treasure like his sister LeeAnn, the dream would be
that much sweeter.

Twenty minutes later he pulled up in front of Jasmine's
two-story home. He parked in the driveway behind Jasmine's candy-apple-red Porsche and stepped out into the
twinkling twilight of the late-spring evening. Hopefully,
Jasmine wouldn't make this any more difficult than it had
to be. He walked up the short lane that was braced on either side by emerald-green hedges, stopped at the front
door and rang the bell.

Jasmine opened the door moments later. There was
no denying that Jasmine DuBois was a stunning woman.
Wherever she went, heads turned, with men wanting to
know her and women wishing they were her. There was
a small corner of Justin's ego that enjoyed the fact that
she was on his arm. But as the old saying goes, beauty
is only skin deep. What Jasmine exuded on the outside
ended there. In the months of their dating, it had become
more and more apparent how shallow and self-absorbed
she really was.

"Hey, sweetie." She extended her slender hand and led him inside.

"Hey."

Justin closed the door behind him and before he could barely turn, Jasmine had wrapped herself around him, enveloped him in her kiss, pressed the curves of her body against his. It was clear what she wanted.

Justin clasped her upper arms and pulled away, holding her in place. Her eyes flashed. Her chest heaved.

"What's wrong? What is it?"

"You know what's wrong, Jazz. Us."

She tugged away as if she'd been slapped. "What are you talking about?"

Justin crossed the space into the front room and turned to face her. "We want two different things, Jasmine. The life you want to lead is not my life. There's so much more than the next social event, and island hopping and new clothes and cars. There are people out there hurting."

"And that's my fault," she cried incredulously. "Simply because I've been fortunate enough to have the things I want, I should what…turn it all over to some, some bum on the street! Devote my time to those less fortunate," she said in nasty singsong. She threw her hands up in the air.

"No. That's not it, and you know it. You'd be content with me working for your father or practicing a form of law that I hate in order to keep up the front of prestige and power and privilege. That's not who I am."

Her fine-boned features hardened, and hazel eyes glinted with fury. "That's what you think," she said with a tone of superiority in her voice. "You pretend to be holier than thou, but you're just like me. We were cut from the same cloth. You think that hiding behind a veil of the do-gooder makes you better." She laughed. "It doesn't, and it never will. Your name, where you came from, is who you are and who you'll always be. A Lawson!" She tossed her head.

Justin shook his head sadly. "That's exactly why we can never be together, Jasmine. Because I *am* more than a name and the weight that comes with it. What I intend to do with the weight that comes with the Lawson name is something you'll never be able to understand."

"Fine! Get out. Go save the world." Hot tears rolled down her cheeks. "You'll regret it. I swear to God, you will."

"No, I don't think so." He turned and walked out, shutting the door softly behind him and the sound of breaking glass hitting the door.

Chapter 6

Bailey had all but given up on seeing Justin again. With each day that passed, she put him further in the back of her mind. Her stomach didn't do that twirly thing every time the door to the Mercury Lounge opened—at least not as much as it once had, and she didn't imagine that she saw him in every other handsome face that she passed in the streets of Baton Rouge. She had all but moved on when Justin walked through the door.

Whatever lie she'd been telling herself—that she'd put all thoughts and budding feelings about him behind her—fell by the wayside when his searching eyes found her, and his smile lit a fire in her soul.

He moved through the crowd, and to Bailey it felt like slow motion. Her pulse began its rapid ascent while a tingling sensation rippled through her limbs as he came closer.

"Hey."

The pounding in her chest nearly drowned out his greeting. She swallowed and glanced away, focusing on the bar top. "Hi. What can I get you?"

"You could start by looking at me."

Her throat tightened. Her lashes rose, and her gaze connected with his. Big mistake. She sank into the depths of his dark eyes and was swept away.

He reached out his long, slender finger and touched her cheek. "That's better," he crooned. "I want to see those eyes."

Her cheek flamed beneath the tip of his finger.

"How have you been?"

"Fine." She took a step back. "And you?"

"Better now."

"Your regular?" she asked, trying to regain some clarity.

"Sure." She felt his eyes on her when she walked away. Bailey returned with his shot of bourbon.

"Thanks." He lifted his glass and took a sip without taking his eyes off her. "I was hoping that we could get together on your next night off."

Her heart thumped. "Get together?"

"Yes. Away from here. Just me and you."

She glanced away. "I don't think that would be a good idea."

"Why not?"

"I don't go out with my customers."

"Cardinal rule?"

"Something like that."

"Hmm." He tossed back the rest of his drink, pulled out his wallet and passed her his credit card.

"Is that all you're having?"

"Yep." He set his glass down and stared at her.

She drew in a breath, snatched up his card and walked to the register. Her hands shook as she processed the payment. Was that it? Was he simply going to walk out? She didn't give him much of a chance. *Fine. Go.*

Bailey returned with his receipt and his card. She placed them in front of him.

"Thanks." He tucked both away and slowly stood. "You take care."

"You, too," she managed to eek out.

Justin strode away, and Bailey's heart sank to the pit of her stomach.

For the rest of her shift she worked like an automaton. She handed out drinks, took orders and managed the bar all by rote. If anyone asked her what her night was like, she wouldn't have been able to tell them. The hours dragged by, and all she wanted to do was have her night end so that she could go home and crawl into bed. Thankfully, it was a weeknight, and they closed at eleven.

"You okay?" Mellie asked as they tallied up the night's receipts.

"Yeah. I'm fine. Why?"

"You seem a little out of it, that's all."

"I'm fine. A little tired."

"You go back to school in the fall, right?"

"Doesn't look good, but I'm still hopeful."

Mellie patted her on the back. "Everything will work out."

Bailey briefly glanced at her. "That's what I keep telling myself." She gathered her things and took the receipts and the cash drawer. "I'm going to put these in the safe, then I'm heading out. Get home safely."

"You, too. See you tomorrow."

Bailey went to the back offices to put the receipts and cash drawer in the safe and was surprised to see Vincent's light on. She tapped on his door.

"Come in."

"Hey, you're here late."

"Actually, I was waiting for your shift to end."

She frowned. "Oh. Is something wrong?"

He leaned back in his seat. "Come in for a minute. Close the door."

She did as he asked and sat in the chair in front of his desk.

"I've been thinking about things."

"Yes…" she responded with caution.

"You've been here for a while now, and I know how hard you work, and I tried to make sure that you were compensated for it, by promoting you to Assistant Manager."

Where was this going? Wherever it was, she didn't like the direction.

"And...I don't usually do this...but I want more."

"Excuse me?"

"I did all of that for you because I like you, Bailey. I like you a lot, and I was hoping that you could put aside whatever reservations you may have about relationships with your boss."

She blinked rapidly. "What...are you saying?"

"I'm saying that I want to take our business relationship and make it personal."

Her stomach did a three-sixty. "Vincent... I..."

He held up his hand. "You don't have to answer me now. Think about it. That's all I ask."

Bailey stood up slowly. This was the last thing she expected or needed. Her thoughts ran at a dizzying speed. There were no good choices. She needed her job and no matter what she did or said, things would never be the same. That much she was certain of.

"I, umm, I'll see you tomorrow."

He nodded. "Good night, Bailey, and please think about it."

Bailey walked out. Stunned could hardly describe how she felt. She closed the door behind her, made the deposit into the safe and mindlessly left the lounge. Her thoughts were still twisting in her head when she stepped outside, so much so that she thought for sure that she was imagining her name being called.

She glanced over her right shoulder, and there was Justin, perched on the hood of a gleaming Jaguar convertible as calm as if he was posing for a commercial. She squeezed her eyes shut and opened them, certain that she was seeing things. But she wasn't. Justin hopped down off the car and strode casually toward her, his hands slung in his pants pockets.

He stopped directly in front of her. "I hope I didn't scare

you." He held up his hand before she could respond. "And I'm not stalking you." He grinned that grin, and she knew she'd believe whatever he said.

"Okay," she said, dragging out the word. "What *are* you doing? You left hours ago."

"You made it pretty plain back there that you didn't mix business with pleasure, and I can appreciate that. And you don't go out with your customers." He gave a slight shrug of his left shoulder. "But I figured since I'll never be coming back to the Mercury Lounge again, you'd have to come up with some other reason why I can't take you to dinner."

Her throat went dry. She looked up and into his intense gaze, and there were a dozen comeback lines in her repertoire that she routinely doled out to would-be suitors at the job, but for the life of her, she couldn't think of any and didn't want to. She shifted her purse from her right shoulder to her left.

"Any reason you can think of?"

The air fluttered in her chest. "Not really."

Justin tossed his head back and laughed. "Woman, you sure give a man a hard way to go."

Bailey grinned. "So now what?"

He took her hand. "So now, you give me your number, and I'm going to call you, and you're going to tell me what night is good for you." He took out his cell phone. "Ready when you are."

Bailey dictated her phone number, and Justin added it into his contacts. "Done." He punched in her number and her phone trilled in her purse. She took it out. "Now you have mine." He put his phone back into his pocket. "Let me walk you to your car."

"It's on the corner."

They walked quietly side-by-side, and Bailey felt as if she was in a dream. She stopped in front of her Honda. She turned to him. "Thanks." She dug in her purse for her keys.

Justin took them from her shaky fingers, opened her

door and handed the keys back to her. He leaned down and placed a kiss so featherlight on her cheek that it sent a ripple through her limbs. Her heart banged in her chest. She ran her tongue across her bottom lip.

"Good night."

"Night." She slid in behind the wheel. He shut the door and stepped back.

Bailey managed to stick the key into the ignition and start the car. She slowly pulled off while stealing glances at him in her rearview mirror until she turned the corner, and he was gone.

Chapter 7

Bailey was grinning inside all the way home. She kept replaying their exchange in front of the Mercury Lounge and was still blown away that he'd actually waited outside, that he was willing never to come back simply because he wanted to honor her personal rule of not dating her customers. If it wasn't so late, she would call Addison.

By the time she shut her apartment door and kicked off her shoes, her cell phone rang.

"Hello?"

"Wanted to make sure that you got home safely."

Bailey's stomach flipped. "Yes. I just walked in the door."

"Good." He paused. "Rest well. I'll call you during the week."

"Okay. Good night." She pressed End on her phone then held the phone to her chest like a prize and did the happy dance. The heck with it being late. Waking Addison up from a well-deserved slumber with this hot bit of news was worth it.

After talking Addison's ear off for nearly a half hour, and listening to her squeals of delight and "I told you sos," Bailey bid Addison good-night, took a long, hot bath and then sank into her bed.

For the first time in quite a while, her night was filled with the sweet dream of possibility.

* * *

It had been only a couple of days since his talk with Jasmine, and already Justin detected the shift in the atmosphere at work. The partners were cordial and professional, of course, but there was an invisible distance between him and them that wasn't present before, as if they'd put up a shield to protect themselves from the inevitable fallout. Justin was sure that the only reason he hadn't been confronted by Mr. DuBois himself was because he'd been out of the country and was scheduled to return to the office that afternoon.

However, if he could withstand the rant of his father, who told him in no uncertain terms that he'd ruined his career and any chance at a partnership, and let that roll off his broad shoulders, he would deal with whatever Mr. DuBois had to say about "breaking the heart of his baby girl."

Justin turned his focus to the intellectual rights case that he'd been working on for the past few weeks. Although it was important to the client and he knew he would give it his best, this kind of work was so far removed from his real passion of working for those who really needed legal services but couldn't afford it.

His desk phone rang.

"Lawson."

"Mr. Lawson, Mr. DuBois is in his office, and he'd like to see you."

"Thanks, Rebecca. I'll be right there."

"Oh, and he said to bring the Warren file."

His sat up a bit straighter. The Warren file was the intellectual rights case that he was working on. This request didn't bode well.

"Sure. Thanks." He hung up the phone, put on his jacket and tucked the folder under his arm.

Mr. DuBois, Senior Managing Partner, had an office on the top floor. The elevator ride seemed to last an eternity, and when Justin strode down the long corridor, with the senior partners' offices on either side, to his boss's domain, it was the equivalent of walking the gauntlet. There were quick, sidelong glances from the secretaries and awkward smiles from the attorneys. Everyone seemed to know something was amiss.

Justin tapped on Mr. DuBois's door.

"Come in."

Justin walked in.

"Shut the door, Lawson," DuBois said, while covering the mouthpiece of the phone. He returned to his call.

Justin shut the door behind him and moved to the opposite side of the room. He took in the space. Massive and ostentatious were understatements. The room reeked of old money, power and prestige from the mahogany cabinets and bookshelves, to the persian rugs and twenty-seat conference table. The view from the floor-to-ceiling windows spanned one side of the room and overlooked the entire city of Baton Rouge. One wall was lined with degrees, certificates and photos of DuBois with his famous friends and wealthy clients.

"Have a seat, Lawson."

Here we go. Justin turned from scoping out the photos and approached DuBois's oversize smoked glass and cherrywood desk. He placed the Warren file on the desk. "The file you asked for." He unfastened his one-button jacket and sat opposite DuBois.

DuBois reached for the file and pushed it aside. He leaned back and rubbed his chin. "Are you happy here, Lawson?"

"Yes, sir, I am." It was a white lie but…what the hell. He rested his hands on the arms of the chair.

"You see yourself moving up within the firm?"

"I would hope so."

DuBois murmured in his throat. "To move up in the firm, I expect that my staff—all of them—are loyal, that they are dedicated to ensuring the success of the firm, first and foremost."

Justin waited for the ax to fall. He didn't have to wait long.

"There is little chance of success when the boss—me— is distracted by the actions of his employees."

"Sir?"

DuBois steepled his fingers. "I'm turning the Warren case over to Stevenson."

He tapped down his rising temper and leaned forward. "I've worked on that case for the past two months."

"I'm sure you've done the best you can with it." The dismissive tone was apparent.

Justin's eyes tightened at the corners. "You want to tell me the *real* reason why you're taking the case? Because I know it has nothing to do with my abilities in the office or in the courtroom, and if the client had an issue, I would have known about it."

DuBois glared. "The last time I checked, my name was on the door, and as long as it stays there, I don't have to tell you anything I don't think you need to know." He lifted his chin in challenge. "Maybe there's something you want to tell me."

Justin knew exactly what DuBois was doing, and he wasn't going to fall into a pissing match with him. He wanted Justin to get angry. He wanted Justin to steer the conversation in the direction of Jasmine. Justin wasn't going for it. He stood up slowly and refastened his jacket.

"If Stevenson needs any additional information on the Warren case, he can see me." He gave a short nod of his head, turned and walked out.

The faces were a blur as Justin moved steadily down the corridor toward the elevator. His jaw was so tight that his temples began to pound. He jammed his finger repeatedly on the down button as if that would magically make the elevator appear. Finally, it did.

It was clear that things were only going to get worse from here. DuBois was notorious for his ability to annihilate his opponents in the courtroom and in his life. Justin had now become his opponent, but he had no intention of allowing DuBois to pick him apart.

Justin returned to his office and shut the door. Once word got out that DuBois had pulled a case from him, it would only be a matter of time before everyone around him would know his career had derailed. He'd seen it happen to several other attorneys. Two eventually quit, one remained and basically did the required pro-bono work that big firms handled.

Justin leaned back in his seat and looked up at the ceiling. Everything happened for a reason. He'd been riding the fence long enough. He and Carl had been mapping out their future for months. There was no time like the present to seize the moment. How could he in good conscience stand up for others if he was unwilling to do the same for himself? He turned on his computer.

The confrontation with DuBois was the last bit of incentive that he needed. In one fell swoop he'd divested himself of the weight of a toxic relationship and a job that was sucking the life out of him.

He put his fingers on the keys and drafted his letter of resignation. He couldn't remember feeling better when he printed out the letter and signed his name. He smiled with satisfaction. This called for a toast.

Bailey was stepping out of a well-deserved shower after a long run in the park when her cell phone began to dance on the nightstand. Draped in her striped oversize towel that she loved, she quickly grabbed the phone and a jolt of excitement shot through her. "Justin."

"Hey, how are you?"

"Just getting out of the shower."

"I was hoping you were off tonight."

"As a matter of fact, I am. Why?"

"There's a jazz concert in the park tonight. Thought you might like to go if you don't have plans."

Bailey spun around in a giddy circle. "Hmm. What time?" she asked, not wanting to make it too easy.

"Show starts at nine. I thought I'd stop by the gourmet deli, get some sandwiches, snacks and some wine. We can throw down a blanket and eat outside."

She grinned as if he was asking her to accompany him to the inaugural ball. "Okay. Sounds good."

"Plus, I have some celebrating to do."

"Celebrating?"

"Tell you all about it tonight. What's your address? I'll swing by and get you by seven."

She gave him the information. "I'll be ready."

"See you soon." He disconnected the call.

Bailey floated around her bedroom getting ready and replaying the conversation over in her head. She never even asked who was playing tonight. Not that it mattered. It could have been the Three Stooges for all she cared. The main thing was that she was going to spend the evening with Justin and not as his bartender but his date.

She pulled out a pair of denim capri pants and a plain white spaghetti-strapped T-shirt. Accessories were the key with a simple outfit. So she selected a thick, bronze-toned metal bracelet, matching hanging earrings and a fabric belt that tied at the waist. She gathered up her springy spiral curls into a loose knot on the top of her head, added a splash of pink lip gloss and a hint of mascara. She appraised herself in the mirror. In all total her outfit might have cost eighty dollars, but she knew she looked like a million bucks. A plain canvas tote and simple platform slides finished off the look, and she was ready.

The doorbell rang and she went to the intercom. "Yes?"

"It's Justin. Ready?"

"Yep. Be right down."

"Oh, do you have a blanket?"

"Sure."

Bailey took one last look in the mirror, grabbed her tote, cell phone, keys and a blanket from the hall closet and headed out.

When she stepped outside, she wasn't sure what to expect or how she was going to feel seeing Justin, but no matter what she may have thought or felt, nothing prepared her for the impact of the real thing.

Justin was leaning casually against the side of an ink-black Jaguar that gleamed with a life of its own. He was surveying the neighborhood, which gave her a moment to take him in. He was just long, lean and fine. All caps. That's all there was to it. From the top of the sleek waves of his hair, the yummy caramel of his skin, the broad shoulders and hard chest with abs outlined in a black fitted T-shirt, down to the length of his powerful thighs and legs hidden beneath low-riding black jeans.

He turned, sensing her and slid the dark shades from his eyes. Her heart jumped. He came toward her and met her at the bottom step.

"Hey."

"Hey yourself."

He took the blanket from her, leaned down and kissed her cheek. "Good to see you," he said, soft as a prayer. He placed his palm at the small of her back and led her to the car, opened the door and helped her inside before rounding the car and getting in next to her.

Justin put his shades back on and turned the key in the ignition. "You look great," he said then put the car in Drive and pulled out.

Bailey adjusted herself in the seat and briefly wondered if he could hear her heart banging in her chest. *Damn, he smelled good.* "So…who's playing tonight?" she managed.

Justin shrugged slightly. "A local group. The name didn't ring a bell, though."

"You keep up with the local talent?"

"Pretty much. My brother, Rafe, plays. When he's in town he usually sits in on a couple of sets. So I try to keep up." He turned to her with a grin that made her stomach flip.

"Are you musically inclined, as well?"

"If you can count singing in the shower then I'm a star, baby."

Bailey laughed. "That remains to be seen."

He stole a quick glance at her before turning the corner. "I hope so."

Chapter 8

When they arrived at Greenwood Community Park, the crowds had already begun to file in. People were unloading coolers, lawn chairs, blankets and festive attitudes. There was a party energy in the air, and the buzz was that there was a special guest that would be making a surprise appearance.

"Wonder who it could be," Bailey said and took the blanket while Justin grabbed the cooler with their food.

"Looks like we're in for a show." He put his arm possessively around her waist and led them across the lawn to a space beneath a willow tree.

Bailey spread out the blanket while Justin took out some plates, napkins and clear plastic cups. "Hope you like shrimp po' boys." He took out the sandwiches and placed one on each plate. "There's chopped barbecue also."

"Oh, no, you didn't," she said, her stomach already screaming hallelujah.

Justin grinned. "I take that to mean that the menu meets with your approval."

Bailey sat with her legs tucked, spread a napkin on her lap and took the plate with the shrimp po' boy. "Catch me if you can," she teased and took a mouthwatering bite.

"I plan to do just that," he said in a slow, seductive tone that had nothing to do with eating sandwiches.

Bailey's pulse quickened when she glanced into his eyes and registered the intensity that danced there. For a moment she didn't breathe until he looked away and took out his choice of food.

"I got beer to go with the sandwiches." He plucked a bottle of Coors from the cooler. "The wine is for later." He winked.

Inwardly, Bailey smiled. This was a whole other side of Justin. She'd grown accustomed to seeing him order his bourbon and fancy dinners, show up in his expensive suits, not to mention the glitz and glamour that surrounded him the night of his grandfather's party. Justin Lawson was steeped in money, class and power. He was a man who could have anything and anyone he wanted. Yet, here he was, hanging out at a free concert in the park, eating sandwiches off paper plates and drinking beer from a bottle. Maybe there was a possibility for them.

Justin leaned on his elbow and faced her. "It's good to see you like this."

"Like what?"

"Relaxed. Unhurried. No distractions."

She briefly glanced away. "To tell you the truth, it's good to be out."

"What do you like to do in your free time?"

Bailey gave an abbreviated chortle. "Free time. Ha. What's that? With the hours that I put in at the Mercury Lounge, when I do have a day off, I usually sleep."

"We have to change that." He opened the bottle of beer and took a long swallow. "Hmm, forgot how good an icy-cold brew could be." He looked across at her. "How about we make a deal?"

"Depends. What kind of deal?"

"On your day off we plan to spend it together."

Her stomach fluttered. "How are you going to manage that? You have your day job."

The corners of his eyes tightened ever so slightly. "Let me worry about that."

She studied the calm but determined, unflinching look

on his face, the set of his mouth, and she knew that whatever Justin Lawson wanted he'd make a way to get it. "I think I'd like that."

"I just love it when negotiations go smoothly."

Bailey laughed. "Always the litigator."

"That's about to change."

She frowned. "Why? What do you mean?"

The voice of the emcee was amplified through the mic and filled the night air. "Good evening, and welcome to Greenwood Park's Jazz series. We have a show for you tonight. So sit back and enjoy the cool sounds of In Touch." The lights on the stage shifted to spotlight the quartet, and they launched into their first number.

"Tell you about it later," Justin said. He patted the space beside him. "Come. Next to me."

Bailey shifted her position and moved closer to Justin, close enough to feel the warmth of his body waft off him. She forced herself to focus on her surroundings and not the proximity of Justin, the feel of his hard thigh against hers, the woodsy scent of him that seeped into her pores and short-circuited her senses.

Fortunately, the band was excellent and able to distract her overly stimulated senses, and it wasn't long before they were both bobbing their heads and tapping their fingers in time to the music.

Now that the sun had fully set, the air had cooled, and a sensual breeze moved among the throng. Even in the midst of all the people, there was a feeling of intimacy that the music evoked that drew everyone closer—Justin and Bailey included. He'd adjusted his position so that his back was against the tree, and he'd pulled Bailey between the tight ropes of his thighs. He draped his arm loosely around her waist and intermittently he'd lean in and whisper something in her ear about the notes that were played, or a couple that he noticed or a star in the heavens that sparkled more than the others.

Each whisper against her neck, the words uttered like secrets, shimmied through her. Every now and then he would place his hand on her thigh, or tuck a stray wisp of hair behind her ear or trail the tip of his finger along her collarbone, and it took all that she had not to moan with every contact. There was a subtle sensuality, an understated eroticism about Justin that made it impossible to pretend that he was like every other man. He wasn't. The realization unmoored her because her thoughts got all crazy and fuzzy when she was around him, and her insides twirled, and her body screamed for him. All for a man that she barely knew. She'd always prided herself on her clearheadedness, and her focus, which was how she was able to put her own needs and wants aside, hold down two jobs and take care of her siblings for years. When she was around Justin, her sense of good and evil, left and right, up and down, were all screwed.

"How's the sandwich?"

Bailey blinked into reality. She angled her head over her shoulder. "Delish." She forced herself to take a bite. Her stomach was so jumpy with him being this close that she could barely swallow. Not to mention that food was the last thing on her mind. "How about you?"

"You want to know the truth?" He gently stroked her shoulder.

She didn't dare look at him. "Always."

He leaned down so that his lips brushed against her ear. "The only thing I've been able to think about is you—how you feel between my legs, that scent of yours that's driving me crazy, the texture of your hair, the softness of your skin. What it will feel like to make love to you."

Her breath hitched. She turned her head, and the hot sincerity that shot from his gaze lit the pilot light in her belly. She didn't move, didn't breathe, as he curved toward her, and his mouth slowly covered her own. He cradled her head in the palm of his hand and took full possession of her lips. A deep groan rumbled in Justin's throat while a sensation of light-headedness overtook Bailey. If he had not been holding her, she would have lifted away on the night wind. The music, the chatter, the world eased into the background, leaving only them imprinted in this one moment.

Justin slowly leaned back. The warmth of his chocolate eyes feasted on her face. He brushed his thumb across her slightly parted lips. Her eyes fluttered.

"Better than I imagined," he murmured.

Bailey swallowed. "Was it?"

The corner of his mouth curved into a smoldering grin. "Yeah, it was. So much better that I can't wait to taste you again."

Oh, damn. "You're very sure of yourself, Mr. Lawson."

"Yeah, I am. I'm sure that I've been walking in a fog since I met you. I'm sure that whatever it is that's pulling us together is something new for me, and I want to take my time figuring out what it is. And…I'm sure that you feel the same way."

Bailey slowly dragged her tongue across her bottom lip.

The air was suddenly filled with cheers and applause as the music came to an end, saving her from a response. The emcee took the mic. "Let's hear it for In Touch!" The applause rose again then slowly settled. "We promised everyone a special guest tonight, so please put your hands together for Tony award-winner Audra McDonald with her incomparable rendition of Billie Holiday."

The crowd went crazy.

"What!" Bailey squealed, and her eyes widened in stunned disbelief.

Justin tossed his head back and laughed, wrapped his arms around her waist, kissed her cheek, pulled her back against his chest and let the music and the voice do the rest.

"I still cannot believe we saw Audra McDonald," Bailey said, shaking her head while she fastened her seat belt.

"Pretty impressive for a first date, huh?"

Bailey cracked up. "I have to give it to you. I'm impressed, even if you had *no clue whatsoever* that she would be there."

"Ha! Minor detail."

"That's your defense, counselor?" She giggled and leaned back against the headrest.

Justin gave her a quick glance. His voice dipped and stroked her right where she needed it. "I'm far from resting my case." Justin winked, and her clit jumped. He turned his attention back to the road.

Bailey pressed her knees together and concentrated on breathing.

"Guess we have two things to celebrate."

"Two things?"

"A fabulous night *and* my personal celebration."

"Which you have yet to tell me about." She folded her arms.

"And we still have the bottle of unopened wine." He threw her a quick look.

"You're right. And where do you plan to open this *alleged* bottle of wine, counselor?"

Justin chuckled. "Alleged. Very funny." They stopped for a light. Justin angled his body in the seat to face her. "Well…there *are* some options. I can take you home, and you can invite me up, and I can tell you all about it, and then you can send me on my way. Or, I can take you to my place, I can tell you all about it, and I can fix you breakfast in the morning."

Heat scorched her cheeks.

Justin grinned and drove across the intersection. "Your choice. But the deal will be off the table when I hit the next exit. Right, my place. Left, yours."

"Are you serious?"

"Very."

The car seemed to slow.

"Exit coming up… Right or left?"

Her stomach flipped. "Right," she managed.

"Not a problem." He signaled, moved into the right lane and took the exit.

Chapter 9

Bailey's heart clapped in her chest. There was no doubt about Justin's intentions, and she'd just agreed to them. She linked her fingers together and stared out the passenger window. It's what she wanted—*needed* was a better word. She drew in a long, deep breath and stole a glance at Justin's profile. *Yes, needed.*

"You okay?"

Bailey's insides jerked. She turned. "Yes. Why?"

"You're sitting so close to the door, I'm thinking you might jump out."

The quip broke the knot of tension in her stomach, and Bailey laughed in relief. "Really?"

Justin chuckled. "Yeah, really." He made the turn onto the street that led to his house. The Lawson mansion loomed in front of them.

She had not been back to the house since the party. Without all of the people and food and decorations and music, it was much like any other home—only bigger. There was certainly a feeling of grandeur about the house, but there was still a sense of intimacy, from the simple but elegant decor to the array of family photos that told a story of not a dynasty but a real family.

Justin took Bailey's hand. "Make yourself comfortable." He led her into the living space. "I'll get the wine."

Bailey put her jacket and purse down on the club chair

while Justin took the bottle of wine and walked over to the minibar.

He popped the cork and poured two glasses. "Want to hear some music?"

"Sure."

"You pick."

Bailey strolled over to the stereo system that looked so complicated, a degree from NASA was needed to operate it. She skimmed through the revolving rack of CDs and selected some of her favorites—Kem, Luther Vandross and Kurt Whalum. "Here're my picks." She held them up in her hand. "But I have no idea how to work this thing."

Justin grinned. "Help is on the way." He crossed the room with the wineglasses and gave one to Bailey, tapped his glass against hers then leaned down and lightly kissed her lips. "Hmm, sweet." He turned his attention to the system, pressed a few buttons and the CD tables opened. He slid them in.

Bailey's insides vibrated every time he touched her. She couldn't even imagine what making love to him would feel like. Inadvertently she moaned.

Justin tipped his head toward her in question.

"The wine...it's really good." At least she was still thinking quick on her feet.

"Glad you like it."

Luther Vandross's sultry crooning wafted around them.

Justin took Bailey's glass from her hand and placed it on the side table. "Dance with me."

Bailey sputtered a nervous laugh. "Dance with you?"

"Yes." He stepped to her, slid one arm around her waist and eased her close. "Like this," he murmured against her hair.

Bailey's pulse roared in her ears. Her eyes drifted closed when she rested her head against his chest, and she silently prayed that he didn't feel her body trembling.

"This feels good." He held her closer while they swayed to the music.

Bailey lifted her head and dared to glance up. Justin was gazing right down at her, and the heat that flamed in his eyes started a campfire in her core. The world receded into the background as he lowered his head. She held her breath. Light as cotton his lips touched hers, and she melted into his body to deepen the kiss. The sweet tip of his tongue grazed her bottom lip, sending jolts of sizzling desire through her veins. Her soft moan of assent was all the invitation that he needed before fully capturing her mouth.

Justin's long fingers cupped the back of her head and threaded through the riot of tight spirals, then slowly trailed along the column of her neck while his tongue danced with hers. He pulled her tight against him, bending her back ever so slightly so that she could feel his growing need for her.

Bailey's sigh of desire was instantaneous, and she lifted her pelvis to meet the hard throb of his arousal. A groan seeped from his lips and into her mouth, erupting in her center.

The song ended, another one began, and they didn't miss a beat, finding their own rhythm that glided between the notes. Justin unsealed their kiss and braced Bailey's face in his hands. "I want you," he said, his voice thick with aching need. "I want to make love to you." His thumb stroked her cheek.

Her breath caught in her chest. It's what she'd longed for, this moment, this time. She'd seen them together, felt them together in her mind almost from the moment they met. *That* was pure fantasy. *This* was the real thing.

"Say yes."

She ran her tongue across her bottom lip, tasted him there. "Yes."

Without another word, Justin took her hand and led

her across the room, up the winding staircase and along the hallway to the suite of rooms at the end. He lowered the handle on the door and pushed it open. He turned in the threshold and looked at Bailey, searching for any sign of doubts, second thoughts. He backed into the expansive room. She followed and shut the door behind her.

Bailey quickly took in the room. Justin's essence filled it; from the decidedly sleek masculine furniture in deep chocolate woods and leather to the scent of him that teased her senses. French doors opened to a small terrace, and one wall held a mounted flat-screen television of undetermined size. The little things that personalized the space and made it feel lived in dotted the room: a pair of shoes by the side chair, a discarded jacket tossed across its back, a stack of magazines on an end table and his robe casually tossed across the foot of the king-size bed.

Justin came to her and placed his hands on her shoulders. "Change your mind?" he gently asked.

She shook her head, unsure of her voice.

He leaned down and kissed her so tenderly that it made her knees weak. His hands moved from her shoulders down her arms then snaked around her body. The kiss intensified, and their bodies connected.

Justin grasped the hem of her top and lifted it up and over her head. He clenched his jaw when he gazed upon the swell of her breasts. He placed a heated kiss on one side and then the other while he reached behind her and unfastened her bra. He slid the straps over her shoulders and plucked the delicate fabric away to fully reveal the tempting treasures that awaited him. He cupped the weight of her breasts in his palms and grazed the swollen nipples with his thumbs, bringing them to a tight head. Bailey's breath caught. Her chest rose.

He emitted a ragged groan as her fingers unfastened his belt and slid down his zipper.

Justin made quick work of relieving her of her pants and

panties before lifting her high in his arms to dip his face into the concave of her belly. She whimpered as the muscles of her stomach rippled beneath the erotic strokes of Justin's wet tongue. He walked with her in his arms across the carpeted floor to his bed and gently laid her down.

Bailey's heart pounded. Justin stood above her. The hard outline of his sleek body was outlined by the moonlight that slid through the open French doors. Her gaze was drawn from the broad expanse of his shoulders down to the rippling abs that led to the trail that gathered dark and thick around the heavy, long cock that lifted toward her. The dewy head glistened in the moonlight.

She had to touch him. Needed to touch him. Purposefully, she reached out. Her fingertips brushed the smooth skin. His hard member jumped in response. She wrapped her fingers around him and ran her thumb along the thick vein that throbbed on the underside of his sex. Power filled her when she heard his deep groan and felt the weight of his member pulse in her palm. She stroked him, slow and steady, letting only the tips of her fingers graze him. Each stroke stiffened him further. She could just make out the subtle tremors of his inner thighs. She ran her thumb across the dampened head, and he gripped her wrist.

"No more," he rasped. The dark embers of his eyes moved painstakingly slow across her face. Her fingers released him, and he kneeled on the side of the bed. "Turn over," he demanded.

Bailey's eyes widened. Her lips parted.

"Turn over."

She couldn't resist the command and did what he asked. Hot blood pumped through her veins. And then he was above her, his legs straddling her supine form. The tip of his erection brushed the curve of her spine. She gasped. Her body stiffened.

His tongue flicked that soft spot at the nape of her neck.

He clasped her arms that were at her sides and gently raised them toward her head and held them there.

Justin leaned forward and placed a kiss behind her left ear then her right. Her body shuddered. His tongue played with the tender skin, drifted along her collarbone and then slowly down the center of her spine. The nerves beneath her skin jumped and fluttered in response every time the wet heat of his tongue teased her. He blew his hot breath against her damp flesh, and the sensation was electric. Her soft whimpers aroused him as he continued down along her back to the dip then across the firm globes of her rear to the backs of her thighs. He teased her behind each knee and tenderly nibbled the strong calves. She shuddered and pressed her face into the downy fluff of the pillow.

"Don't hide. I want to hear you want me," he said. He spread her thighs and slid his arm beneath her, lifting her to press against the throb of his cock. Bailey flinched. He reached around her and stroked her slick split with his fingers.

"Ahhh…"

He teased the hard knot of her stiffened clit, and her entire body quaked. The sounds of her whimpers intensified and charged through his veins. He groaned, rose up and turned her onto her back.

Dark hunger sparked in his eyes. "Only if you want me," he said in a ragged whisper. "Tell me."

"Yes," she managed. She spread her legs and drew her knees upward.

Justin's jaw tightened as he held back the explosion that threatened to undo him. He rested back on his haunches, reached over to the nightstand and pulled out a condom packet. He tore it open and gave it to her.

Bailey's fingers shook as she slowly unrolled it over the length of him. He held his position above her and continued to finger her until her head thrashed against the pillow, and her hips rose and fell.

Justin braced his weight on his forearms and lowered his head to taste her mouth. The mixture of wine on her lips and tongue and her own sweet essence fueled him. His tongue danced with hers, savoring the flavor. She thrust her hips against him. He pulled back.

"Not yet." He captured one dark, full nipple between his lips and teased it with his teeth until she cried out in sweet agony then cupped her round rear in his palms and kneaded it until she trembled.

She was simpering with need, and that only intensified his want of her. He pressed the head of his sex against her slick opening. She gasped and gripped his shoulders. He pushed just a little to open her to him, and she cried out as her body gave way, and he pushed long and deep inside her wet walls.

Justin hissed through his teeth as the hot, wet warmth of her enveloped him.

The length and heft of him filled her in ways that she'd never before experienced. The fullness stole her breath and made her heart tumble in her chest. Shock waves jolted through her limbs as he began to move slowly in and out of her. By degrees her body adjusted to the feel of him, and she began to meet him stroke for stroke, lifting and rotating her hips, drawing groans that rose from his belly and tumbled from his lips. His body grew damp, as did hers as the pace escalated, and the sound of flesh slapping against flesh mixed with their moans and cries.

Justin rose up on his knees and pulled her hips tight against him as he plowed into her. Bailey gripped the sheets in her fists and bit down on her bottom lip, but it didn't stop her scream that vibrated through him.

The tremor started at the balls of Bailey's feet and scooted up her legs. Justin's buttocks tightened, and his sac filled and tightened. Bailey thrust her pelvis against him, and he blew like a volcano while her insides flexed and contracted in an orgasm that exploded in hundreds of white-hot lights.

"Oh, Goddddd…" Her neck arched. Her body vibrated as if hit with a bolt of lightning.

Justin's growl of release bordered on animalistic before he collapsed on top of her, breathing hard. He pushed her damp hair away from the sides of her face before cupping her cheeks and tenderly kissing her wet, swollen lips.

Bailey caressed his damp back, felt the hard tendons flex beneath her fingers. She had no words for the riot of feelings that poured through her. Thoughts and images of the two of them ran in a kaleidoscope through her head. Whatever she thought making love with Justin would be like, she was wrong. The empty space that lived inside her no longer echoed. The sound was dull and distant, receding into the background. She felt alive, vibrant, happy. Maybe it was only the effects of sexual release and afterglow. Whatever it was, she wanted to hold on to it for as long as she could.

She nuzzled Justin's neck, and she felt his smile. He lifted his head and gazed down at her.

"You okay?"

She nodded. "You?"

He chortled deep in his throat. "I passed *okay* a long time ago." He brushed his lips against hers, tasted the salty skin and sighed into her mouth. "Humph. Woman…you could easily become my guilty pleasure." He eased up off her and turned on his side. He braced his head on the palm of his hand. His eyes were at half-mast, only lifted by the satisfied smile on his lips.

Bailey ran her fingers down the length of his arm. Her eyes didn't leave his. "You never told me what you were celebrating." She took his hand, lifted it to her lips then drew the tip of his index finger into her mouth.

His breath hitched, and she sucked a bit harder. The dark pupils of his eyes grew larger.

"Tell me."

"What? That you're making me hard again sucking on my finger?"

"Oh, that." She tickled the tip of his index finger with her tongue. "What I asked you was to tell me what your surprise was," she said between little sucks.

He slowly extracted his finger from her mouth, turned onto his back and tucked his hands under his head.

"Well, I handed in my resignation today."

Her head snapped toward him. "What?"

"Yep." He glanced at her.

"But…why?"

He drew in a deep breath and exhaled. "It's been a long time coming. Today only sped up the process." He told her of the showdown with his boss as a result of his firmly telling Jasmine they had no future and how he'd come to his decision. "Things would only get worse at the firm if I'd stayed, and this way at least I can walk away with my head up and can move on to pushing my dream forward. Which is what I've wanted to do all along."

Bailey was a breath away from asking him if he could afford to leave his job when the reality of who he was kicked that thought to the curb. He was a Lawson. He could do what he wanted. Money was no object. The realization unsettled her. The fact that he could walk away from his job and pursue his dream was a stark reminder of just how different they were; how far apart their lives would remain.

"Something wrong?" Justin traced the outline of her ear.

She shook her head and forced a smile. "Nothing." She turned to face him and slid her leg between his. "It was wonderful," she whispered, easing close.

"It was more than wonderful." His eyes moved slowly over her face while he caressed the rise of her hip. "I want you to get used to having me in your life and many more amazing days and nights like this one."

Her heart thumped. She swallowed.

He leaned in and kissed her. His mouth moved over hers firm and insistent, sucking and teasing her bottom lip until her lips flowered, and his tongue dipped inside to savor her taste. And whatever notions she had in her head about their differences were pushed into the back of her mind as she welcomed him deep within her.

Chapter 10

Justin's eyes flickered open against the morning light that sifted through the draped windows. His body flexed and ached in a good way as memories of his night with Bailey rushed back. He turned his head. She was curled on her side, her wild hair shielding her face from him. Just looking at her got him hard. He stroked his shaft wanting to put it where it could find release—buried inside her.

Bailey stirred and sighed softly. She stretched her legs and arched her back. Justin was about to lose his mind watching her. He stroked a little faster. Bailey turned on her back and stretched her arms above her head, causing her full breasts to rise. The sheet slid down revealing her heavy mounds and the dark, hard nipples, and Justin's cock jumped in his hand. This was better than any strip show. Bailey moaned while she slid her hand down her body and between her legs. Justin nearly lost it. Sweat dampened his skin. He gritted his teeth as he watched the totally erotic show, imagining her fingers in all the slick places that his had been.

Bailey's lips parted. Her breathing escalated. "Ohhhh," she moaned. Her eyes fluttered open, and she turned to him. Her skin was flushed. "Justin," she said in a hoarse whisper. She reached for him, grabbed his hand and put it where hers had been. Her hips arched, and her eyes slammed shut.

Justin fingered her then put his slick fingers in his mouth to taste her. He pulled her on top of him. He cupped her breasts in his palms while she rose up on her knees and positioned herself before lowering her hips to suck him inside her.

"Good morning," she whispered before covering his mouth with hers and riding them both to satisfaction.

"Hope you like omelets," Justin said from his spot at the stove. He glanced over his shoulder and nearly dropped the spatula when he glanced at her barely covered in a towel and her hair dangling in wet tendrils around her face. "Hey."

"Hey yourself." She sauntered closer and stopped at the counter that separated them. Her gaze took in the broad bare back that curved into a perfect V, and the drawstring pajama pants that hung low on his narrow hips. She tugged on her bottom lip with her teeth.

"Coffee or juice?" He turned away to keep from doing something other than fixing breakfast.

"Coffee would be great."

"Help yourself." He ladled the omelet onto a platter and placed it on the center of the counter along with a bowl of fresh-cut fruit.

Bailey took the coffeepot off the heated inset on the table and poured coffee into a mug. "You want some?" She held up the pot.

The corner of his mouth rose. "That, young lady is a loaded question, especially with you standing in my kitchen with nothing on but a towel."

Bailey innocently glanced down at her scanty attire as if seeing it for the first time. "Oh...I can go change."

"Don't. I like the view."

Her cheeks heated. She lowered her gaze and slid onto a bar stool. "Now that you're unemployed, what are your plans?"

Justin sat opposite her and scooped fruit onto his plate and then a portion of the omelet. "Actually, I'll be going into the office for the next few weeks to clear up some pending cases and bring everyone up to speed on what I have on my desk."

Bailey nodded her head as she chewed on a forkful of omelet. "Mmm, is this feta cheese?"

"Yep. You like?"

"Very much. So...tell me more about your business venture."

His eyes lit up.

"It's been something I've been working on for about a year now. Along with my buddy Carl Hurley. He was with me the first night I came to the Mercury Lounge." He looked at her over the rim of his coffee mug. "I guess I need to thank him."

"For what?"

"He was the one that insisted I stay after he had to leave for a meeting. If I didn't, we may have never...gotten this far."

Bailey blushed. She took a mouthful of food.

"Anyway, it's called The Justice Project. Our goal is to handle cases for defendants that can't afford high-priced attorneys and those who we believe have been wrongly convicted."

"Really?"

He nodded. "That's the plan. We had scouted some locations for a small office. And there are more cases than we will probably be able to handle." He gave a slight shrug. "So this unscheduled departure is a blessing in disguise."

"Well...how do you go about selecting which cases to accept?"

"It's a process. Carl and I will review the case material, interview the defendant, any witnesses, and if we feel we can do some justice, we'll take the case." He angled his head in question. "Something's on your mind."

"No. I was just curious."

"I'm sure we'll need a staff," he said with a raise of his

eyebrow. "You already have some law school under your belt, and you plan to finish up, right?"

She focused on her plate and pushed her food around with her fork. "That's the plan."

"You don't sound very sure. I thought that's what you wanted."

"It is."

Justin studied her closed expression and decided to let it go. "So when do you go back to work?"

"Tonight. I should probably get myself together and go home."

"Now?"

"Yeah, I have a lot to do. Aren't you planning on going into the office?"

He heaved a sigh. "Around noon."

She nodded her head. "Looks like both of us need to get in gear." She pushed back from the table and stood.

Justin reached across the table and clasped her wrist. "What is it?"

"I don't know what you mean." She avoided looking at him.

"I feel like you did a one-eighty on me, and I'm not sure why."

"I don't know why you would think that."

He released her. "My bad." He took his plate to the sink. "Give me a few minutes to get dressed, and I'll drive you home."

"Thanks," she murmured and walked out of the kitchen.

Bailey put on her discarded clothing then stood in front of the bathroom mirror to try to put some order into her hair. She'd spent the most incredible night with a man she'd had a wet spot for since the night they'd met. Her body still hummed with pleasure. She smiled at the memories. There was no doubt that there was more than a physical connection between them. They vibed on so many levels. But… Her smile slowly faded. She didn't want to risk disturbing the magic, the one time in her life when there was someone for her—just her—by inserting the drama of her family life into the mix.

A sensation of guilt crept into her conscience. She couldn't turn her back on her siblings. She was the glue that held them together. The reality of her situation angered her. She shouldn't feel guilty for wanting her own life. But she did.

Roughly, she twisted her damp hair on top of her head and tucked it into an untidy knot. She turned away from her all-seeing reflection and returned to the bedroom to get her purse and shoes. Justin was pulling a shirt over his head. Her stomach twirled at the sight of him, the way his muscles rippled when he stretched and moved. She shook her head to scatter the hot thoughts that tried to dominate her good sense—which was telling her to go home.

Justin tugged down on his T-shirt, and Bailey came into his line of sight. "Ready?"

She leaned against the frame of the door. "Pretty much."

He nodded noncommittally, turned to his dresser and grabbed his wallet, keys and cell phone.

"Justin…"

He turned toward her with his brows raised in question. "Yeah… I… You were right."

"About what?"

"I did do a one-eighty."

"Wanna tell me why?"

She drew in a breath. "I want to…just not right now."

"My mama raised me to be a gentleman. I'd never make a lady do anything she didn't want to do." He gave her that half grin that sent shock waves up her spine. He strolled slowly toward her, tucked a finger under her chin and lifted it. "There's no rush…about anything. I don't plan on going anywhere."

Her heart knocked in her chest and for some reason,

her eyes filled with hot tears. She blinked rapidly, swallowed the knot in her throat and nodded her head. "Thank you," she whispered.

He pulled her into the protective arc of his arms and held her close. He didn't say a word. He simply held her, and to Bailey that was the most intimate thing he could have done.

Justin helped Bailey into her seat and shut the door, got in behind the wheel and flipped on the radio. The Tom Joyner morning show was on and host Cousin Tommy made a prank phone call that had them both laughing out loud. The prank call to a local pizza parlor was followed by the news that spewed out one bad story after the other, including the forecast that predicted a major storm complete with dangerous lightning and flash flooding.

They drove in companionable silence, bobbing their heads to the music and laughing at the outrageous members of the morning show. Before long, they were coming up on Bailey's street.

After they pulled onto her street and Justin got out to open Bailey's door, two police cars raced right down the block with their dome lights spinning. He held open the passenger door and helped Bailey out of her seat just as the nerve-jangling sound of police sirens wailed in the gray-tinged morning. Justin shut Bailey's door. His gaze followed the cars to the corner where they turned and then silenced, indicating that they'd reached their destination. He slowly rounded the car and fully took in the neighborhood. Several of the buildings on the opposite side of the street were boarded up while others were in disrepair. A small group of men of undetermined age sat on the steps of a corner house drinking out of brown paper bags. Justin walked Bailey to her front door. He didn't comment, but for the first time, Bailey saw her world through his eyes.

"Are you sure you have to work tonight? Weather report doesn't sound good."

"No choice. As long as Vincent opens the lounge... I'm on duty."

"I wish you didn't have to go in. These spring storms are notorious for always being worse than the forecast." He didn't want to tell her that what he was most concerned about was her coming home at night in this neighborhood. But it wasn't for him to say...at least not now.

"Thanks, but I'll be fine."

"Well, I'll try to stop by later this evening."

She forced a brave smile. "Okay. Look forward to it."

He leaned down and gently kissed her on the mouth. "You want me to come up?" he said against her lips.

"And neither one of us will get anything accomplished today." She pressed her finger to his lips.

"That would be the point, wouldn't it?" He gently nibbled the tip of her finger.

"Bye, Justin."

"Agggh, you wound me," he teased, pressing his hand to his chest and stumbling backward.

"Right." She shook her head and chuckled as she went up the three steps to her front door. "Talk to you later."

"Count on it." He waited for her to get through the front door before getting back into his car. He took one more look around before taking off.

Bailey opened the door to her apartment, and the sensation of being suffocated overwhelmed her. She shut the door, and at that moment saw just how small her place was. She'd grown used to the kitchen table that wobbled, the sink that dripped if you didn't turn the faucet just right and the sound of sirens that peppered the night. She tossed her purse on the used couch.

She'd prided herself on her "unique finds" as Addison put it, and made a habit of haunting the local flea markets and used-furniture stores. She felt her one-bedroom apartment had an eclectic character. Now it seemed shabby. She plopped down on the sofa and looked around. This is what Justin would see. And she didn't want that. This was why she didn't want to get involved with someone like Justin. It was the road that her mother had taken, and it had ultimately taken her.

Oh, how easy it would be to slip into a lifestyle that she knew Justin could offer. All of her worries would be over. She drew in a long, slow breath. She wasn't her mother.

Her cell phone buzzed inside her purse. She dug around and pulled it out. Her sister Apryl's number lit the face of the screen.

"Hi, sis," Bailey greeted. At least Apryl rarely needed money. But if men were dollar bills, her baby sister would be a wealthy woman. "What has you calling so early?"

"I *do* have a job that requires me to be at my desk by nine," she playfully tossed back. Apryl, at the tender age of twenty, worked for an up-and-coming urban men's fashion magazine as a copy editor. A job that suited her perfectly. Apryl had always done well in school, and the chance to meet gorgeous men on a regular basis was right up her alley.

Bailey chuckled. "Okay, so what's up?"

"Well…" she lowered her voice. "There is this *f-i-n-e* brother who has been doing a shoot here all week, and well…we kind of hit it off. I was wondering if you could hook me up a nice table at Mercury."

Bailey's brows pinched together. "Why are you taking him out?"

"B…get with the program. Hello…women take men out all the time."

"They do?"

Apryl sighed into the phone. "Can you do it or not?"

"I guess so. When?"

"Tonight."

"You heard about the storm, right?"

"Oh, yeah," she said, dragging out the last word. "Are you working tonight?"

"Yes."

"Okay, well, if it looks too dicey we can make it another night."

"Fine, sis. Let me know when you know."

"Will do."

"Great," she said, cheerfully. "Anyway, gotta run. Hugs."

"Hugs." Bailey dropped her phone back into her purse and pushed up from the couch. She had some errands to run, and nothing would get done sitting on the couch.

She went into her bedroom and looked at her queen-size bed that resembled a doll bed compared to Justin's. It would never work. They were from two different worlds. But for once she was going to be selfish and do this for her...at least for a little while.

Chapter 11

Justin arrived at the office a bit before noon. The moment he pushed through the glass doors to the reception area, he could feel the change in the air. Dina, the front desk receptionist, was almost apologetic in her greeting and wouldn't look him in the eye. The associates that he passed in the hallway murmured veiled greetings. He stopped at his assistant's desk to check for messages.

"Mr. Dubois was looking for you. He wanted to see you when you got in."

"Thanks. Tell him I'll be there in a few minutes."

She picked up the phone while Justin walked into his office and shut the door.

He was sure that Dubois would have been more than happy to accept his resignation, considering the conversation they'd had. So he couldn't imagine what else they had to talk about. He made a couple of calls then took the elevator ride to Dubois's office.

"He's waiting for you," Dubois's secretary said. "Go right in."

"Thanks." He adjusted the knot in his silk tie and strode toward the closed door. He knocked lightly and went in.

"You wanted to see me."

"Lawson. Have a seat." He pursed his lips and leaned back in his chair.

Justin took a seat opposite Dubois's desk.

Dubois reached for the letter on the desk. Justin knew what it was. He waved the letter in front of him then tossed it on the pristine desk. "This is the route you decided to take." It was more of a challenge than a question.

"The right one. It's clear that we've come to a cross-roads. I'll clear up my cases, bring my replacement up-to-date and be out of here by the end of the month." He stared him in the eye until Dubois looked away.

Dubois stood, a tactic that Justin knew was only to create a sense of control. "Don't be a fool. You have a future here."

"Do I?"

His eyes tightened at the corners. "My employees don't walk out on me. *I* let them go."

Justin didn't respond.

Dubois blew out a breath filled with frustration. He looked hard at Justin, who didn't flinch as most would have done. "Whatever issues you may have with my daughter shouldn't interfere with your job here."

He'd finally put it out on the table. Justin crossed his right ankle over his left knee. "It never did."

Dubois's jaw tensed.

This wasn't a matter of Dubois wanting him to stay. He simply was not used to anyone defying him. Justin knew this, and that's why he had the upper hand. If he'd decided to stay, he could probably negotiate for whatever he wanted. However, it was too late for that. He'd made up his mind. Dubois would have to find a way to deal with his wounded ego.

Dubois slid his hands into his pockets. "As I said, Lawson, I think you are making a big mistake. Most would have been begging to stay. Not you." He snorted. "But...I respect you for it." He lifted his chin.

Justin's brows rose in surprise. "Thank you, sir." He knew that wasn't easy for Dubois to say.

"Keep me posted on the progress of your cases."

Justin stood. "I will."

Dubois turned away, ending the meeting.

"Thank you for the opportunity."

Dubois murmured a grudging acknowledgment deep in his throat. Justin smiled to himself and walked out.

When he returned to his office, Carl was waiting for him.

"You could have given me a heads-up, man."

Justin held up his hand. "I know. It wasn't planned."

Carl plopped down in a chair. Justin closed the door.

"So…what happened?"

Justin ran down to Carl what had transpired between him and Dubois and what prompted him to file his resignation, up to and including the last conversation.

Carl lowered his head and shook it slowly. "Wow. So now what?"

"So now I can move ahead with the plan—full-time."

Carl massaged his right knee. "I'll do what I can from here. I can't say I'm ready to follow in your footsteps."

"I don't expect you to. You have a wife to think about. I'll work on getting us set up. You jump in when you can."

"Cool."

"Knee acting up again?"

"Yeah. Played a short game of pickup last night." He chuckled. "Not as young as I used to be."

Carl could have made it to the NBA, but he was injured in his sophomore year of college, and his knee had never been the same.

"Where were you last night? I called you. Wanted to see if you wanted to play."

Justin grinned. "I was with Bailey."

Carl's eyes widened. "Get out. So…what happened?"

"I don't kiss and tell. But I will say it was…great."

"Ha! My man."

"I really dig her, man."

"I hear a *but* in there."

Justin leveled his gaze with Carl's. He knew him all too

well. "I took her home this morning and—" he hesitated "—she lives over on Chestnut."

"Hmm. Rough area."

"I know. I don't like the idea of her having to come in and out at all kinds of crazy hours from her job."

"Not much you can do about it unless you're going to morph into her sugar daddy and set her up somewhere."

The idea ran pleasantly through his head. "I wouldn't mind waking up to Bailey every morning."

"Say what?" Carl croaked. "She got you whipped like that already?"

Justin grumbled in his throat. "I like her. A lot. End of story."

"Told you, man. The right woman can change your whole mind."

"Don't you have work to do?"

Carl gingerly pushed up from his seat. "Don't hate the messenger." He chuckled. "Talk to you later."

"Yeah. Later."

Justin sat down behind his desk and thought about his comment to Carl. He'd never considered living with a woman or taking care of one. Bailey was different. She wasn't like the women he'd known. She clearly didn't have everything handed to her. She worked hard for whatever she wanted. She was smart, sexy as all hell and easy to be with. When he made love to her…it was like coming alive. Yeah, he liked her. A lot.

Chapter 12

Vincent came behind the bar. "You going to be okay getting home?"

"I'll be fine." Bailey wiped down the bar top and continued stacking glasses in the rack for washing.

"I can drive you home. You'd be a lot safer in my truck than your car in this weather."

Her honey-toned eyes flicked toward him. Their once, easygoing friendship had grown tense since he'd made his overture several weeks earlier. She'd made it a point to keep her distance and steer clear of having to respond to his "offer." This was the first time they'd actually been in the same space long enough to have a conversation. She moved farther away.

"We haven't had a chance to talk in a while." He lined up the bottles on the shelf, something he never did. "I wanted to give you some time and distance...to think about what I said."

Her heart pounded. "Vincent." She turned to face him and folded her arms. "We have a good working relationship, and I truly appreciate everything that you've done for me." She paused. "I'm seeing someone and even if I wasn't, I don't think that taking a business relationship and making it personal is wise, or something that I would do. I hope you understand that."

His gray eyes grew stormy, darkening like the skies. "I see."

"I don't want this to affect anything."

He placed another bottle on the shelf. "Get home safely." He turned and walked away.

Bailey let out a breath she'd held and realized that she was trembling inside. The look in his eyes actually chilled her. She made quick work of closing out the register and took the night's receipts to the safe. There was no way she was going to try to make it to the bank. She'd take care of it in the morning.

On her way out, she checked her phone. Apryl was supposed to have stopped by. She was sure the weather was a deterrent, but she was surprised that she hadn't heard from her sister. Knowing Apryl, she was more than likely curled up with her new man somewhere. Something she wished she was doing instead of navigating the flooded streets of downtown Baton Rouge.

The windshield wipers were working overtime, but she managed to see enough to pull over so that she could make the call to Justin. She put on her hazard lights, just in case, and pulled her cell phone from her purse. Just as she was ready to call, the phone rang in her hand. She didn't recognize the number. She pressed the talk icon.

"Hello?"

"Is this Bailey Sinclair?"

"Yes. Who is this?"

"I'm calling from the admitting office at St. Barnabas Hospital. Your sister Apryl was in a car accident. She asked that you be called."

"Oh, my God. Is she all right?"

"She's listed as stable. Do you think you can make it to the hospital?"

Bailey peered into the night, looked around to try to get her bearings. "Yes, yes. Um, I'll be there as soon as I can."

She tucked the phone into her purse, gripped the steering wheel and lowered her head. She whispered a prayer.

The drive to the hospital was nerve-racking to say the least. So many of the streets were flooded that she had to detour around them, and lights were off in some areas making it nearly impossible to see in front of her. Shaken, she finally arrived at the emergency entrance of the hospital, found a parking spot and raced inside.

"My sister Apryl Sinclair was brought in. She was in a car accident," she blurted out the instant she reached the intake desk.

The clerk behind the counter checked her computer screen. "Do you have ID?"

Bailey rolled her eyes in annoyance and fished in her purse for her ID, practically shoving it in the woman's face.

The woman looked it over and handed it back. "Sorry, but we have to be careful," she said, mildly soothing Bailey's ire. "Your sister was admitted, but they haven't taken her to her room yet. She's still in the emergency area. Walk straight through those swinging doors. You'll see a reception desk. Someone there can tell you where she is."

"Thank you."

"Good luck." She smiled.

For an instant Bailey felt bad about the awful things she was thinking about doing to the woman. "Thanks."

She hurried down the corridor and through the swinging doors. The nurses' station was on her right. "Hi. My sister Apryl Sinclair was brought in earlier. Car accident." Her heart was racing so fast she could barely catch her breath.

The nurse checked her register. "Yes. She's in the fourth cubicle down on your left. The doctor is with her now, I believe."

"Thank you." She raced off. Curtain number one, two, three, four. She stopped, steeled herself, and said a silent prayer for strength, not knowing what to expect when she pulled the curtain back. She didn't have to. A young, ready-for-television-looking doctor pulled the curtain back and stepped out, nearly colliding with Bailey.

"Sorry," he said, grinning, showing deep dimples in his smooth chocolate face. "I'm Dr. Phillips. Relative?"

"Yes, Doctor. I'm her sister." She tried to peek over his height and broad shoulders to get a glimpse at the body beneath the white sheet. "How is she?"

"Very lucky. She has a concussion, bruised ribs and a badly sprained wrist. The car didn't fair as well, I understand."

Bailey pressed her hand to her mouth and sighed in relief. "Can I see her?"

"Sure, but only for a few minutes. They need to get her to a room."

"How long is she going to have to stay?"

"At least overnight. The main thing is the concussion. We want to monitor her for the next ten to twelve hours. If everything looks good tomorrow, say midday, she can go home. She'll experience headaches for a while, and she'll need some help until her ribs and wrist heal, but other than that, she should be fine." He flashed those dimples again.

Perfect for Addy. "Thank you, Dr. Phillips."

"She may seem a little out of it. But it's to be expected. I don't want you to be alarmed."

Bailey nodded. She tugged in a breath and stepped behind the curtain. Her heart jumped at seeing her sister appear so helpless. Her eyes were closed, and there was an IV in her arm. Her left hand was in a soft cast. Bailey slowly approached. She stroked her sister's fingers.

Apryl's eyes fluttered open. "Sis," she croaked.

"Hey," she said softly. "How are you feeling?"

Apryl groaned. "Like I was in a car accident," she said, trying to make light of her situation.

There was a bruise on her cheek, and her eyes looked

slightly swollen. Her lip was cut, but other than that, she looked like herself. That was a relief.

"The doctor said that you'll probably go home tomorrow. You're going to stay with me until you're feeling better. No argument."

She tried to smile but winced instead.

"What happened?" Bailey pulled up a chair and sat next to the bed.

"It was so freaking dark, and the rain was crazy," she said in a halting voice. "The next thing I knew I'd hit a divider."

"Where in the world were you going in this weather?"

"I was going to see John, the guy I was telling you about. Never made it."

Bailey slowly shook her head. "The main thing is you're okay." She lightly squeezed her hand.

"You mean you're not going to fuss me out?"

"Not this time." She offered a soft smile. "I'm just happy that it wasn't worse."

A nurse pulled the curtain back. "We're ready to take you to your room, Ms. Sinclair." An orderly followed the nurse into the tight space.

Bailey squeezed by and stepped out while they unlocked the wheels on the bed and connected the IV to a hook on the bed.

"What room will she be in?" Bailey asked as they began to wheel Apryl out.

"Third floor. Room C14."

"Thank you."

"You won't be able to come up, but you can come back in the morning." She offered an apologetic smile.

"Okay." Bailey walked with them to the elevator and held Apryl's hand the entire way. "I'll see you in the morning." She tenderly brushed her forehead then placed a kiss there. "Get some rest."

The elevator doors opened, and they pushed the bed inside. Bailey finger-waved at her sister as the doors closed. For several moments she stood there staring at the door and replaying the events of the evening. Suddenly, a wave of exhaustion overtook her, and she felt like her body was going to give out. She squeezed her eyes shut for a moment and took deep breaths. She opened her eyes and looked around at the rush of nurses and doctors, the anxious faces of family members, heard the clang of metal, orders being barked out and the cries and moans of the sick and injured. She had to get some air.

When she stepped outside, the wind seemed to have died down, but the rain continued. All she wanted to do was go home and crawl into bed. She dashed for her car and stepped into a puddle that reached her ankles. Perfect. By the time she got to her car she was soaked through and through. Her shoes were soggy, and her clothes were sticking to her.

"Just get me home," she said and turned on the ignition.

The drive home was riddled with obstacles from stalled cars to flooded streets. Finally, there was daylight at the end of this seemingly endless tunnel. She was two blocks away from home, and then her car shut off in the middle of the street.

"Oh, hell, no. Not tonight." She turned the car off then back on. All she heard was a click. She tried again. And again. *Click. Click.* She pounded the steering wheel in fury.

Clearly she couldn't stay there. She gathered her belongings, checked the glove compartment and took out all of her important papers and stuck them in her purse. She checked around the interior of the car for anything of importance then got out. She locked the door and prayed that it would be there in the morning.

The streets were beyond dark. There were no streetlights and only intermittent light coming from scattered windows. By the time she reached her front door, she was beyond soaked and felt like a leaking pipe with water dripping off her from everywhere. She left a watery trail up the darkened staircase.

She opened her apartment door, whispered a silent prayer and flicked on the light switch. Nothing. She felt her way into the kitchen and found two old candles in the overhead cabinet. She was sure she had a flashlight somewhere but didn't have the energy to look for it. She lit a candle and lighted her way to the bathroom, where she peeled out of her clothes and left them in a wet heap on the floor. She didn't have the energy for the shower that she desperately needed, but instead dried off with a towel, took her nightshirt off the hook on the back of the bathroom door and put it on. She padded back into the kitchen and poured herself a glass of water before plopping down on the couch. She blew out the candle, and the room was sufficed in darkness. Better to hide the tears of exhaustion and frustration.

The sound of sirens and the oppressive heat woke Bailey the following morning. She blinked against the blazing light coming in through the window and slowly sat up. Every muscle in her body ached from having fallen asleep on the couch. She rotated her neck and then pushed up from the couch. Her knees ached. The clock on the microwave was flashing. At least the electricity was back on. She walked to the window and looked outside. The neighborhood was slowly coming to life, and then the events of the night before stiffened her spine. Her sister!

She hurried over to her purse and pulled out her cell phone. She plugged it in and while it charged she took her much-needed and long-overdue shower. When she'd finished, she felt human again. She checked her phone and there were three messages from Justin. Her stomach fluttered. She went into her voice mail and listened to his calls. He sounded genuinely worried and asked her to please call him no matter what time. His last call was at 3:00 a.m. She tugged on her bottom lip with her teeth, literally biting back a smile. He was thinking about her. He was worried about her. She would call him back and let him know she was fine.

But, first things first. She needed to call the hospital and get the update on her sister, which she did. The on-duty nurse told her that the doctors had not made their rounds and would make a determination then about her discharge. Rounds would be completed about 11:30 a.m. She could call back after that time. Bailey thanked the nurse and hung up. According to the clock on her phone it was just after eight. She had some time to get her place in order for her sister and fix some coffee to get rid of the remaining cobwebs.

With a mug of coffee in hand, she checked her phone that was now fully charged. She sat down at the kitchen table and called Justin. He picked up on the first ring as if he'd been watching the phone, waiting for her call.

"Bailey! I was worried sick. Are you all right?"

"A little worse for wear but I'm okay. Sorry I missed your calls. My phone was dead. We didn't have any power…and my car… Oh, damn."

"What? What happened to your car? Were you in an accident?"

"Not me, my sister Apryl." She ran down the events of the evening up to her car dying on the street.

"I'm getting dressed right now. You stay put."

"I can take care of it."

"I know you can. That's not the point. Wait there."

"Justin, you don't have to come. I can handle it."

"Goodbye, Bailey. I'll be there soon."

"Justin!"

"Goodbye, Bailey." The line went dead.

She sucked her teeth in an attempt at being annoyed, but she was bubbling inside. As much as she may protest, she didn't want to deal with the day ahead alone. Now she didn't have to.

Chapter 13

"Girl, you had some kind of night," Addison said. "Is your car still there?"

"I sure hope so." She sighed.

"At least Justin is coming. He'll take care of everything. And worst case, he can take you to pick up Apryl from the hospital."

"You know that depending on men rubs against me like sandpaper. Dependency leads to nothing but trouble and heartache."

"Don't even start with that mess. Independence is fine. Shouting *I am woman, hear me roar* from the rooftops is fine, but there comes a time when there's nothing wrong with asking for and accepting help from a man. It's not going to diminish your womanhood. Did it occur to you that he's doing this because he cares?"

"Too late to stop him now," she groused. "But let me tell you about this gorgeous doctor that is taking care of Apryl. Perfect for you."

"You are always so concerned about and fixing everybody else's life."

"Don't go there again, Addy. Not today." She had to fix and worry about everyone else. It was the only way she could keep the past at bay, but it was always lurking in the shadows, following her wherever she went. What scared her in a place deep in her soul was that she was mirroring the life of her mother—as much as she tried to fight it.

Phyllis Sinclair was forty-seven when she took her own

life. Saddled with three kids and no man. That was what drove her mother to do the things that she did and to ultimately take her life. Her mother had been gone for five years, and she missed her every single day. The only way she could avoid the path that her mother had taken was never to need or depend on a man. She would maintain her independence at any cost.

"I have to go, Addy."

"Okay, one last thing."

"I couldn't stop you if I wanted to."

"Fine." She paused a beat. "Let him help you, B…this one thing. Accept it gracefully. If for no other reason than because it will feel good, girl." She laughed.

Bailey pushed out a breath. "Okay, you've badgered me into submission."

"That's what besties are for. Hugs."

"Hugs back." Bailey put down the phone, looked around her apartment and made a mad dash to put everything in order. Justin had never been to her apartment. Suddenly, the sheer white curtains that let in all the sunshine on Crescent Street looked cheap and flimsy. The crack above the sink seemed to be grinning at her. The bedroom was not much better. Her bed, that was always her oasis, appeared bland and insignificant. She closed her bedroom door just as the bell rang. She'd meet him downstairs. There was no reason for him to come up.

Bailey opened the downstairs front door, and that indescribable sensation sizzled through her at the sight of him. The only reason to be as damned fine as Justin Lawson was to torment all the women who couldn't have him.

"Hey," she said, playing it casual as she trotted down the three steps.

"Hey yourself." He looped his arm around her waist and pulled her close. Her chin brushed against the baby-soft fabric of his gray fitted sweater. The tempting V at the neck dared her to touch him. He took her mouth and her breath away as if they were his to own.

"I needed that," he murmured against her mouth.

Bailey was on fire. Her body of its own will yielded to him, longing for him to command it to do whatever he wanted.

"Do you smell this good all over?" He breathed into her ear before easing back.

His eyes were endlessly dark as they descended upon her, making her heart race and her pulse roar in her ears to block out the world around them. It was only the two of them until the blare of several car horns intent on out-blasting each other snapped the spell in half.

"Woman, you could make me forget what I need to do." He grinned that sly, sexy grin, and the dampness between her legs intensified.

"So, where's the car?"

Bailey blinked. "Um, two blocks over." She pointed in the direction.

"Did you call a tow service yet?"

"No. My phone was dead last night...and this morning...I want to make sure it's still there." She didn't know what she was going to do if it needed to be towed.

"It will be, and if it's not, I'll take care of it." He took her hand.

His long, slim fingers enveloped her hand. She wanted to tug away, remind him that *she* would take care of it. Somehow. She drew in a breath, and even Addison's warning words didn't stop her from verbalizing the fear that lurked in her heart. "You really didn't have to do this." She felt his entire body tighten.

Justin stopped walking. "What exactly shouldn't I have done—come to see if I can offer some assistance to a woman that has taken up residence in my head, be here if she wants to talk or just be a decent kind of guy who doesn't want to see a hardworking, beautiful, fiercely independent, sexy-as-hell woman stranded? Any of those strike a chord?"

Bailey twisted her lips to keep from grinning. "Fine. The defense rests."

"Hey." He lowered his head and lifted her chin with the tip of his finger. He looked deep into her eyes. "Never think or imagine in a million years that you'll ever have to be on the defensive with me. Okay?"

She nodded her head. "Okay."

He took her hand again, and they continued on for the block and a half and there was her car, right where she left it.

Bailey pressed her hand to her chest and exhaled in relief. "Thank goodness it's still here."

Justin squeezed her hand and kissed the top of her head. They hurried over to the car, and a quick inspection turned up no apparent damage, not even a parking ticket.

"So far, so good," Bailey said before unlocking the driver-side door. She got in behind the wheel and turned the key in the ignition. Nothing happened.

"I'll call a tow service," Justin offered as he slid into the car next to her. He pulled out his phone, scrolled through his contacts, found the number and placed the call. Shortly after, he was giving his info and then asked Bailey for her plate number. "They said about a half hour."

"Thank you." She released a breath of relief.

"What time do you need to be at work?"

Bailey groaned and pressed her hand to her forehead. "Late shift. Seven to twelve. I'm going to need to get a rental."

"You can use my car."

She snapped her head toward him. "Your car?" Her brows knitted.

"I can drive...my other car."

Her cheeks heated. Of course he would have more than one car. "I couldn't ask you to do that. I can get a rental."

Justin lowered his chin. "Let me ask you something. Why is it so hard for you to accept any help...at least from me?"

The slight hitch in his voice caught Bailey by surprise. She tightened her grip on the steering wheel. "It's not you," she whispered.

"Okay. That's a good start. Then what is it? Seriously."

"It's complicated."

"I'm listening."

She couldn't look at him. "It's... I've seen firsthand what depending on someone can do to you."

Justin rocked his jaw. "Seen? Who? What did you see that was so damned foul that it keeps you second-guessing and keeping at arm's length anyone that wants to get near you?"

Bailey's features flinched. Her throat worked as the words clung there, stuck against her tongue and struggled to get past her pinched lips.

"My mother," she finally blurted.

Justin kept his surprise behind a neutral expression. "Must have been rough."

Bailey reached for the handle and opened the door. "It was." She needed air. "And I really don't want to talk about it." She stepped out of the car.

Through the car window, Justin watched Bailey pace. He didn't know what she meant by "her mother" but whatever happened, it had dug a deep hole in her soul that had been refilled with doubt, suspicion and fear. He'd leave it alone for now, but he had every intention of digging all of that crap out and filling her up with what she really needed.

He took out his cell phone and spent the waiting time answering a couple of emails and checking into the office to let his assistant know that he would be there by early afternoon. He spotted the tow truck coming down the street, got out of the car and went around to stand next to Bailey. He draped his arm around her shoulder and felt her relax against him.

The driver checked the car, hooked it up to his truck and gave Justin instructions to the garage where it would be taken.

Bailey thanked him as she watched her precious baby being towed away.

"So what do you want to do, get a rental or drive my car?"

Bailey slid her gaze across Justin's polished two-seat Mercedes Benz. "Um, maybe I should get a rental. I wouldn't forgive myself if something happened to your car."

Justin chuckled. "It's only a car, Bailey. But if you feel more comfortable, do the rental. The family has an account with a private car rental agency. I'm sure I can get you something you'd feel more comfortable with."

The gleam of sunlight bounced off the hood of the car. "Well…maybe the Benz won't be so bad."

Justin tossed his head back and laughed. "That's what I'm talking about! Come on, get behind the wheel and get comfortable. We'll go pick up your sister, and I'll take a car service from there."

Bailey got behind the wheel and sighed as the lush leather seats cushioned her like a lover. The brand-new, off-the-showroom-floor scent still lingered. The dashboard was a series of blue lights and glass and panels. Daunting. She turned the key in the ignition, and the engine purred to life. She gave Justin a quick look, and he simply adjusted his seat back and closed his eyes. She drew in a breath and pulled off.

At the first stoplight, Bailey scanned the dash to figure out what button to press to turn on the radio. She finally found the icon, and the local jazz station joined them for the ride. Containing a satisfied smile, Bailey maneuvered the dream machine in and out of the growing traffic, or rather the Benz did the driving. The ride was so smooth and the vehicle handled so well, it was akin to gliding on a cloud. It would be so easy to get used to this.

She stole a quick glance at Justin, who was completely in relax mode, eyes closed, head back, fingers lightly tapping the armrest in time to the music. Not a care in the world. The life of money and privilege.

Not too long after, the hospital loomed ahead. Bailey drove into the visitors' parking lot. Justin opened his eyes and sat up.

"Hmm. Safe and sound." He yawned. "Ready?"

It was on the tip of her tongue to tell him that he didn't have to come with her, but this time she refrained from what, to her, was instinctual. "Sure." She swallowed. "Thanks."

"I was supposed to call and find out what time they were releasing her," Bailey was saying as they pushed through the revolving glass doors. "I totally forgot."

Justin checked his watch. "If the hospital is true to form, she won't be released before noon."

They stopped at the information desk and received passes to enter the ward.

"Why is that?" She pressed the button for the elevator.

"After twelve they can charge for another day." He gave an offhand shrug. "Capitalism."

The elevator doors opened. Justin and Bailey stepped aside to let the passengers off, one of whom was Dr. Phillips.

"Bailey." He smiled warmly.

"Dr. Phillips. I was coming to pick up my sister. How is she?"

The elevator doors closed.

"She had a restful night. The tests look good, so I've already put in the discharge order along with instructions for aftercare."

"Thank you." She extended her hand, which he shook.

"Thank you so much. Dr. Phillips, this is Justin Lawson." She turned her attention to Justin.

The two men shook hands. "Lawson...Senator Lawson's son?"

"That would be me," he said without humor.

"Pleasure to meet you. Tell your father he has my vote in the next election."

Justin only returned a shadow of a smile.

"Well, make sure your sister gets plenty of rest. No driving while she's on the medication. It's pretty strong. She should come back in two weeks for a follow-up, but of course if there are any problems, she should come in right away."

"Thank you."

"Mr. Lawson. Ms. Sinclair." He gave a short nod of his head and walked away and out the door.

"On a first-name basis," Justin said with a hint of sarcasm in his voice.

The elevator doors opened. They stepped aboard.

"What?"

"He called you Bailey."

She blinked in confusion, then it hit her. "I met him for the first time last night. He calmed me down when I got here and explained everything that was going on with my sister." She took his hand and looked into his eyes. "That's about it."

"Look, it's not a problem. I was wondering. That's all."

She linked her fingers through his. Her insides smiled. He was jealous.

The doors opened on the third floor, and they walked to the nurses' station to get Apryl's room number.

"I'll wait here. I don't want to walk in on your sister," Justin said. "She doesn't know me."

Bailey reached up and lightly kissed his lips. "Thanks." She hurried off down the corridor.

When she arrived at Apryl's room, she was up and dressed and sitting in a chair by the window.

"Sis." She smiled then winced.

"Hey." Bailey crossed the room. "How are you feeling?"

"Tired. Head hurts, and this cast and sling are annoying, but I'm here."

"I ran into Dr. Phillips, and you're all set to go home."

A nurse entered the room. "I have your discharge papers, Ms. Sinclair, and your prescriptions." She handed the papers to Apryl then turned to Bailey. "You'll be taking her home?"

"Yes."

"I'll get a wheelchair."

"I don't need one."

The nurse smiled. "Sorry. Hospital policy. I'll be right back."

Bailey sat on the edge of the bed. "I, uh, brought someone with me."

"Who? Addison?"

"No. A friend. His name is Justin."

"Oh, a man friend." She grinned. "Good for you, sis. It's about time."

Bailey made a face. "Anyway, we'll be taking his car to my place."

"His car? What happened to yours?"

She blew out a breath. "The short version...I had to get it towed. Finally conked out on me last night after I left here."

"Oh, damn. You need your ride."

"Yeah, I know."

"Sure can't use mine," she said and grimaced at the memory.

The nurse returned with the wheelchair and helped Apryl to sit. "You have all of your belongings?"

"Yes, thank you."

The nurse pushed Apryl out of the room and down the

corridor with Bailey right alongside. Justin rose from his seat as they approached.

"That's him?" Apryl whispered in awe.

"That's him."

"Yummy."

Justin joined the trio en route to the elevator.

"Justin, this is my sister Apryl."

The resemblance was remarkable. Apryl was a carbon copy of her older sister. Where Bailey kept her hair long, wiry and wild, Apryl's natural curls were cut close to her head. Bailey's more serious, worldly eyes were offset by Apryl's mischievous ones.

"Lucky lady," Justin said and hit her with his mega-watt smile.

"I don't always look like this," she joked. "Nice to meet you, though, and thanks for looking after my sister."

"It's been my pleasure to look after Bailey," he said on a deep note that stroked Bailey's insides with innuendo. He winked at Bailey, and her cheeks flushed.

They rode down in silence, and the nurse wheeled her out to the front. Justin went to get the car and when he pulled up in front of them, Apryl let out an expletive of shock and pleasure.

"Apryl," Bailey said in admonishment.

"What?" she innocently retorted.

The nurse helped her up while Justin grabbed his garment bag, jumped out and held open the passenger door. He helped her with her seat belt then walked around the other side to Bailey.

He stepped up close. "I'll call you later." He draped the garment bag over his shoulder and leaned down and kissed her slow and deep, letting his tongue play for a moment with hers. When he broke the kiss, Bailey felt light-headed. She blinked and slid her tongue across her bottom lip to savor the taste of him.

"Okay," she managed. "How are you going to get to the office?"

"I called a car service while I was waiting. It should be here in about ten minutes."

"Thank you…for everything."

"Whatever you need." He cupped her chin in his palm. "Whatever." He pecked her on the lips, turned and bent down to wave goodbye to Apryl then headed back inside, out of the heat, to wait for the car.

Bailey watched him until he blended in with the visitors and hospital staff then got in the car.

"Girl, you done hit a grand slam!"

"It's not like that, Apryl." She put the car in gear and eased away from the curb.

"If it's not, it should be."

Bailey turned on the music.

"So, spill. Where did you meet Mr. Fine?"

"At work."

"And?"

"And nothing. We're just friends."

"A friend with benefits." She laughed lightly.

Bailey shook her head. She wasn't going to feed into her sister's penchant for scintillating details. Apryl had no qualms about divulging her most intimate details about her various male friends, and believed that her sisters should reciprocate. Bailey didn't agree.

"Fine, don't tell," she said with a pout.

"I didn't intend to." A smile mirrored on her recently kissed lips.

"Does he have any brothers?"

"I haven't met his brother."

"How long have you known him? What does he do for a living to be able to afford this ride?"

"He's an attorney."

"Niiiice. Right up your alley. And speaking of right

up your alley, when do you start school? You are going back, aren't you?"

Bailey heaved a sigh. "I don't know." With so much going on in her life recently, she hadn't had a moment to focus on the upcoming fall semester. She still had no positive response for the grants and scholarships she'd applied for, and time was running out.

Then Apryl being Apryl zipped off topic to prattle on about the guy she'd met. Bailey half listened. She only wished she could be as carefree as her sister. But if she was, there was no telling where any of her siblings would be.

Chapter 14

By the time Justin arrived at his office building it was nearly one.

"You're pretty casual today, Mr. Lawson," his assistant teased.

"Hectic morning. Any messages?"

"A few." She handed him the slips of paper. "Mr. Hurley stopped by to see you. He asked that you give him a call when you get in."

"Thanks." He started for his office.

"Mr. Lawson…"

He stopped and turned. "Yes?"

"You have a three o'clock with Mr. Turner on his infringement case. Do you want to reschedule?"

"No. Thanks. Pull the files. We can meet in the small conference room."

"I already have it blocked for you from three to four."

"Hopefully it won't take that long," he said.

"I allowed for Mr. Turner's long-windedness." She smiled.

Justin went into his office and locked the door. He got out of his sweater and jeans and changed into his dark blue Italian-made business suit, winter-white shirt and pinstriped navy tie. He took his black wingtips from the bag and slid them on his feet. Reviewing his messages he decided that they all could wait until he'd spoken with Mr. Turner.

The afternoon sped by and true to form his client, Mr. Turner, took up the entire hour—all of which was billable.

Justin loosened his tie and put in a call to Carl, who told him that he'd gotten a call from the Realtor, and he had a place for them to look at that evening. Justin told him they'd have to ride together as Bailey had his car. Carl couldn't hide his shock knowing how much Justin loved that car. He'd never let anyone drive it—ever—not his siblings and not even him—his best friend.

"She got you whopped, my brother," Carl taunted.

"Call it whatever you want to call it. Just meet me out front at five-thirty."

Carl chuckled. "See you then."

Justin disconnected the call, sat back and gazed upward. Bailey Sinclair had certainly done something to him. Whatever it was, he liked it.

The space was located in Downtown Baton Rouge, about a mile away from their current office. It was a suite on the tenth floor, with space for reception and enough cubicle space for at least four employees with an additional two small offices.

"What do you think?" the Realtor asked once they'd completed the tour.

Justin exchanged a look with Carl. "It has everything that we're looking for. How long would the lease be?"

"We can do a one year or a two."

"How soon do you need an answer?" Carl asked.

"As soon as possible. Space in downtown is premium and rare, especially at this price."

Justin slung his hands into his pockets. "We'll get back to you first thing in the morning."

"Fair enough." He led them out and locked up.

"It's your call, man," Carl said as they pulled away from the building.

"I think it will suit our purposes as a start-up. We don't

need more space than this. I would have preferred a stand alone, but I think this will work."

"I'm down if you are."

Justin grinned. "Then I guess we go for it."

"I'll give him a call in the morning. I'm sure there'll be papers to sign."

"This is it, bro." Justin glanced at Carl.

"Yep, this is it."

"So let's hear it. What happened with Bailey?" Carl asked as he drove Justin home.

Justin brought him up-to-date on what had transpired up to him meeting Bailey's sister.

"Humph. You really dig this woman, don't you?"

Justin's smooth brows drew close. "Yeah, I really do."

"All I have to say on the subject is don't let the thrill of something new screw with your head. 'Cause let's be real. Bailey is not the type of woman you usually deal with. Your ready for all that?"

"Ready for what?"

"For bringing her into a world that…maybe she's not used to. You know the circles your family travels in."

"I can't believe you're saying this shit, man." His jaw tightened as he glared at Carl.

Carl held up one hand and kept the other on the wheel. "I'm being real. I'm not throwing shade on her. She is the exact opposite of every woman you've ever been with. That's the truth. So are you with her because she's different and you think you can 'rescue her' or is it real? I'm just asking. I wouldn't be a friend if I didn't bring it up."

Justin fumed, but there was some truth to what Carl said. Bailey was the polar opposite of every woman who'd slept in his bed. It *was* refreshing, and he *did* want to help her, do things for her. But he knew how she made him feel—truly alive in a relationship for the first time in his life. And he wanted more of it. He wanted more of her.

"I'll keep that all in mind," he grumbled. He and Carl

were always honest with each other, even if it pissed the other one off. He didn't have to admit that to Carl. It was an unspoken understanding.

They pulled up on Justin's street.

"You coming in for a minute?"

"Naw. I need to get home. Wife is waiting." He winked. "Talk to you tomorrow. You plan to call the Realtor or you want me to take care of it?"

"I'll give him a call when I get into the office. I have an 8:00 a.m. meeting, so I'll call when I'm done."

"Good. Then we can get the lease signed and get this show on the road."

They gave each other a fist bump and Justin got out. "Later."

Carl pulled off, and Justin headed inside, feeling truly inspired, and he wanted to share it with Bailey.

It was good having her sister with her. Apryl was truly entertaining with her tales of escapades with her line of suitors. She kept Bailey in stitches while she fixed them dinner. She checked the pot of jerk chicken that was simmering on the stove.

"Girl, you are a hot mess," Bailey said.

"You only live once, sis. I want to enjoy life and the men that come along with it. If I'm lucky, the right man will find me in the process."

Bailey caught the wistfulness in her voice. She looked at her. Apryl was staring off into the distance. Of all the children, Apryl had taken their mother's loss the hardest. She was the youngest and she'd needed a mother even more than her sisters, and with their father out of the picture and the string of men that their mother had brought home, Apryl grew up looking for love. She was still looking.

"A good man would be lucky to have you, Apryl. And probably when you stop looking…he'll find you." She gave her a warm smile.

"Like Justin found you?" She gave her sister a knowing look.

Bailey felt flush all over at the mention of his name. She turned away from the stove, wiped her hands on a towel then sat down at the shaky kitchen table. She blew out a breath. "He's...special. The way he makes me feel. But..."

"But what, sis?" Apryl reached her good hand across the table and covered her sister's clenched fist.

Bailey raised her gaze to her sister's questioning look. "It's so hard to explain. We come from two different worlds. Justin Lawson comes from one of the wealthiest families in Louisiana."

"And that's a bad thing, how?"

"You don't understand." She pushed up from the table.

"You're right, I don't."

"Every time I think about me and Justin...I think about mama and what happened with her."

Apryl's eyes searched her sister's face. "What really happened to Mom?"

Bailey lowered her head. "She chased after a dream... and believed that the right man could provide it for her..."

By the time Bailey finished telling Apryl about their mother, they were holding each other and shedding silent tears.

Bailey was cleaning up the kitchen when Justin called. "Hi."

"Hey, babe. How is everything?"

"Good. Just finished dinner. Apryl is resting, and I'm getting ready for work."

"I'll stop by the club. Have some things to tell you. Plus, I love to see you walking back and forth behind the bar."

Bailey giggled. "You are so bad."

"Oh, baby. I thought you told me I was so good." He chuckled.

"Bye, Justin."

"See you later, babe."

She hung up the phone with a big grin on her face then went to get ready for work.

"You sure you'll be okay?" she asked Apryl.

"I'll be fine." She yawned. "These pills will have me knocked out before you get to the front door."

"Okay, but call me if you need me."

"Mmm-hmm."

Bailey parked Justin's car and checked three times that it was locked before she went inside. Being responsible for that piece of beauty was nerve-racking to say the least. She didn't want anything to happen on her watch.

She pushed through the doors of Mercury and immediately felt the pulse of energy that flowed throughout the lavish space. She had to admit, Vincent had transformed what was once a three-story warehouse into one of the hottest spots in Baton Rouge. Every detail from the arrangement of the seating, the lights, private dining rooms, linens, live music, top-shelf liquor and mouthwatering cuisine to the hardworking and devoted staff combined to outshine every other club in the area. Although this was not her "dream job" she was happy to be part of the success and actually looked forward to coming to work. Not everyone could say the same thing. The only glitch in the program was the come-on by Vincent. That threw her for a loop and created a feeling of awkward tension—at least for her. Now, instead of seeking Vincent out for updates about Mercury and general conversation, she tried to avoid him, and it didn't feel good.

Bailey smiled and waved hello to the staff members that she passed on her way to her office. She had about fifteen minutes before she needed to hit her spot behind the bar, and she wanted to do a quick review of the weekly staffing schedule and the status of the private party.

She went into her office and closed the door behind

her, thankful that she hadn't run into Vincent in the narrow hallway. Quickly, she booted up her computer and reviewed the schedule and the arrangements for the private party. Everything looked good. The only item outstanding was the confirmed guest list for the party with several RSVPs still outstanding. The final head count would determine staffing. She hoped that the number would come in soon. She shut off her computer, locked her purse in her desk and stuck her cell phone into her pocket and headed out. Her luck was holding out, and she got to her station without running into Vincent.

"Hey, Mellie. How's it going?" She tied an apron around her waist.

"Busy." She grinned. "But what else is new on a Friday night? You have a particular glow about you," she said, looking Bailey up and down. "I bet it's that fine hunk that put a light in your eyes."

"Don't start, Mel."

"You can tell me, you know," she said, angling for information.

"I think a customer wants your attention," she said with a lift of her brow, unwilling to engage in conversation about her and Justin.

Mellie pouted. "Fine. Don't tell, but I say you hit paydirt landing a man like Justin Lawson." With that she sauntered down the length of the bar to a waiting customer.

Bailey blew out a breath and shook her head. *Paydirt.* Addy believed the same thing. But Bailey didn't want to entertain the idea that Justin was some meal ticket. For her it could never be that. She wouldn't allow it. Even if Justin could change her entire life and open her world to things she only read about, she wasn't going down that road. With that thought, the heartbreaking conversation she'd had with Apryl bloomed anew and reaffirmed her commitment to stand on her own. Period. Yet the unequal balance between her and Justin nipped at her conscience.

The steady flow of thirsty and hungry customers kept Bailey busy and totally focused on serving and entertaining those that sat in front of her. She felt on point tonight, exchanging barbs with some of the regulars and making newcomers feel welcomed enough that they would be sure to return. She'd spotted Vincent a few times from across the room, and her stomach tightened from the pensive looks he threw in her direction, but he didn't make any move to approach her.

It was nearing ten when Mellie sidled up to Bailey. "He's here," she teased, and gave Bailey a playful nudge with her elbow.

Bailey's heart jumped in her chest. She knew exactly who *he* was without looking because the tiny hairs on her arms had begun to tingle.

Slowly she turned around, and Justin was coming toward her. If she didn't know better she'd swear the seas parted as he strolled through the room with that confident swagger that only comes from one who knows exactly who they are and what they want. He was looking straight at her as if no one in the entire space existed.

Tonight he was totally casual. His black shirt had three buttons open and was tucked into expertly tailored black slacks, looped by a black lizard belt. He wore a diamond stud in his ear, something he left at home during office hours, and it picked up the light and gleamed against his smooth chocolate skin. He lifted his chin in greeting to Mellie and slid onto an available bar stool.

"Hey, babe," he whispered for only Bailey's ears.

She felt like some dumbstruck teen who'd met her rockstar idol.

"Hey." The smile was in her eyes. "Your usual?"

"Sounds good."

She turned away toward the shelf of bottles and went about preparing his drink, commanding herself to breathe and focus. She placed his glass of bourbon in front of him, and he intentionally brushed his fingers across hers. Electricity shot up her arm. She moaned.

"Dinner?" she whispered.

"I'll have plenty to eat when I take you home."

Her eyes widened for an instant.

Justin lifted the glass to his lips, and she envisioned what those lips could do to her.

"What do you think about that?"

The problem was she couldn't think, not with him burning a hole through her with his eyes. Her pulse quickened, and she didn't see Vincent until he was right beside her.

"I want you upstairs," he barked.

Bailey jerked back. "What?"

"I said I want you upstairs."

"Why? You have a staff up there and that will leave Mellie alone. We're busy."

He lowered his voice and stepped closer. "Last time I checked, this was my establishment. Let Steven know he should come down here."

Bailey's nostrils flared, and her skin burned with humiliation that Justin was a witness to her being dressed down.

"Fine." She couldn't look at Justin when she walked away. Her feet felt as if she was lifting them out of thick mud while she took the stairs to the upper level.

Unshed tears of humiliated frustration burned her eyes. She blinked them back, pasted on a smile and told Steven that he was needed on the main level. He was shocked but thrilled to have the chance to work the front lines. That's where all the action happened.

Bailey checked on the seated guests to ensure that their service was up to par then went behind the bar. She knew what Vincent was doing with this little stunt. He wanted to remind her that he could pull the plug whenever he wanted, and there wasn't anything that she could do about it. If she didn't need this job so badly, she would walk the hell out and tell Vincent exactly what he could do with himself. But she couldn't. All she could do for now was count the minutes until her shift was over.

Justin watched the entire exchange go down between Bailey and her boss with brewing fury. It took everything he had not to reach across the bar and grab that SOB by the collar and throw him onto the floor. He tossed back the remnants of his drink and paid his tab.

His dark eyes scanned the main floor. He spotted Vincent at the hostess podium. He glided off his seat and walked in that direction.

"I want to talk with you for a minute," he said, coming up behind Vincent.

Vincent turned and came face to chest with Justin. He looked up at the withering glare.

"Can I help you?"

"Why don't we step over here," Justin said with a tilt of his head that was away from the hostess.

Vincent pursed his lips. "Of course."

They stepped over to a quiet corner.

"I'm a friend of Bailey Sinclair. Justin Lawson."

"And…"

"Man to man. I know why you pulled Ms. Sinclair away from the bar. If you have a thing for Bailey, I can totally understand." His grin was nasty. "Man to man." He stepped closer. "She's taken. And you are not going to ever speak to her like that again."

A red flush began at Vincent's collar and raced to his cheeks. "Just who do you think you are coming into my establishment and telling me how to talk to my employees?"

"I already told you who I am, and I'd rather not have this conversation again—Vincent." His voice lowered to a mere rumble. "And I'm sure that Ms. Sinclair will have no further problems." With that he turned and left Vincent standing in place.

The hostess greeted him by name on his way out.

Vincent came up to her. "You know that man?"

She frowned. "Sure. Mr. Lawson. He comes in about two or three times a week. He's one of the Lawson heirs. Senator Lawson's son. Is there a problem, Vince? Did he complain about the service?"

He gritted his teeth. "No problem." He spun away and went directly to his office and shut the door. He turned on his computer and searched for Justin Lawson on Google. Almost instantly, a long list of articles and pictures were displayed about Justin Lawson.

Vincent clicked on the first link. It was an article about Justin Lawson, joining the law firm of Lake, Martin and DuBois, three years earlier. The article went on to detail his family tree and how the legacy of the Lawson name and brand would carry on as Justin was destined to move up the ranks in the legal world, having already made his mark on a major corporate case in his first six months at the firm.

Disgusted and infuriated, Vincent turned off the computer. Not only did Bailey have a man, but a man like Justin Lawson that could buy and sell him on a whim, too—one word from him and he could dry up Vincent's business.

Vincent wasn't a man used to feeling impotent. He worked too hard to get to where he was to have some privileged pretty boy millionaire ruin all that he'd accomplished—over a woman. Even if that woman was Bailey. Defeat wasn't an emotion that he'd ever had to deal with, but that's what he felt. Worse, if he didn't know before, he knew now that he'd never have a chance with Bailey.

"Bailey, what in the hell happened with you and Vincent?" Mellie asked in a harsh whisper when Bailey stopped to say good-night.

"Nothing. He just needed some help upstairs."

Mellie gave her a questioning look. "I didn't hear what he said, but I saw how he was talking to you. It didn't look friendly."

"Don't worry about it, Mel. Everything is fine." She forced a tight-lipped smile and made a move to leave.

"Well, it might have been *nothing* to you, but Justin didn't seem to take it too kindly."

Bailey stopped in her tracks. "What are you talking about?" Her heart began to race.

She gave a slight shrug. "He paid his bill right after you left, and I caught a glimpse of him and Vincent talking. That didn't look like a friendly conversation, either."

Bailey tried to beat back the thoughts that were running around in her head. If Justin… "See you tomorrow, Mel."

She stalked toward the exit with every manner of reprimand dancing on her tongue. What was it tonight with the humiliate Bailey routine? First Vincent and now Justin. She already had a good sense about Justin's take-charge attitude and his penchant for wanting to fix things. She and her life didn't need fixing!

Bailey pushed through the door with such force that it swung back and banged against the wall. Her eyes lit with anger when they landed on the Benz, reaffirming the undeniable truth of her position in her life. Her shoulders dropped. She blinked rapidly to stem the sting of tears building in her eyes. "Shit!"

And then, like all knights in shining armor, Justin was in front of her.

"Hello," he said tenderly, so sweet that her heart felt like it was fracturing into a million brilliant pieces.

Her throat tensed and whatever she wanted to spew at him clung there, held back by the gentleness in his eyes and in his touch as he stroked her chin.

"You okay?"

She could only nod, afraid that her voice wouldn't respond.

"Sure?"

"I am now," she managed.

He let his finger trail along the curve of her jaw. "Do you need to go home? To see about your sister?"

He was giving her an out if she needed to take it, and the realization softened her even more.

"Apryl said the pain meds knock her out." Her gaze lifted to meet his magnetic one, and it drew her closer. "She said she would sleep through the night."

"Perfect." He leaned in and stroked her lips with his, sending a shiver of need through her limbs.

"Follow me home," he said against her mouth.

"Okay."

"I'm parked across the street. Black Navigator."

She spotted it.

Justin crossed the street. The alarm chirped, and he got in. The headlights illuminated the street—the path that she couldn't seem to resist taking. She drew in a steady breath, got into the Benz and pulled off behind Justin.

Chapter 15

"Make yourself comfortable. I'll fix us a drink. Wine or something stronger?"

Bailey put her purse on the side table. "Wine. Please."

"Yes, ma'am."

Bailey took off her shoes and tucked her legs beneath her. Once again, she slowly took in the understated opulence of how Justin and his family lived. It was a lifestyle that had always been out of her reach. And now she could touch it. She could reach out and wrap her fingers around it. Her stomach fluttered. It would be so easy to simply give in.

"Here you go."

She blinked. Justin handed her the glass of wine.

"Thanks."

He sat down beside her. She took a sip and sighed with pleasure.

"Love that sound."

Her lids fluttered open. She looked at him. "What sound?"

"That purring sound that you make in the back of your throat."

Warmth flowed through her as Justin teased the fine hairs at the back of her neck with his fingertips. If he kept this up, she would come all over herself.

"I didn't...realize I did that."

"There is a long list of things that you do that make me crazy." He angled his body toward hers. "Like the way that tiny pulse flutters in your throat when I get close to you, or the way your lips move, the sway in your hips, the way you pour my drinks, the light that sparks in your eyes when you talk about the law, your laughter, the huskiness in your voice, the brilliance of your mind, the way you move under me when we make love." His jaw tightened. "The list is long."

Her chest rose and fell in rapid succession as she tried to breathe. No one had ever spoken to her like that. No man had ever made her feel that she was more than a nice time before moving on. Most couldn't deal with the luggage that she carried around with her—the responsibility that she felt for her siblings. Would Justin feel the same way once he knew the entire story?

Justin sensed that his "confession" had made her uncomfortable. It wasn't his intention. He took a sip of his drink. "Hungry?"

She grinned. "Starved."

He got up and took her hand, pulling her to her feet. "I know about some of your talents, Ms. Sinclair. Let's see how you do in the kitchen."

"Oh, baby, don't even go there. I get down in the kitchen."

"You're on."

Bailey took a look in the fridge and cabinets. In short order she'd diced and sliced all the ingredients for a Food Network–worthy omelet, stuffed with spinach, cheddar cheese, shrimp, peppers and spices and cooked light as cotton. She cut up strawberries, kiwi and melon slices and placed them in two small bowls. Then she fixed them both mimosas to go with their late-night, early morning feast.

"Well?" she asked after Justin had taken his first mouthful.

"Babe…your case…is rested." He picked up another fork of food and chewed with relish. He pointed his fork toward her self-satisfied grin. "You have skills."

Bailey giggled. "This is light work. One day maybe I'll cook a *real* meal for you."

"You're on." He tasted the mimosa. "Good stuff. Not my usual, but good. Goes down well with the meal."

"Of course," she joked. "It's what I do." She focused on her plate and then popped a strawberry in her mouth.

Justin watched the shift in her demeanor when she mentioned what she did. He knew where it stemmed from. He wouldn't push it. But if that piece of work calling himself her boss gave her any more grief, he would have a real problem.

"Hey, we found a location today."

"You did? Where?"

"Downtown. Nice office spaces. Exactly what we need for now. We should sign the lease this week."

Bailey beamed. "Congratulations. That's wonderful. Big step. This makes it real."

"Yep."

She scooted her chair closer and covered his hand with hers. "I'm really happy for you. There's no greater feeling than seeing your dreams materialize."

"I want to make a difference."

"You will."

He leaned in and kissed her, tasting the sweetness of the strawberries on her lips. He wanted more. He lifted a strawberry from his bowl and put it on the tip of his mouth and came to her. She parted her lips and bit down. The sweet juice dribbled over their lips. She sucked the rest into her mouth, and Justin went after it, delving into her mouth with his hungry tongue.

Bailey moaned, and the sound incited him. He threaded his fingers through her tight mass of curls and pulled her to him. Tongues and lips tasted and suckled and danced in and out. He nibbled her bottom lip, and electricity sparked through her. Justin ran his hands down the column of her spine, and her body arched toward him. Her nipples hardened to tight pebbles, and she wanted to free them from the maddening sensation of them brushing against her bra.

He knew what she wanted. He unbuttoned her blouse, and a groan rose from the pit of his belly when the soft full flesh made an appearance. He buried his face between the swell of her breasts then ran his tongue along the deep valley. He cupped her breasts in his palms and lifted them higher, nuzzling the delicate fabric away until he could take the pleading nipple into his mouth.

Bailey cried out.

Justin tugged her shirt off and tossed it aside. His dark eyes deepened as they scorched across her face and down along her lush body as he slowly disrobed her. He reached into the bowl and picked a piece of kiwi, squeezed the juice along her skin then licked it away.

Prickly heat raced along her flesh. Her head spun from the thrill, the growing need. His hands and mouth seemed to be everywhere at once. She was on fire. She fumbled with the buckle of his slacks, unzipped and freed him. His groan intensified the heat that roared through her. She held him in her palm, stroked him, felt him grow and throb.

Justin pushed her black panties aside and found her slick welcome. He fingered her and felt her entire body shudder.

"You feel so good," he groaned hot in her ear. He lifted her as if she weighed no more than a loaf of bread and pushed her up against the refrigerator. Bailey locked her long legs around his back.

"Ahhhhh," she cried out when he pushed deep inside her and buried her face in the hollow of his neck.

Justin's muscles tensed as the thrill of feeling her envelop him raced through him. "So good," he groaned as he moved in and out of her.

"More," she whispered, pressing her fingers into his back.

He tightened his hold on her rear, kneading the firm

flesh and plunged deeper, harder, faster until the only sounds in the kitchen were the slapping of skin against skin and their moans that rose and fell in a chorus of ecstasy.

After, they stumbled laughing and naked up to his bedroom and tumbled onto his bed. Bailey draped her damp body across Justin's. She placed tiny kisses across the expanse of his chest.

Justin held her, feeling her heart beat hard and steady against him. He hadn't expected to feel this way so soon, so fast, about anyone. But the more he was with her, the more he wanted, and he would do whatever he must to make that happen.

"I know you said something to Vincent," she whispered into the darkened room.

He stroked her back.

"You didn't have to. I can handle Vincent."

"He's not going to talk to you like that. No one is. Not when I'm in your life."

Bailey sat up, made out his face. "I don't need you to come to my rescue, Justin."

He rose up and balanced his weight on his elbow. Her body was outlined by the moonlight. "What kind of men are you used to, Bailey? The kind that sit back and let things happen to the woman they care about? I'm not that man."

She turned her head.

"Look at me."

"Is that really the kind of man you want? Because that's not what you deserve."

Her features tightened. "You don't understand."

"No. I don't, so tell me. Be honest with me."

Her mouth worked, but no words came out.

He reached out to her, held her arm. "Talk to me, babe."

"My mother committed suicide when I was twenty-seven. Never knew who or where our father was." Her throat tightened. "He could have been any number of men that came in and out of our lives." She sniffed and was glad for the darkness that masked the shame in her eyes.

Justin gently squeezed her arm, stroked her thigh.

"I had just started law school but after two years, I had to drop out to get a job to take care of my siblings, so I put my dreams of continuing law school on hold."

"That was quite a sacrifice for you," he said in admiration.

She uttered an abbreviated laugh. "I had no other choice."

"Tell me about your siblings," he quietly urged.

She tugged in a breath. "My younger sister Tory is under the misconception that she was destined to live the high life, no matter the cost. And my baby sister, Apryl, humph, there isn't a man that misses her radar..." Bailey sighed heavily. "It's hard to keep them on track."

"And all the weight fell on you."

"Yeah. I had to take care of them. I still do. They depend on me."

"I'm no psychologist but it sounds like your mother's life and death affected each of you the same way."

"The same way?"

"Yeah, everyone is looking for something to fill the loss. Including you."

She vigorously shook her head. "No."

"Think about it."

She pushed up from the bed. "Don't you get it, Justin? I don't want to think about it. I don't want to talk about it anymore, either." She stalked off to the bathroom and solidly shut the door behind her.

Justin tucked his hands beneath his head and stared into the dark room. There was more to the story, that much he knew for sure. The feelings that he had for Bailey only deepened by her revelations. She may not need him or want him to *rescue* her, but he felt deep in his gut that it was exactly what she needed—to be truly loved—the way he wanted to love her.

His insides jerked as if shocked. *Love.* Was he falling in love with Bailey? He glanced toward the closed bathroom door. He was in it to find out.

Chapter 16

They didn't talk anymore that night about her past, the thing that haunted her. They talked about little things, the getting-to-know-you things, how she got to be a bartender, what it felt like being the youngest Lawson, places they'd been, favorite lines from movies. Those kinds of things that couples finding their way to each other talk about.

"You all set up for school for the fall?"

"Hmm, it's coming together."

"I know you don't want to hear this, but if you want me to make a couple of calls…"

"No, Justin."

"All right. All right. All right," he said in a pretty damned good imitation of Matthew McConaughey, that made her burst out laughing. He kissed the back of her neck, and she spooned closer.

"Do you have plans for tomorrow?"

"Spending the day with you, if you let me." He kissed her again.

"I'd like that."

"Yeah, me, too." He held her closer, and they drifted off to sleep.

Bailey awakened and found herself alone in the massive bed. She rubbed the sleep out of her eyes and languidly stretched. Everything ached in a good way, and it brought a smile to her face thinking about why she felt the way she did.

She heard Justin's voice coming from downstairs, and another male voice. What time was it? She checked the bedside clock. It was after ten.

"Damn." At least she didn't have to tiptoe downstairs in search of her clothes. Justin must have brought them up while she was asleep. She scrambled to get dressed. Apryl was definitely up by now, and she must be worried. She checked her phone for messages. There was only one from Addison, calling to see if she wanted to catch a movie before her shift.

Her shift. Her stomach rolled. She had no idea what Justin said to Vincent, and she didn't want to know. But what she was certain of was that Justin made himself clear to Vincent. And she had a strong feeling that Vincent wouldn't be giving her a hard time going forward. As much as she didn't want to, it gave her a little thrill to know that Justin dealt with Vincent—for her.

Bailey gazed into the mirror, studying her reflection. She looked exactly the same, but something inside her was changing. Justin's laughter rose up the staircase. It was because of him, and she wasn't sure if she could stop it, or if she wanted to.

Bailey came downstairs and followed the sound of voices that led her to the living room.

"Hey, babe." Justin rose from the arm of the side chair and came up to her. He placed a hand on her hip. "Hope we didn't wake you," he said quietly while his eyes scanned her face.

"No. I needed to get up." She inhaled his intoxicating scent, and that crazy need for him began to simmer.

Justin stepped closer, blocking her from his guest. "I want you…" He placed a light kiss on her forehead, took her hand and turned around. "You remember Carl. He was with me the night we met." Justin led her fully into the room.

Bailey couldn't think straight after that sexual gauntlet that he'd just thrown.

Carl stood. "Good to see you again."

Bailey remembered to smile. "You, too."

"I told Carl that I owe him big-time.

Bailey glanced at him. "Why?"

Justin slipped his arm around her waist. "If he hadn't insisted that I come to the Mercury Lounge that night and then told me to stay after he had to leave, we would have never met." He kissed her full on the lips, lingering for a moment before guiding her over to the couch.

Bailey felt so off balance, unaccustomed to public displays of affection directed at her. But as she was quickly coming to understand, that's the kind of man Justin was— ready to take a stand and have his position made clear.

"We were going to play a quick game of tennis out back while you go and check on your sister. I can swing by and get you about one—then we'll find something to do. How's that sound?"

"Great. I'll be ready."

"There's coffee and tea in the kitchen, and there's a plate for you on the warming tray. I'd love to take credit, but our housekeeper fixed everything."

It was awkward enough that she had to do the "morning-after walk" in front of Carl, but the housekeeper knew she was there, too.

"Tough life this brotha has," Carl teased.

"Very funny." He turned to Bailey. "I'll get your plate." He walked off before she could protest.

Bailey eased over to the club chair and sat. "So… Justin's been telling me about the venture."

"Yeah, he's been talking and working on this for a couple of years. His father wanted him to go the corporate route and eventually follow in his political footsteps. It's a major bone of contention between them. But Justin went along with the whole working-in-a-law-office thing for as long as he could—to make his father happy, but his heart was never in it. For a man who has everything, all he's ever wanted to do was help others. Now he has that chance."

Bailey's heart softened even more hearing about Justin from Carl.

"You've made quite an impression on him."

Her eyes flicked toward Carl. "I have?"

"Definitely. To be honest, you're not the type of woman he usually dates. Don't get me wrong. It's just that in the circles that his family travels in—there are a lot of *takers*—for lack of a better word. All surface and no substance. From everything he's told me about you—you're nothing like them, and it's what he's been looking for."

"What who's been looking for?" Justin placed Bailey's plate on a lap tray and gave it to her. "What lies has he been telling you?"

"Oh, my," she said, taking in the cheese grits, turkey sausage, eggs and fruit. "This is too much."

"Eat what you want," Justin said offhandedly.

She smiled up at him. "Thank you."

"Anything you need," he said only for her ears.

"We were talking about The Justice Project," Bailey said and shot Carl a conspiratorial look. She took a spoonful of fruit and had a momentary flashback of the night before.

"Carl is going to stay with the firm for a while until we're fully operational."

"Yes, my lovely wife has grown very accustomed to a comfortable lifestyle." He chuckled. "Happy wife, happy life. As a matter of fact, you should bring Bailey to the house for dinner. Gina always wants to have a reason to lay out a spread."

"He's right about that," Justin added.

"Besides, maybe once she meets Bailey, she'll stop trying to play matchmaker."

Justin looked down at Bailey. "I've definitely stopped

looking," he said quietly. "Let us know when," which was as much a statement as a question.

"I'd like that," Bailey said. She took a sip of orange juice.

"Probably after the fund-raiser," Carl said. "Gina is on the committee, so I know she's busy until then."

"Right." Justin arched his neck back. "Totally forgot about that." He sat down on the arm of Bailey's chair. "It's a pretty big deal, and I want you to go with me." His voice lowered. "So I can show you off."

Bailey swallowed back the rise of anxiety that bubbled up from her stomach. She'd never been to any foundation fund-raiser and could only imagine the glitz and glamour that she could never match.

Justin registered the hesitation in her eyes. "We'll talk about it, and you let me know," he said, gallantly giving her a way out. "I know how crazy your schedule is."

"I'll let you know."

He leaned down and kissed her forehead. "Whatever you want, babe."

Her throat burned with unspoken emotion. He *understood*. She gave him a smile of thanks. "And speaking of stuff to do…" She placed the tray with her half-eaten food on the table. "I've really got to go." She stood. "Thank your housekeeper for me."

Carl rose from his seat, and Bailey realized how tall he was. He had Justin's six feet three inches beat by at least two inches. The two friends cut an imposing figure. He extended his hand.

"I'll be looking forward to seeing you again."

"Me, too. Take care."

Justin walked her to the door. "Sorry we couldn't have the morning to ourselves. I'd forgotten about the tennis game." He leaned against the frame of the door, folded his arms and sucked her in with his gaze. "Seems like I'm forgetting a lot of things lately."

"Why is that?" she asked, a bit breathless.

Dark orbs traversed her upturned face. "Because you're all I think about."

Bailey's heart thumped. Her breath hitched as he lowered his head and kissed her with an intensity that made her knees weaken. She gripped the tight ropes of his arms.

"Mmm, sure you have to go? I can get rid of Carl," he murmured, pulling her tight against his arousal.

She gasped. "I can't…"

Justin drew in a tight breath and reluctantly stepped back. "I will see you later."

"Definitely." She raised up and pecked him on the lips then quickly turned in time to avoid him snatching her back.

Her laughter brightened the late-morning air.

Justin watched her until she'd left the driveway before returning to Carl, which also gave him some time to tame the tiger.

"I like her," Carl said when Justin came back. "Something genuine about her." He finished off his orange juice. "I'm happy for you, man."

A wistful grin lifted the corner of his mouth. "I like her, too. More than I thought I would. And you're right. She does make me happy. Happier than I've been for a while." *If only she'd let me get past some of the walls she's put up*, he thought.

Chapter 17

Bailey jogged up the three flights of stairs to her apartment with the spring and bounce of a teenager.

Apryl was up and resting on the couch. A pang of guilt thumped in Bailey's chest. She had been so involved with her and Justin that she'd totally neglected to think about the help that Apryl would need just to fix something to eat or bathe or get dressed.

"Sis, I'm so sorry. I should have been here when you got up." She tossed her purse onto the table and went straight to the kitchen sink to wash her hands. She dried her hands on a dish towel and pulled open the fridge. "What do you want to eat? I have eggs, bacon—"

"I'm not hungry," she said petulantly.

Bailey spun around. She leaned against the sink and folded her arms. *Here we go.* "What's the problem, Apryl?"

"*You* asked me to come here," she snapped, rocking her neck as she spoke. "*You* said you would take care of me. *You* didn't even bother to call. *You* didn't know if I was dead or alive."

"Apryl…really?" She tilted her head to the side and squinted at her sister, who actually had the nerve to pout. "What did you say to me before I left last night?"

"This is what Mom would do!" She threw a side glare at Bailey. "Just leave us…for some man."

Bailey rocked back on her heels as if she'd been pushed in the chest. Her gaze fell on the pile of the unpaid bills that mirrored her own dreams put on hold and the half life she lived because she'd always put her family first—above herself—wanting to be for them everything that their mother had never been. She'd mistakenly believed that in finally telling Apryl the truth about their mother, Apryl would realize what she'd been trying to do all these years.

A pain that she had no name for opened up inside her. She felt ill. Addison's words of wisdom about her family echoed in her head.

"Sorry you feel that way." She tossed the dish towel across the counter and walked off to her bedroom.

Bailey sat down hard on the edge of her bed. She'd spent years of her adult life looking out for her siblings: coming to the rescue, covering finances, providing refuge, being the sounding board for their woes. And for what? A rude and painful awakening. An awakening that had always been there but she'd refused to see it. She had no choice but to see it now.

She stripped out of her clothes and tossed them in the hamper then turned on the shower full blast until the room filled with steam. She stepped beneath the beat of the shower, letting the water pelt her skin as the sting of her tears flowed down the drain.

The sound of one of the midday talk shows filtered into her room. It sounded like that doctor that Oprah made famous. For a moment Bailey saw herself in the guest seat surrounded by her siblings and wondered what sage advice the good doctor would have for her. How many hours of counseling would the Sinclair family need?

Bailey fastened the button on her black jeans and pulled a black fitted T-shirt over her head, dug in her top dresser drawer and pulled out a burned-orange-and-gold oblong scarf. She piled her hair on top of her head and then fashioned the scarf into a headband. She added a pair of silver hoop earrings and then threaded a silver-toned belt through the loops of her jeans.

All the little details of getting ready to go out with Justin kept her mind off what Apryl had said. Almost.

She leaned closer to the mirror to coat her lashes with mascara, and as she looked into her reflection, she wondered if her other sister saw her the same way that Apryl did.

Bailey straightened, drew in a steadying breath and turned away from the truth. She barely heard the faint *ping-pong* of the downstairs doorbell cut through the sound of applause coming from the television; a sure sign of another successful intervention from the good doctor. She glanced at her watch. It wasn't even twelve thirty. It couldn't be Justin. She walked barefoot to the front of the apartment, but Apryl had already buzzed the door.

"Who was that?"

Apryl shrugged. "I thought I pressed Talk but I guess I pressed Door. She plopped down on the couch and winced from the impact.

Bailey huffed and shook her head in concert with the knock on her apartment door. She peered through the peephole. Justin. Damn it. She'd intended to meet him downstairs. She opened the door and as tense and off balance as she felt, the sensations began to dissipate when she looked into Justin's eyes and watched the heart-melting smile illuminate the space around them.

"Hey."

"Hey yourself."

"I know I'm a little early. I made quick work of whipping Carl's ass so that you and I could spend more time together."

Bailey grinned. "Humble, aren't we."

"When you got it, you got it." He winked.

Well, she couldn't stand there in the doorway making small talk. He'd have to see where and how she lived at some point. She took his hand. "Come on in. I need some shoes." She glanced down at her bare feet.

"Yep. I would say so."

Bailey led him inside.

"Apryl, hello. How are you feeling?" He came over and sat next to her on the couch.

Bailey hesitated for a moment then went to her room. The quicker she got ready, the better.

"Coming along," Apryl said.

"You had your sister really worried. We're glad that you're okay. Listen—" he lowered his voice "—I wanted to thank you."

"For what?"

"For hanging tough last night. Bailey needed some downtime. She's been dealing with a lot lately." He flashed that smile.

Apryl's stiff demeanor softened. "It's not a problem. I told her she needs to enjoy herself. The pain pills had me in la-la land anyway."

"I still wanted to thank you."

"Ready," Bailey announced.

Justin pushed up from his spot next to Apryl. "You take it easy. When you're up to it maybe we can all do something together."

"Three's a crowd."

"Never. You're Bailey's sister. Family."

Apryl's gaze drifted toward her sister.

Bailey's chest tightened. She didn't want to believe that she saw regret in her sister's demeanor. It was what she wanted but not what she expected.

Justin draped his arm across Bailey's shoulders, and they walked out.

"Everything okay?" he asked while he opened the door to the Navigator.

"Yes. Fine. Why?" She hopped up inside, and Justin shut the door.

He got in behind the wheel and secured his seat belt then turned on the ignition. "Because things seemed kind of strained between you and your sister." When Bailey only looked straight ahead, he continued. "Am I wrong?"

"Not entirely."

"You want to talk about it?"

She shook her head. "Not now. Maybe later."

Justin studied her profile. He was used to sibling squabbles. Growing up in a house full of strong-willed, opinionated people, conflict was inevitable. This was something different. For now he'd leave it alone. Bailey was as stubborn as he was. She'd tell him when she was ready.

"So," she said, shoving cheer into her voice. "Where are we going?"

"Thought I'd drive us down to the pier and we could board the Ole Miss for the midday cruise. How's that sound?"

Bailey beamed a genuine smile. "I've always wanted to do that."

"You mean you're a born and raised Louisiana girl and you've never been on Ole Miss?"

"Nope."

"That ends today. As a matter of fact, I'm going to make it my mission to take you to all the places you've wanted to go but have never been."

Bailey adjusted her body toward him. They stopped at a light.

"Why?" she whispered.

Justin frowned. "Why what?"

"Why do you do what you do for me?" She needed him to look her in the eye. She needed to know that it was more than just sex, more than simply taking a walk on the other side, more than one of his projects that he thought he could fix.

"Can't it simply be because I care about you, really care about you? I want to see you smile. I want to see the light in your eyes when you're excited. I want you to be happy."

"What makes you think I'm not happy or that I need you or any man to make me happy?"

His features constricted as if struck with a sudden pain, but she couldn't stop the words that continued to flow.

"Men always think that the poor, helpless woman needs the big strong man to rescue her from her mundane life." Flashes of the numerous "uncles" ran through her head. "I don't. I'm not one of those women." She wasn't like her mother.

Bailey watched his jaw tighten and his fingers grip the steering wheel.

"For what it's worth, Bailey, I'm not one of those men," he said quietly.

The midday cruise on Ole Miss was strained to say the least. They made small talk about the weather, avoided eye contact and murmured about the cuisine.

The drive back home to her apartment was more awkward than the past couple of hours.

Justin kept his eyes on the road and hummed tunelessly along to the music coming from the speakers as if she wasn't there. She couldn't blame him.

Bailey knew she'd gone too far. She'd intentionally hurt him when that unnamed fear put those words into her mouth, even though deep in her soul she knew she had nothing to fear from Justin. But that didn't stop the phantom of her past from materializing.

They pulled up in front of her apartment building. Justin popped open the lock from the panel on his armrest.

"Safe and sound."

Bailey focused on her entwined fingers. "Thanks. The cruise was great."

Justin didn't respond.

Bailey reached for the door handle, stopped, glanced over her shoulder then opened the door and got out. The Navigator pulled off before she could reach her front step.

Chapter 18

"You said what?" Addison ground out from between her teeth, practically leaping over the bar in the process.

Bailey pushed Addison's mimosa in front of her. "I know. I know." She ran her fingers through her twist of curls.

The Mercury Lounge was relatively quiet. Bailey was grateful for that. It was hard to concentrate with flashes of her crazy rant at Justin running through her head. When Addison had called her earlier, she couldn't keep the ache out of her voice that Addison easily picked up on. Addison was insistent on coming straight to Bailey's apartment, but Bailey didn't want Apryl to overhear anything. She still had Apryl's revelation to deal with, but it stung too much at the moment. She knew if she talked to her sister with the mental space that she was in, she'd say something to Apryl that she wouldn't be able to take back. So she'd finally agreed to talk with Addison at the bar.

Addison took a swallow of her drink. "What would make you say something like that?"

Bailey slowed her busy work of wiping the bar top and gripped the edge with her fingertips. "I'd gotten into a thing with Apryl." She replayed the conversation.

"That little ungrateful…" She held up her hand to stop herself. "I know she's your sister, but give me five minutes with her in the bathroom."

Bailey laughed for the first time in hours. "Addy, you need to stop."

"Humph, you think I'm joking." She rolled her eyes. "So instead of enjoying your afternoon with that fine specimen of a man, you jump all over him instead of Apryl."

"Something like that," she admitted.

"That's only part of it."

Bailey's gaze rose to meet Addison's all-seeing one. "What do you mean?"

"You know what I mean. The instant anyone gets close to you, you get radioactive." She touched Bailey's fingers. "At some point you've got to stop being afraid that to allow yourself to love, to open your heart, that you're going to turn into your mother."

Bailey's nostrils flared. "You don't know what you're talking about."

"Don't I? I'm your friend, B. Your best friend. I've been hip to hip with you through all the bull. So, yeah, I do know. At some point you're going to have to step out of Phyllis's shadow and walk in your own light."

"I heard myself," she said in a faraway voice. "I heard the words. I saw what they were doing, and I couldn't stop myself. I wanted to hurt him..."

"Before he hurt you."

Bailey blinked back the water in her eyes.

"The way I see it, you can chalk this up and blow maybe the best thing that's happened to you in a while, or you can take your ass over there and be honest with him—about everything. If he can't deal then it wouldn't have worked anyway. But if he can—" she looked into Bailey's eyes "—happiness is waiting for you."

Justin stepped out of the shower and draped a towel around his waist. He used a hand towel to wipe away the steam on the mirror. He examined his reflection. He could see the hard line of his father's jaw and the warmth of his mother's eyes. His mother would be proud of what he'd accomplished and would have been rooting for his success with The Justice Project. His father, on the other hand, grudgingly accepted his decision to leave the firm while at the same time reminding him that he was ruining his career. It would always be difficult for his father and his uncles to understand and accept that their children were just as stubborn and driven as they were, and that they'd carve their own paths.

Justin ran his hand across his chin. A quick shave was in order. He plugged in his electric shaver and turned it on just as his cell phone began to dance and vibrate on the sink. Bailey's name and image appeared on the face. He let it ring, watching her face smile back at him. He'd taken that picture the night of the concert. Things certainly had changed since then. He pressed the green talk icon.

"Hello."

"Justin, it's me, Bailey," she said inanely.

"I know."

He wasn't going to make this easy, but she refused to be discouraged. "I wanted to talk with you about today, the things I said."

"Not sure what there is to say, Bailey. You were pretty clear."

She squeezed her eyes shut. "I know you think I was, but you don't have all the facts, counselor. Before you make a decision...don't you want to hear all of the evidence?"

Justin's mouth flickered in a grin. "I'm listening."

"I'm outside."

"Excuse me?" He tightened the towel around his waist and walked out of the bathroom.

"I'm in front of your house. The things I need to say need to be said face-to-face."

Justin jogged down the stairs to the main level, looked out the front window. The headlights of his Benz spread softly against the driveway. His mama always said it was ungentlemanly to keep a lady waiting.

He went to the front door and pulled it open. For a moment his towel-clad body was framed by the beam of the car's headlights. Bailey turned off the car, and the space around them dipped into a silhouette of intimacy.

She knew without a doubt that he had nothing on beneath the towel, and his bare chest only made it more difficult for her to concentrate on what she'd come to say. His body blocked her way, forcing her to stare at him. Her breathing escalated, and for a moment she thought he might not let her in.

Justin finally stepped aside to let her pass then shut the door with a thud. "Have a seat. I'm going to put something on."

Bailey wanted to tell him that he was fine just the way he was, but she held her tongue.

Too nervous to sit, she slowly paced the expansive space then walked over to the glass doors that opened onto the pool and the grounds that appeared to go on forever. This was the life, the world he lived in, and she wasn't sure that she could ever be a part of it. But she wanted him. She wanted Justin, and somehow she was going to have to convince him of that and let go of her past.

"Can I get you something?"

Bailey turned toward the sound of the voice that she heard in her dreams, and her breath caught at the sight of him.

Yes, he'd gotten out of the towel, only to put on a pair of low-riding drawstring sweats that drew the eye to the rock-hard abs and the thin trail of hair that led to hours of pleasure. She tore her eyes away.

"Um, some water is fine."

He went into the kitchen and returned shortly with a glass of water with ice, handed it to her then went to lean against the mantel. "So…what do you want to talk about?"

"First…I'm sorry. I shouldn't have lashed out at you. It has nothing to do with you. You were just the recipient of all the stuff that I've been dealing with." She swallowed. Justin hadn't moved; his expression hadn't changed. "I was the one that…found my mother. I'd come home from school—first year of law school. I'd stopped off after class to the law library then a local diner. I knew I was stalling. I didn't want to go home." She had a distant smile. "It was October tenth. Around five. It was already getting dark. The apartment was quiet. I figured my sisters were at friends' houses." She took a swallow of water.

"I went to my room, and that's when I saw water coming out from under the bathroom door. The first thing I thought was that my lazy sister Tory had left the water running. I…I didn't expect…to find my mother in the tub. She'd cut her wrist and taken some pills. There was water and blood, and I started screaming. I tried to wake her. I did CPR…" She shook her head at the vision. "It was too late."

"Bailey…"

She held up her hand. She had to get it out now, or she never would. "My mother struggled for years to feed and clothe us and keep a roof over our heads when my father left her and us—we were too young to even remember him. My mother was beautiful." She smiled wistfully. "Men flocked to her beauty, and she believed that was all she needed. She discovered that she could use her looks to get men to give her things, to pay for things, to keep her company. So the 'uncles' started to come and go. But they would tire of her looks, tire of her neediness, tire of her three kids." She took another sip of water. "She spent her days trying to catch that man that was going to take care of her, but they all eventually abused her emotionally, and then they were gone." Tears streamed down her cheeks.

"I tried to protect my sisters from seeing stuff. I made excuses for the times when Mom wouldn't come out of her room or when she would disappear for days at a time and leave us alone." She sniffed hard then swiped at her eyes. "After...I had to drop out of school, get a job to take care of them. I had to be there..." She lowered her head.

Justin crossed the distance between them and gathered her into his arms. "I can see how hard you try to be strong and independent at the expense of your own happiness. It's okay to need someone, Bailey. I don't want to take away your independence, babe." He stepped back a bit and lifted her chin so that she would have to look at him. "I only want you to be happy."

"Sometimes I feel like I'm failing my sisters."

"Bailey, there comes a point in everyone's life when they have to take responsibility for their own choices and stop using the past as an excuse for their future. Your siblings are all adults. What happened with your mom was horrible, and it affected each of you in a different way. But you can't blame yourself, and you can't save people who don't know they need to be saved."

She wiped her eyes. "I've been told that a zillion times by Addy."

Justin grinned. "Smart girl."

"She thinks so, too." She exhaled a long breath. "My head tells me all of that is true. It's my heart that keeps getting in the way."

Justin slung his hands in his pockets. "You may not want to hear this, but I'm going to take a chance and say it anyway. You still feel guilty."

She frowned. "Guilty? About what?"

"That you didn't come straight home that day. That if you had come home, you could have saved her."

The air caught in her chest. Her temples began to pound. She'd never told anyone, not even Addy that she was late getting home that day. She'd never said it out loud. Her shoulders shook as the sobs overtook her.

Justin held her, stroked her hair, her back, cooed softly that it was okay; she would be okay.

Bailey sank into the security of his arms and his words.

All this time, guilt had been the phantom that stalked her. It was the voice in the recesses of her subconscious. She blamed herself, but even understanding that didn't make the guilt go away.

"Let me fix you something a little stronger." He kissed her forehead and walked her over to the couch. "Thank you for telling me," he said as he fixed her a shot of scotch and him a bourbon. He sat beside her and handed her the glass. He touched his glass to hers. "To getting over the hurdles...together."

Bailey's smile trembled around the edges. She took a sip of her drink and hummed as the heat of the honey-brown liquid flowed down her throat and ignited in her belly. She knew her liquors, and this was definitely the good stuff. Of course, she wouldn't expect anything less from Justin.

"I didn't tell you all of that for you to feel sorry for me."

Justin bit back a smile. "I know." He put his arm around her shoulder. "You make it very difficult to feel sorry for you."

Bailey made a face. "I told you about my family, tell me about yours, stuff that's not in the papers."

"Well, this is family news. My oldest sister, Lee Ann, is expecting twins!"

"Wow. How exciting."

"Second set of twins in the family. Desi and Dom thought they had a lock on it." He chuckled. "I'm sure you've heard about my brother, Rafe."

"I've seen a couple of pictures of him. You two look a lot alike."

"Yeah, he swears he's the better-looking one, but you and I both know that's a lie." He winked.

"You are absolutely right."

"Anyway, Rafe is off in Europe, playing with his band. Says he loves it and isn't sure when he'll be back. But I know my brother. He has his eye on a woman he met here at my grandfather's birthday party. He keeps asking about her, which is so unlike my brother. He'll be back."

"Sounds like you all are close."

"We are. Growing up, we were inseparable. Not to mention the host of cousins that lived here off and on, or spent summers and holidays here."

Bailey stared into her drink. "That's what I wanted," she said softly. "A close family that loved each other, supported each other, us against the world. You know." She took a sip, and her eyes fluttered closed for a moment.

He tossed her a smile. "Hey, do you swim?"

"I can manage in the water. Why?"

"Let's go for a moonlight swim."

She giggled. "Are you kidding?"

"Absolutely not."

"I don't have a bathing suit," she hedged.

He put his glass down, swung his long legs off the table and stood. "The water is always warm. No one here but us."

There was that smile again, and her heart started jumping.

Justin extended his hand. "Great way to relax," he continued to coax.

Bailey suddenly beamed a smile, took his hand and jumped up. "Let's go for it."

"Now you're talking."

They ran out back like two giddy high school kids who had the house to themselves while their parents were away.

"You sure no one can see us?" Bailey asked as she slowly began to strip.

Justin stepped out of his drawstring sweats. "If they could—" he voice grew thick as he looked at Bailey's lush body unveiled in front of him "—they would be very jealous that they could only see and not touch."

Her flesh heated from the lascivious look in his eyes.

"Woman, you could make a man lose his mind." He

stepped to her, reached around her back and unfastened her bra. He peeled it off and tossed it onto a lounge chair. He murmured something deep in his throat before letting his thumbs trail teasingly across the dark brown areolas. Bailey moaned softly. Justin lowered his head and took the right nipple into his mouth, let his tongue play and tease it until it was large and hard, and he could feel her body shiver against his. He hooked his fingers beneath the band of her panties and inched them down across her hips. She wiggled out of them.

Justin caressed her round hips and slid a finger inside her very moist slit. Her legs wobbled. She gripped his shoulders and rocked her pelvis against his hand. She then reached between them and took his hard phallus in her hand. Justin groaned as she stroked him, ran her thumb across the swollen head, and felt his dew dampen her fingertip.

He backed up to the lounge chair and sat. His hot gaze beckoned her. Bailey came to him, spread her legs on either side of the chair and slowly lowered herself on top of him. As always, that initial contact took their breaths away. For a moment, neither of them could move and then, slowly, Bailey began to ride him as he leaned back and took everything that she threw at him, returning the favor in kind.

Justin grabbed the globes of her rear and thrust up and deep. She cried out, and he pushed harder, holding her in place so that she was totally his for the taking. Bailey arched her back and thrust her hips forward, taking him even deeper inside.

"You're mine. All mine," he groaned between the valley of her breasts. "Mine," he repeated.

Bailey felt her world begin to shatter as the tingles raced up the backs of her legs, and her pulse roared in her ears. She threw her head back, and the moon and the stars looked down upon her as a volcanic orgasm snapped through her, shook her limbs, arrested her breath, clenched her walls to suck the essence of Justin out of him in an explosion that vibrated through the night.

She collapsed against his chest, and he held her. Their hearts banged and pounded as they tried to regain control over their breathing, that slowly turned to satiated laughter.

Justin kissed the hollow of her neck. "Woman…"

"Hmm…"

"I have no words."

"Hope that's a good thing."

"Trust me, it is." He cupped her face in his palms. His dark eyes skimmed her face. "I'm in love with you, Bailey."

She blinked rapidly.

"Don't say anything. I want that to sit with you for a while." He stroked her bottom lip with his thumb. "See how it fits."

"I don't have to see how it fits. I love you, too." She felt him pulse inside her.

"We'll make it work, babe."

She caressed his jaw. "I know." She slowly gyrated her hips against him.

Justin hissed between his teeth. "It's more than this," he groaned, thrusting up inside her. "Believe that."

She draped her arms around his neck and pressed her cheek against his. "I know," she whispered.

Chapter 19

"I need to go to Atlanta for a couple of days," Justin said while he prepared breakfast the following morning.

"Really? What's in Atlanta?"

"Hmm, just some business to handle."

"Okay. When are you leaving?"

"Tomorrow afternoon. I'll be back late Monday." He turned and spooned the omelet from the pan onto a platter.

Bailey looked at him. "Is everything okay?"

"Yeah, just some old business with a client that I need to tie up."

She bobbed her head and cut a slice of the omelet and put it on her plate. "I have to work Sunday anyway. We're hosting a private party."

Justin swung onto the stool. "No more issues with Vincent, I hope?"

"No. He's been cool. Distant but cool."

"Good. I know you were pissed that I said anything to him, but that's who I am. I can't sit around—" he leaned across the counter "—and have the woman I love disrespected. It's not gonna happen." He gave her a light peck on the lips.

Bailey's cheeks flamed. Love. Wow. This is what it feels like. A bubbling joy that could barely be contained. A warmth that flowed through your veins. A feeling that no matter what, that special someone was in your corner. She'd never had that. Never. It was hard to wrap her mind around the enormity of it, the responsibility of it. She'd felt love before, for her siblings, for Addy, but love had always been on the back burner when it came to her own life. Now, here it was. Right in front of her. This man loved her, and she was in love with him. A man who could have any woman he wanted. He chose her. Her.

"You okay? You're not eating," he said, breaking into her thoughts.

"Oh." She grinned. "Just thinking."

"About what?"

"About the fact that we never did get to swim last night."

Justin chuckled. "Yeah, I think we got a little distracted."

"Ya think!"

They both laughed.

"Listen, I know your car is still in the shop. What did they say about the repairs?"

Her expression drooped. "Hmm, the engine is shot."

"That's major."

"I know. Replacing the engine will cost more than the car is worth at this point."

Justin was thoughtful for a moment while he chewed his food. "Well, you can drive the Benz as long as you need to."

"I really can't do that. I can get a rental or something until…"

"Why do that when you have a car at your disposal?"

"Are you sure? You need your car."

"You need it more. And I have the Navigator." He didn't tell her that he also had other vehicles parked in the garage.

"If you're sure."

"Absolutely. Now eat up." He checked his watch. "I have some errands to run this morning."

"And I definitely need to get home and change, and check on Apryl."

"Speaking of home…I was thinking that since you'll

be spending more time here that you should bring some things over."

Her pulse quickened. "Bring some things over?"

Justin frowned and looked around the room. "Do you hear an echo?"

Bailey laughed. "Very funny. You sure?"

"Stop doubting what I say. Yes, I'm very sure."

She drew in a deep breath then grinned. "Okay. I will."

"Good. Then it's settled." He pushed back from the table and took his plate to the sink. "You think anymore about going with me to the foundation gala?"

"Not really. I've never been to anything like that before."

"And what was my promise to you?" he asked when he turned to face her. He rested against the sink.

She twisted her lips. "That you promise to take me to all the places I've wanted to go and have never been," she said softly.

"Exactly. So when you say the word, I'll make it happen."

He looked into her eyes, and she instantly knew that he understood the why of her reluctance.

She nodded her head in agreement. "Okay."

"Good. I'm going to grab a shower. You're welcome to join me." He gave her that tempting grin that made his eyes sparkle.

She got up from her seat and took her plate to the sink. "And we'd never get out of here." She lightly kissed his cheek that was slightly rough against her lips. "I think I like this rugged, after-five look on you." She caressed his jaw.

"Whatever makes you happy, babe." He lassoed his arms around her and pulled her close. "You like it, then I love it." He lowered his head and brushed his mouth against hers then slowly deepened the kiss, tasting the meal that they'd shared on her tongue, and he grew hungry again.

* * *

"I'm leaving for real this time," Bailey said over her laughter while Justin tried to entice her to stay in bed with him, where they'd eventually wound up. She scrambled out of bed as he tried to snatch her back. "And don't follow me," she said with a warning wag of her finger.

"I could make it worth your while."

"I'm sure you could." She gathered her clothes and went into the bathroom, shutting and locking the door behind her.

When she was dressed and ready to leave, she came out of the bathroom.

"I'll call you later," Justin said.

She reached up and gave him a quick kiss. "Okay. I go in tonight at six to set up for the private party. I'm off at one."

"Come here when you're done."

"Sounds inviting. I'll let you know. Okay?"

"Fair enough." He snatched her back before she crossed the threshold. "I love you."

Her pulse leaped. "I love you."

"Go, before I seriously change my mind about listening to you."

"Talk to you later." She spun away and practically skipped to the car. When she got behind the wheel of the Benz and looked at the expanse of the Lawson mansion in front of her and the man who loved her standing in the doorway, she felt as if she was in a dream, someone else's life. But it could be her life now, if she was willing to step into it. She turned the key in the ignition and slowly pulled out of the driveway. One day she was serving drinks behind those doors, and now she was sleeping with the man of the house.

When she arrived at her apartment, it seemed smaller than ever. She locked the door and put her purse on the kitchen table. She flipped through the mail that she'd taken

out of the mailbox on her way in. Bills, bills, overdue notices. There was one letter from Xavier University. Her
pulse quickened. She tore the envelope open. Her eyes
raced across the page. Her heart stopped. "We're sorry,
but at this time…" She didn't need to read any further.

She plopped down in the chair at the kitchen table. The
table rocked. What was she going to do now?

"Hi."

Bailey glanced over her shoulder. "Hi."

"Something wrong?"

"Nothing out of the ordinary." She stuck the letter back
in the envelope.

Apryl pulled out a chair and sat. "Sis, I'm really sorry
about the things I said. I was so out of line. You didn't
deserve that."

"How's your wrist?" she asked.

"Did you hear what I said?"

"I heard you."

"And? No response."

"What can I say, Apryl? You hurt me. Really hurt me
in a way I don't think you understand. I accept your apology, but that doesn't make the hurt go away. That's going
to take time." She glanced away. "How's your wrist?"

"Better. At least if you accept my apology, that's a
start."

Bailey offered her sister a shadow of a smile. "We all
have to start somewhere."

"I love you, sis."

Bailey's stomach jumped. Apryl had never said that to
her, not that way, not like she really meant it.

Apryl squeezed Bailey's hand. "Thanks for everything."
She pushed up from the table. "I think I'll go for a walk.
I need to get out of the house. I'll probably go home to-
morrow, give you your space back."

Bailey was speechless. Maybe her sister was growing
up after all.

* * *

Justin planned on using the family's Learjet. As long as someone else didn't need it, it should be available. If not, he'd book a quick round-trip flight to Atlanta. He put in a call to the hangar and spoke with the supervisor. Luckily, Desiree and her husband had just come back from Cancun that morning. After servicing and refueling, the supervisor told him it would be ready for Justin's trip to Atlanta. He'd have his usual pilot, Paul Harris. Although both Justin and Rafe had their pilot's license for a number of years, Justin preferred to relax this time. He had a lot to think about, and unwinding on the flight was exactly what he needed.

With that bit of business out of the way, Justin made a few phone calls, checked his email and was surprised to find one from Jasmine. She wanted to apologize for how she acted, the things she'd said. She missed him, and she hoped that they could find a way to fix things between them.

Justin pressed Delete, and the email zipped into the trash can. Next on his agenda was a trip into town to meet up with Dominique. His sister's keen eye for fashion was just what he needed. He knew what he liked to see on a woman, but Dominique knew what a woman wanted to be seen in.

Dominique was waiting for him in front of Femme Boutique. She'd assured him that something designer ready-to-wear could be found there.

"Hey, baby bro," she greeted.

"Hey yourself. Thanks for meeting me."

"Anything for you, sugah." She gave him a hug. "When am I going to get to meet this new lady of yours? Bailey, right?"

"Soon."

She hooked her arm through his. "Well, let's get this shopping party started."

Justin held the door open for her, and they walked inside.

"You can't go wrong with the little black dress," Dominique said, strutting through the aisle. She fingered a silk scarf as she passed. "I'm thinking cocktail length."

They were approached by a sales clerk. "How can I help you?"

"We're looking for a black cocktail dress, size ten. Flirty, but classy. Maybe something by Vera Wang."

"Right this way."

About an hour later, they were walking out with a dress that Justin couldn't wait to see Bailey in so that he could get her out of it."

"What about accessories?"

"Hmm, hadn't thought about that."

"Follow me over to my shop. I'm sure I can find the right thing."

Dominique had launched her business, First Impressions, nearly five years earlier. At first it was an outlet for the overflow of clothing that she'd acquired. Her idea was to provide a wardrobe jump start to women who were returning to the workforce, had hit on hard times or simply needed a designer outfit at rock-bottom prices. The business did so well, and her clientele was so devoted, that she expanded First Impressions to include GED classes and financial management courses. Both of which were always full with a waiting list. The expansion of her original building space was how she'd met her husband, Trevor—contractor extraordinaire. The one man on the planet that had been able to tame Dominique's wild ways—or at least rein her in a bit.

When they arrived at First Impressions, Dominique showed Justin the jewelry case that was lined with what looked like very expensive jewelry. She picked a rope choker coated in cubic zirconia that sparkled like diamonds, a real pair of diamond studs and a matching cuff bracelet. "On the house," she teased and put the items in a gift box.

"Thanks so much."

"I hope she appreciates you," Dominique said while she walked him to the door.

Justin stopped at the door. He looked at his sister. "I truly believe she does."

Justin kissed his sister's cheek. "Thanks for today, sis. Gotta go." He climbed into his Navigator and pulled off.

Chapter 20

Bailey picked through her closet and her dresser drawers and put a few items into a small carryall. A couple of tops, a pair of shorts, jeans, undies and lotion. The rest of her things were generally in her purse. She'd pick up a toothbrush and her favorite deodorant from the drugstore on her way to work.

She was still in a state of euphoria. She was in love, and the most incredible man was in love with her. Her sister, her flighty sister, finally admitted that she loved her. Bailey was in a good place in her soul. Better than she'd been in a long time—bills and no scholarship be damned. For now she was going to enjoy her time in the sun.

"Going away?" Apryl asked, appearing in the doorway of Bailey's room.

"No. Just putting a few things together to leave at Justin's place."

"Well, well. Sounds serious." She came into the room and sat on the side of Bailey's bed.

"Getting there," Bailey offered without saying more.

"I've left more of my *things* around town to fill a small boutique," she said in a self-deprecating way.

Bailey took a quick glance at her sister and was surprised to see the unhappiness that hung around the downturn of her mouth.

"One of these days I may get a drawer all my own." She looked up at her sister. "You're lucky. He really cares about you. I can tell. He'll make space for you in his closet and in his life." She snorted a laugh. "I know these things. My own love life may be shot to hell, but I can always predict someone else's."

Bailey sat down next to Apryl. "When you stop looking and when the time is right, the perfect man is going to walk right into your life. Stop chasing after love, sis."

Apryl rested her head on Bailey's shoulder the way she used to do when she was much younger. It still felt good. "I'll try to follow your advice."

Bailey arrived at the Mercury Lounge by six. The private party was scheduled to begin at eight. The third floor had been reserved, and the waitstaff was already setting up. They were expecting a party of seventy-five, some corporate bigwigs and their wives and guests. The party organizer had ordered top-shelf everything from the appetizers to the dessert.

Vincent was on his way down when Bailey arrived on the third level.

"Everything looks good," he said without preamble. "You can take it from here."

"Thanks."

He breezed by her without saying anything further. Bailey breathed a relieved sigh and entered the dining room. She reviewed the inventory and checked all of the carts. The third floor had its own kitchen for events like this, so she went to meet with the chef to ensure that he had everything he needed. With that last item out of the way, she met with the waitstaff supervisor for the event to go over the guest list and the staff for each table.

"I'll check in shortly. And you can reach me on the bluetooth if anything comes up throughout the night."

"Yes, Ms. Sinclair."

Bailey gave one last look around then went to the main level. She'd be doing double-duty tonight, but that was fine. It made the night go by faster.

On her first break of the evening, she called Justin to tell him to wait up for her, that she would come by when she got off work. He told her he was more than looking forward to it and would definitely make it worth the ride over.

With so much to look forward to, the night seemed to glide by. She felt good, deep-down-in-her-soul good. She went up to the third level to check on the guests and the service.

"Aren't you the one from the party?"

Bailey stopped short. She tilted her head in question. And then she recognized the woman in front of her. She was with Justin the night of the party, the one who made the catty remark about talking to the help.

"Good to see you again. Welcome to Mercury."

"What does he see in you?"

"You'd have to ask him."

"You'll never measure up," she said, stepping close. "He's intrigued for now. Something new. But he'll be back once he realizes that slumming isn't all it's cracked up to be."

"As long as you keep believing that. The real question is not what he sees in me but what did he ever see in you?"

Jasmine's eyes flared, and if looks could kill, someone would be preparing Bailey's eulogy. She took a sip from her glass of champagne and spun away.

Bailey was trembling inside. Fury spun in her gut like a tornado needing to let loose on someone or something. She conducted her work with professionalism even as she wanted to smack the smug look off Jasmine's face each time she fell into her line of sight. And every time, Jasmine would lean close to her conversation companion, giggle behind her hand and look in Bailey's direction.

Bailey went about her duties and instructed the staff before returning to the main level.

"What. Is. Wrong. With. You?" Mellie asked. "Who are you going to push out into traffic?"

Bailey wouldn't put the words together. To do so would give them more power than they were worth. Thinking about her brief run-in with Jasmine and her comments about Justin did leave her unsettled, though. How much truth was there in what Jasmine said? Hadn't she said the very same things herself? "Nothing," she finally said. "You know how the money folks can act."

"Hmm," she groused. "I know that's right. But at least they're good tippers."

"Yeah," Bailey said absently then walked down to the other end of the bar to serve a customer. *Just slumming.*

Bailey parked the car on the winding driveway of Justin's home. The lights on the ground floor were on. She could hear the faint sound of music coming from the house. This was the life that Jasmine claimed as hers, the life that Bailey only read about. Would Justin grow tired of her once he realized that she didn't fit in?

The front door opened, and Justin stood in the archway. He trotted down the steps and crossed the driveway to where Bailey was parked. She let the window down.

"Everything okay?" he asked, concern lacing his voice.

Bailey smiled. "Fine. Was just taking a minute."

"Rough night?"

"A little." She pressed the button to raise the window, shut off the car and got out.

Justin took her carryall, draped his arm around her shoulder then kissed the top of her head. "Let me see what I can do to make you feel better. I ran you a bath. Water's hot, wine is cold, and I've been known to give a mean massage."

She glanced up at him, and her spirit began to rise. "I like the sound of all of that."

"Right this way."

As promised, a hot bath was waiting, and the room held the aromatic scent of jasmine. The lights were dimmed, and candlelight flickered from the votives set strategically around the spa-size bath.

"Oh, Justin…" She turned to him and was greeted by his smile. Her heart swelled. "This is…" She was at a loss for words.

"This is all for you." He placed his hands on her shoulders. "Take as much time as you need. I'll bring you some wine. Want to hear some music while you unwind?"

"Sure," she whispered. "That would be wonderful."

"Your wish is my command." He crossed the heated mosaic tiles and pressed a button on a panel by the door. Soft, instrumental music floated through the air.

"Perfect."

Justin winked. "Be right back."

While he was gone, Bailey got undressed and stepped into the steamy water. Every muscle in her body moaned with pleasure as she slowly descended into the fragrant water. She leaned back against the headrest and closed her eyes, allowing the water to loosen her limbs.

"Here you go, babe."

Bailey's eyes fluttered open. Justin was sitting on the edge of the tub with a flute of wine in his hand.

She sighed with pleasure and took the glass. "Thank you."

"You can turn on the jets in the tub if you want."

"Thanks, I will."

He leaned over and kissed her lightly on the lips. "See you when you're done."

She nodded with a closemouthed smile.

Justin walked away and closed the door behind him. Bailey pressed the start button for the jets in the Jacuzzi, sipped her wine and experienced heaven.

She'd actually drifted to sleep, long enough that the hot water was now warm. She turned on the faucets and added more hot water, finished bathing and got out. A thick aqua-blue towel was laid out across a table. She dried off and wrapped herself in the towel that reached beyond her knees then opened the adjoining door that led to Justin's bedroom.

"Hey, feeling better?"

"Much."

"You can put whatever you want in the top two drawers and make whatever space you need in the closet if you have things you want to hang," he said from his seat by the window.

This was really happening. She was actually putting her clothing in Justin's home. He'd made space for her. This was no simple act; this was taking their relationship to another level.

"You're sure about this?"

He glanced up from what he was doing on his laptop. "Sure about what, babe?"

She felt silly asking, but she needed to hear the words. "Sure about me...taking up space."

Justin closed the cover of his laptop, set it on the table next to him and got up. He crossed over to where she was standing. He placed his hands on her shoulders and gazed down into her eyes. "Listen, you can take up all the space you want with me, in my home and in my life. Okay?"

Bailey blinked back the sudden burn in her eyes. "Okay."

"And don't you think for one minute that you don't belong here. You do. You belong here because I want you to be here." He stepped closer and put his arms around her waist. "Now that we have that out of the way, you hungry or do you want to turn in?"

"I'm really tired. I think I'll turn in."

"Cool. I have a few cases to review. As soon as I'm done, I'll give you that massage that I promised."

Bailey grinned. "Looking forward to experiencing your skills."

"Oh, baby, you have experienced my skills." He winked and walked back to his seat by the window.

While Justin worked, Bailey unpacked her carryall, putting undies and some tops in the drawer and her toiletries in the bathroom. She had brought two pairs of jeans and blouses for work that she hung in the deep walk-in closet. He had enough designer clothes and shoes to start a small boutique. She added her meager belongings.

"There's a box on the bottom shelf. It's for you," Justin called out.

Bailey looked at the sleek black box with the gold embossed letters of Femme Boutique. Her heart pounded. She gingerly lifted the box and brought it out of the closet. She placed it on the bed.

"Go ahead. Open it. I swear it won't bite."

"Justin…"

"Open it."

She lifted the cover, and her breath caught when she lifted back the scented tissue paper. Tucked in the box was a black dress that seemed to glisten from the hand-sewn insets across the bodice. She tenderly lifted the dress and held it up. It was a dress straight out of one of the top fashion magazines. The bodice was sleeveless and fitted, sprinkled with stones that looked like diamonds. The top was heart-shaped and tapered down to a flounced skirt of silk and tulle, that was both sexy and flirty.

Bailey held the dress up to her body and imagined herself in it. "Oh, Justin…it's beautiful." She spun toward him and was rewarded with his devastating smile.

"There's more."

"More?" She whirled back to the box, and beneath the tissue paper was two boxes from First Impressions. She opened the long box that held the bracelet and choker. She couldn't believe her eyes. Then she opened the smaller box and a pair of diamond earrings twinkled back at her. "Oh, my God. I don't believe this."

"Can't wait to see you in it."

"Justin…this is too much."

"Naw. I thought it would be a good incentive for you to get all dressed up and come with me to the foundation gala. And I wanted to do something special for you."

She clung to the dress as if she couldn't believe it was real. "You've done so much already."

Justin crossed his right ankle over his left knee and leaned forward. "Babe, anything I do for you is because I want to."

"But I can't do anything for you...nothing like this."

"This isn't tit for tat. I'm not looking for anything. What you can do for me is be happy and let me be there for you." He got up and came to her. He took the dress from her hands and put it on the bed. "Let me love you, Bailey."

Her body flooded with heat. That was the second time he'd uttered the word *love*. Was it simply an endearing phrase that he used, or did it have real meaning? Did he love her? Really love her?

"Love me?" she murmured.

"Yes, love you. And I don't mean *make* love to you. I mean love you, the way a man loves a woman, the way I want to love you, totally and without reservation." He paused and searched her open expression. "Let me." He didn't give her time or room to respond. He covered her mouth with his and reconfirmed his declaration.

She melted against him, sank into the essence of him, absorbed him through her pores and when her towel fell away and tumbled at her feet, she loved him back with every ounce of her being.

Chapter 21

Justin pulled up in his driveway just as twilight was beginning to settle, that in-between time when it's hard to determine fact from fiction. But whatever doubts and feelings of uncertainty he'd been having today about his career path were erased when he spotted the Benz already parked. His wavering spirits soared.

Bailey was curled up on the couch intently watching the new Omari Hardwick series when Justin walked in. She hopped to her feet, and he pulled her into his arms. She'd never felt so good to him as she did now. He held her close, kissed her cheeks, her ears, her lips as if he had to assure himself that she was really here. That this was real.

"You don't know how much this means having you here now, today," he breathed into her hair.

She stepped back, looked up at him and cupped his face in her palms. Her eyes scored his taut expression. "What is it? What's wrong?"

He looked away and released her then walked over to the bar and poured a quick glass of bourbon. "You want something?"

"Do I need something?"

He tossed the drink down his throat, savored the warmth then set the glass down. He leaned back against the bar, folded his arms. Bailey sensed that she needed to sit down and she did.

"I had a conversation with my father today. He is tying himself in knots about me leaving the firm to launch The

Justice Project. He went on and on about how I was going to ruin my legal career, mess up my connections to some of the most influential people in Baton Rouge." He shook his head with annoyance. "I told him in no uncertain terms that it was long past the time when he could dictate my life to me. He was either going to support me, or…walk away." He took a swallow of his drink. "He then said he had an 'important call coming in.' and had to go." He snorted a laugh then shrugged. "Branford Lawson isn't used to his way not being 'the' way."

She pushed up from her seat and walked up to him. She took his hands. "I'm here. We're in this together, whatever way it works out."

Relief softened the lines around his eyes. A smile of thanks lifted his mouth. "This is why I love you," he whispered, before covering her lips with his.

They spent the rest of the evening talking about what the future would hold for both of them—Justin's pursuing his new venture and her returning to law school.

"So have you heard anything yet from the schools that you applied to?"

She shook her head. "I can pretty much go wherever I want *if* I had the money to pay for it." She snorted a laugh. "I've gotten a couple of partial scholarships but nowhere near what I need. But I'm hopeful. I'm still waiting on the big one—Harvard. They're really trying to elevate their diversity, and they have money."

"Harvard… You'd have to leave…"

She stole a glance at him and nodded slowly. "But I still haven't heard anything. The letters should be going out soon."

"I can help you."

"Help me? What do you mean?"

"I can pay for your classes."

"Are you kidding me? No. I don't want you to do that, and I didn't tell you about it because I wanted a handout!"

He levered up on his elbow and clasped her bare shoulder. "It's not a handout, Bailey. Why is it so hard for you to accept anything from me? I'm not like those other men, and you're not your mother."

She swung her head away. It was a constant war that she waged within herself. More so now than ever before in her life. She could easily see herself falling headlong into all the trappings that came with a life that Justin could offer. First the car, then space in his closet, then keys to his door, the dress, jewelry and now he was offering to help pay her tuition. What next? How much of her independence was she willing to lose?

"I can't let you do that," she said softly. "This is my dream—just like you have yours. I need to do this for me. And if I can't, then I guess it wasn't meant to be."

"I moved some stuff into Justin's house," Bailey said as she sorted through her mail.

"Wow. So now what?"

"Now we…" Her heart thumped. "Addy…its a letter from Harvard." Her fingers trembled.

Addison jumped up from the couch. "Open it!"

"I'm scared. What if I don't get in?"

"But what if you do? Open it."

Bailey drew in a breath and stuck her thumb under the flap of the envelope and peeled it open. Slowly she unfolded the letter. Her eyes raced across the words. "Oh, my God, oh, my God!" She squeezed the letter to her chest.

"What? What?"

"I got a full-year scholarship to freaking Harvard!" She jumped up and down and spun in a circle of joy.

Addison started screaming, too, as if she'd won the lottery and then wrapped Bailey in a hug. "I'm so happy for you. Everything is coming together for you. Finally. And you deserve it, girl. You deserve it."

Tears pooled in Bailey's eyes. "Thank you," she sniffed

and then read the letter again through her misty eyes. "This is so incredible." She sat at the wobbly kitchen table and stared at the letter—at her future.

"So…when would you have to leave?"

Leave. The word rocked her inside. That was the reality. She would have to leave. Leave her family, her life here—Justin.

"Classes start in five weeks," she said softly.

"How do you think Justin will take it?"

"I don't know."

"I'm sure the two of you will work it out. He wants you to have your dream as much as you do. Long-distance relationships can work if the couples are willing and committed to it. Besides, your man has the means to see you whenever you want."

"Yes," she said almost to herself. "He certainly does."

Chapter 22

Bailey stared at her reflection in the full-length mirror. The dress fit as if it had been made especially for her. The garment hugged her upper body, showcasing her narrow waist and full breasts that teased above the heart-shaped dip of the bodice. From the waist the silk-and-tulle skirt floated out and around her knees. Her jewelry sparkled, and for the first time in her life she felt like she was living the fairy tale of her dress.

"Oh, baby…" Justin murmured in deep appreciation.

She turned from the mirror and gave him the full effect but was hit by a jolt of lightning when she laid eyes on him.

The cut of his tuxedo accentuated his broad shoulders and washboard abs. He opted to go tie-less, which gave him an elegant yet cavalier appearance, and the slight shadow around his jaw only added another level of delicious sexiness.

Bailey beamed then gave him a little twirl before dancing over to him. He looped his arm around her waist and gently swayed with her. "You'll be the most beautiful belle at the ball," he said then lowered her into a dip that had her giggling with happiness.

"Exactly how many cars do you have?" Bailey asked, wide-eyed when Justin opened her door to the Lexus.

He gave an indifferent shrug. "A couple." He shut her door and came around to the driver's side and got in.

"How many is a couple?"

He turned the key, and the car purred to life. The lush leather seating enveloped her, and she felt as if she was being held in the palm of a hand. The dash gleamed with lights and buttons and the sound system was to die for.

"The Benz, the Navigator, the Jaguar, this…and a Mustang convertible," he added.

Bailey shook her head in amazement. What could one person need with so many cars? But the reality was, if he didn't have more than one car, she would have been in debt with a rental, since she'd told the mechanic to junk the car.

"I have a confession to make," Bailey said.

"What?"

"I'm sure you must have guessed it, but I've never been to one of these things before, at least not as a guest."

"No big deal, really. Just a lot of people who got all dressed up to drink and gossip and spend money—for a worthy cause. It'll be fine. And as soon as I make the rounds, shake a few hands, we can leave if you want. Deal?"

"Deal." She relaxed against the headrest.

Justin drove with his left hand and placed his right hand on her thigh. A shiver fluttered up her leg.

"I'm going to be shaking hands really quickly," he said, his voice having grown thick, as his fingers stroked her inner thigh.

Bailey's lids drifted closed. She covered his hand with hers to stop his trip up her skirt. "We'll never get there and get back if you keep that up."

Justin snatched a look at her. "Yeah, real fast handshakes."

The foundation gala was being held at the Ritz Carlton Hotel, and the decked and bejeweled guests were out in force. Bailey felt as if she'd stepped into the pre-Oscar show hour as she and Justin walked arm in arm down the length of the red carpet and up the marble stairs to

the entrance. The annual foundation gala for cancer re-
search brought out the media, who took as many pictures
as possible as the well-heeled guests arrived, calling out
to them, asking who they were with and what the women
were wearing.

Bailey was overwhelmed and held on tight to Justin,
who seemed to be less than interested in the hoopla or
maybe it was the fact that he was so accustomed to these
things that it no longer fazed him.

Once inside, they were directed to the main ballroom,
which was something right out of a magazine. Crystal
chandeliers splashed diamond-like light across the expanse
of the room that was dotted with large circular tables—to
seat ten—all topped with bursts of flowers in tall glasses,
gleaming silverware and hand-designed china. Waiters
floated around with trays of champagne.

Justin reached in his pocket and pulled out the invitation. "We're up front. Table three." He stuck the invitation back into his pocket before stopping a waiter. He took
two glasses of champagne from the tray and handed one
to Bailey. "May this part of the evening fly by," he said
with a wink and tipped his glass to hers.

Bailey's teasing glance caught him over the rim of her
glass. "Let the handshaking begin."

They settled themselves at their table after Justin ran
into several of the guests that he knew, and each time
he proudly introduced Bailey as "my lovely lady." She
couldn't remember ever having been claimed like that by
a man in public. It made her feel valued in a way that she
hadn't experienced before. And he didn't say the things
he did, or do the things he did for her because he could
get something out of it. She had nothing to offer but herself. And that seemed to be enough for him, which made
keeping the news from him about the letter from Harvard that much more difficult. She knew she couldn't wait
much longer.

Shortly after they were seated, Carl and his wife, Gina, arrived, and Gina and Bailey hit it right off. Before long they were talking like old friends that had plenty in common. Bailey wanted Gina to meet Addison, and they talked about setting up a girls' night.

The entrées were served, and the formal part of the evening was under way. The waiters were taking away the plates and preparing to serve the next course when Jasmine appeared at the table with her cousin Stephanie.

"Justin. Hello."

"Jasmine."

Her light brown eyes roamed the table, acknowledged Carl and Gina then settled on Bailey. "I wouldn't expect to see you here."

"And why would that be?" Bailey tossed back.

Jasmine gave a shrug. "I mean, I didn't think that you could get time off from bartending."

Stephanie snickered.

Justin rose, towering over her. He got close, lowered his voice to a stern whisper. "I'm going to tell you this for the last time. We're done. We will never be. Bailey is with me. You don't have to like it. I don't give a damn. But you will respect her."

The color beneath her cheeks heightened. Her nostrils flared as if she couldn't breathe as she blinked back the sting in her eyes.

Stephanie took her arm. "Come on. There's nothing going on over here."

Jasmine looked at Justin with a defeated pain in her eyes before she turned and followed her cousin.

Justin's chest heaved. He sat down, his face stoney. Bailey covered his clenched fist. "Thank you," she mouthed. He leaned over and kissed her lightly.

"Now that we've got that bitch, I mean, business, out of the way, let's eat," Gina said, breaking the last lock of tension at the table.

* * *

As promised, once the meal was over, Justin and Bailey began inching their way to the exit before all the long-winded speeches and awards were presented. He'd already made his five-thousand-dollar contribution, so there was nothing keeping him there, and he was eager to get Bailey out of that dress that had been driving him crazy all night.

This time she didn't stop him when his fingers roamed higher and higher up her skirt to tease the thin covering over her crotch. She could feel herself growing slick with need as she pressed her hand over his to cup it in place. It had taken twenty minutes to get to the hotel, but it seemed to take an eternity to get home.

"I think you'd better take that off. If I get my hands on it I may rip up a perfectly beautiful dress."

"With pleasure," she cooed and blew him a kiss before giving him her back to undo her zipper. "And for now, be gentle."

He made slow work of unzipping her, kissing each inch of succulent flesh as it exposed itself to his hungry eyes.

Bailey quivered as the heat of his kisses shimmied up and down her spine. He peeled the dress away, and she stepped out of it. Justin turned her around; her bare, full breasts brushed against his tux jacket and lit her nipples afire.

"Damn," he groaned before embarking on the feast of her offerings. He lifted the weight of her breasts in his palms and guided them to his mouth. His tongue teased each nipple, nibbling and laving them until they were hard, dark pebbles.

Bailey's fingertips dug into the hard knots of muscle in his arms while she arched her back to give him better access.

"I want to take you, right here, just like this," he said, his breath a hot hiss against her skin. He hooked his fingers along the elastic of her black panties and tugged them down, slid two fingers inside her that took her breath away.

She kicked her panties away and pulled his jacket from his body. The buttons of his shirt were determined to stay in place, but she was just as determined. With his shirt finally undone, the hard span of his chest was hers for the taking, and she took. Her tongue danced along his skin, suckled his nipples, teased the hard lines of his arms while she unfastened his buckle and unzipped him. She took him in her palm and felt him pulse along with the almost painful moan that left his lips. Bailey lowered herself, bit by bit until the head of his cock brushed her lips. She flicked her tongue along the dewy head and was rewarded with his outcry of her name. Little by little she took him in, sucking and licking until he filled the cavern of her mouth to the back of her throat. She wanted all of him, but she'd taken in all that she could. She stroked the rest until he began to rock his pelvis against her mouth. His fingers dug into her hair.

"Ahhh, babe…" He sucked in air through his teeth. He grabbed either side of her head. "Gotta…stop," he managed, even as he continued to thrust against her willing mouth. Then he pulled out and stumbled back, breathing heavily. His eyes were blazing dark pools as if an oil field had been set on fire.

Bailey's wet, puffy lips parted as she looked up at him with her own kind of hunger. He pulled her to her feet and unceremoniously scooped her up and carried her up to his bedroom.

When Justin entered her, she exploded. The sudden intensity of her orgasm slammed through her like an electric charge. Her body vibrated, and she cried out. The pitch of her joy hung in the torrid air. Justin wasn't ready to let go yet. He wanted to remain buried inside her heat and held captive between her thighs.

Bailey moaned and rotated her hips as Justin continued to move within her as her own release began to ebb, then by degrees rise to meet the thrill that Justin stirred inside her. She felt that she would burst from his fullness while his ride toward release intensified with every thrust that became faster, deeper, harder. His breathing escalated, a sheen of sweat dampening his skin. His groans grew heavier. She tightened her hold on him.

"Come. Come to me," she whispered deep in his ear.

The erotic words mixed with the quick sucking of her insides on his throbbing member sent him hurtling over the edge.

"That was…there are no words," Bailey said.

"My sentiments exactly." He kissed the back of her neck and pulled her closer. He sighed in satisfaction. "It's good having you here." He kissed her again.

"I like being here."

"There's plenty more room in the closets," he said suggestively.

For an instant, she froze. "What are you saying?"

"I'm saying that I have no problem with you being here…full-time."

She turned over. Her eyes searched his face in the dimness. "Move in?"

"Why not? Plenty of space."

She paused. "Justin, I need to tell you something." She felt him tense.

"What is it?"

"I got the letter from Harvard. They offered me a scholarship for a year, and…I'm going to take it."

The seconds of silence were eternal.

"Babe, that's amazing. I'm so happy for you. I know how much you want this." He gathered her close, bringing her into the hollow of his neck. He stared out into the darkness. "Harvard. That is big-time. When would you have to leave?"

"Umm, five weeks. I have to look for off-campus housing." She fluttered a laugh. "I think I'm a bit old to live in a dorm."

Justin chuckled absently. "Very true...not saying that you're old or anything," he added in jest.

Bailey nudged him. She drew in a breath. "I know this is going to change things between us...the distance. But I want us to find a way to work it out." She clutched his shoulder and tried to gauge his expression.

He kissed the top of her head. "Of course we will. Let's not worry about that now. You have plans to make."

Chapter 23

"Harvard. That's major," Carl said. He lifted his bottle of Coors and took a long swallow. "How is that going to play out with you two?"

Justin stretched out on the lounge chair on the back deck, tucked his hands beneath his head and closed his eyes against the setting sun. A light evening breeze ruffled the trees.

"Good question. We were just settling into a rhythm. I gave her a key."

"You what?"

"Yeah, man."

"That's a serious move."

"That's how I'm feeling about her—serious."

"Man. Well, they say that long-distance relationships can work," he said without much conviction.

"They who?"

"You know. Them. Those people that take those surveys."

"And you would know that how?"

"I hear things."

Justin cut him a look. "Whatever, man." He paused. "Would you do it?"

"Have a long-distance relationship?"

"Yes."

"I guess it depends on how long and how invested I was."

"What if it was Gina?"

"Hmm. If you'd asked me that before we got married, I probably would have said no. Now…it would be hard, but I'd do it if it would keep us together. I can't see myself without Gina."

Justin sighed heavily. Maintaining a relationship was tough enough with all the curves that life could throw, then add in long distance and you were asking for trouble.

"What about Xavier or LSU?" Carl asked, cutting into Justin's thoughts.

"She's going on scholarship."

Carl's brows rose then fell. "Oh."

"Oh, what?"

"Nothing. I'm just saying, oh." He waited a beat. "If it's about money…maybe you could help her out and then she could stay."

"Ha! You don't know Bailey. She's so damned independent and determined to do everything on her own, her way, that she'd cut my head off for even suggesting it. I hinted at it once before and she went nuclear. Naw, not an option."

"Then you don't have much of a choice. She's going to Harvard, and you are either going the long-distance route or walking away."

Justin closed his eyes. Walking away wasn't in the plan.

Bailey hurried through the main level of the Mercury Lounge and went straight to her office. Since the one-on-one between Vincent and Justin, Vincent had remained on the perimeter of her life. They only spoke about business, and to be honest, she missed their former camaraderie— at least what she thought was a friendship. Soon it would all be moot anyway. She had to give her notice, and she needed to do that sooner rather than later.

She stowed her purse in her desk drawer, locked it then turned on the computer to verify the staffing for the night. With that out of the way, she wanted to have the conversation with Vincent and get that out of the way, too. She didn't want the knowledge of her departure and the ensuing conversation to hang over her head longer than necessary.

Bailey stepped out of her office, locked the door and then walked farther down the hall to Vincent's office. She hoped he was there and that she wouldn't have to make a "special time" to talk to him.

A stream of light peeked out from under his door. She moved forward. Stopping in front, she drew in a breath of resolve and knocked on the door.

"Come in."

Bailey opened the door and stepped in. "Vincent, I want to talk to you."

"What is it?" he asked without looking up.

Bailey stepped closer and sat down in the chair by his desk. "You know that my long-term goal was to go back to law school."

He glanced up at her through his lashes then looked back at what he was writing. "And?"

"Well, I got accepted to Harvard. Classes start in five weeks. I'm giving my two-weeks' notice."

Vincent put down his pen, pushed back and leaned in his seat and looked at her. "Congratulations. I know that's what you wanted."

"Yes, it is." She dared to smile, being hard-pressed to contain her excitement.

He was thoughtful for a moment, and his steady stare was making Bailey uncomfortable.

"You're going to be hard to replace. But there comes a time when we all have to move on to bigger and better things. Good luck."

"Thank you, Vincent. And thank you for giving me a chance here." She pushed up from her seat and stood. "I better get to my station."

"No need."

"Huh?"

"You can leave tonight. No reason to drag out the inevitable."

Her mouth dropped open. "But I still have three weeks to work," she cried.

He gave a slight shrug. "We'll mail you your check."

She was so furious that she could barely see in front of her. He was really going to screw her like this? Her entire body was white-hot with rage, but she'd never let him see her sweat. "Fine. I'll get my things and be gone." Her throat tightened. She spun away and walked out.

When she unlocked the door to her office her hands were shaking, and tears of fury and impotence stung her eyes. Was he really that vindictive? What was she going to do for money? She had bills to pay and plans to make. Damn you, Vincent!

Through blurry eyes, she went through her desk and took out any personal items, which were few. She put her files on a flash drive that she kept in her purse, took a last look around and walked out.

When she arrived at what would have been her post for the night, Mellie instantly knew that something was wrong.

"What's going on? Are you all right?"

Bailey blinked away the sting of her tears. She took her office keys out of her purse and placed them on the bar top. "I no longer work here."

"What!"

Bailey gave her the abbreviated version.

"I'm happy for you, Bailey. I know how much you wanted it. This is your shot, girl, but I'm going to miss you like crazy." She shook her head slowly. "I can't believe that bastard did that to you."

"I can't worry about it."

"Are you going to be okay money-wise?"

"I'll work it out."

Mellie reached across the bar and covered her hand. "Stay in touch, okay?"

"I will. Promise." She offered a tight smile, turned and walked out. By the time she walked the half block to where she'd parked, the tears were flowing in earnest. A wave of panic assaulted her. What was she going to do? Five weeks without an income?

She'd told Justin earlier that she would come to his house when she got off, but she wasn't up to seeing him. She couldn't have him know how bad things were and how scared she was. But he'd be expecting her. She'd call him when she got home.

When she got home, all she had the will to do was stretch out on her bed and stare at the ceiling. She had to figure something out, but her thoughts kept swimming in endless circles. At some point she must have dozed off, and it was the ringing of her cell phone that jerked her out of a restless sleep.

She fumbled with the phone in the dark. Justin.

"Hey," she said, trying to sound cheery and wide-awake.

"Hey yourself. How's everything going? You sounded like you were sleeping." He chuckled.

"I...was actually."

"Sleeping on the job?"

"I'm home."

"Are you sick? What's wrong?"

"Silly me, I got my schedule wrong. I wasn't on for tonight."

Justin let the silence hang there for a minute. "What happened, Bailey? As organized and precise as you are, that would never happen."

"Can we talk tomorrow? I'm really tired."

"You're not going to tell me what's wrong?"

"Nothing. Nothing that I can't handle with a little sleep."

"This isn't cool. I'm not going to ask you anymore. But know that this isn't cool. Whatever is going on with you, we are in it together. But we can't be if you want to keep walking the line by yourself when you don't have to."

"Vincent let me go tonight."

"Say what?"

She squeezed her eyes shut and visualized the steely look that she was certain was on Justin's face. "I told him that I would be leaving in five weeks for school and I was giving my two-weeks' notice. He basically told me there was no reason to finish out my two weeks and that tonight was my last day."

He muttered an expletive. "I'm coming over. Answer the door."

"Justin!"

He'd already hung up.

Bailey got up from the bed and began pacing her apartment. Justin was right; she should feel comfortable enough to tell him anything, and not be leery of asking for advice or help or support. But old habits die hard. She was constantly battling the demons of her past. Already she could see herself falling into the trap of being taken care of by a man. The car. The dress. His coming to her defense the first time with Vincent. The key to his house. All of those were small things when looked at singularly. But together they added up to becoming dependent on someone else for your survival, for your happiness. She couldn't do it. Even though he'd said he loved her, it was still hard to let go.

More than an hour had passed since she'd spoken to Justin. It didn't take that long to get from his part of town to hers. She hoped nothing had happened and went to the window to see if his car was coming, just as her downstairs doorbell rang. She buzzed him in.

When she pulled open the door and saw him standing there with nothing but love in his eyes, her soul opened up, and she fell into his arms. She inhaled him like fuel for an engine and he held her, not saying a word. He didn't need to, because she realized that his being there said everything.

"Come in," she finally said when she could let him go.

Justin closed the door behind him. "Apryl here?"

"She went back home. She said she wanted to give me back my space. Can I get you anything?"

"No. I'm good." He sat on the couch and extended his hand to her. She took it and sat beside him. He draped his arm around her shoulder. "First of all, if that's the way he wants to treat you after the time and service that you put in to make his establishment successful, the hell with him. It's his loss. And it shows you the kind of man he really is." He reached in his pocket and pulled out an envelope. "After our little chat, he seemed to understand the error of his way of thinking." He handed her the envelope.

"What is this?"

"Open it and see for yourself."

Hesitantly she took the envelope and opened it. Inside was a check for easily twice the amount that she was owed. She stared at the numbers in disbelief then turned wide eyes on Justin.

"What is this? How…?"

"He owed it. He paid it."

"Justin. What did you do?"

"I didn't break his knees, if that's what you're thinking," he said in jest. "I simply had a talk with him. When I finished talking, he understood how wrong he was and wanted to make it up to you."

She studied his expression, which didn't change from its matter-of-fact demeanor, as if convincing people to do what he wanted, to buy into his idea, was second nature. The truth—it was. He was a seasoned attorney who molded, spun and presented information for a living—a good living. She had no idea what she was going to do being out of a job and with no money in sight. Now, thanks to Justin, it was a non-issue. Then she felt that old demon slip in under the door and take a seat in between them. This was all part of the same pattern of turning yourself over to someone else; giving them the power over you and the direction your life would take. It was easy to succumb when your back was against a wall, easy to simply "let it happen," because there was no other way, until one day you didn't know who you were, and when your almighty benefactor left, you were left with nothing and no one.

Bailey stared at the check. Her thoughts twisted in her head. "Thank you," she said finally.

"You take what is owed to you. All the time. Every time. If you are going to be a lawyer, that's one of the first lessons of making a deal. You must make your opponent believe that negotiating is to their benefit, when in the end, its yours." He leaned over and kissed her forehead.

"I'll try to remember that."

"Speaking of becoming a lawyer, what are you going to do about someplace to live?"

"The school mailed a list of off-campus housing. I'm going to make a few calls. Now that I have time on my hands…"

"How do you see things working out between you and me?"

She sighed heavily. "To be honest, I don't know." She turned her body toward his. "I want us to work. I need us to work. Whatever it takes. I know it won't be easy."

"And with me working to get The Justice Project up and running, it will put us to the test." He stroked her face. "I always did well on tests," he said, his voice dropping an octave.

Bailey grinned. "So did I. Top of my class."

He leaned in. "Impressive," he uttered before melding his lips with hers. "Me, too."

Chapter 24

"Girl, not only is the man wealthy and sexy as hell, he's a damn superhero, too."

Bailey burst out laughing. "Addy, you are a pure fool."

"What else do you call a man who 'comes to the rescue?' He's been there for you from the start. You are one lucky woman."

"I know that I should feel lucky. I know that I am."

"But?"

"But I feel that the more he gives, the more he offers, the more I will lose of myself."

"Do you know how many women would love to be in your shoes?"

"Hmm." She continued cutting up the cucumbers for the salad. Addison had a bridal shower that she was catering for, and since Bailey had the time, she offered to help with the preparations.

"I'm going to miss you when you leave."

Bailey began to rinse and devein the shrimp. "I'm going to miss you like crazy," she said just above a tight whisper. "But we can visit, write. I'll try to come down on breaks…"

"But it won't be the same." Addison sighed.

"I know," Bailey said as she tossed the shrimp shells onto a layer of newspaper.

As much as she tried to pretend that life would remain virtually unchanged, she knew she was deluding herself. But this was her chance. She had to take it or she would never forgive herself, even if taking that chance meant leaving the ones you love behind.

During the next few weeks leading up to her departure, she realized day by day what a blessing in disguise it was to be let go early from the Mercury Lounge. Every day there was an endless list of things to do. She'd finally decided on a one-bedroom apartment, about six blocks from campus. She'd taken a virtual tour, spoke with the landlord and then mailed her month's rent and security. The next step was packing and having her belongings shipped up. Fortunately, her current lease was month to month, and she'd given her current landlord plenty of notice.

Bailey came back from The Home Depot with more boxes. She stopped at her mailbox and checked for mail while also making a mental note to stop by the post office and have her mail forwarded.

Her sisters were already in her apartment to help with the packing when she returned. Seeing them together, laughing and teasing each other, filled her soul with a kind of joy that was hard to name.

"Hey, folks," she announced, dropping the boxes by the door and tossing the mail on the table. She stood in the center of the chaos with her hands on her hips, taking it all in.

"I sorted all the clothes," Tory said. "By season. Your warmer things are marked. You'll need those first."

"Your books are all boxed up, and I just finished up with your pots and dishes. I left a couple out for you to use until...you leave," Apryl said.

"You guys are so wonderful. I'm practically packed." Bailey grinned.

"We wanted to do this. You're forever putting your life on hold for us, sacrificing for us. It's way past time that we took care of ourselves and let you have a life, go after your own happiness," Apryl said.

Bailey could barely believe the words she was hearing. She'd longed for them, but never thought she'd hear them. "Thank you," she choked.

"That doesn't mean that I'm not still going to be a pain in the ass," Tory teased.

Apryl threw a pillow from the couch at Tory and they all laughed and hugged and laughed some more.

When her sisters had piled out of her tiny apartment, she looked around at the stack of boxes and the empty cabinets. A chapter of her life was closing, and a new one would begin very soon.

So much had happened in the past few months. If anyone would have told her that she would have found the love of an amazing man, got admitted into one of the top law schools in the country, would be leaving her home state of Louisiana and had forged a new and mature relationship with her sisters, she wouldn't have believed it. Life.

She stepped around the boxes stacked neatly in her living room, picked up her mail from the kitchen table and took it to her bedroom. She tossed it on the nightstand, and the familiar Louisiana State University logo, sticking out from a magazine, stopped her cold. She lifted up the magazine and plucked out the letter that had been stuck in between the pages. She flipped the envelope over and ripped open the flap. Her heart raced as she read the letter of congratulations. The letter stated that she was being considered for a full scholarship at LSU for the fall, and the admissions committee wanted to arrange an interview on August 10. Tomorrow!

Bailey spun around in a circle of crazy excitement. She read the letter three times to make sure that she had not misread it. She didn't. They wanted to meet with her.

She tucked the letter back into the envelope, picked up her cell phone and called Justin. She was so giddy with excitement, he had to ask her to slow down and repeat herself.

"Babe, that is incredible. Talk about the eleventh hour. What time tomorrow?"

"Noon."

"Okay. I was going to tell you to come over, but you need a good night's sleep so that you will be at the top of your game tomorrow. But I know you are going to wow them. It's probably all formality. It's yours. I just know it."

"Oh, Justin. This would mean I could stay here."

"It would. Are you willing to let go of the idea of Harvard?"

She was quiet for a moment. "I would still get to attend law school and I would be here with you."

"I want you to be happy."

"I am, Justin, happier than I have been in a very long time, and I owe so much of that happiness to you."

"I love you, Bailey. Whatever it takes to show you…"

"The way you love me…"

"What, babe? The way I love you, what?"

"Makes me feel…like someone who'd been dying of thirst and that thirst is finally quenched. I feel whole, valued."

"And for as long as you let me, I'm going to do everything in my power to keep you feeling that way. Now, you get some rest. Call me in the morning."

"Okay. I will."

"Good night."

"I love you," she said softly.

"And I love to hear you say it. Now, go to bed. Dream of tomorrow and us."

She grinned from the inside out. "Night."

Bailey had taken extra time preparing for her interview. She'd gone over and over in her head the kinds of questions that might be tossed at her so that she could be ready for any eventuality. She arrived with more than twenty minutes to spare before her scheduled appointment. She cooled her heels in the reception waiting area and bided her time watching the comings and goings of staff. Finally, the assistant to the dean of admissions came over and said to follow her.

She was led down a long, carpeted corridor, whose walls were dotted with large framed photographs of the learned and somber faces of past college presidents and chairmen. It was a bit intimidating, but Bailey took it in stride. She deserved to be here.

The assistant opened a heavy mahogany door and stepped aside so that Bailey could enter.

"Dean Withers, this is Ms. Sinclair."

Coleman Withers removed his half-frame glasses and smiled up at Bailey. He rose from his seat and came around his desk. "Ms. Sinclair." He extended his hand, which she shook. "Thank you for coming."

"I should be thanking you."

"Please have a seat. Can I get you anything?"

"Water would be fine."

He looked to his assistant. "Would you bring us some water, Diane?"

"Right away."

"Have any trouble finding us?" he mildly joked.

Bailey smiled. "No, not at all. Parking is a bit of a maze."

He chuckled. "Yes, it's been the battle cry for years, but—" he gave a slight shrug "—we've accepted it as part of the LSU charm."

Whatever anxiety that Bailey had been feeling peeled away. Dean Withers made her feel totally comfortable and relaxed.

His assistant returned with a glass pitcher of water and glasses on a tray. She set them on the table. "Will you be needing anything else?"

"No. Thank you, Diane.

"So, tell me about yourself and why you want to come to LSU."

Bailey had gone over this part of what she was going to say at least a dozen times. The words flowed easy as the Mississippi.

"You are exactly the kind of candidate that we want in our law department here at LSU," he said once she'd finished. "And I can guarantee that the program and the sense of family here at the university will make your time with us years that you will cherish."

Bailey listened and felt like she was on cloud nine. Yes, she had Harvard on a lock, but LSU offered her everything she wanted, as well, and she could stay in Baton Rouge and with Justin.

"It isn't often that we give full-ride scholarships. But with your grades, your statement of purpose essay and of course meeting you…I have no doubt that we made the right decision." He smiled broadly. "And of course any friend of the Lawson family is a friend of ours. One of our biggest benefactors."

Bailey's heart seemed to stop then banged in her chest. "Lawson?"

His face turned almost crimson. He cleared his throat. "Wonderful family," he stuttered.

Bailey felt sick. Justin did this. He arranged for the entire thing. Was her scholarship a real one, or was he paying for that, as well? Her temples began to pound. She pushed up from her seat and extended her hand. "Thank you for your time, Dean Withers."

Before he had the chance to react to his faux pas, Bailey was out the door and practically running down the hallway. How could he do this to her? Manipulate her life? Where would it all end?

Bailey could barely see through the cloud of tears that continued to fill her eyes and the wall of fury that boiled and bubbled up from her stomach. She was giving him back his damned car, his freaking keys and the fairy-tale life that he thought he was going to shove down her throat. She'd called Addison and told her to meet her at Justin's house. Even as Addy pressed, Bailey wouldn't get into details on the phone because she knew that Addy would try to talk her out of it.

Addison had actually beat her there and was parked on the road leading to the entry gate of the house. Bailey slowed and pulled up alongside Addison.

"I'll be right back." She screeched onto Justin's driveway, before Addison could blink, spitting up dirt and dust and came to a halt right at the front step. She snatched her belongings from the passenger seat, got out and stomped up to the front door. She didn't bother to use her key or ring the bell; instead she left the house keys on the mat along with the keys to the Benz. She drew in a shuddering breath, spun away and hurried down the winding walkway and out to the road where Addison was parked.

Bailey tugged the door open and flung herself into the seat. She jammed the seat belt buckle in the slot and folded her arms defiantly in front of her.

Addison knew that when Bailey took that stance and that hot look burned in her eyes, that it was best to keep distant until she was ready to talk. Otherwise one risked getting their head bitten off. She pulled out and got back on the main throughway that led back to their part of town. Periodically, Addison stole furtive glances in Bailey's direction. Her stoic countenance never changed. The suspense was killing her.

"I guess you must know that it's over," Bailey finally said, her voice raw and hoarse.

"I figured as much. But why, B? You were head over heels happy."

"Just proves what I've been saying all along about

relationships—" her voice cracked "—and men wanting to control your life."

"You really sure this is how you want to deal with this?"

"The whole meeting at LSU was manipulated by Justin!" she blurted out, hurtling the conversation in a different direction. "The scholarship, admittance, everything. He used his family name to get me in and pulled the strings to get the full-ride scholarship."

Addison frowned. "And you're pissed...why? Girl, do you have any idea what a lucky damned woman you are?"

"You don't understand, Addy." She folded her arms tighter as images of the trail of uncles drifted across her line of vision, the tears, the breakups, the highs and lows that her mother endured, just to have a man take care of her. No, she would never go down that road, not even for Justin Lawson.

"You're right. I don't understand. The man loves you. You love him. Maybe he shouldn't have pulled strings without telling you, but damn, girl, I know how you are, and I'm sure he does, too. Did it ever occur to you that he did it because he would be crazy lonely without you?"

Bailey pressed her lips together. "Doesn't excuse what he did. And what next? This is my time, my life, my dream, and I'm not going to have anyone twist it to suit themselves. I've held off on doing me for a long time, Addy. This is me time, on my terms, not the me that he wants me to be."

Addison blew out a breath and slowly shook her head. "I still think you're making a big mistake."

"It wouldn't be the first time."

They spent the balance of the drive to Bailey's apartment in silence. Addison pulled up in front of Bailey's building. "Want me to come up?"

"No." She unfastened her seat belt. "I need some time."

"If you want to talk..."

Bailey turned toward her friend and managed a pained

smile. "I know. Thanks for coming." She leaned over and kissed Addison's cheek, then got out of the car.

"Call me!"

Bailey raised her hand in acknowledgment, mounted the three stairs to the front door of her building and went inside. The moment she was safely on the other side of her door and looked around at her life stacked in boxes, the well of tears that she'd held in abeyance, broke loose. She slid down to the floor until she came to rest on her haunches, covered her face with her hands and wept.

Chapter 25

Justin pulled into his driveway and was thrilled but surprised to see the Benz parked right in front of the house. Bailey must have decided to come straight to him after her interview. As he got out of the Lexus, the feelings of happy anticipation began to dissipate. The angle of the car was all wrong, as if it had been thrown to a stop. He walked past the car and up the steps to the front door and saw the house key and the keys to the car tossed on the welcome mat.

Slowly he bent down and picked them up. He turned back to look at the car. Whatever idea he may have had about Bailey being home to greet him was wishful thinking. This was bad, very bad.

Justin put the key in the door and then shut it behind him. The multi-bedroom, two-story mansion echoed with emptiness. The weight of the silence pressed down on him in a way that it had never done before. The enormity of his aloneness bounced off the walls and settled around him.

He pulled off his jacket and tossed it on the chair. He dug his cell phone from his pants pocket and held it in front of him. No matter when he placed the call it wouldn't be good. He pressed number one on the keypad to speed-dial Bailey, and paced the room while he listened to the phone ring until her voice mail came on.

"Bailey, it's me. We need to talk. Call me." He started to hang up. "Please." He disconnected the call then tapped in Carl's number.

"Damn, man. Sounds like you really ticked her off," Carl was saying after hearing what Justin had found when he got home.

"That's an understatement. I had doubts about interfering..."

"But you stopped thinking with your head," Carl said.

"Man, don't go there. It's more than that."

"I know. I know. So what are you going to do?"

"I can't do much of anything until I get to talk to her."

"Maybe you should just go over there. Plead your case, counselor."

"No. If I know Bailey she won't listen. She probably wouldn't let me in." He exhaled.

"Hopefully, she'll call and you two can work it out."

"Yeah," Justin groused, not feeling at all confident.

Justin called Bailey three different times throughout the evening. Each time his call went to voice mail. He could sit in front of her house. She had to come out sometime. Then what? He wouldn't get into a personal squabble on the street. All he could do was wait.

At some point he'd drifted off. Sunrise was making its way above the horizon. He groaned. He'd fallen asleep in the armchair. His muscles were in knots. Then the events of the previous night came flooding back. He snatched up his cell phone that had fallen onto his lap and stared at the face for a list of missed calls. There were no calls, and there were no texts from Bailey. He tossed the phone across the room and ran his hand across his stubbled chin then pushed up from the chair with a mild groan.

Shower and coffee, then he'd figure out what to do next.

"How many times did he call?" Addison asked.

"All together, six."

"B, you need to talk to him."

"There's nothing to talk about, and I'm not going to

give him the opportunity to sweet-talk me into believing that his going behind my back was for my own good."

"Fine. Don't call."

"That's it? You aren't going to badger me to death about calling him?"

"Nope. I'm out of it. This is your decision. You need me to come over and help with anything?"

Bailey sighed. "Everything is done. I called a moving company. They are going to pick up my boxes this afternoon."

"This afternoon!"

"Yes. I decided that I may as well go up there a little earlier and...get settled."

"You really mean get away from Justin and this asshole decision you've made."

"I thought you didn't have anything else to say about it."

"I lied."

"It's part of it," she finally admitted.

"You don't have to do this."

"Yeah, I do. I already called and confirmed the off-campus apartment and paid my deposit over the phone—thanks to the money I got from being fired." The money that Justin had gotten for her. She shook away the thought. "I'm leaving this weekend."

"Bailey! That doesn't give me any time."

"For what?"

"To plan a going-away party or something. You can't just leave like this."

"No fanfare. Just us girls. Promise."

"Okay, my place. Thursday night."

"Sounds fine. I'll be there. I'll call my sisters."

"Love you."

"You, too."

Bailey held the phone to her chest and closed her eyes. She missed him. Deep down to the soles of her feet, she missed him. But she was so angry and disillusioned and betrayed. What he'd done scared her. She knew it was a ridiculous emotion, but she couldn't help it. The idea that Justin had the power to mold the direction of her life, strip her of her independence so that she relied on only him, terrified her.

Getting away was what she had to do. *Justin. Justin. Justin.*

Justin called her at least three times a day for the next four days. He'd sent flowers, cards, text messages. All he wanted to do was talk to her, he'd said. It was most difficult at night when she was alone staring at the crack that ran across her ceiling. She wanted to call him, hear his voice; she wanted to feel his touch, taste him. She wanted to wrap her legs around his broad back and feel him fill her to her throat. Instead, she stared at the crack in the ceiling.

Her apartment was empty of the boxes and clothes that she'd had shipped to her new apartment. Tory got a new job that would pay her a decent salary and pay for her to return to school. Apryl swore that she was going to work on herself before she got involved in another relationship. All things considered, Bailey felt comfortable leaving her siblings. It really seemed like they were going to be able to stand on their own two feet. Of course, she was only a phone call away. It was definitely ladies' night, and Addison was in her element from the spread of food, wine and great music. The girls laughed and shared stories of all of their crazy antics growing up, all the secrets they'd shared, the losses and heartaches.

This was good. This is what she needed, to be reminded that all she'd sacrificed over the years was worth it. Her sisters were going to be fine, and so was she.

The ringing doorbell snapped through the laughter and music.

"The strippers are here!" Tory screeched in delight and gave a high five to Apryl.

Addison left her living room to go to the door. Moments later she returned, and Justin walked in behind her.

Addison, Apryl and Tory all shared a knowing look, offered their greetings and eased out of the room and out to the back deck.

"Hey," Justin said softly. He stuck his hands in his pockets and kept his distance.

Bailey's heart was pounding so loud and so fast, she didn't respond. Justin took a step toward her. "Addison told me that you were leaving tomorrow."

Bailey swallowed and nodded her head.

"You weren't going to say goodbye?"

"Thought I did that already."

The muscles in his face jerked. "I wasn't trying to run your life, Bailey."

"Really? What do you call it when you manipulate and maneuver a situation for your benefit without regard to anyone else?"

"I did it for you, Bailey. And yes, I had selfish reasons." He took a step closer. She curled tighter in her seat. "I didn't want you to leave. I didn't want to risk what we were starting to build. I was wrong." He lowered his head, shaking it slowly. "It was your decision, and I took it away from you." He looked directly into her eyes. "I did it because I love you, and I didn't want to lose you."

Bailey pushed herself up from her seat and walked over to him. "You can't run my life in the name of love, Justin. It will never work between us if you do. I know you have connections and power and money and stuff that I can only imagine, but when we are together it's got to be about us, the decisions made about our relationship have to be made by both of us."

"Whatever you want." He reached out and clasped her shoulders.

His touch thrilled her to the marrow of her bones. Inwardly, she sighed.

"I'm sorry, baby." He stroked her cheek with his finger. "I need you to forgive me. Can you do that? Can you forgive me?" He lifted her chin so that she had to look in his eyes.

"I'll think about it," she taunted.

"It's a start." He slowly lowered his head until his lips touched hers, and the contact shot through him with such force that it pushed his groan of want up from the center of his being and across his lips.

Bailey inhaled his need that fed her own. She sank into his body, and the security of his arms wrapped around her, holding her, assuring her that whatever it would take, he would do.

"I don't know what I would have done if I'd lost you," he murmured against her mouth before tasting the sweetness of the wine on her tongue. "You leave in the morning…" He caressed her waist.

"Yes," she managed as he trailed kisses along her neck.

"Then we don't have much time. Come home with me."

"What about…" She jerked her head toward the back deck.

"Believe me, they'll understand. Get your things."

It was clear that it wasn't a question. It was a statement. But this time she didn't care that he wasn't asking what she wanted, but telling her what she needed—a night with the man that she loved.

Chapter 26

"If it's okay with you, I'll fly you up in the morning."

Bailey sighed and stretched her limbs that had gotten a serious workout from the moment they'd crossed the threshold of his home. She smiled in the darkness. "I'd like that."

"So glad that you approve, Ms. Sinclair." He chuckled and caressed her bare hip, and the simple action had him growing hard again. "Hmm. Turn on your stomach," he said deep in her ear.

Bailey glanced at him then turned onto her stomach.

Justin pulled one of the overstuffed down pillows from the top of the bed and pushed it under Bailey's pelvis, raising her round derriere to bring it closer. He kissed the back of her neck, nibbled her ears and stroked the curve of her spine with his tongue until she was one electrified nerve. He reached between her and the pillow and toyed with the hard bud of her sex until her body shuddered, and her soft whimpers rose to cries, begging him to make her come.

"Not yet," he whispered. His fingers played with her until they were slick with her need, and then he entered her in one deep thrust that forced the air out of her lungs. He grabbed her hips to control exactly how fast and how deep he wanted things to go. She was totally at his mercy. He took his time to make her beg for release. And she did, again and again.

* * *

"I've never been on a private plane," Bailey said as she stepped on board. She had to admit, even if not to Justin, that this beat flying commercial any day.

"Make yourself comfortable." He stowed their carry-on luggage in the overhead bins.

A flight attendant came by with a tray of refreshments. Bailey opted for an iced tea and settled down into the plush leather seat. "Do you know how to fly?"

"Mmm-hmm." He buckled his belt, turned to her and grinned.

"What else do I need to know about you?"

Justin grinned. "We have years to unwrap all of my secrets."

"I like the sound of that…years."

"So do I."

When they landed in Boston, Justin had a car waiting for them to take them to her new apartment. They stopped at the management office where she picked up her keys.

The apartment was just like the pictures, open and airy with modern touches. The one bedroom was small but cozy, and there was a small terrace that added a bit of ambiance. The delivery company had brought in all of the boxes. Her new bed was being delivered, so for the time being she'd have to sleep on the pullout couch that came with the apartment.

"This is nice," Justin said, looking around and taking inventory. "I'm going to like staying here."

"Staying here?"

"I thought I'd wait until you got here before I told you."

"Told me what, Justin?"

"I'm going to be relocating…to Boston. My work, The

Justice Project, can succeed from here as well as from Baton Rouge. Carl can handle things on that end."

"Justin…"

"I know you have this thing about anyone other than you moving the puzzle pieces of your life around. But this time, Bailey—" he stepped up to her "—I'm making an executive decision for the both of us. Now, if you have a problem with that, tell me now."

Her heart thundered, and her soul swelled with happiness. She stepped into his arms. "Whatever you say, Mr. Lawson."

He pulled her tight and sealed their pact with a kiss.

* * * * *

DR CINDERELLA'S MIDNIGHT FLING

KATE HARDY

For Fiona – my very best friend and the sister I wish
I had – with much love.

CHAPTER ONE

'CINDERELLA, you are *so* going to the ball,' Sorcha said as Jane opened her front door.

Jane stared at her best friend. 'But I've only just got in from late shift.'

'Perfect timing, then.' Sorcha glanced at her watch. 'The taxi's going to be here in thirty minutes, so you don't have time to argue.'

'I don't have anything to wear.'

'Yes, you do. Right here. It's an unbirthday present from me because I saw it when I was in town and thought the colour was just perfect for you.' Sorcha waved a carrier bag at her. 'Go and have a shower and wash your hair. I'll dry it for you and do your make-up.'

'But—' Jane began, and then subsided. She knew from past experience that, once Sorcha was in full bossy mode, there was no stopping her.

'It's not as if you've got anything better to do tonight,' Sorcha added. 'And ironing and cleaning your bathroom don't count. You didn't go to a single one of the Christmas nights out, you're always switching your duty so you can avoid team nights out, and it's well past time you stopped letting Shaun ruin your life.'

Jane didn't have an answer for any of that. She knew it was all true.

Sorcha hugged her swiftly. 'I know he hurt you badly, Janey, but you can't hide behind work for the rest of your life. Look, I'm not telling you to go and have a wild fling with the first man you meet. Just come out with me tonight and enjoy yourself. Have some fun.'

Jane wrinkled her nose. 'There's a teensy problem. I don't actually have a ticket for the ball.' She'd given a donation toward the funds instead.

'Actually, you do have one. From Maddie and Theo, with their love—and she says if you say you can't accept it, then she'll accept a promise of babysitting one evening in return, but you're coming to the ball and that's final. And Theo echoed the lot.'

Jane knew when she was beaten. 'I can hardly argue with my boss,' she said wryly.

'Attagirl.' Sorcha smiled at her. 'You've got twenty-seven minutes. Go, go, go!'

By the time the taxi arrived, Jane hardly recognised herself. She normally kept her hair tied back in a pony-tail at work, but Sorcha had blow-dried it into a sleek bob. Her make-up was light but still managed to emphasise her hazel eyes and make them sparkle. And the dress was the prettiest she'd ever seen, with a swishy skirt that made her feel light on her feet; it fitted as if it had been made to measure.

'Perfect,' Sorcha said with an approving nod. 'Let's go.'

'What do you mean, you can't make it?' Ed asked.

'I'm stuck in Suffolk,' George explained.

Ed's heart skipped a beat as a nasty thought hit him. 'Is Dad all right?'

'As far as I know. I'm not at the hall.'

'Uh-huh.' So there could only be one other reason why his older brother was standing him up, Ed thought. He'd had a better offer than a hospital charity ball. 'A girl,' he said with a sigh.

'No, actually. My car had a slight argument with a tree.'

'*What*? Are you all right?'

'I'm fine. Nobody's hurt, except the car. Stop fussing,' George said. 'Metal's easily fixed.'

'I'm a doctor. If you tell me you've crashed your car, of course I'm going to fuss,' Ed retorted.

'Honestly, I'm fine. Not a scratch on me—unlike my poor car. I'll be back in London later in the week. I'm just sorry I've let you down.'

'Just as long as you're really OK. What happened?'

'I took the corner a bit too fast,' George said cheerfully. 'But I've learned my lesson, so don't nag. I spent *hours* polishing that chrome to perfection. I'll be more careful in future.'

Ed could see exactly why his stepmother had begged him to talk some sense into his older brother. Not that he thought George would actually listen to him, but maybe some of Ed's seriousness and common sense would rub off on George and he'd steady down a bit. 'OK. I'll see you when you're back. Try not to break your neck.'

George just laughed. 'Have a good time tonight.'

Ed replaced the receiver and straightened his bow tie. Well, it wasn't the end of the world that he had to go to the ball on his own. It was a chance to meet some of his new colleagues and have some fun, as well as raising money for specialist equipment at the London Victoria.

He'd liked Theo Petrakis, the senior consultant, at their first meeting. And the photograph of the three little girls on his desk had sealed the deal: Theo was very clearly a family man. Just as Ed was, too; his decision to move back to London from Glasgow was less to do with being promoted and more to do with being nearer to his brother and his sisters. Prompted partly by a quiet phone call from Frances saying that George desperately needed someone to talk sense into him before he broke his neck doing some extreme sport or other.

That was Ed's slot in the family: the younger son of Lord Somers was the sensible, serious one who fixed things. George, the heir to the barony, dated a different gorgeous girl each week and would be the first one down a double black diamond ski run, making him a firm favourite with the paparazzi. And sometimes Ed really worried that his brother was going too far. Still. There was nothing he could do about it tonight. Once George was back in London, he'd take his brother out to dinner and see if he could talk him into calming down just enough to stop the rest of the family worrying themselves sick about him.

'Jake's over there—and he's on his own,' Jane pointed out as she and Sorcha walked into the ballroom.

'And?'

'Sorcha, this is the *ball*. It's your chance to get him to notice that you're stunning as well as good at your job.'

Sorcha shrugged. 'Some other time. I'm not aban-

doning you on your first night out since...' Her words
tailed off.

Jane met it head on. 'Since Shaun.' Her ex-fiancé.
Who'd cheated on Jane with her twin sister and shattered every illusion Jane had. 'I know. But it's not as if
I don't know most of the people here. I can look after
myself.' Jane smiled at her. 'And anyway, I need to find
Maddie and Theo to thank them for the ticket. Go and
talk to Jake.'

'Are you sure?'

'Very sure.' Jake and Sorcha would make a great
couple; Jane thought he just needed to wake up and see
what was right under his nose. 'Go for it. I'll see you
later. Good luck!'

Once Sorcha was on her way over to Jake, Jane
sought out her boss and his wife. 'Thank you so much
for the ticket.'

'Our pleasure, Janey,' Maddie Petrakis said, hugging
her. 'I'm just glad Sorcha talked you into it.'

'But I'm definitely babysitting for you. Two nights,'
Jane added.

'Janey, you look lovely.' Theo, the senior consultant
on the maternity ward, gave her an appreciative smile.
'If I was single, I'd be sweeping you off your feet.'

'Yeah, yeah.' She flapped a dismissive hand.
Everyone knew that Theo only had eyes for his wife.
But the compliment still pleased her.

'I love your shoes,' Maddie said. 'And have you had
your hair done? It's gorgeous.'

'Sorcha nagged me into letting her blow-dry it,' Jane
confessed.

'Good for her. Keep it like that,' Maddie said. 'Even

if it means getting up twenty minutes early. Because it really suits you.'

Again, the compliment warmed Jane. Maddie was one of her favourite colleagues, and had been a real rock when the hospital grapevine had been buzzing about her last year. Having been through a similar thing with her first husband, Maddie understood exactly how Jane felt about Shaun's very public betrayal. And she'd joined with Sorcha in helping Jane keep her head held high and ignoring the gossip.

'Have you bought your tombola tickets yet?' Maddie asked. 'The prizes are brilliant this year.'

'If there's a balloon ride among the prizes, Dr Petrakis,' Theo said, 'then we're buying every single ticket until we get it.'

Maddie actually blushed, and Jane laughed. 'I won't ask you what *that's* about. But, yes, I'll buy tickets. And I'll do a stint selling them, if you want.'

'No backstage stuff for you, Dr Cooper. You're here to dance your feet off,' Maddie said. 'Tonight's all about having fun.'

'And raising money for hospital equipment.'

'That, too. OK, you can go and buy loads of tombola tickets—and then you get on that dance floor,' Maddie said. 'Actually—that's senior consultant's orders, isn't it, Theo?'

'Certainly is,' Theo agreed with a smile. 'Actually, I'm trying to keep an eye out for our new consultant. He doesn't start officially until next week, but Maddie bullied him into buying a ticket for the ball.'

'I was off duty when he met everyone else in the department,' Jane said. 'What's he like?'

'A nice guy. He'll fit in to the department, no problems,' Theo said. 'You'll like him. Which is just as well, as he's going to be working with you.'

'So if I don't see him tonight, I'll meet him on Tuesday morning.'

'Yes. Now, go and enjoy yourself,' Maddie ordered with a smile.

Jane had got halfway over to the tombola table when her phone beeped. She looked at the screen automatically—the senior midwife had promised to get in touch if there were any complications with Ellen Baxter, a patient Jane was worried about—but the message wasn't from Iris. It was from her twin, the one person Jane didn't want to hear from tonight. She groaned inwardly. Right now, she was feeling good about herself, and Jenna always managed to change that within the space of ten seconds.

Even the title of the message stung: PJSB. Short for 'Plain Jane, Super-Brain', the nickname Jenna had coined when they were ten and Jane had won a scholarship to the local private school. Jenna had inherited their mother's genes and was tall and beautiful and effortlessly skinny; compared to her, any woman would look plain. But Jenna had always been quick to point out that Jane was six inches shorter than her, plain and dumpy—especially during their teenage years, and Jane's confidence in the way she looked had reached rock bottom. Jenna had spread the hated nickname among the popular girls at school, to the point where Jane had simply retreated into her books to avoid them.

She meant to close the screen without reading the message—she'd learned the hard way that Jenna only ever contacted her when she wanted something, so it could wait until tomorrow—but she accidentally pressed the wrong button and the words came up on the screen.

Soz it came out lik dis. U shda dun da i/view.

Interview? What interview?

Then Jane remembered. Jenna's publicist had wanted her to be interviewed a few months ago for a *Celebrity Life* feature about twins, along the lines of Jenna being the beauty and Jane being the brains. Jane had been in the middle of exams and simply hadn't had time to do an interview, much less spend a day on a photo shoot. She'd explained why, and thought that was an end to it—but clearly they'd gone ahead with the idea anyway.

Even though she knew it was a bad move, she couldn't help clicking on the attachment.

And then she really wished she hadn't done it. She definitely hadn't posed for that photograph. It looked as if it had been taken after she'd been at the tail end of a busy week on night shifts. She was wearing ratty sweat pants and an old T-shirt under a zipped hooded jacket that had seen better days, with her hair tucked under a woolly hat—clearly ready to do her daily run before crashing into bed. There was nothing in the article about what Jane actually did for a living; it was all about Jenna and unidentical twins.

Worse still, the magazine was going to be on sale in the hospital shop, where everyone could see it. She'd better warn Theo, because it wasn't going to look good for the department. But not right now; it wasn't often that he and Maddie had a night out, and Jane didn't want to spoil things for them. There wasn't anything anyone could do about it right now in any case, so leaving it until tomorrow was the right thing to do.

She closed the phone, but the question buzzed round

her head. Why did Jenna hate her so much? Jane had tried and tried and tried to be supportive to her twin. She knew it wasn't easy, being a supermodel. You were always in the public eye; you had to watch what you did and said and ate and drank, and whatever you did people would twist it to suit their own ends. Plus there were always new models coming along, ready to take your place in the spotlight. Not to mention those who were quick to take advantage. It was a lonely, precarious business that had left their mother fragile and prone to bouts of serious depression. Jenna, too, suffered from headaches and what she called 'nerves', whereas Jane had the constitution of an ox and hardly ever caught so much as a cold. But she'd tried to be kind. She'd looked after them both. She'd never complained, never said or done anything to make them feel they were a burden to her.

And yet nothing she did could ever please Jenna or Sophia. They seemed to resent her and look down on her in equal measure, and Jane had no idea how to change that.

She blew out a breath. Sorcha had talked her into coming to the hospital ball and Jane wasn't going to let her twin get to her tonight. All the same, instead of going to the tombola table, she went to the bar and drank a glass of champagne straight down before ordering a second. The bubbles, to her relief, hit immediately. They didn't take the magazine picture out of her head, but they did at least dull the edge of her misery.

She'd just bought her second glass of champagne and was turning back to the dance floor to go and find someone she knew to chat to and dance with when someone jogged her arm and the entire glassful went over the arm of the man standing next to her, soaking his white tuxedo.

'Oh, no! I'm *so* sorry,' she said, horrified. 'Please excuse me.'

'It was an accident. It's not a problem.' He took a handkerchief from his pocket and mopped up the spill.

The handkerchief wasn't enough; she knew the champagne was going to leave a stain over his sleeve.

'Please, send me the cleaning bill.' She was about to grab a pen and pad from her handbag to scribble down her details for him when she realised: she didn't have either. The dinky little bag she'd brought tonight was less than an eighth of the size of the bag she normally used—the one that Sorcha always teased her was big enough to carry the kitchen sink as well as everything else. In this one, Jane could just about cram her door key, her wallet and her mobile phone into, and even that was pushing it. She was about to pull out her phone and offer to text him her details when he smiled.

'It's fine,' he said. 'Really. But if you want to make amends, you could dance with me.'

She blinked. What? The guy looked like James Bond. Dark hair, piercing blue eyes, and a smile that made her feel as if her temperature had just gone up six degrees. He was the kind of man that attracted third glances, let alone second. 'Dance with you?' she asked stupidly.

He shrugged. 'It's what people are supposed to do at a charity ball, isn't it?'

'I…' Yes. But this man was a stranger. The epitome of a tall, dark, handsome stranger. 'Well, if you're sure. I'm J—'

'No names,' he cut in, smiling to take the sting from

his words. 'I rather like the idea of dancing with a gorgeous stranger. Cinderella.'

Gorgeous? Even Sorcha's skill with make-up couldn't make her look as stunning as her mother and her sister. Jane knew she was just ordinary. All the same, she smiled. 'If I'm Cinderella, does that make you Prince Charming?'

'Are you looking for a Prince Charming?'

'No. I don't need rescuing,' she said. Though it wasn't strictly true. Right now, she could really do with dancing with the best-looking man in the room. To take the sharpness of that article away. Honestly compelled her to add, 'Besides, your toes might really regret that offer later. I have two left feet.'

'I don't. So dance with me anyway,' he said, his eyes crinkling at the corners.

'If you have bruised toes tomorrow, don't say I didn't warn you,' she said.

He laughed. 'Somehow, I think my toes will be just fine.'

And then Jane discovered that Prince Charming could dance. *Really* dance. Moving round the floor with him was like floating. Effortless. He was guiding her, so her footwork couldn't possibly go wrong. She'd never, ever danced like this before, and it was a revelation. This was what it was like not to be clumsy.

When the music changed to a slower number, he didn't let her go. It felt completely natural to move closer. To dance cheek to cheek with him.

His skin was soft against hers, with no hint of stubble—clearly he'd shaved just before coming out tonight—and she could smell the citrus tang of his aftershave. She closed her eyes, giving herself up to the moment. Right now she really could imagine herself as Cinderella, dancing with her Prince Charming as he spun her round the floor.

And then she felt him move slightly. His lips brushed against the corner of her mouth.

If she pulled away, she knew he'd stop. All her instincts told her that her gorgeous stranger was a gentleman.

But what if she moved closer? Would he kiss her properly?

Even the idea of it made her pulse rate speed up and her breathing become shallower.

And then she did it. Moved just a little bit closer.

His arms tightened round hers, and his mouth brushed against hers. Sweet, tempting, promising: and it sent a shiver all the way through her. It had been way too long since she'd been kissed; she couldn't help responding, tipping her head back just the tiniest bit to give him better access to her mouth.

She kept her eyes closed, concentrating purely on the touch of his lips against hers. The way it made her skin feel super-sensitised; the way he coaxed her into responding, kissing him back. Tiny, sweet, nibbling kisses, almost like a dance in itself, leading each other further and further on.

She couldn't help opening her mouth, letting him deepen the kiss. And either that glass of champagne had seriously gone to her head, or Prince-Charming-meets-James-Bond was the most amazing kisser she'd ever met, because he made her feel as if she were floating. As if there was nobody else in the room, just the two of them and the music.

He kissed her through the rest of the song. And

maybe the next, too, because when he broke the kiss she realised that it was a fast dance, and they were sway-ing together, locked in each other's arms as if it were still a slow dance, even though the band was playing something uptempo.

He blinked then, as if he were just as shocked.

'Wow. It's been a long time since someone's had that effect on me, Cinders,' he said softly.

'You're telling me.' She couldn't remember reacting like this to anyone, ever. Even to the man she'd once planned to marry.

He leaned forward and stole a kiss. 'Let's get out of here.'

Leave a ballroom where she knew most of the people there, to go to some unspecified place with a complete stranger she'd only just met and whose name she didn't even know? She'd have to be crazy.

Or very, very angry and hurt. Enough to think that going off with the most gorgeous-looking man she'd ever seen—a man who'd kissed her to the point where she'd forgotten where she was—would make her feel much, much better.

'What did you have in mind?' she asked.

'I have a room here,' he said. 'So I was thinking room service. More champagne. Freshly squeezed orange juice. And a toasted cheese sandwich.'

If he'd said caviar or lobster, she would've said no. But the homeliness of a toasted cheese sandwich… Now that was seriously tempting. 'Yes. On condition.'

'Condition?'

'No names. No questions.'

His eyes widened. 'Just one night? Is that what you're saying?'

'Yes.' Tomorrow morning she'd be back to being Plain Jane, Super-Brain. Well, not quite, because she was off duty and she'd actually be Plain Jane who needed to catch up with cleaning her flat. But he'd just made her feel beautiful. Cherished. And she wasn't quite ready to let that feeling go. 'One night.'

'Allow me one question. You're not involved with anyone?'

That was an easy one to answer. 'No.' Though she appreciated the fact that he'd asked, because she needed to know the same thing. The fact that he'd asked first made it easy for her. 'Are you?'

'No.' He caught her lower lip briefly between his. 'Then let's go.'

She walked with him into the hotel reception; while he collected his key, she texted Sorcha. *Bit of a headache, having an early night. Enjoy the rest of the ball, J xx*

It wasn't that far from the truth. She was having an early night. Just…not at home. And the headache excuse was enough to make sure that Sorcha didn't ring the flat to see how she was and worry when there was no answer.

'Everything all right?' Prince Charming asked.

'Fine.' She smiled back at him. 'Just texting my best friend to say I'm leaving, so she doesn't worry that I've disappeared.'

'Which means you're all mine. Good.'

CHAPTER TWO

ED USHERED his Cinderella over to the lifts. Her face
was incredibly expressive; as the doors closed behind
them, he could see that she was starting to have second
thoughts. And third.

She was definitely the responsible, thoughtful type,
because she'd made sure that her best friend wasn't
worrying about her rather than disappearing without a
word. And she was clearly wondering whether she was
doing the right thing now.

He took her hand, pressed a reassuring kiss into her
palm and curled her fingers over the imprint of his lips.
'Stop worrying,' he said softly. 'You can say no and it
won't be a problem. Just come and have a drink with
me.'

'I don't normally do this sort of thing,' she muttered,
and more colour flooded into her face.

'Me, neither,' he said. 'How shockingly bold of us.'

To his relief, she responded to the teasing note in his
voice and smiled back. 'I guess so.' And she made no
protest when he unlocked his room and gestured for her
to go inside.

'Take a seat,' he said. Though he wasn't surprised
that she pulled the chair out from under the dressing

table rather than sitting on the bed. 'Shall I order some champagne?'

She gave him a rueful smile. 'I think I've already had enough. So unless you're planning to drink the whole bottle yourself...' She wrinkled her nose. 'Probably not.'

'You spilled most of your glass over me,' he pointed out.

She winced. 'I know, and I'm sorry.'

He shook his head. 'I didn't mean *that*. I wasn't intending to make you grovel, just pointing out that you haven't had a drink tonight.'

'Actually, I have.' She bit her lip. 'This is going to sound terrible, but I drank one glass straight down before the one I spilled over you.'

Now that did surprise him. She'd looked slightly vulnerable when she'd first met him, but he'd assumed that was simply embarrassment at spilling her champagne over him. 'Why? Didn't you want to come to the party?'

'No, it's not that. The hospital ball's always fun.' She blew out a breath. 'We said no questions, remember.'

He shrugged. 'Fair enough.' Though he still wondered. Why would a woman with such beautiful eyes and such a perfect mouth need to bolster her courage with champagne?

'Why do you have a room here?' she asked.

He smiled. 'And who was it who just reminded me, "no questions"?'

'Sorry.' She bit her lip. 'I'm not much good at this. I never go off with complete strangers whose name I don't even know.'

Neither did he. But then again, he hadn't responded so powerfully to someone for a long time; if he was honest, he hadn't felt like that about his wife. And he'd avoided dating since his marriage had disintegrated.

His sisters were all nagging him to have some fun and start dating again. And the way Cinderella had kissed him back on the dance floor had really stirred his blood. He had the feeling that this was something they *both* needed. Except she was clearly worried about him being a stranger. 'That's an easy one to sort. My name's—' he began.

'No,' she cut in. 'We're at a charity ball for the hospital. So the chances are, if you were a complete snake, you wouldn't be here. Or else someone would've warned me about you beforehand and I'd know to avoid you.'

He blinked. 'The grapevine's that fast?'

'Yup.'

'So you work at the hospital,' he said thoughtfully.

'No questions,' she reminded him.

He smiled. 'It wasn't a question. It was a logical deduction. This is a charity ball for the hospital, and you clearly know people, plus you've been to the ball before and you know how fast the grapevine works. QED.'

'And you had an expensive education.' She smiled at his raised eyebrow. 'Again a logical deduction. Most people don't use Latin abbreviations in everyday speech.'

'So the fact you recognise it says the same about you,' he parried.

'Not necessarily. I might be a crossword addict.'

'I like fencing with you,' he said. 'Almost as much as I like dancing with you.' His gaze held hers. 'And almost as much as I like kissing you.'

Colour bloomed in her face, but this time it wasn't shyness. The way her lips parted slightly and her pupils grew larger told him that she liked remembering the way they'd kissed, too.

He took her hand; this time, instead of kissing her palm, he kissed her wrist right where her pulse was beating madly. The longer his mouth lingered, the more her pulse sped up. Her skin was so soft. And she smelled gorgeous—some floral scent he couldn't quite place, mixed with something else. Soft and sweet and gentle. Irresistible.

'You do things to me, Cinders,' he said softly. 'But I'm not going to push you. Do you mind if I…?' He ran his finger round the collar of his shirt and grimaced.

'Slip into something more comfortable?' she asked, raising an eyebrow.

He laughed. 'Hardly. I just want to feel a bit less—well—formal.'

'Sure.'

'Thank you.' He stood up and removed his jacket, hanging it in the wardrobe. Then he undid his bow tie and the top button of his shirt and let the tie hang loose, and rolled the sleeves of his shirt up.

She sucked in a breath.

'What?' he asked.

'Forget Prince Charming. You're all James Bond,' she said.

He raised an eyebrow. 'Is that a good thing?'

'Oh, yes.' Her voice was husky. 'My best friend and I saw the last film three times at the cinema.'

'Well, just for the record, I hate martinis.'

She smiled. 'So do I.'

'And I don't have a licence to kill.'

She spread her hands. 'The only licence I have is a driving licence.'

He laughed. 'Snap. I like you, Cinderella.' His voice deepened, softened. 'Come here.' It was an invitation, not an order. She paused, clearly weighing it up, then nodded, stood up and crossed the short distance between them.

He cupped her face with both hands. 'A perfect heart shape,' he said softly. 'And right now I really, really want to kiss you. May I?'

'Yes.'

Ed smiled and lowered his mouth to hers. Teasing, enticing, more of those little nibbling kisses that had her twining her fingers through his hair and opening her mouth so he could deepen the kiss.

And, just like it had been between them on the dance floor, he felt desire lance through him.

He pulled away slightly, spun her round and undid the zip of her dress. She arched back as he stroked his way down the bare skin he uncovered. Her skin was so soft; and touching her like this wasn't enough. He wanted more. A hell of a lot more.

Gently, he slid the dress from her shoulders and let it fall to the floor. He drew her back against him, his hands splayed across her midriff and his thumbs stroking the undersides of her breasts through the lace of her bra.

'I want you,' he whispered. 'I want to be with you, skin to skin.'

'Me, too.' The admission was low and throaty, and sent a kick of sheer need through him.

She turned to face him, untucked his shirt from his trousers and undid the rest of the buttons of his shirt. Her hands were gentle and yet sure as she slid her palms across his pecs. 'Nice,' she said appreciatively.

'Thank you.' He inclined his head, acknowledging the compliment. 'I like it when you touch me.'

She smiled back, and pushed the cotton from his shoulders; his shirt pooled on the floor next to her dress. She traced the line of his collarbone with one finger.

Good, but not enough. He needed more. He kissed her again, his mouth teasing and demanding at the same time.

He unsnapped her bra, tossed the lace to the floor and then cupped her breasts properly. 'You're beautiful, Cinders.'

No, I'm not. Her thoughts were written all over her face.

Someone—presumably her ex—had really done a number on her. Just as much as Camilla had made him wary of trusting anyone.

'Whoever he was,' Ed said softly, 'he was an idiot.'

'Who?'

'Whoever put that look in your eyes.'

She shrugged. 'You're wearing too much.'

She'd said 'no questions'. And now he had a pretty good idea why. This was starting to look like rebound sex. For both of them.

But they'd agreed from the start that this was one night only. A night out of time. The new hospital was big enough for their paths never to cross again. And if he could make her feel good about herself again tonight, the way she was making him feel good about himself, then that would be a bonus for both of them.

He took her hands and drew them down to his belt. 'Since you think I'm wearing too much, why don't you even things up?' he invited.

Her hands were shaking slightly as she undid his belt,

then the button of his formal trousers, and slid the zipper down.

'You are beautiful, you know,' he said softly. 'Your eyes—I'm not sure if they're green or grey or brown. The colour keeps shifting, and it makes me want to know what colour they are when you're really aroused. And your mouth.' He traced her lower lip with one fingertip. 'It's a perfect cupid's bow. It makes me want to kiss you until we're both dizzy. And here...' He dipped his head and took one hardened nipple into his mouth.

She gave a sharp intake of breath and tipped her head back in pleasure.

Part of Jane knew that this was a seriously bad idea. He was a stranger. And she'd never had a one-night stand before.

Then again, this wasn't a relationship. She didn't have to take the risk of trusting him and then discovering that he had feet of clay, the way she had with Shaun. In a weird kind of way, this was safe—because this man wasn't going to get close enough to her heart to break it.

His mouth teased her lower lip, demanding and getting a response. Jane wasn't sure which of them finished undressing whom, but then he'd lifted her and was carrying her to the bed. She felt the bed dip with his weight, and then the mattress shifted again as he climbed off. She opened her eyes.

'Condom,' he said in answer to her unspoken question.

At least one of them was being sensible. It hadn't even occurred to her. How reckless and stupid was that?

He rummaged in his trousers for his wallet, took out the foil wrapper and placed it on the bedside table.

'You look worried.' He stroked her face. 'If you've changed your mind, I'll understand. I've never forced a woman, and I don't intend to start now.'

'I just…' She hadn't even dated anyone since Shaun's betrayal, let alone slept with anyone. She'd turned down the couple of offers she'd had, not wanting to risk the same thing happening all over again. 'I'm not used to this kind of thing,' she admitted.

'Then let's get used to it together.' He bent his head to kiss her again; his mouth was gentle and promising, rather than demanding. Until she responded, when suddenly the kiss turned hot, turning her into a mass of sheer aching need.

This time, when he touched her, the shyness was gone. She gave herself up to the sensation as he stroked her, teased her, let her touch him in return.

His hand slid between her thighs and she gasped in pleasure.

It really shouldn't be this good for a first time. They didn't even know each other's names, for pity's sake. But it felt as if Prince Charming knew exactly where she liked being touched, exactly how to make her respond to him.

She was near to babbling when she heard the rip of the foil packet and the snap as he rolled on the condom to protect her. Then he eased, oh, so slowly into her. And it was heaven. This was a man who knew exactly what to do—how to give pleasure, how to take her right to the edge and keep her there until she was practically hyperventilating.

And then wave after wave of pleasure surged through

her as her climax hit. He held her tightly, and she felt the answering surge of his own body against hers.

Gently, he withdrew. 'I'd better deal with the condom. Excuse me a moment,' he said softly.

Jane pulled the sheet back over her, the pleasure replaced by a rush of awkwardness. What did you do on a one-night stand? Did you stay for the whole night, or did you get dressed and leave straight after having sex? She didn't have a clue. She'd never done this kind of thing before; she'd always hung out with the nerdy students, not the wild ones.

He reappeared from the bathroom—still naked, and looking completely unembarrassed about the situation. Clearly he had some idea of the rules; whereas she felt totally at sea.

He climbed into bed beside her and drew her against him. 'What's wrong?'

She sighed. 'If you really want to know, I don't have a clue what the rules are. What you're supposed to do next on a one-night stand.'

'Once you've had sex, you mean?' He stroked her hair. 'I don't think there are any rules. What we do next is entirely up to you.' He smiled. 'Though my vote would be for you to stay a bit longer and for us to order something from room service.'

'Your toasted cheese sandwich?'

He shrugged. 'Or whatever you like from the menu.'

Funny how something so homely could make her feel so much more at ease. 'Toasted sandwiches would be lovely, thank you. And orange juice.' She smiled at him. 'And can I be really greedy and ask for coffee as well?' The champagne she'd gulped down was still fizzing through her and she really didn't want to spend the next day with a hangover. OK, so she was a lightweight, hardly ever drinking more than a single glass of wine; but she didn't need alcohol to have a good time.

He smiled back at her. 'Coffee sounds great to me.'

'And of course I'll pay my half,' she added.

He shook his head. 'My room, my idea and my bill. Don't argue.'

There wasn't much she could say to that, unless she offered to treat him some other night. Which would definitely be breaking the rules—by definition, a one-night stand was for one night only. 'Then thank you,' she said.

'You know,' he said, 'when I came out tonight, didn't think I was going to end up sitting in bed with a perfect stranger, eating comfort food. But I'm really glad I met you, Cinders.'

'Me, too,' she said softly, meaning it.

The sandwiches, when they arrived, were gorgeous. The orange juice was freshly squeezed. And the coffee was among the best she'd ever tasted.

'That was fabulous. Thank you,' she said when they'd finished.

'My pleasure.'

He really was gorgeous. Those piercing blue eyes made her heart skip a beat.

But she didn't want to overstay her welcome. 'And I guess this is my cue to leave.'

'If that's what you really want.' He stole a kiss. 'Or you could…' He paused. 'Stay. Tonight.'

The heat was back in his expression. How could she resist? 'Yes.'

CHAPTER THREE

THE next morning, Jane woke with a start. She was in an unfamiliar bed, in an unfamiliar room, with a body curled protectively round hers.

For a moment she thought she was having some peculiarly vivid dream, remembering what it was like being part of a couple and waking up in her man's arms. But then the body next to hers shifted and pulled her closer.

She was definitely in bed with someone else. And she'd split up with Shaun eight months ago. Which meant that the body curled round hers belonged to... She swallowed hard. She was still in bed with the handsome stranger she'd spilled champagne over last night.

Talk about out of the frying pan and into the fire. What a stupid thing to do: spending the night with a complete stranger, without telling anyone where she was. Even if he did have lovely manners and had given her more pleasure in one night than her ex-fiancé had given her in two years, he was still a stranger. Anything could've happened.

Oh, for pity's sake. Dr Jane Cooper was known for being ultra-sensible. She didn't *do* this sort of thing.

Except...she just had.

At least she hadn't told him her name. Hopefully their paths wouldn't cross so they could avoid an embarrassing situation. Even if they both worked at the London Victoria, the hospital was big enough for her not to know at least half the staff; and she definitely hadn't met him before, or she would've remembered those beautiful eyes.

She'd needed practically no persuasion to spend the whole night with him. And they'd spent most of the night making love. They'd actually run out of condoms, and she'd felt like the bad girl she'd never actually been.

It wasn't that she had regrets about last night—how could she regret the way he'd made her feel?—but she really didn't have a clue how to face him this morning. What to say. How to deal with the situation. Plus she needed to be somewhere. So the best thing she could do would be to slip quietly away before he woke. It would avoid embarrassment on all sides. Gradually, she worked her way out of his arms; when he moved to pull her back again, she gave him the warm pillow she'd been lying on, and he cuddled that closer.

Cute.

Jane smiled regretfully. Maybe if they'd met under other circumstances... But there was no point dwelling on it, and she really needed to check on a patient and talk to her boss.

She picked up her clothes from the floor and quickly dragged them on, rescued her handbag and her shoes, tiptoed over to the door, and unlocked it very quietly. When she glanced back towards the bed, she could see that he was still sleeping. 'Thank you,' she mouthed silently. 'For making me feel beautiful.'

Then she remembered. His jacket. Considering it

had been her fault, the least she could do was pick up the dry cleaning bill.

There was a leather folder on top of the dressing table, with the hotel's crest stamped on it. Just as she'd hoped, it contained paper and a pencil. She slid the top sheet quietly out of the folder and scribbled a quick note on it. Then she took some money from her purse and left it on top of the note, then put the pencil on top of the banknotes to weigh them down. Finally, she closed the door behind her and fled.

Back at her flat, Jane showered—trying not to think about what Prince Charming had done with her in his shower last night—and changed into jeans and a plain T-shirt. Once she'd downed a mug of coffee, she flicked into her phone and read the article again, just to be sure that she wasn't making a fuss over nothing.

She wasn't.

She sighed and closed her eyes briefly. There was no point in trying to call Jenna to task over it. Her twin would simply open her big brown eyes and claim innocence, say it wasn't *her* fault the journalist had written it that way. And then somehow their mother would get wind of the row and she'd have a panic attack; and the blame for that would be laid firmly at Jane's door. Been there, done that, worn the T-shirt until it was in rags.

So instead of asking Jenna what her problem was and why she couldn't play nicely for once, Jane sent her a very polite email, saying simply, *Thank you for letting me know.* Even Jenna couldn't twist that.

And now she was going to have to do some damage limitation, as well as check up on how Ellen Baxter was doing this morning.

'You're supposed to be off duty, Jane,' Iris, the senior midwife, said as Jane walked into the department.

Jane smiled. 'I know. Thanks for sending that message through Theo last night.'

'Did you have a good time at the ball?'

'Yes, thanks.'

'Are you sure?' Iris gave her a concerned look. 'You're looking a bit…well, worried, this morning.'

'You know me. Always worrying about my patients,' Jane said lightly. She knew Iris would be sympathetic if she told the midwife about that horrible article, but she needed to tell Theo first. And if anyone was too nice to her right now, she might just bawl her eyes out—from frustration as much as hurt. 'Talking of patients, I'm just going to see Ellen.'

Ellen Baxter was listlessly flicking through a magazine, but she brightened when Jane walked into her room. 'Dr Cooper!'

'Good morning, Ellen.' Jane's smile was genuine. 'How are you doing?'

'OK. I hope.' Ellen grimaced. 'I'm trying to relax.'

'But it's hard when you're on bed rest and you want to be at home.' Jane patted her hand sympathetically. 'Let me have a look at your charts.' She read through them swiftly. 'OK. Can I check your blood pressure and your temperature?'

'You can stick as many needles as you like in me, if it means I can go home!' Ellen said.

Jane laughed. 'You're safe from needles today.' She checked Ellen's blood pressure and temperature, then marked them on the chart. 'That's good. Any twinges or spotting?'

'None. And, believe you me, I'd say if there was,'

Ellen said feelingly. 'I don't want anything to go wrong. I can't lose this baby.'

'I know,' Jane soothed. 'We're all rooting for you.'

'Everyone's being so nice here, but it's just not home.' Ellen flushed. 'And I know it's wet of me, but I can't sleep properly without Rob.'

'It's not wet. It's perfectly understandable.' It had taken Jane weeks to get used to sleeping on her own after she'd split up with Shaun. Luckily she'd been the one to move, so at least there were no memories of him in her flat. 'Ellen, I'm happy with your obs. If Rob can come and pick you up, then I'll discharge you this morning. With conditions,' she added firmly.

'Anything,' Ellen said, her eyes shining.

'Firstly, you take it easy. Secondly, any worries at all—no matter how small or how silly you think they might be—you call me. Thirdly, any twinges, you get straight here to the department. OK?'

'OK.' Ellen's eyes filled with tears. 'You've been so lovely. If it wasn't for you...' Her voice cracked.

Jane squeezed her hand again. 'That's what I'm here for.' She smiled at Ellen and got off the bed. 'You call Rob, and I'll get the paperwork sorted with Iris.'

'Thank you. Thank you so much.' Ellen's eyes glittered with tears.

Warm and soft in his arms... Ed snuggled closer, then realised drowsily that he wasn't holding someone, he was holding some*thing*. He opened his eyes. A pillow.

She'd left him asleep, holding a pillow.

Unless maybe she was in the shower? He listened, but he could hear nothing from the bathroom. And the sheet on her side of the bed was stone cold. She'd been gone for a while.

Well, he supposed it was one way to avoid the awkwardness. Though it stung that she hadn't waited for him to wake up.

On his way to the bathroom, he saw the note on the dressing table.

Dear Prince Charming, Thank you for last night. Hope this covers the dry cleaning bill. Cinders.

So she'd played the game right to the end. He damped down the surge of disappointment that she hadn't left him her number or told him her real name.

And there was the fact that she'd left him some money. He knew she'd meant it to cover the cleaning bill for his jacket, but it still made him feel cheap.

Still, it was his own fault for acting on impulse. He was better off being his usual sensible, serious self. And he wouldn't make that mistake again.

Once the paperwork was done, it was time to start the damage limitation. Jane knocked on Theo's open office door.

He looked up from his desk. 'Janey, you're supposed to be off duty. What are you doing here?' He raised one hand to silence her reply. 'Oh, don't tell me. Ellen Baxter.'

'Yes. I'm discharging her this morning. She'll call me if she has any worries and she'll come straight back here if she has the slightest twinge.'

'And did you come in to tell me that, or to bring me coffee?' he asked, looking hopeful.

'Actually, a large brandy might be more in order,' she said ruefully.

He frowned. 'What's up, Janey?'

She dragged in a breath. 'I need to show you something. I'm sorry, I had absolutely no idea about it until I got the email last night.' She pulled the article up on her phone and handed it to him.

Theo read through it, his mouth set in a grim line; when he'd finished, he looked up at her. 'I've never seen such utter spite in my entire life. I can't believe this is focused on something so shallow and it doesn't even say what you do! Are you all right?'

No. She was ragingly angry and desperately hurt. She yanked the emotions back. No more tears. Just smiles. 'I'm fine,' she fibbed. 'But this is going to look really bad for the department. If you want me to resign, I understand.'

'Resign? You must be joking. Janey, you're an excellent doctor and this rubbish has got nothing to do with you.' He flicked out of the screen. 'When does the magazine go on sale?'

'I'm not sure. This week, I think.'

'Right. I'll have a word with the shop manager and make sure it's not on sale in the hospital this week. If necessary, I'll buy their entire stock of the magazine myself. I can't do anything about people who buy it elsewhere and bring it in, but my guess is that anyone who knows you—staff or patient—will be fuming on your behalf.' He looked grim as he handed the phone back to her. 'And those who choose to spread gossip or make stupid comments to you—well, their opinions are worth nothing in the first place, so just ignore them, OK?'

'Thank you.' She felt humble beyond belief that her

boss was prepared to buy up the entire stock of magazines to try and spare her from an awkward situation.

'I take it that—' he said something in Greek that she didn't understand, but from the expression on his face it definitely wasn't anything complimentary '—sister of yours was behind this?'

Jane spread her hands. 'She asked me to do the interview months ago. It was meant to be a feature about twins, "the beauty and the brains". Except I was up to my eyes with work and exams, so I said I couldn't do it. I thought she'd just forgotten about it.'

'More like she used it to have another dig at you, because she's incredibly jealous of you.'

'She can't be. There's absolutely nothing to be jealous about. She's a supermodel,' she reminded Theo.

'She's also heading towards thirty and she's not going to get the same kind of work opportunities she had when she was eighteen. Looks don't last, but education does. You're clever, your career will be going from strength to strength while hers is starting to go more slowly, and everyone who meets you really likes you. *That's* why she's jealous,' Theo said. He sighed. 'Do your parents know about this?'

'Probably not. But I'm not going to say anything. You know my mum's fragile.'

'I know depression's tough to overcome,' Theo said gently, 'but it doesn't mean you can just give up on being a parent to your children. When have either of your parents ever put you first?'

Jane didn't want to answer that. 'It's OK.'

Theo gave her a sympathetic look. 'You've got more patience than anyone else I know.'

'It's not easy for Mum. She was right at the height of

her career when she fell pregnant with Jenna and me and had to give it all up.' According to Sophia, pregnancy had ruined her skin and her figure; and, with the crippling post-natal depression she'd suffered afterwards, she'd never been able to return to her modelling.

'You know, Maddie could say the same thing. Being a mum means that she's had to give up some of her career choices, and I've turned down offers as well because I don't want a job that'd mean I can't give her and our daughters enough time. But neither of us would change a thing, because the girls have brought so much joy to us,' Theo said softly.

Jane had to swallow hard. What would it be like to have a family who loved her unconditionally, the way Maddie and Theo felt about their children, instead of making her feel guilty for being born? What would it have been like if Jenna had supported her and cheered her on through the long years of studying medicine, instead of pulling her down and mocking her all the time?

Though it was pointless dwelling on it. She couldn't change the way they were. All she could do was try to love them as best as she could—and, since Shaun had betrayed her with Jenna, that had meant from a safe distance. Which, she supposed, made her just as bad as them.

Theo reached out and squeezed her hand. 'Sorry. I'm overstepping the mark. It's not my place to criticise your family. Though I wish they'd appreciate you for who you are.'

He paused. 'Do you want me to call Maddie? Or Sorcha?'

'No. I'll be fine.'

'Hmm.' He looked at her. 'Is that article the reason why you disappeared from the ball so early last night?'

'No.' Not exactly. She definitely wasn't telling him the real reason behind that.

'Sure?'

'Sure,' she confirmed.

'I'll believe you—for now.' He smiled at her. 'Now, go and have two nice days off, forget about that stupid article, and come back all bright-eyed on Tuesday morning, yes?'

'OK, Theo.' She dragged in a breath. 'And thank you.'

'Any time.'

On Tuesday morning Jane had just checked up on her first patient when Theo walked in. 'Janey, have you got a moment?'

She looked over at him, saw the man in the white coat next to him, and her knees went weak as she recognised him.

Oh, my God.

He couldn't possibly be… Could he?

Theo's next words confirmed it. 'I'd like to introduce you to our new consultant.'

If Theo said his name was James or Bond, she was going to collapse in a puddle of hysterical laughter.

'Edward Somers,' Theo continued. 'Ed, this is Jane Cooper, one of our F2 doctors, but it's not going to be long before she makes registrar.'

She could feel her face going bright red and there was a tiny, tiny smile lifting the corner of Ed's mouth. Oh, please, don't let him say anything about Saturday night…

'Good to meet you, Jane,' he said politely.

Then she realised she'd been holding her breath, waiting for him to spill the beans. Clearly he wasn't going to do that: because it wouldn't reflect too well on him, either. She smiled at him in relief. 'You, too, Edward—or do you prefer Ed?'

For a second, she could swear he mouthed 'James Bond', but then he said, 'Ed. May I join you in your rounds?'

'I—well, sure.' She spread her hands. 'You're the senior. I guess you should lead.'

Ed smiled at her. 'Patients are much more important than protocol. You already know them, so I'm happy for you to lead and introduce me while we're there.'

'I'll leave you in Jane's capable hands,' Theo said, and headed back to his office.

'Very capable,' Ed said softly.

Oh, help.

'I, um… Look, we probably need to talk, but for now can we keep this…well, just work?' Jane asked.

'For now,' he agreed.

Before she could take him to the next patient, Iris hurried over. 'We've just had a call from the ED. The mum's twenty-four, she's eleven weeks pregnant and she can't stop being sick. Marina thinks it's hyperemesis.'

'We're on our way,' Jane said.

In the emergency department, she swiftly introduced Ed to Marina Fenton, the specialist registrar.

'I'm pretty sure it's hyperemesis. Poor woman— morning sickness is bad enough,' Marina said. 'I've already done bloods and sent them off for electrolyte levels, blood count and renal.'

'Thanks, Marina—that's great.'

'Mrs Taylor's through here.' She showed them to the cubicle where a young woman was retching miserably into a bowl.

'Mrs Taylor? I'm Jane Cooper and this is Ed Somers. Dr Fenton asked us to come down and see you. Can I get you a drink of water?' Jane asked.

Mrs Taylor shook her head. 'I can't keep anything down.'

'Taking small sips might help you feel a little bit better,' Jane said gently, and stuck her head out of the cubicle for long enough to ask one of the auxiliaries to bring in a glass of water.

'How long have you been feeling like this?' Ed asked.

'About a month. I knew you got morning sickness, I just didn't expect it to be all day and all night and as bad as this.' She retched again. 'Sorry.'

'You don't have to apologise,' Jane said, squeezing her hand.

The auxiliary brought in the water Jane had asked for, and Mrs Taylor managed a small sip. 'Thank you. That's made my mouth feel a bit less disgusting,' she admitted.

'Good. Have you talked to your family doctor or your midwife about your sickness?' Ed asked.

'I didn't want to bother them.' She shook her head. 'My sister had it bad, too. She lost weight and felt lousy all the time for the first bit.'

Jane and Ed exchanged a glance; hyperemesis was known to run in families. But it was also more common in women carrying twins—or, more rarely, it could be caused by something more sinister. They needed to run some tests to rule out the nasties.

'My boss made me come in. I was sick over a client.

It was her perfume that set me off—it was so strong.'
Mrs Taylor bit her lip. 'I really hope he forgives me.'

'I'm sure he will. He sent you in because he was
worried about you,' Ed reassured her. 'So, you're about
eleven weeks. Have you had a scan yet?'

'No, that was meant to be next week. My Jason's
getting the day off to come with me.' Worry skittered
across her face. 'Is there something wrong with the
baby? Is that why I keep being sick like this?'

'I think you have something called hyperemesis—it's
basically really bad morning sickness,' Ed said. 'I've
treated mums before who've had the same thing. It's
really miserable for you, but you're in the right place
and we can do something to help you feel a lot better.'

'Really?' Mrs Taylor looked as if she didn't quite
dare believe them.

'Really,' Jane confirmed.

'And it won't harm the baby? Only my nan said she
knew someone who took stuff to make them stop being
sick and the baby was…' She shuddered. 'I feel like
death warmed up, but I'd rather put up with that than
risk anything happening to the baby.'

'We won't give you anything that's not safe for the
baby,' Ed reassured her. 'Dr Fenton told us she's already
done some blood tests, so we need to wait for the results
of those. But in the meantime we'd like to give you a
scan and see how the baby's doing.'

'Has anyone called your husband, or would you like
us to call someone to be with you?' Jane asked.

'Jason's on his way,' Mrs Taylor said.

'That's great. We'll to take you up with us to the maternity unit, then,' Jane said.

'And, because you're quite dehydrated from being

sick, I'd like to keep you in for a little while and put you on a drip to replace the fluids you've lost. That'll make you feel a lot better, and we have one or two things that will help you stop being sick but won't affect the baby,' Ed reassured her.

By the time they'd taken Mrs Taylor up to the maternity unit, her husband had arrived. Ed ushered them in to the consulting room with the portable scanner, and Jane noticed that he was careful to make sure that the Taylors couldn't see the screen, in case it was bad news.

'What I'm going to do is to put a bit of gel on your stomach—sorry, it's a bit cold, whereas down in ultrasound it's always warm. All it does is help us get a better picture of the baby,' Jane explained. 'It's not going to hurt you or the baby—I'm sure your midwife's already told you this, but it's all done by sound waves.'

Mrs Taylor retched again, and her husband held the bowl for her; when she'd finished, Jane wiped her face with a damp cloth.

'This baby's going to be an only child,' Mrs Taylor said. 'I'm not going through this again. Ever.'

Jane made a soothing noise and glanced at Ed. Please, don't let it be a molar pregnancy causing the sickness, she thought.

Ed returned her glance; as if he could read her mind, he gave her a reassuring smile and the tiniest nod.

Thank God.

'I'm pleased to say that the baby's doing fine.' Ed turned the screen to show them. 'I did wonder if you might be having twins, because that sometimes makes the sickness much worse; but you're having just one. Here's the heart, beating nicely.' He pointed out the baby's heart. 'Everything's looking just as it should do.'

He made some quick measurements. 'And you're eleven and a half weeks.'

Mrs Taylor brushed back a tear. 'The baby's really all right?'

'The baby's absolutely fine,' Ed reassured her.

'Can we have a picture?' Mr Taylor asked.

'Unfortunately, this is a portable scanner, so we can't print anything from it. But when you have your proper scan next week, they'll be able to give you pictures then,' Jane explained.

Ed ran through the treatment plan, explaining what they were going to try and why; Jane found herself chipping in from time to time. It was as if she'd worked with him for years, instead of only half a morning. Whatever the complications caused by their fling on Saturday night, she was definitely going to able to work with this man. He fitted right in to the team, and he treated the mums with respect and dignity. And she liked that. A lot.

'I like your bedside manner,' she said when they'd left the Taylors.

He raised an eyebrow. 'Funny, I find sometimes women run from it.'

Jane felt the colour shoot into her face. 'I didn't mean *that* kind of bedside. I meant how you are with the mums. In my last hospital, I worked with a consultant who was incredibly brusque and treated everyone like idiots, mums and staff alike. He had all the social skills of a piranha, and I swore I'd never become like that myself or be forced to work with anyone like that again.' She gave him a wry smile. 'Though I guess I knew you wouldn't be like that, or Theo would've refused to appoint you.'

He smiled. 'I was teasing you, Jane.'

Her face was burning. 'Sorry. Everyone says I'm too serious. I'm afraid you drew the short straw and you've got the nerdy one to work with.'

'Nerdy's good,' he said. 'I like clever people. Come on, let's finish our rounds.'

She introduced him to the rest of her patients. When they'd finished, he said, 'I think we need to talk. Probably not where we're likely to be overheard, so do you know a quiet corner somewhere?'

Here it came. Retribution for her acting so madly, so unJanelike, on Saturday. And Sunday. 'Believe it or not, the most private place is probably going to be the hospital canteen; it's noisy and people don't get a chance to eavesdrop.'

'Good. Let's go.'

CHAPTER FOUR

'I'M BUYING,' Jane said, trying not to think of the last time they'd had coffee together. 'Black, no sugar, isn't it?'

'Yes, thanks. You have a good memory.'

'Doctors are supposed to be observant,' she said with a smile. She ordered a black coffee, plus a cappuccino for herself. 'Do you want a muffin with that?' she asked.

'No, I'm fine with just coffee, thanks.'

When she'd paid, she found them a quiet corner. 'Thanks for not bringing up what happened on Saturday in the department.'

He shrugged. 'No problem. But we do need to talk about Sunday.'

'Sunday?' She'd expected him to talk about Saturday and how they needed to set some boundaries. They were colleagues, nothing more, and what happened on Saturday wasn't going to be repeated.

'Sunday,' he confirmed. 'I was kind of expecting to see you when I woke up.'

She stirred her coffee, avoiding looking him in the eye. 'You were still asleep when I woke, so I thought it might be less awkward if I just left quietly.'

'Maybe. But when you wake up and someone's left

you money after they spent the night with you, it tends to make you feel a bit like a gigolo.'

She nearly choked on her coffee. 'The money was to cover the cleaning bill for your jacket. I didn't mean it to—oh, help. OK.' She blew out a breath. 'Theo didn't introduce me properly. Dr Jane Cooper. Good with patients, but her social skills need a bit of polishing.'

'Want to know how I see it?' Ed asked softly. 'Dr Jane Cooper, who's charming and warm and kind; and, even more charmingly, clearly doesn't have a clue just how lovely she is.'

It was a far cry from Shaun's damning assessment of her when she'd asked him why he'd cheated on her with Jenna. He'd said that she was twenty pounds too heavy and six inches too short. Jane knew it was ridiculous—she couldn't change her height and she had no intention of tottering around in uncomfortable high heels just to please someone else—but it had knocked her confidence as well as destroying her trust. He'd homed in on exactly the same criticisms that Jenna and her mother had always made about her: everything was about appearances, not what lay beneath. She'd thought Shaun was different, that he'd love her for who she was. How rubbish her judgement had turned out to be.

She frowned. 'Look, I'm not fishing for compliments, Ed. I know who I am and I'm comfortable with that.'

'Which is just how things should be,' Ed said.

This was crazy, Ed thought. He didn't do mad things. He was sensible. But on Saturday night he'd swept Jane off her feet and surprised himself. And he wanted to do it all over again.

According to his sisters, he was too reserved and needed to get a life. If he could swap a bit of his common sense for some of George's recklessness, they'd both be a lot more balanced.

Since the divorce, Ed hadn't even dated. He hadn't trusted his own judgement. And it looked as if Jane too had an ex who'd hurt her badly and had made her wary of relationships. Which left them...where?

He'd felt that they'd had a real connection on Saturday night. Not just the sex—there was something about Jane. Something that made him want to get to know her better. Something that made his customary reserve feel totally wrong where she was concerned. Something that made him want to take a chance.

He'd seen her work. She was calm, competent and knew how to work as a team. So it wouldn't be that much of a risk...would it?

'Given that I didn't get to see you on Sunday, how about you make amends this evening?' he asked.

She looked surprised. 'How do you mean?'

He shrugged. 'Have dinner with me.' He could see the panic skittering across her face. 'Unless you'd rather go and see a film or something?'

The teeniest twinkle of mischief appeared in her eyes. 'Would that be a James Bond film?'

Just how he'd hoped she'd respond. He grinned. 'If you know where one's showing, sure. Or, if not, we could go and find a DVD—though we'd have to watch it at your place. My hotel room doesn't have a DVD player.'

'You're still staying at the hotel?'

He nodded. 'I do have a flat lined up, but I can't move

in until the weekend. So the hotel was really the only choice.'

'Don't you have family or friends you can stay with?' Then she grimaced. 'Sorry. I'm being horribly nosey.'

He spread his hands. 'I don't think our "no questions" rule applies any more—and of course you'd want to know more about a new colleague. I was working in Glasgow, but I came back to London to be near my family.'

She frowned. 'So why are you staying in a hotel rather than with them?'

He smiled. 'I love my family. Dearly. But they'd drive me crazy if I went back to live with them after fourteen years of being away—there'd be questions all the time. Far more questions than you ask,' he added, seeing the colour rise in her cheeks. 'And living with my older brother's a definite no-no.' He'd thought about it, on the grounds that maybe he'd be a steadying influence. But then again, George was too strong a character to be influenced by anyone.

'Because you don't get on with him?' Jane asked.

Ed laughed. 'No. I get on fine with George. It's just that I'd never be able to keep up with him. He tends to burn the candle at both ends.'

'And you disapprove of that?'

'Not disapprove, exactly. I worry about him overdoing things. So I guess I'd drive him crazy, the same way the girls always nag me about working too hard.' He paused. 'What about you?'

'I have my own flat.'

Sidestepping again, he noticed. OK. He'd ask her straight out. 'Do you have family in London?'

'No.'

And he noticed she didn't say where her family was. 'You really don't like talking about personal stuff, do you?' he asked softly.

She spread her hands. 'What do you want to know? I'm twenty-eight, I'm working towards being a specialist registrar and I love my job. My parents used to live in London, but they're retired now and they have a place in Cornwall overlooking the sea.' She paused. 'And that's about it.'

Her body language was definitely telling him to back off. So he changed the subject to something he thought she'd find easier. 'What made you want to be a doctor?'

'I'm a fixer,' she said. 'I like to make things better. So it was the obvious career choice.'

'Me, too,' he admitted. 'Why obstetrics?'

'I was interested in IVF,' she said. 'I loved the idea of being able to give people hope, give them the family they'd dreamed about and longed for. Really making a difference.' Giving them the dream family she'd so wanted herself. She pushed the thought away. 'But then I did my rotation on the maternity ward, and I discovered just how much I like babies. There's absolutely nothing to match seeing those first magical seconds of a newborn taking in the world. Oh, and I'd better warn you in advance—it makes me cry every single time.'

He'd guessed she was soft-hearted. From what he'd seen of her at work so far, she really cared about her mums.

'But Theo knows I'm interested in IVF and I worked with the specialist team for a while, so my list tends to include more IVF mums. It means I've got the best of both worlds—I get to deliver babies, and I also get to look after mums who need a bit of extra care.' She looked at him. 'What made you choose obstetrics?'

'The same thing, really. I'm the fixer in my family, too. Right from when I was small, I used to bandage the dogs' paws and pretend I was making them better.'

'So you wanted to be a vet?'

'When I was that young, yes.' He laughed. 'Luckily the dogs were very indulgent. They'd let me listen to their heart with my stethoscope and stick a bandage on their paw. I was forced to use them as my patients because George—my older brother—was never still for long enough for me to bandage him.' He turned his coffee cup round in his hands. 'My sister Alice got meningitis when she was two. Luckily she was fine, but we spent a lot of time at the hospital, and I was desperate to make her better and make everyone in the family happy again. That's when I decided that I wanted to be a doctor. I thought about being a children's doctor, but then Frances had Bea. She was this little red-faced squeaky thing—just like Alice was—and everyone was smiling and so happy. And I knew then that was what I wanted to do—bring little red-faced squeaky things into the world and spread all that joy around.'

She laughed. 'Do your sisters know you call them red-faced squeaky things?'

'Yes.' He grinned. 'And I'm not going to tell you what they call me. Or what Charlotte calls me, for that matter.'

'Alice, Bea and Charlotte. You're Edward, and you have a brother George,' she mused. 'So who are the D and F?'

He liked the fact she'd picked that up. 'My father's David, and my stepmum's Frances.'

'Are there an H and an I, too?'

'No. And I really hope the girls aren't planning to make me an uncle to H and I before they've finished their education.'

'They're a lot younger than you, then?'

He nodded. 'I'm six years older than Alice. She's just about to be called to the bar, Bea's training to be an architect and Charlotte—the baby—is in the last year of her degree. She's on course for a First, so she's planning to do a PhD in a really obscure bit of Roman history.'

'So you're all clever.' Jane smiled. 'What does George do? Is he a professor of astrophysics or something?'

'He's—' Ed stopped. How much had Theo told the team about him? Or had Jane worked it out for herself that Ed's older brother was the Hon George Somers, heir to the barony? From what he'd seen of Jane, she was very straightforward and absolutely everything showed in her face, so it would be obvious if she read the gossip rags and knew who George was.

'He works in the family business,' Ed prevaricated.

Jane knew a sidestep when she saw one. Probably because she'd learned to be so skilled in sidestepping herself. Ed didn't want to talk about his brother as much as she didn't want to talk about Jenna. And yet he'd sounded affectionate when he'd said he worried about his brother. Something didn't quite add up, here. Though it was none of her business and she didn't want to pry—in case he started asking questions back.

She glanced at her watch. 'We need to be getting back to the ward.'

'Of course. So are we having dinner or going to the cinema tonight?'

Help. She'd hoped that getting him to talk about himself would've distracted him enough to make him forget the idea of going out. 'It's really nice of you to ask, but I can't make tonight. Some other time?' Though she was careful not to give an excuse that he could easily topple over, or to suggest anything specific—like an actual date when she could go out with him.

'Sure.'

Back on the ward, they were both kept busy, and the rest of the day shot by.

'See you tomorrow,' Ed said. 'Have a nice evening, whatever you're doing.'

Dinner for one and a pile of textbooks. But she liked it that way. 'You, too,' she said with a smile.

Even so, she couldn't get Edward Somers out of her head all evening, and she caught herself mooning over him when she was supposed to be studying. Which was ridiculous. And she was glad when the phone went and the caller display showed her best friend's number.

'Am I interrupting your studies?' Sorcha asked.

'I was about to take a break anyway,' Jane said.

'Hmm. Just checking on how you're doing.'

Jane knew exactly why Sorcha was calling. Because today was the day that horrible magazine had come out. 'I'm fine. Honestly, I am. Nobody on the ward's mentioned that article, and Theo's gone well above the call of duty and arranged that the hospital shop won't sell the magazine this week.' She bit her lip. 'Actually, I think he bought all the copies.'

'If he hadn't, Maddie and I would've clubbed together and done it,' Sorcha said. 'I'm not going to nag you about Jenna, because I know it's hard for you.'

'Good.'

'But I still think she's incredibly mean to you and you're a saint to put up with it.'

'Do you mean doormat?' Jane asked wryly.

Sorcha sighed. 'No, because you don't do it because you're weak. You do it because you're nice, and I guess family relationships are complicated. Though I'd disown her if she was mine. You know, just because you're related to someone, it doesn't mean you have to like them—or put up with them behaving badly towards you.'

Jane just coughed.

'OK, OK, I'll shut up. So what's your new colleague like?'

The gorgeous stranger I spent the night with on Saturday, and still haven't told you about, Jane thought. My guilty secret. 'Fine.'

'Come on. Deets.'

'There aren't any.'

'Well, is he nice?'

'Yes.'

'Single?'

Yes, but she didn't want to tell Sorcha that. Or that Ed had asked her out to dinner tonight. Because then Sorcha would nag her about letting Shaun's betrayal ruin her life. And Jane already knew her best friend's 'the best revenge is living well' speech by heart. 'It's hardly the first thing you'd ask a new colleague.' She really needed to change the subject, now, before she ended up telling Sorcha more than she intended. 'How's Jake?'

'He's wonderful.'

'Good.' Jane smiled. 'It was about time he noticed you. I'm so glad it's working out.'

'I just wish I had a magic wand and could find someone nice for you,' Sorcha said.

'There's no need, honestly. I'm fine on my own.'

'Really? Because I worry that you're lonely. I think what happened with Shaun last year broke something in you.'

It had. 'I guess I learned my lesson the hard way,' Jane said lightly. 'I'm sticking to friendship from now on. It makes life a lot easier.'

'Not every man's as shallow as Shaun was.'

'I know.' Ed definitely wasn't shallow. But she didn't want to analyse her feelings about him too closely. She'd thought she had a future with Shaun, that with him she'd make the close family she'd always wanted, filled with unconditional love. And she'd been so wrong. What was to say that she wouldn't be wrong about Ed, too? One night was just one night, and she was fine with that. 'I'm fine, Sorcha. Really.' Protesting a little too much, perhaps. But she'd get there.

'Well, you know where I am if you need to talk. Even if it's stupid o'clock in the morning.'

'I know, and thank you. I'm just glad you're my best friend.'

'Me, too. Now, don't study too late.'

'I won't,' Jane promised.

'And I'll see you for lunch tomorrow. Call me if you get held up, OK?'

'Will do. See you tomorrow.'

CHAPTER FIVE

'ED, I'VE got one of my mums on the way in. She's bleeding. And I could do with another view on the situation,' Jane said. 'Would you mind?'

'Sure. Fill me in on the background. Is she one of your IVF mums?'

Jane nodded. 'Pippa Duffield. She had a low-lying placenta at her twenty-week scan.'

'Nearly a third of women do. You know as well as I do, in most cases, it stops being a problem as the uterus develops further,' Ed said. 'I take it you're thinking placenta praevia in Pippa's case?'

Jane nodded. 'She's got more than average risk factor. IVF increases the chances of her placenta growing in the lowest part of the womb and covering the opening of the cervix, plus she's having twins.'

'OK. How many cycles did she have, and how old is she?'

'This was the fourth cycle, and she's thirty-eight.'

'So her age is another risk factor.' He looked grim. 'Let's hope for her sake that it's praevia and not an abruption.'

Jane hoped so, too. An abruption, where the placenta tore away from the uterus, could be life-threatening for both the babies and the mum.

Ed looked thoughtful. 'How far is she?'

'Thirty-two weeks.'

'So we'd be considering delivery at thirty-five weeks anyway. Provided we can get the bleeding under control, if the ultrasound shows it's praevia, I'd like to keep her in the ward on bed rest until delivery, so we can keep an eye on her and monitor the babies,' he said. 'Are you happy with that?'

She spread her hand. 'Hey, you're the consultant. It's your call.'

'She's one of your mums. You asked me for my opinion—I'm not muscling in and giving orders you're not happy about.'

'Thank you. Though, actually, my clinical decision would be the same as yours.'

'Good.' He smiled at her. 'I'm glad we're on the same wavelength. It feels as if I've worked with you for years, not just for a day or so.'

Funny how that warmed her. 'Me, too. And that makes life so much easier for our mums.' She smiled back at him. 'I should warn you, Pippa's desperate for a natural birth—the way she sees it, it'll make up for the fact she couldn't conceive without help.'

'That really depends on the ultrasound,' he said. 'If the placenta's within ten millimetres of her cervix, then it's too much of a risk to go for a normal delivery—both for her and for the babies.'

'Agreed,' Jane said.

Jane had asked one of the porters to meet Pippa's taxi and bring her up to the department in a wheelchair; just as she and Ed were sorting out the consulting room, Joe brought Pippa's wheelchair in.

'Thanks, Joe. I appreciate your help,' Jane said with a smile. 'Pippa, how are you doing?'

'I'm so scared, Jane. I can't lose my babies. Not now. Not after all we've been through. I just *can't*.' Pippa's face was blotchy with tears. 'When I started bleeding…' She dragged in a breath. 'I'm just so scared.'

'Of course you are. Any mum-to-be would be worried, in your shoes, and you did exactly the right thing by coming straight in,' Jane soothed, giving her a hug. 'But first of all remember that you're thirty-two weeks now, so even if the twins arrived today there's a very good chance of them being absolutely fine. And secondly, there are all sorts of reasons why women start spotting or even having quite a big bleed. Until we've examined you, I can't tell you what's happening, but you're in the best place right now. And the best thing you can do for your babies is to take some big, deep breaths for me.'

She coached Pippa through the breathing until the other woman was calmer. 'Brilliant. That's got your blood pressure back down a bit. Now, I'd like to introduce you to our new consultant, Mr Somers. Ed, this is Pippa Duffield.'

'Oh, my God.' Pippa's eyes widened. 'The bleeding's serious enough for me to see a *consultant*?'

'No. I'm just the new boy, it's my first week here, and I'm working with Jane,' Ed said cheerfully.

'And he's very good,' Jane said. 'More experienced than I am. So between us you're in great hands.'

Pippa gave her a wan smile.

'May we examine you, Mrs Duffield?' Ed asked.

'Call me Pippa,' she said. 'Yes.'

'Thank you, Pippa. And I hope you'll call me Ed.'

She nodded.

Gently, he examined her. 'Are you feeling any kind of pain?'

'No.'

'Good. Are you having any kind of contractions, even practice ones or tiny ones?'

'I don't think so.'

He nodded. 'Jane, would you mind checking the babies' heartbeats?'

Jane did so. 'The good news here is that their heartbeats both sound normal. Now, at this stage, we're not going to do an internal exam, Pippa.' Until they were sure it was placenta praevia and not an abruption, she didn't want to take the risk of causing a much worse bleed. 'But we'd like to do an ultrasound so we can get a better idea of what's causing the bleeding, if that's OK with you, Pippa?'

'The babies are all right. Thank God.' Pippa closed her eyes briefly in seeming relief. 'Do whatever you need to, Jane.'

'I'll also need to take some blood,' Jane said.

She swiftly took blood samples and assessed how much blood Jane had lost, before putting a line in for IV access; meanwhile, Ed had gone to locate the portable ultrasound scanner.

The scan showed exactly what she and Ed had expected.

'Your placenta's right near the bottom of your womb and it's partially blocking your cervix,' Ed said. 'What happens in the last trimester of pregnancy is that your cervix starts to get thinner and stretch, ready for the birth, and in your case some of the blood vessels have broken—that's what caused the bleeding. Jane tells me you haven't lost a huge amount of blood, so I'm not too worried. We can keep an eye on you. The good news is that there's a really strong chance that we can deliver the babies as originally planned, at thirty-five weeks.'

'And the bad news?' Pippa asked.

'Jane tells me you were hoping for a normal delivery.' He took her hand and squeezed it. 'I'm sorry, we can't do that, because the placenta's going to be in the way. You could end up losing a lot of blood, and we just can't take that risk—for you or for the babies.'

A tear trickled down Pippa's cheek. 'I couldn't conceive normally and I can't even have a normal birth. I'm going to be a rubbish mother.'

'No, you're not,' Ed said. 'Lots of women need help with conceiving, and lots of women end up having a Caesarean. But the good news is that we can plan it, so you won't have to go through a trial of labour first, then end up in emergency surgery because the babies are in distress and you're exhausted. It's tough enough being a mum to twins without all that on top of it.' He smiled at her. 'Right now, I'd guess you're feeling disappointed and relieved and worried, all at the same time. In your shoes, I think I'd be bawling my eyes out. So I'd say you're doing just fine.'

Pippa bit her lip. 'So what now? I go home and have to rest?'

'No. We'd like to keep you on the ward,' Jane said, 'so we can keep an eye on you.'

'Overnight?'

Ed shook his head. 'Until you have the babies.'

'Three weeks? But—I can't.' Pippa looked horrified. 'I haven't sorted out the nursery yet! I only went on maternity leave last week.' She shook her head in distress. 'I've been so careful not to overdo things and rush around like I normally would. I've taken it really easy and waited for Mike to paint the walls instead of grabbing the step ladders and doing it myself. And now…' She rubbed a hand across her eyes, scrubbing away the tears. 'I don't want Mike's mother taking over and making the room what she thinks it should be like, instead of what I want.'

'Can your mum maybe step in and bat your corner for you?' Ed asked.

'No. She died from breast cancer, two years ago.' More tears slid down Pippa's cheeks. 'I wish she was here. I wish she was going to meet my babies. She would've been such a brilliant grandmother. She wouldn't take over and try to boss me around all the time, like Mike's mother does.'

'Ed, would you mind calling Mike for us while I sit with Pippa for a bit?' Jane asked.

'Sure.' Moving so that Pippa couldn't see his face, he mouthed, 'I'll give you a yell when he gets here and we'll talk to him.'

Jane sat with Pippa, holding her hand and soothing her until she'd calmed down. 'I know this is rough on you, but we can work round things. Ed and I are happy to talk to anyone you need us to, so they know exactly why you're in and that you need a bit of TLC.'

'I don't think Mike's mother knows how to give TLC,' Pippa said wearily. 'And he never stands up to her.'

'You'd be surprised how much it changes you, becoming a parent,' Jane said softly. 'Where you might not stand up for yourself, you suddenly find that you do for your children.' At least, you stood up for your favourite one. But Pippa didn't need Jane dumping her own inadequacies on her; she needed support.

Rosie, one of the midwives, came in. 'Jane, sorry, Ed needs a quick word with you in his office.'

'Sure. I'll be back in a minute, Pippa.' She smiled at the midwife. 'Rosie, would you mind sitting with Pippa for a bit?'

'Of course I will.'

When Jane got to Ed's office, Mike Duffield was sitting on the chair at the side of Ed's desk.

'Jane, is Pippa all right? And the babies? Ed's just been telling me what happened. Can I see her?'

'They're all doing OK,' Jane reassured him. 'Mike, I know you're worried and you want to see Pippa, but we wanted a word with you before you go in.'

'Why? Is there something you haven't told her?'

Jane shook her head. 'We want to keep her in so we can keep an eye on her, and she's really upset about it.'

Mike frowned. 'So there *is* something wrong.'

'I've told you everything, Mike,' Ed said gently. 'We want to keep an eye on her because she might start bleeding again. We can monitor her and the babies here; if things get sticky and we need to deliver the twins, then there won't be any delay. Pippa's upset because she hasn't finished decorating the nursery.'

Mike's face cleared. 'Well, I can sort that out for her, and my mum will help.'

Just what Pippa had been afraid of. Jane steeled herself for a difficult conversation. 'Mike, there isn't an easy or tactful way to put this, and I apologise in advance if I'm stepping over the line here, but that's one of the things that's worrying Pippa—that she'll end up having the nursery your mum wants, not the one that *she* wants.'

Mike looked taken aback. 'You what?'

Ed glanced at Jane and gave a tiny nod. 'Is there a chance maybe you could talk to your mum?' he asked. 'Maybe you could tell her that Pippa's upset about being in hospital and not able to do things the way she wants, and ask her if she'd consider helping you carry out what Pippa planned. But most importantly she needs to come and see Pippa, to reassure her that it's going to be *her* choices that matter.'

'I…' Mike blew out a breath. 'To be honest, Mum and Pip tend to clash a bit. They both have strong ideas. If Mum thinks that Pip doesn't want her help, then it'll put her back up.'

And clearly Mike didn't relish being stuck in the middle. Jane's father was like that, so she understood exactly why Pippa hated the fact that Mike would never stand up for her. 'Is there someone else you can ask to help with the nursery? A friend, another relative?' Jane asked. 'Because Pippa needs to rest and be as calm as possible, for her sake and that of the babies. People who haven't gone through IVF often don't really understand the kind of emotional and physical strain it involves, and maybe your mum doesn't appreciate what Pippa's gone through.'

Mike grimaced. 'Mum doesn't actually know we had IVF. Pip didn't want her to know. She's got this thing about how people are going to think she's not a proper mum because she couldn't conceive without help.'

'She did say something like that,' Ed said, 'and I told her that of course she's going to be a good mum—it's got nothing to do with the way the babies were conceived or how they're going to come into the world.' He looked thoughtful. 'What about Pippa's dad? Or does she have a sister who can help?'

'Her dad's a bit frail, and her sister...' Mike wrinkled his nose. 'They're not close. I really don't think Pip would want me to ask her.'

Jane could appreciate that. She knew all about difficult sisters, too. Jenna would be the last person she'd ask for help—because she knew the answer would be no. 'What about her best friend? That's who I'd want to help me, if I were in Pippa's shoes. And if that would reassure Pippa, then as her doctor my advice to you would be to talk to her best friend.'

'Well, I could ring her,' Mike said slowly. 'Shelley's a bit bossy.'

'So's my best friend,' Jane said with a smile. 'It's one of the things I love about her. She gets things done.'

'All right. I'll call her,' Mike said. 'And I'll tell Pip not to worry about the nursery. I'll make sure it's how she wants it.'

'Thanks. Taking something big like that off her mind will really help a lot. I'll take you through to her.'

Jane ended up spending the rest of the morning with the Duffields; when she went to collect her handbag from the rest room at the beginning of her lunch break, Ed was there, too.

'How's Pippa?' he asked.

'Much more settled. And thanks for having a word with Mike. That really helped.'

'Any time.' He smiled at her. 'Got time to have lunch with me?'

She shook her head regretfully. 'Sorry, I'm already

meeting someone.' She glanced at her watch. 'And I'm going to be late! Gotta go. Catch you later.'

Jane didn't see Ed for the rest of the afternoon. She did a last check on her patients, making especially sure that Pippa had settled, at the end of her shift. She was about to leave the ward when she passed Ed's open door.

'Jane? Can I have a word?'

'Sure.'

'Close the door.'

She frowned, but did so.

'Tell me honestly, do I have a personal hygiene problem?'

She stared at him, puzzled. 'No. Why on earth would you think that?'

'Because, unless I'm also suffering from a bad case of paranoia, you seem to be avoiding me.' He sighed. 'Jane, I like you. And on Saturday I thought you liked me, too.'

She did. But she didn't want to risk getting hurt again.

Not knowing what to say, she stayed silent.

'So do I take it you've had time to think about it and you want to be strictly colleagues?' he asked.

'Yes.' She saw the disappointment in his eyes just before he masked it.

Oh. So he *did* really like her.

'And, if I'm really honest, no,' she admitted. 'Look, I don't want to go into details right now, but I don't exactly have a good track record when it comes to relationships.'

'Join the club. I'm divorced,' he said, surprising her. From what she'd seen of Ed, he was thoughtful and kind and charming. Not to mention the way he made her feel physically. So why on earth would someone want to break up with him? Unless he, too, had completely lousy judgement when it came to relationships, and had picked someone who really wasn't suited to him.

'I won't pry,' she promised.

'There isn't much to tell. We wanted different things.'

'I can identify with that,' she admitted. She'd wanted a family, and Shaun had wanted Jenna. 'Except I didn't get quite as far as marriage.'

'Sounds to me as if we have a lot in common,' Ed said. 'Including not wanting to get hurt. So how about it? We go for a pizza, somewhere really crowded with lots of bright lights, and I walk you home and kiss you very chastely goodnight outside your front door?'

'You actually want to go out with me?'

'Yes.'

He meant it. OK, so Jane's track record in judging men was pretty rubbish, but she'd seen the way he was with their patients. Totally sincere, kind, taking the time to listen. Ed Somers was a nice guy, as well as being the hottest man she'd ever met.

'Pizza, and a chaste kiss goodnight outside my front door,' she checked.

'There might be two chaste kisses. But I promise they'll be chaste. Unless—' there was a glint of mischief in his eyes '—you decide to kiss me unchastely. In which case all promises will be on hold.'

It was tempting. So very tempting.

Dared she trust him, let him get close to her? Maybe her best friend was right and she needed to just get out there, enjoy herself, and put the past behind her. Dating Ed, maybe ending up back in bed with him, didn't mean that she was going to fall in love with him. He'd been hurt, too. They didn't have to rush this or make any promises, just see where it took them. They could both enjoy this and keep their hearts intact.

'OK. I'd love to go for pizza.'

'Great. Give me five minutes to save this file and shut down the computer, and I'm all yours.'

All yours. Jane rather liked the sound of that. 'See you in five, then.'

CHAPTER SIX

JANE knew exactly the place to go: a small trattoria that was busy and brightly lit, and the food was fantastic.

'Excellent choice,' Ed said after his first taste of the pizza. 'The food's fantastic.'

'I normally come here with Sorcha—my best friend,' she explained. 'Because of the food.'

They spent the whole evening talking, discovering that they had similar tastes in music and books and films. And when Jane finished her third coffee and glanced at her watch, her eyes widened in surprise. 'Blimey! We've been here for four hours.'

Ed looked awkward. 'Sorry—I didn't mean to keep you that long.'

'No, I've really enjoyed it.' She was aware how surprised she sounded—and how bad that was. 'Sorry. I didn't mean to imply I thought I wouldn't enjoy your company. Just that it's been a while since I've gone on a date and I thought it might be a bit, well, awkward.'

'Snap. Except it wasn't,' Ed said softly. 'I've enjoyed tonight, too.'

He walked her home, escorted her up the steps to the entrance to her block of flats, and gave her a chaste kiss right at the corner of her mouth.

'Wasn't that meant to be my cheek?' Jane asked.

'Technically, it *is* your cheek,' he pointed out.

'Hmm.'

He kissed the other cheek, but this time Jane moved slightly and Ed ended up kissing her on the mouth. He pulled back and looked her straight in the eye. 'Jane, are you going to kiss me?'

'Would it be a problem?'

He smiled. 'No. It'd be a delight.'

And it was a delight for her, too. Hot enough to let her know that he found her attractive, but not so pushy that she felt pressured.

Finally, Ed broke the kiss. 'I'd better go back to the hotel.' He stroked her cheek. 'I'm not going to ask you to let me come in, even though I'd like to, because I don't quite trust myself to behave honourably.'

Was this his way of letting her down gently? she wondered.

He stole a kiss. 'You know, your face is really expressive. Never play poker, will you?'

Jane could feel her skin heat. 'Sorry,' she mumbled.

'This isn't because I don't want to come in, because I do. But we started this all the wrong way round. It might be a good idea to give us time to get to know each other properly, this time,' he said softly. 'See where it takes us.'

'I guess.'

His kiss was sweet and warm. 'See you tomorrow. Do any of your windows overlook the street?'

'The kitchen. Second floor, middle window.'

'Good. Put the light on and wave to me when you're in, OK?'

'OK.' Jane had never dated anyone who was quite

that gentlemanly before. And she loved the fact that he actually waited until she was safely indoors and had waved to him before he sketched a salute back and left for his hotel.

'Mr Somers—do you have a moment?' Jane asked the following afternoon, leaning against the jamb of Ed's office door.

'Sure. Want me to come and see one of your mums?'

'No. I was just wondering, are you busy tonight?'

'No.' He looked pleased that she'd asked. 'What did you have in mind?'

'You said yesterday about watching a film. I was wondering, maybe you'd like to come over to my flat and see a film this evening. Say, about eight?'

'I'd like that,' he said.

'Comedy or serious drama?'

'I'll leave the choice to you.'

'You might regret that,' she warned.

He grinned. 'You said that about dancing with you. I didn't have any regrets then, so I doubt I'll have any regrets tonight, either.' He winked at her. 'See you later, Jane.'

At precisely eight o'clock, Ed walked up the steps to Jane's apartment block and pressed the buzzer.

'Come up. Second floor, first door on the left next to the stairs.' Her voice sounded slightly crackly through the intercom.

By the time he reached the second floor, her door was already open and she was waiting for him. 'Hi.'

'For you.' He handed her the flowers he'd bought on the way back to the hotel from the hospital.

'Oh, they're lovely, all summery and…' She buried her nose in them and inhaled deeply. 'I adore the smell of stocks. Thank you, Ed. They're gorgeous.'

'My pleasure.' He'd thought that roses might be too obvious, and was glad he'd opted for the pretty, scented summer flowers instead.

And he'd also guessed that she'd like crisp white wine. She beamed at him when he handed her the chilled bottle of Chablis. 'This is my favourite—and you really didn't have to, you know.'

'I know. I just wanted to.'

'Come in. I'm going to put these gorgeous flowers in water—make yourself at home,' she said. 'The living room's through there. I take it you'll have a glass of wine, too?'

'Thanks, that'd be lovely.'

Her flat was exactly what he'd expected it to be: small, but warm and homely. The living room had an overstuffed sofa and soft furnishings in rich autumnal colours. He couldn't resist browsing her bookshelves; there was an eclectic mix of thrillers, poetry and medical textbooks, and another shelf held a selection of films, a mixture of serious dramas and comedies.

On the mantelpiece there were several framed photographs. Ed knew he was snooping and Jane was cagey about her personal life, but he looked anyway. One of the photographs was of Jane on her graduation day with an older couple he guessed were her parents, though they didn't look much like her; another was of Jane with a bubbly-looking redhead he guessed was her best friend. There was also a photo of a much younger version of Jane with a Springer spaniel draped all over her and the widest, widest smile, and another of Jane with an elderly woman.

'Gorgeous dog,' he said when she came into the living room, carrying two glasses of wine.

'That's Bertie. He was my great-aunt's,' she said. 'I always wanted a dog, but my mum didn't really like them. She said they were too messy and she always moaned about dog hair on her clothes whenever we visited Sadie.' She shrugged. 'Sadie had a quiet word with me and told me that I could share Bertie with her, and she'd look after him between visits.'

'And I guess, working hospital hours and living in a flat, you can't really have a dog here,' he said.

'No.' She looked regretful. 'I adored Bertie. He was the sweetest, gentlest dog ever.'

'Is that Sadie?' he asked, pointing to the photograph of the elderly woman.

She nodded. 'Sadly, she died last year. But she was lovely. I was privileged to have her in my life.'

'That's how I feel about my sisters,' he said. 'And George.'

For a moment, he could've sworn that she flinched. And her smile didn't quite reach her eyes when she said, 'It's good to have people like that around.'

'Are these your parents?' He indicated the picture of her with the older couple.

'Yes.'

'And I'm asking too many questions?'

'No, it's OK.' She shrugged. 'It's an old picture now, but my mum's barely changed in the last thirty years. I guess that's the thing about supermodels—they have wonderful bone structure.'

'Your mum was a supermodel?'

She nodded. 'She's retired now.'

He studied the photograph, and it made him wonder. Jane's mother was classically beautiful, but there was something remote about her. Plus by Jane's own admission her mother was fussy about dog hairs and mud. He had the strongest feeling that Jane's childhood hadn't been anywhere near as happy as his own. He couldn't remember that much of his own mother, but his stepmother Frances had always been warm, welcoming and loving—not to mention completely unbothered about the amount of hair their assorted dogs and cats shed. Clearly Jane's mother wasn't like that; she didn't sound like the easiest of people to be close to.

'I think you have her eyes,' he said eventually, trying to be diplomatic.

'Maybe.' She handed him one of the wine glasses. 'Here.'

'Thanks.' He took the hint and put the photograph down. 'So what did you pick, in the end? Serious drama or a comedy?'

'Comedy,' she said.

'Sounds good.'

When she sat next to him on the sofa, he slid one arm round her shoulders and she relaxed into him. The film wasn't bad, but he couldn't take his attention off Jane. So much for his good intentions. But they'd spent hours talking last night, getting to know each other better. One kiss wouldn't hurt, would it?

He shifted slightly so he was half-lying on the sofa. When she leaned into him, he shifted further, and moved her so that she was lying on top of him.

'Hello,' he said softly, and reached up to kiss her.

He had meant it to be soft and sweet, but then she

opened her mouth, letting him deepen the kiss, and his control snapped. His fingers slid under the hem of her T-shirt, moving further up until his hands were splayed against her back. And the way she was lying, she'd be in no doubt of how much she turned him on. He could feel the softness of her breasts against his chest, and also the hardness of her nipples; so he had a pretty good idea that it was the same for her, too.

'Sorry. That wasn't meant to happen,' he said when they surfaced from the kiss. 'I was trying to be a gentleman. But you leaned into me.'

'Hmm,' she said.

But there was a twinkle in her eye, so he grinned back, moving so that he was sitting upright and she was still straddling him.

He wrapped his arms round her. 'You know what I was saying about taking it slowly and getting to know each other first? I've had a rethink.'

'And?'

'I reckon we need to do some speed dating.'

She frowned. 'Speed dating?'

'So we get to know everything about each other. Like now. And then I can do…' He paused. 'What I think you'd like me to do, too.'

He loved the fact that she blushed spectacularly.

'Before I met you, I never behaved like this. For pity's sake, we haven't even known each other for a week,' she said.

'No. It's completely illogical and irrational…and irresistible.' He kissed her. 'Your eyes are very green.'

'What does that mean?'

'I noticed on Saturday. You know I said your eyes

change colour? When you're turned on, your eyes go green.'

Her blush deepened even further. 'You make me sound like—I dunno, some kind of siren. I'm ordinary. Plain Jane.'

'If you were ordinary,' he said softly, 'I wouldn't be reacting like this to you.' He kissed her again, just to prove it. 'I was intending to go home. To be gentlemanly.'

'But?' Her voice was very, very soft.

'But what I really want to do right now is carry you to your bed and drive you as crazy as you drive me.' He shook his head. 'I don't do this sort of thing. I'm the serious one in the family, the one who plays by all the rules. But something about you makes me want to be different. To take a chance and follow my feelings instead of my head.'

'Like James Bond.' She stroked his face. 'You already know I think you'd give him a run for his money.'

Actually, he thought wryly, the James Bond-alike would be George, not him. 'Thank you for the compliment, but hardly.'

'Come off it. Half the hospital's swooning over you.'

'Since when?'

'I told you, the grapevine works fast at our place.'

He raised an eyebrow. 'Would you mind very much if they talked about us?'

She grimaced. 'I don't like being the hot topic.'

Of course. She'd probably been there after her ex. 'Did he work at the hospital?'

'No.' She sighed. 'I guess I ought to tell you what happened. Though it's not pretty. I came home early one day—I'd forgotten to tell him I was on a half-day—and found him in our bed with someone else.'

Ed sucked in a breath. How on earth could the guy have betrayed Jane like that? 'I'm sorry he hurt you like that. That's…' He couldn't find the words to describe it, but he needed to say something. To let her know he was on her side. 'That's a really shoddy way to treat someone.'

She shrugged. 'I'm over it now.'

'Are you?'

She nodded. 'But I will admit that Saturday was the first time I'd felt beautiful since it happened.'

'How long ago?'

'Eight months,' she admitted.

'Then I'm glad I could do that for you.' He paused. 'Just for the record, I don't believe in cheating. While I'm seeing you, I won't be seeing anyone else, and that's a promise.'

'Same here.'

'Good.' He stroked her hair. 'I don't know what to say.'

She shrugged. 'There's nothing to say. I gave Shaun his ring back and moved out that same day.'

She'd been *engaged* to the guy when he'd cheated on her? What the hell had been wrong with him?

'Sorcha was brilliant and let me stay with her until I found this place.'

'The more you tell me about your best friend, the more I like her.'

Jane smiled. 'She's the sister I wish I had.'

'The best kind of friend. Since we're sharing difficult stuff, I should tell you…' He sighed. 'My family's, um, fairly well-to-do. And my ex thought she'd have the lifestyle that goes with that kind of family.' Camilla had come from the same kind of background as his own, and she'd had definite expectations. 'I don't think she realised the kind of hours that junior doctors work— or how important my job is to me. I think maybe she expected me to…' How could he put this without scaring Jane away? 'To give it up and join the family business,' he finished. He knew it was selfish of him, but he was truly glad that being the second son meant that he'd never had to face that choice—that he was able to follow his real calling and make a difference to people's lives, instead of doing his duty and trying not to let his family have any idea how trapped he felt.

He sighed. 'I guess I'm selfish. Or I didn't really love my ex enough, because I just couldn't give up medicine for her. Being a doctor, helping mums through tricky pregnancies and helping make their dreams of a family come true—that's who I *am*, not just what I do.'

She kissed him. 'That's how I feel about it, too.'

'But it's not fair of me to put all the blame on Camilla. I dragged her off to Glasgow because I had the chance to work with a top specialist and I wanted to take the opportunity to learn from him. It didn't occur to me how cut off she'd feel from London, and I should've taken her needs into account a lot more than I did,' he said. 'So I'm very, very far from being perfect.'

'You and me both,' she said softly. 'I had this dream and I was so sure that Shaun was the one to make it all come true for me. I expected too much from him. And I guess he couldn't take the fact that I was never going to be tall and skinny and elegant. So he found someone who was.'

'Which is incredibly shallow. It's not what people

look like, it's who they are that's important. And anyway, not all men want a stick insect. Some men happen to like little, cute, curvy women.' He punctuated every adjective with a kiss. Just to make sure she knew he meant it. 'He really doesn't know what he's missing.' He kissed her again, and her hands slid into his hair. He splayed his palms over her spine. 'Jane. Shall we skip the rest of the film?'

Her eyes were very green. 'Yes.' She kissed him back.

He had no idea how they got off the sofa, but the next thing he knew he was on his feet, he'd scooped her into his arms, and he was carrying her out of the living room. 'Which one's your room?'

'First door on the right.'

He nudged the door open and smiled. 'I'm so glad you have a double bed.'

'It's good for spreading papers out on.'

'True.' He stole a kiss. 'But I have other plans.' He set her down on her feet. 'Starting here.' He unbuttoned her jeans, and she sucked in a breath.

'I was in too much of a rush last time. This time I'm going to enjoy it.'

Her eyes widened. 'Ed—the curtains.'

'Wait here—and stop thinking,' he directed. He swiftly closed the curtains and switched on her bedside lamp, then came back to her side. Gently, he encouraged her to lift up her arms, and drew her T-shirt up over her head.

God, her curves made him ache. He didn't know whether he wanted to look at her first, touch her, taste her, or all three at once.

He dropped to his knees in front of her and gradually

peeled her jeans down, stroking her skin as he bared it. He let her balance on him while he helped her out of the denim completely, then sat back on his haunches to look at her. 'Wow, you're gorgeous. All curves.'

She looked shy. 'Do you think you could take some of your clothes off as well? I'm feeling a bit...well, exposed, here.'

'I'm in your hands,' he said, standing up.

She peeled off his own T-shirt, then shyly undid the button of his jeans. He helped her remove them, then traced the lacy edge of her bra. She shivered and tipped her head back in invitation. Smiling, he unsnapped her bra and cupped her breasts. 'You're gorgeous. Lush,' he whispered.

She coloured, but something in her expression told him that he'd pleased her.

Gently, he hooked his thumbs over the edge of her knickers and drew them down. She did the same with his boxers.

He picked her up, loving the feel of her skin against his, and laid her against the pillows. He paused to grab his wallet from his discarded jeans and ripped open the condom packet.

Her hand slid over his. 'My job, I think.'

It thrilled him that she'd refound her confidence with him—just as he was finding his with her. He shivered as she rolled the latex over his shaft. And then he was right where he wanted to be, kneeling between her thighs and buried deep inside her.

Her pupils widened with pleasure, and her eyes were the clearest green.

He took it as slowly as he could, until finally her

body tightened round his, pushing him into his own climax, and his body surged into hers.

Afterwards, Ed went to the bathroom, and returned to see Jane sitting in bed, looking slightly wary.

'I'm not expecting you to let me stay the night, but leaving right now would feel completely wrong,' he said. 'Can I stay for a bit longer?

She smiled. 'I'd like that.'

'Thank you.'

He climbed back into the bed and drew her into his arms; she held him close and he relaxed, enjoying the companionable silence and the warmth of her body against his. He waited until she'd fallen asleep, then wriggled out of the bed without waking her and dressed swiftly.

As he left the bedroom, he realised that the DVD player and TV were still on; they'd been so caught up in each other that neither of them had noticed. He turned them off, took their glasses into her kitchen, then took the top sheet from the jotter block next to the phone and left her a scribbled note propped against the kettle.

Hope you slept well. Can't wait to see you at work this morning. E x

Then he quietly let himself out of her flat.

CHAPTER SEVEN

THE note Ed had left her made Jane smile all the way through her hated early morning run and then all the way in to work.

When she walked into the staff kitchen, Ed was already there, spooning instant coffee into a mug.

'Good morning.'

He glanced round, gave her a sultry smile, and kissed her swiftly.

'Ed!' she said, shocked. 'Supposing someone had walked in on us?'

'They didn't,' he reassured her. 'Though would it really matter if they had?'

'I guess not. I mean, we're seeing each other, but we're both professional enough not to let it get in the way at work.'

'Exactly.' He smiled again. 'Good morning. Did you sleep well?'

'Yes. Did you?'

'Oh, yeah.' The expression in his eyes heated her blood. 'Especially as I had a very, *very* nice dream.'

'Funny, that. So did I.' She glanced at her watch. 'Rounds in ten minutes?'

'Suits me fine.' He gestured to the kettle. 'Want a coffee?'

'No, thanks. I'll pass.' She gave him a sidelong glance. 'I've already had coffee this morning. With a very nice side order.'

'You saw the note, then.'

'Indeed I did, Mr Somers.' And she loved the fact he couldn't wait to see her again. 'See you in ten.' She winked at him, and sashayed out of the kitchen.

Their rounds were routine; Pippa Duffield's condition was stable, and Mrs Taylor was responding so well to treatment that Ed planned to let her go home on Monday, provided she managed to continue eating little and often over the weekend.

But the afternoon saw Iris sending Rosie, one of the more junior midwives, to grab them both. 'Iris says she need a forceps delivery *right now*,' Rosie said. 'Prolapsed cord.'

Rare, and scary, Jane thought.

'And it's not a breech or a footling presentation.'

Rarer still. Jane looked at Ed, knowing how serious the situation could be; given that it wasn't a breech presentation, it meant that the umbilical cord was probably longer than normal and part of it had passed through the entrance to the uterus. There was a real risk of the blood flow being restricted during contractions so the baby wouldn't get enough oxygen, and the baby could be in distress—or even stillborn.

'How far down is the head?' Ed asked.

'The mum's in the second stage, fully dilated, and the head's pretty far down,' Rosie said.

'Too late for a section, then. OK. Iris is absolutely right. We'll need to try forceps,' Ed said, looking grim. 'But if the baby isn't out within three sets of traction, we're talking emergency section under a general.'

As soon as they went into the delivery suite, Iris introduced them to the mum, Tilly Gallagher, who was kneeling with her bottom in the air and her shoulders lowered to slow down the delivery. Iris was clearly following established procedure, pushing the baby's head back up between contractions to avoid extra pressure on the umbilical cord. Pushing the cord back behind the head wasn't an option, because handling the cord could cause the blood vessels to spasm and reduce the amount of oxygen coming to the baby.

Tilly's husband Ray was holding her hand and looking as if he wished he was elsewhere.

'Try not to panic, Tilly,' Ed said, 'but the umbilical cord's causing a bit of a complication and the safest way to deliver your baby is if we give you a little bit of help.' He glanced at Jane, who nodded and took over.

'We're going to use forceps to help deliver the baby. We'll also need to give you an episiotomy.' She talked Tilly and Ray through the procedure while Ed checked the monitor to see how the baby was doing and Rosie went to fetch one of the senior paediatricians, ready to check the baby over after delivery.

They helped Tilly into position for delivery, in stirrups. 'I know it's not very dignified, but it'll help us deliver the baby quickly,' Jane said. 'Ray, if you'd like to stay here by Tilly's side, hold her hand and help her with her breathing?'

Ray looked grateful that they weren't expecting him to view the birth.

Ed administered a local anaesthetic and gave Tilly an episiotomy ready for the delivery. Jane put the forceps together and was about to hand them to him when he mouthed to her, 'It'll be good experience for you to do it.'

Prolapsed cords weren't that common, and Jane knew that he was right about this being good experience for her. Warmed that he had faith in her—and knowing that he would be there to help and advise her if things started to get tricky—Jane smiled at Tilly. 'OK. What I'm going to do is help guide the baby's head down with every contraction. If you're at all worried at any point, just say and we'll do our best to reassure you. Are you ready?'

Tilly took a deep breath. 'I'm ready.'

As Tilly's contractions progressed, Jane synchronised traction with the forceps, guiding the baby's head downwards. She was aware of Rhys Morgan coming into the delivery suite, but was concentrating too much on Tilly and the baby to exchange any pleasantries with him.

She was relieved when the baby was finally delivered; while Rhys and Iris checked the baby over, she and Ed checked Tilly over.

The baby was silent, and Jane was aware of every second passing, every pulse of blood in her veins.

Please let the baby cry. Please let them have been in time. Jane had her back to Iris and Rhys so she couldn't see what they were doing, but she knew they were probably giving the baby oxygen to help inflate the lungs and encourage the baby to breathe.

Please let the baby cry.

Just as she was starting to panic inwardly, she heard a thin wail.

At last. She exchanged a relieved glance with Ed.

She herd Iris calling out the Apgar score, and then

finally Rhys came over with the baby wrapped in a warm blanket and placed the infant in Tilly's arms. 'Congratulations, Mr and Mrs Gallagher, you have a little boy.'

'Oh, my baby.' A tear slid down Tilly's cheek. 'Ray, he looks just like you.'

'He's— Oh, my God,' Ray whispered. 'Our baby.'

Jane couldn't hold back the tears trickling down her own face. 'He's gorgeous.'

'Congratulations,' Ed said warmly. 'There is a little bit of bruising, but that will go down in the next couple of days.'

'And he's going to be all right?' Ray asked.

'He's doing fine,' Rhys reassured her. 'The scary stuff is all past. I'll be in to see you later today, but in the meantime if you're worried about anything you're in very safe hands here.' He nodded acknowledgement to Ed and Jane. 'Catch you both later.'

Ed looked at Jane. 'You're crying.'

'I told you, I always do when I deliver a baby,' she said softly. 'Because it's such a perfect moment, the beginning of a new life, and it's such a privilege to be here.'

Iris put her arm round Jane and hugged her. 'You did well.'

'Hey. Tilly's the one who did most of the work, and your call was spot on,' Jane said.

'I just wish I'd picked it up earlier.' Iris sighed. 'But there were no signs, not until her waters broke and the monitor bleeped to say the baby was in distress.'

'Nobody could've predicted it. And your assessment was perfect,' Ed said.

He and Jane left Iris and Rosie with the Gallaghers

and their newborn son, and Ed shepherded her through to his office. He opened the bottom drawer of his desk, extracted a bar of chocolate and handed it to her.

She blinked. 'What's this for?'

'Sugar. I think you need it.' He blew out a breath. 'That was a scary moment back then.'

'You're telling me.' She broke the chocolate bar in half and handed one piece back to him. 'I was getting a bit worried when I couldn't hear the baby crying.'

'Rhys says he's absolutely fine. They were lucky. And you were a star with the forceps.'

'Thanks for letting me do it. I mean, I've done forceps deliveries before, but they've been where the mum was so exhausted that she needed a bit of help.'

'This wasn't so much different. I knew you'd be fine—and if it had got tricky, I was there,' he said. 'We're a good team.'

Inside *and* outside work. Not that she should let herself fall for Ed too quickly. Even though she knew he wouldn't hurt her the way Shaun had, she also knew it wasn't sensible to rush into this.

'Are you busy tonight?' he asked.

'Don't think I'm pushing you away, but I'm studying.' Which was also a good excuse to keep him at just a tiny distance. Just enough to stop her being as vulnerable as she'd been with Shaun. 'Sorry. I did tell you I was nerdy. And boring.'

'No, you're being sensible and advancing your career. It's much better to study little and often than to cram it all in. You remember it better that way.'

'You're moving to your new flat tomorrow, aren't you?' she asked.

'Yes.'

'I could help, if you like,' she offered.

He smiled. 'I'd like that. Shall I pick you up at ten?'

'That'd be great.'

At precisely ten o'clock the next morning, Ed rang the entryphone, and Jane buzzed him up. Even dressed for moving and unpacking boxes, in soft ancient denims and a worn T-shirt, he looked utterly gorgeous.

'What?' he asked, tipping his head to one side.

She raised an eyebrow. 'Just thinking about Mr Bond.'

'Good.' His smile turned sultry. 'Hold on to that thought.'

'So do we need to go and pick up your things from a storage place?'

'I've already done that. The van's full,' he said. 'If I carry the boxes in, would you mind starting to unpack them?'

'Sure—actually, before we go, do you have coffee, milk and a kettle?'

He looked blank. 'It never even occurred to me. I've been living in the hotel for a week, and my kettle's packed in one of the boxes.'

'So I take it you don't have any cleaning stuff, either?'

'I'm using an agency,' he admitted. 'They bring their own cleaning stuff. And they cleaned the flat for me yesterday. All we need to do is unpack.'

'I'll bring my kettle until we find yours,' she said. She grabbed a jar of coffee, took an opened carton of milk from the fridge, and emptied out her kettle. She put the lot in a plastic bag, locked the door behind her, and followed him outside. He opened the passenger door of the van for her, then drove her to a new apartment building in Pimlico, overlooking the river.

'Want to look round before we start?' he asked.

'Love to.' The flat was gorgeous, really light and airy. There was a large reception room with French doors, containing a couple of bookshelves, a small dining table and four chairs and two pale yellow leather sofas. Next to it was a decent-sized separate kitchen; there was a large bedroom overlooking the river, and an immaculate pure white bathroom. But the best bit for Jane was the riverside terrace leading off from the reception room.

'Oh, now this is gorgeous. You could have breakfast overlooking the river,' she said, gesturing to the wrought iron bistro table and chairs.

'That's what made me decide to rent it,' Ed said.

'If you had some tubs of plants out here for a bit of colour and scent, this balcony would be perfect,' she said. Not to mention eye-wateringly expensive; she knew what prices were like in this part of London, and the river view would add an extra chunk to the rent.

Ed had labelled his boxes sensibly, so it made unpacking much easier. He'd wrapped the crockery and glassware in newspaper to protect it for the move, so everything needed washing. 'Shall I do this while you put everything else where you want it?' she suggested.

By the end of the afternoon, Ed's flat looked a bit more lived-in. Though it was still very much a masculine bachelor pad; the soft furnishings were skimpy in the extreme, and the place had the air of being designed rather than being home.

'You're brilliant,' he said, kissing her. 'Thanks so much. I'd still be doing this at midnight if you hadn't helped.'

'That's OK.' But she was warmed by his appreciation.

She wandered over to the mantelpiece. 'Can I be nosey?'

'Sure.'

All the photographs were in proper silver frames, she noticed. And there was a really nice picture of him with a man who looked so much like him that he had to be Ed's older brother, plus three girls who had the same colouring but finer features and she guessed were his half-sisters. There was a very posh garden in the background; given the way they were dressed, she guessed that they'd been at some kind of garden party.

They all looked close-knit, with arms round each other and affectionate glances, and she suppressed a sigh. Ed was clearly close to his family. How could she explain to him that she wasn't particularly close to hers?

And she really, really didn't want to tell him about Jenna. It had been hard enough telling him about Shaun.

'They look nice,' she said.

'They are. They're noisy and they're nosey and they drive me to distraction, but I love them to bits.'

The warmth in his voice told her that he meant it. Jane felt another pang. She loved her family, too, but they didn't make it easy for her. She'd thought for years that maybe she was the problem—the nerdy, quiet, clumsy one who didn't fit in. She had so little in common with them that it was hard for them even to like her, let alone love her.

But then she'd met Sorcha. The way Sorcha's family had taken her to their hearts, making her feel like one of them—plus the easy camaraderie she had with her colleagues on the ward—made her rethink the position. Maybe she wasn't the difficult one, after all. And you could still love someone without actually liking them, couldn't you?

'Penny for them?' Ed asked, obviously noticing her distraction.

No way. Wild horses wouldn't drag these thoughts from her. 'Nothing important,' she said.

To her relief, he changed the subject. 'How about I order us a takeaway? After making you slave all day, the least I can do is feed you.'

She smiled. 'Thanks. That'd be lovely.'

Jane spent Sunday studying. And it hadn't been as bad a week as she'd expected; nobody at the hospital had said a word to her about that awful article. Jenna had been remarkably quiet, too, though Jane supposed that her twin was probably busy on a shoot somewhere. It was when Jenna wasn't busy that trouble tended to happen.

And she ended up seeing Ed every other night for the next couple of weeks. He took her dancing; for the first time ever she found herself actually enjoying it, because he led her through the moves and was there to catch her before she fell. It turned out that he liked the same art-house cinema that she did; Shaun had always been bored if it wasn't an action flick, and he'd never discussed the films with her afterwards. Ed was different; he insisted on going for an ice-cream sundae afterwards and talking about the film.

He whisked her off to Cambridge one Saturday afternoon, punted her all the way down the river to Grantchester Meadows, then lay in the long grass with her, her head pillowed on his chest. And when he kissed her in the middle of the river on the way back and whispered, 'You're beautiful,' she believed him. The more time she spent with him, the more she liked him; she'd never felt so in tune with someone before.

And maybe, just maybe, Ed was the one she could trust with her heart.

CHAPTER EIGHT

ON TUESDAY Jane was having lunch with Ed when his mobile phone rang.

'Excuse me a second,' he said. 'I'm going into the corridor where there's a better reception.'

He came back white-faced.

'What's wrong?' she asked.

He sighed heavily. 'That was Alice. George has had an accident.'

A road accident? And, given how pale Ed looked... 'Oh, no. Is he OK?'

'He'll live. Would you believe, he crashed into a cliff?'

She blinked. 'Into? Not off?'

'Into,' Ed confirmed. 'It wasn't a car accident.' He rolled his eyes. 'God knows what he was doing. Jet skiing or something like that, I suppose. He's going to be an inpatient for a week, at least. He'll be stir crazy by tonight, so I hate to think what he'll be like by the time the plaster comes off. He loathes being cooped up. The girls and I are going to have a rota to visit him, but he's still going to be bored rigid.'

'Is he in London?'

'Yes, over at the Hampstead Free—they're pinning

his leg right now, so there's no point in me dropping everything and going over, because I can't be in Theatre with him.' He bit his lip. 'I'm going straight after work.'

He looked worried sick. Jane reached across the table and took his hand. 'Do you want me to come with you?'

He looked at her. 'It's a bit of an ask.'

'You'd do the same for me, if my brother had had an accident—not that I've got a brother, but you know what I mean.'

'Thanks, I appreciate it.' He grimaced. 'I'd better warn you in advance, George is a bit of a charmer and a terrible flirt. But I guess even he's going to be held back by having a broken leg and two broken wrists. Not to mention concussion.'

She squeezed his hand, guessing what he was worrying about. A bang on the head could turn out to be very, very nasty indeed; and, as a doctor, Ed would have a pretty good idea of the worst-case scenario. 'Don't build things up in your head. It might not be as bad as you think it is.'

'Yeah, that's the worst thing about being a medic. It's years since I did my emergency department rotation, but I remember seeing head injuries and—oh, God, if he ends up with a subdural haematoma or something…'

'You're building bridges to trouble,' she said gently. 'Alice has probably already told you the worst: a broken leg, two broken wrists and concussion. And, as you said yourself, right now there's nothing you can do.'

'No.' But Ed clearly felt too miserable to finish his lunch.

She was relieved mid-afternoon when they were called in to do an emergency Caesarean section, knowing that concentrating on their patient would take Ed's mind off his worries about his brother. She let Ed close the wound after delivery rather than asking to do it herself, knowing that he needed the distraction.

Finally, it was the end of their shift and they caught the Tube over to Hampstead. On the way, Ed responded to a stream of text messages from his sisters, father and stepmother. He paused when they got to the hospital shop. 'This is crazy, but I've got no idea what to take him. The girls have already stocked him up with grapes and chocolates, there's a no-flowers rule in place and George isn't exactly a flower person anyway.'

'Why not go and see him first?' Jane suggested. 'Then you can ask him what he wants you to bring in for him.'

'Good idea.' He grimaced. 'Sorry. I'm not usually this dense or indecisive.'

'Of course not. You're just worried about your brother.'

He hugged her. 'Thank you for being here—I do appreciate it. Even if I am being grumpy and unapproachable.'

She stroked his face. 'You're worried,' she repeated. 'Come on. Let's go up to the ward and see how he's doing. You'll feel a lot better then.'

'You're right.' He released her from the hug, but twined his fingers through hers as they walked through the corridors. 'Thanks, Jane.'

'May I see George Somers, please?' Ed asked the nurse who was sorting out paperwork at the nurses' station.

'George?' The nurse looked up and then smiled at him. 'Oh, from the look of you, you must be his brother Ed. He's been talking about you.'

'How is he?'

'A bit sorry for himself, bless him,' she said. 'I'll take you through to see him.'

'Thank you.' Ed paused. He knew he was about to break protocol, but he really needed to know, because he was close to going crazy with worry. 'Can I be really cheeky and ask, would you mind me having a quick look at his notes, please? I'm not going to interfere with treatment or anything, but you know how it is when you're a medic.' He gave her an apologetic smile. 'You always start thinking the worst and worrying about the complications.'

'And seeing it all written down stops you panicking.' The nurse looked sympathetic. 'As long as George gives his permission for you to see them, yes—as long as you know that even then it'll be a favour, not a right.'

'Thanks. I won't abuse it,' Ed promised.

She took them through to the small room where George was lying on the bed, his eyes closed and his face covered in bruises.

Ed's fingers tightened round Jane's. Oh, God. He'd known on an intellectual level that George would be in a mess, but actually seeing it for himself made everything seem much more real. If George had been one of his patients, Ed would've coped just fine; he would've been brisk and cheerful and supportive. But seeing his older brother lying there after surgery, with all the associated tubes and dressings, made him feel as if he couldn't breathe. His lungs felt frozen with fear. What if there were post-op complications? What if there was a subdural haematoma they hadn't picked up? *What if George died?*

'Since he's asleep, is it OK to wait here until he wakes up?' he asked the nurse.

'Of course.' She patted his arm. 'Try not to worry. He's doing fine. If you need anything, come and find me.'

Ed sat down on the chair next to George's bed and pulled Jane onto his lap. He really needed her warmth, right now. Thank God she had such a huge heart and wouldn't judge him.

'Do you want me to go and get you a cup of hot sweet tea from the café?' Jane asked.

'No, I'm fine,' he lied. More like, he didn't want her to move. He needed her close.

'You're not fine, Ed,' she said softly.

He sighed. 'I'm better with you here.' He leaned his head against her shoulder. 'Thanks for coming with me. And I'm sorry I'm such a mess right now.'

She stroked his hair. 'Hey. Anyone would be, in your shoes. It's always worse when it's one of your family lying in that hospital bed.'

'I hate to think of how much pain he's been in.' And the fact that George could've been killed… His brother's death would have left a huge, unfillable hole in his life. Not just his, either: his father, stepmother and sisters all loved George as much as Ed did, even when he was driving them crazy with one of his escapades.

He sighed. 'Why does my brother always have to take such stupid risks?'

'Wasn't stupid. Had protective gear on,' a slurred voice informed them.

Guilt rushed through Ed. George needed his rest, and his voice had been too loud. 'Sorry. I didn't mean to wake you.'

'Wasn't asleep. Just resting my eyes. Knew you'd be here.' George gave him a slightly sheepish smile. 'Alice already nagged me, so don't bother.'

'There's no point in nagging you. You won't listen anyway,' Ed said.

'Who's this?' George looked questioningly at Jane.

'Jane. Jane, this is my brother George.'

'She's sitting on your lap. Hmm. She the girl you wouldn't tell me about?'

Ed sighed. 'Yes.' He could see on Jane's face that she was wondering why he'd kept her quiet. Once she'd met his family, she'd understand: they were incredibly full on, and he wanted to be sure where this was going before he let her meet them. He'd explain later. But not in front of his brother.

''Lo, Jane,' George said.

'Hello, George. Nice to meet you, even though it's not in the best of circumstances,' she said politely.

'And you.' George smiled at her, and looked at Ed. 'Jane. Ex'lent. I can call you "Tarzan" now, Ed.'

Jane laughed. 'You can try, but he'll frown at you.'

George grinned. 'She knows you well, then.'

'Yeah, yeah.' Though it heartened Ed that George was feeling well enough to tease him. 'How are you feeling?'

'Bit woozy,' George admitted. 'Gave me enough painkillers to fell a horse.'

'Probably because you needed them, and you've had a general anaesthetic as well so you're going to feel woozy for a day or so.' Ed meant to be nice. He really did. But the fear turned to anger, and the question just burst out. 'What the hell did you do, dive-bomb the cliff or something?'

'No, got caught out by a gust of wind.'

'*Wind*? What the hell were you doing?'

'Paragliding.'

That was a new one on him. Though he knew that George had been looking for another outlet for his energy, since their father had banned him, absolutely, from racing cars.

'How did it happen?'

George grimaced. 'My fault. Not concentrating properly.'

Thinking of a girl, no doubt. 'You could've killed yourself, George.'

''M still here,' George said mildly.

'With what looks like a broken femur, two broken wrists and some broken fingers.' Ed sighed. 'Can I read your notes?'

'Yeah. Can you translate 'em for me?'

'Tomorrow, I will, when you're more with it,' Ed promised. 'Right now, you won't take much in—you're still too woozy even to string a sentence together properly.' And he really hoped it was the combination of pain and the after-effects of the anaesthetic making George slur his words, rather than being a warning signal of something more sinister.

He fished the notes out of the basket at the head of George's bed. 'Yup. Two broken wrists, one broken femur—and...' George had hit the cliff face on, and pretty hard. He'd automatically put his hands up to save his face, which was why both wrists and some fingers were broken; but he'd also damaged his leg. And he'd sustained a blow to his testes, according to the notes. Hard enough to put a question over his future fertility.

Which meant that, even though George was the heir

to the barony, he might not be able to have children. And
that in turn meant that at some point Ed could have to
give up the job he loved and do his duty for the family. Not that that was uppermost in Ed's mind. All he
could see was his brother crashing into the cliff. Lying
on an ambulance trolley. On the table in Theatre. How
nearly they'd lost him. 'You *idiot*. You could've killed
yourself.'

George shrugged. ''M OK. Could be worse. Didn't
break my head, did I?'

'No, just your leg and your wrists. I know you're a
thrill-seeker, and I get that you love the adrenalin rush.
But, for pity's sake, can't you do things the *safe* way?'
Ed asked plaintively.

'Nagging.' George wrinkled his nose. 'Pointless.'

There were times when Ed really, really wanted to
shake his older brother. But maybe not while he still
had concussion. 'Give me strength.'

'Powered paragliding's not dangerous.'

'Says the man who's got a metal rod holding his leg
together and both wrists in plaster.'

'What's powered paragliding?' Jane asked.

'Awesome,' George said, and smiled. ''S a motor like
a backpack for take off, then you glide on the current.
Show you pictures later.'

'I take it you need training to do that?' Ed asked.

'Yes. 'M certified.'

Jane smiled. 'Judging by the look on Ed's face, I
think you might mean *certifiable*.'

George laughed. 'Prob'ly.' Then he sobered. 'Gonna
be stuck here f'r a whole week.'

Given that George barely sat still for five minutes,
this was going to crucify him, Ed thought. 'Think your-

self lucky you're not in traction—you'd be stuck there for a lot longer than that,' he said.

'What'm I gonna do for a whole *week*?' George asked plaintively.

'The girls and I will visit. And Dad and Frances.'

'You're working. Charlie and Bea've got exams. Alice'll nag me. Frances worries.' George sighed. 'Dad's fuming.'

Ed just bet he was. 'So am I,' he pointed out.

'Didn't do it on purpose.' George grimaced. 'Uh. A whole *week*.'

'There's the television,' Jane suggested.

'Can't switch channels.' He indicated his casts. 'Six weeks till the plaster comes off.' He grimaced. 'Can't wait to go home.'

Home? He seriously thought he was going to get up from his hospital bed and go *home*? Oh, for pity's sake. 'Be sensible about this, George. You're going to be here for at least a week. And you'll need physio on your leg and your shoulders when you leave here,' Ed warned. 'How exactly are you going to manage at home, anyway?'

George shrugged. 'Voice-controlled laptop. Don't need to type.'

'I didn't mean work.' Ed already knew his brother couldn't sit still at a desk; he paced his office and did everything with voice control. 'I meant with simple little things like washing, eating…going to the loo.'

'*Ed!*' George rolled his eyes. ''S a lady present.'

'I'm a doctor,' Jane said with a smile. 'I don't get embarrassed about bodily functions. And Ed does have a point. It's going to be hard for you to manage personal care with both wrists in plaster—and I'm not quite sure how you're going to manage a crutch, actually.'

'There's one very obvious solution,' Ed said. 'Come and stay with me until you're properly mobile again.'

'Not 'nuff room.'

'Yes, there is. I'll sleep on the sofa bed and you can have my bed—it'll be more comfy for you with your leg.'

'Thanks, bro.' George shook his head. 'But best not. We'd drive each other mad. You nag too much. I play too hard.' His face softened. 'Love you, Ed.'

Yeah. He knew. Because George had always been there for him. *Always.* George had read story after story to Ed in the nights when he couldn't get to sleep after their mum had left; and, twenty years later, his older brother was the one Ed had turned to after the night shift from hell, a miserable night that had caused him to question whether he was really cut out to be a doctor.

'I love you, too,' he said, his voice thick with emotion. 'But you give me grey hairs. I thought the oldest child was supposed to be the sensible one?'

George smiled. ''M sensible. Sometimes.'

Yeah. Ed knew. It was just the rest of the time.

'I just like doing—'

'—dangerous things,' Ed finished wryly. 'I know.' Though sometimes he wondered. Was George such a thrill-seeker because he was stuck as the heir to the barony and hated it? It was something they'd never, ever discussed. He'd always assumed that George was fine with it. Maybe he was wrong. He'd been so wrapped up in his career that he hadn't even considered that George might've had a vocation, too. They needed to talk about this. Not right now, while George was still feeling rough from the crash and the anaesthetic, but soon. And maybe they could work something out between them.

'The girls said they'd already fixed you up with chocolates and grapes. What can I bring you?'

'Dunno. Can't do a lot with these.' George nodded at his casts, then grimaced. 'Feel sick.'

Jane slid off Ed's lap, grabbed a bowl and was just in time.

'Sorry. Not good to be sick over Ed's new girl,' George said sheepishly when he'd finished.

'Anaesthetic has that effect on people sometimes,' she said. 'Don't worry about it. I'm used to this sort of thing. Really.'

'Thank you. Still sorry, though.' George looked contrite.

She smiled. 'No worries.'

'Look, I'm going to see one of the nurses and ask if they can give you something for the sickness,' Ed said. 'Jane, would you mind staying with George until I get back?'

'Sure.'

'Sorry to be a nuisance,' George said when Ed had gone.

'You're not a nuisance. I think Ed's a lot happier now he's seen you for himself.' Jane gave him a rueful smile. 'It's just as well we had a busy afternoon, because he was going through all the possible complications in his head and worrying himself si—' Given that George was feeling queasy, that wouldn't be the best phrase, Jane decided, and changed it to 'Silly'.

George clearly guessed, because he smiled. 'Sharp.

You'll be good for Ed.' He paused. 'Best brother I could ever have.'

'If it makes you feel any better, he feels the same about you,' Jane said.

'Yeah.' George closed his eyes. 'Sorry. Tired.'

'Hey, that's fine. Just rest. I'm not going anywhere—if you need anything, you just tell me, OK?'

''K,' George said.

Ed came back with one of the doctors, who gave George an anti-emetic and wrote it on the chart.

'Your brother really needs to get some rest now,' the doctor said.

'Of course.' Ed put an affectionate hand on his brother's shoulder. 'Reckon you can stay out of trouble until I see you tomorrow, George?'

'Can't go abseiling, can I?' George said lightly.

'I wouldn't put it past you,' Ed said. 'I'll be back tomorrow night after work. Do you want me to bring anything?'

'Chess set, maybe?' George asked. 'Move the pieces for me.'

'Sure. Get some rest, and I'll see you tomorrow.'

'You'll come back too, Jane?' George asked.

'Maybe not tomorrow—Ed might want some time with you on his own—but yes, I'll come back. And I'll play chess with you, if you like,' Jane said with a smile. 'Take care.'

Ed was silent all the way to the Tube station, and barely said a word until they got to her stop.

'I'll see you home,' he said.

Jane was perfectly capable of seeing herself home, but Ed was clearly upset and she was pretty sure he needed some company. 'Thanks.' She didn't push him into a conversation, but she noticed that he held her hand tightly all the way to her front door.

'Come up,' she said softly.

'I'm not going to be good company,' he warned.

'It doesn't matter.' She stroked his face. 'I hate to think of you going home and brooding. You saw something bad in his notes, didn't you?'

'It's not fair of me to discuss it.' He sighed. 'There's a potential problem, yes. Hopefully it'll sort itself out.'

'OK. I'm not going to push you to tell me. But if you do decide to talk, you know it won't go any further than me, right?'

'I do.' He kissed her lightly. 'And thank you.'

She put the kettle on and made herself a coffee and Ed a mug of tea, adding plenty of sugar.

He took one mouthful and almost choked. 'Jane, this is disgusting!'

'Hot sweet tea is good for shock.'

'Yeah.' He sighed. 'That's what George made me drink, when I decided I couldn't be a doctor any more.'

She blinked. 'You were going to give up medicine?'

He nodded. 'I was on an emergency department rotation. There was a major pile-up, and—well, you know what a majax is like. I wasn't used to losing patients. Kids, some of them. And I just couldn't handle it.' He blew out a breath. 'When I got home the next morning, I knew George had been out partying all night and had probably only just crawled into bed, but he was the only one I could talk to about it. So I called him.'

'And he made you a mug of tea like this?'

'Yeah. He came straight over and cooked me a fry-up.' He smiled wryly. 'George is a terrible cook. The bacon was burned and the eggs were leathery. I had to cover everything in ketchup to force it down. But it was the best breakfast I've ever had. He made me talk until it was all out. And then he told me it was just one shift in a department that wasn't right for me, and if I gave up medicine I'd regret it and I'd make everyone around me miserable. He said I'd be a great doctor, as long as I found the right department for me.'

There was a huge lump in Jane's throat. What must it be like to have a sibling who supported you like that, instead of taking and taking and taking all the time? 'He was right,' she said softly.

'Yeah.'

'And he's in good hands. The Hampstead Free has a really good reputation.'

'I know.' Ed sighed. 'It's just…'

'He's your brother. And you worry about him.' She walked over to stand behind him and slid her arms round his neck. 'I don't have the right stuff in the fridge to cook you a fry-up, but I have the makings of other comfort food. Like a toasted cheese sandwich.'

'Thanks, but I'm not sure I could eat anything.'

'Trust me, some carbs will help you feel better.'

He lifted her hand to his mouth and kissed her palm. 'You're wonderful. I hope you know that.'

'Sure I do,' she said. She kept her voice light, but the fact that he felt like that about her made her feel warm from the inside out.

'I'm not sure I could've got through seeing George like that without you there.'

She gave a dismissive shrug. 'Of course you would.'

'But you made it better. Only you,' he said softly.

'Hey.' She kissed him lightly, and busied herself making toasted sandwiches before she did something really stupid—like telling him she thought he was pretty wonderful, too.

'George liked you,' Ed said. 'Though he's going to torment me about the Tarzan thing. As soon as his hands have stopped hurting, he's going to start beating his chest and doing the yell.'

'And are you telling me you wouldn't do the same to him, if he was seeing a girl called Jane?'

Ed looked faintly sheepish, and she laughed. 'He's very like you, you know.'

'Apart from being in plaster and covered in bruises, you mean?'

'No. I mean, he's like you but without the brakes. He must drive his girlfriends crazy with worry.'

'Not to mention his parents and his siblings,' Ed said dryly. 'He did go through a spell of racing cars, but Dad had a word with him.'

'And that stopped him?'

'Surprisingly, yes.' Ed frowned. 'He wouldn't tell me what Dad said to him, but it must've been pretty tough.'

'So he's always done dangerous sports and what have you?'

Ed nodded. 'You know you were saying I remind you of James Bond? That's actually how George is. He thinks nothing of skiing down a double black diamond run.'

'As I know nothing about skiing, I take that means it's a really hard one?' Jane asked.

'Yes. But he's been crazier these last six months,' Ed said thoughtfully. 'He's taken a lot more risks.'

'Did something happen six months ago?'

Ed thought about it. 'Yes. I should've made him talk to me. But I guess I was still getting over the divorce and I wasn't paying enough attention.' He sighed. 'Now he's stuck in a hospital bed, he's not going to have any choice—he'll have to talk to me. And maybe I can help him sort out whatever's going on in his head.'

Ed relaxed more after they'd eaten, though he seemed more comfortable in the kitchen than anywhere else, so Jane didn't suggest moving. Eventually, he squeezed her hand. 'You were going to study tonight. I'd better go. I've held you up long enough.'

'It's OK. I can catch up some other time—it's not as if I've skipped studying for weeks on end,' she said lightly. He looked so lost. She couldn't possibly make him go back to his flat where he'd be on his own, brooding and worrying all night. 'I think tonight you could do with not being on your own. So if you want to stay...' She took a deep breath. 'There are no strings. Just—if you want to stay, you're welcome.'

'I'd like that. I'll have to leave at the crack of dawn so I can get some clean clothes before work, but if you're sure?'

She smiled. 'I'm sure.'

CHAPTER NINE

ED LAY awake; he was brooding, but not as much as he would've done had he been alone in his flat. Jane was sprawled all over him and it just felt better, being here with her. She had a huge heart and, even though he guessed that asking him to stay had put her in a vulnerable position, she'd seen exactly what he needed and hadn't hesitated to offer.

He held her closer and, in response, her arms tightened round him.

Their lovemaking that night had been so sweet, so tender, and he felt that Jane really understood him—far more than anyone he'd dated before. OK, so they'd only known each other for a month, but it was long enough for him to have worked out that there was something special about her. Not just the calm, confident way she was with people at work, treating everyone with respect and kindness. Not just the physical stuff that made his heart beat faster. He liked her instinctively. He'd never felt so in tune with someone like this before. And he really hadn't expected to fall for someone so fast.

He couldn't tell her. Not yet. She'd come out of her shell a lot with him, but even so he didn't want to take this too fast for her and risk her backing off again. But he was starting to hope that this was more than just a rebound fling—for both of them.

The next morning, Ed woke early; for a moment, he was disorientated, but then he remembered where he was. In Jane's flat. In Jane's arms.

Last night, he'd leaned on her. This morning, it was time to even up the balance. He gently disentangled himself from her arms, climbed out of bed and made coffee for them both.

'Thank you for last night. For being there,' he said softly, kissing her as he climbed back into bed.

'It's no problem. You would've done the same for me,' she said.

'Of course I would. You're on the list of people who could call me at three in the morning and I wouldn't yell at you for waking me up—I'd come straight to your side. And it's not that big a list,' he said. His parents, his siblings and his very closest friends. And Jane.

She smiled. 'Snap.'

Funny how something so simple as drinking coffee in bed with her made his world seem brighter. He finished his coffee. 'I'd better go back to my flat and get some clean clothes, but I'll see you at work, OK?'

'OK. And if you're not busy at lunchtime,' Jane said, 'perhaps you might like to have lunch with Sorcha and me.'

He realised immediately what she was saying. Yesterday, he'd asked her to meet the closest person to him; and now she was returning the compliment. Letting him that little bit closer. 'I'd like that,' he said simply. 'Very much.'

* * *

The ward was incredibly busy, that morning; Jane called Ed in to help her with a difficult delivery.

'Just after his head emerged, his neck retracted and his cheeks puffed out.'

It was a classic symptom of shoulder dystocia, where the baby's shoulder was caught on the mother's pubic bone so they couldn't deliver the baby.

'Is the baby big for his dates?' Ed asked.

'And ten days overdue. But there weren't any indications that it was going to be a problem.'

Shoulder dystocia was always a tricky situation, with the risk of the baby dying during delivery from not getting enough oxygen. Even if the baby was delivered alive, there was still a risk of a fractured collarbone or damage to the nerves in the baby's neck.

Quickly, Jane introduced Ed to the mum and her partner and explained the situation to them.

'If we can change your position,' Ed said, 'it'll move your pubic bone and that should give us enough leeway to deliver the baby safely. Try not to push just yet, OK?'

'OK.'

Gently, he and Jane guided the mum onto her back, with her bottom to the edge of the bed and her thighs guided back towards her abdomen.

'Jane, do you know the Rubin manoeuvre?' he asked.

'I know the theory.'

'Great.' Though it meant that she'd yet to put it into practice. Well, that was what he was here for. He directed her where to put suprapubic pressure over the baby's anterior shoulder so it moved towards his chest and would slip free. 'I'll tell you when to press,' he said. 'Rosie, can you get the neonatologist down?' This baby would definitely need careful checking over in case of nerve damage or fractures.

He really, really hoped the manoeuvre would work; otherwise, given that the mum already had an epidural and wasn't mobile, it would mean giving her an episiotomy and moving to more advanced intervention.

At the next contraction, he said, 'Now,' and gradually applied traction to the baby's head.

To his relief, it worked, and the baby finally slipped out.

'Well done,' Ed said to the mum.

The neonataologist checked the baby over, then came over with a broad smile and gave the baby to the mum for a cuddle. 'I'm pleased to say that he's a very healthy little boy—he had a bit of a tough time coming into the world, but he's absolutely fine.'

Ed and Jane exchanged a loaded glance. The outcome could have been so very different. Luck had definitely been on their side.

The mum was in tears of relief. 'Oh, my baby.' She looked at Ed. 'Thank you both so much.'

'It's what we're here for. Congratulations,' Ed said with a smile.

'He's gorgeous,' Jane added. She stroked the baby's cheek, then wiped the tears away from her own. 'Sorry. Newborns always make me cry. They're so perfect.'

'I think I need some sugar after that,' Ed said.

'Me, too.' Jane blew out a breath. 'That was a scary one. Thanks for talking me through it.'

'I barely needed to do that—you already knew the theory.'

'Which isn't *quite* the same as doing it in practice, knowing what could happen if you get it wrong.'

'But you got it right. And you're a quick learner—you won't need a word from me next time.'

'Hopefully not.' Jane glanced at her watch. 'Perfect timing. Lunch.'

In the canteen, a gorgeous redhead was already waiting for them—a woman Ed recognised from the photograph in Jane's flat.

'Caught up in the delivery room?' she asked.

'Yup. And it was a scary one.' Jane introduced them swiftly. 'Sorcha, this is Ed, our new consultant; Ed, this is Sorcha, my best friend—she's a rheumatologist.'

'I hope you don't mind me gate-crashing your lunch,' Ed said, shaking Sorcha's hand.

'Not at all. It's nice to meet you,' Sorcha said.

During lunch, Ed could see her watching him and trying to work out what his relationship with Jane was—whether it was strictly work, or if there was more to it than that. So had Jane been keeping him as quiet as he'd been keeping her? he wondered. And for the same reason?

He could see the second that Sorcha worked it out. Because she smiled very sweetly at her best friend. 'I am *so* desperate for a cappuccino. And a tiny, tiny bar of chocolate.'

'And it's my turn to fetch the coffee,' Jane said, getting up. 'OK. See you in a second.'

'So how long have you been seeing Jane?' Sorcha asked when Jane was out of earshot.

'Seeing her?' Ed asked.

She sighed. 'Don't play games. It's obvious in the way you look at each other—apart from the fact that she already knows exactly how you take your coffee and whether you're a chocolate fiend or not. I noticed she didn't even need to ask you what you wanted.'

'Right. Not long.'

Sorcha's eyes narrowed. 'I see. And this is a casual thing, is it?'

Well, if she was going to be that open with him, he'd give her the same courtesy. 'No, I don't think it is. And I'm glad she has someone to look out for her. My brother was still woozy from anaesthetic when he met her last night, or he would've been asking exactly the same questions. And, believe you me, my sisters are going to be every bit as careful as you when they meet her.'

'You're close to your family?'

'Yes. My family's great.'

Sorcha looked approving. 'Jane's like a sister to me.'

'So she told me.'

'She's got the biggest heart in the world,' Sorcha said, her gaze challenging.

'Absolutely.' He knew that first hand.

'And she's vulnerable.'

He knew that, too. 'Thanks to Shaun.'

'*Him.*' She rolled her eyes. 'I tell you, if he had a heart, I'd be first in the queue to remove it with a rusty spoon.'

Ed got the message. Very firmly. Hurt Jane, and Sorcha would be on the warpath.

'So she actually told you about him?'

'Yes.' He could see in Sorcha's face that she hadn't expected that. Clearly Jane didn't usually talk about what had happened. 'Look, I know Jane's special. I'll be careful with her, Sorcha. You don't have to worry.'

'Good.' Sorcha bit her lip. 'I can't believe she actually told you about Shaun and J—'

'OK, Sorcha, you can stop doing the guard dog act now,' Jane cut in, carrying a tray with three mugs of coffee. 'Sorry, Ed.'

'Nothing to apologise for. I think Sorcha and I understand each other. Which is a good thing. We know we're on the same side.' He held Jane's gaze. 'Yours.'

'Thank you. I think. But no more discussing me, OK?'

'Unless we need to,' Sorcha said.

Ed laughed. 'I'm so tempted to introduce you to my brother, Sorcha. I think you might be the only woman in the world who'd have the ability to keep him under control.'

'Too late. She's already spoken for,' Jane said.

'Shame. You don't happen to have a clone?' he asked Sorcha hopefully.

Sorcha laughed. 'No. But I think you and I are going to be friends.'

Jane didn't go with Ed to visit George that evening, knowing that he needed some time alone with his brother so he could start persuading George to open up about whatever was bothering him. But she made it clear that Ed was welcome to drop in on his way home if he needed a hug and someone to talk to. As always, a hug turned to something more, and Ed ended up staying the night again. And she somehow ended up staying at his flat after they'd visited George on Friday night.

This was all going crazily fast; and yet she trusted Ed instinctively. She knew he wouldn't hurt her. He wasn't like Shaun. He had integrity, he thought of others and he learned from his mistakes.

On Monday, she had a day off, and dropped in to see George in the morning.

'I thought you could do with a fresh challenger at chess,' she said.

'Janey! How lovely to see you.' He brightened when he saw what she was carrying. 'Are they for me?'

'Yup. Fresh English strawberries. And I've already washed and hulled them.'

'Oh, wow. Has anyone told you lately that you're wonderful?' Then he looked at his hands. 'Um, think they might be a bit cross with me if I get the casts covered in strawberry juice, and I'm not very good with cutlery right now.'

'No. Breaking your wrists *and* your fingers is pretty harsh.' She produced a spoon. 'Bearing in mind that I'm a doctor, I think it might be OK for me to feed them to you. As I would do for any of my patients if they were in this state.'

'I don't expect any of your patients would end up with all these breaks,' he said.

'Not usually, though I did once deliver a baby where the mum had a broken ankle,' she said with a smile, and set up the chess board on the table that slotted over his bed. 'And I'd better check before I give you these— you're not allergic to strawberries, are you?'

'No. And I *love* strawberries. Thank you.'

She sat on the edge of the bed, so it would be easier for her to move the chess pieces according to his directions, and fed him the strawberries.

'I can see why Ed's so taken with you,' he said when she'd finished. 'He tends to be a bit cagey about letting us meet his girlfriends. Probably because we're all so full on and we've been nagging him about...' His voice tailed off. 'I'll shut up. I was about to be really tactless.'

'Nagging him about it being time he got a life after his divorce?' Jane asked.

George raised his eyebrows. 'He told you about Camilla?'

'Yes.'

He blew out a breath. 'I told him he was making a huge mistake, but she'd told him she was pregnant, and Ed *always* does the right thing—so he married her.'

'Pregnant?' Ed hadn't told her that bit.

It must have shown in her expression, because George grimaced. 'So he didn't tell you everything. Sorry. I didn't mean to be tactless.'

'That's OK. So are you telling me that Ed has a child?' But there hadn't been any photographs of a baby in his flat. He hadn't mentioned a child. And she just couldn't see Ed turning his back on his child. He wasn't that kind of man.

'No. She lost the baby just after they got married.' George left a very significant pause. 'Or so she said.'

Ah. Now Jane understood. And she was relieved that she hadn't been wrong about Ed. 'And you think she was lying to him in the first place, to get him to marry her?'

George nodded. 'Even though she was from the same kind of background as us, they really weren't suited. She wanted different things and she definitely didn't want to be a doctor's wife. But Ed thinks it was all his fault for not giving her the life of luxury she wanted, and he's been wearing a hair shirt ever since.' He looked at her.

'You've been good for him. You're definitely helping him lighten up.'

Jane couldn't help laughing. 'That's so ironic.'

'How come?'

'They used to called me "Plain Jane, Super-Brain" at school.' Jenna had managed to get the whole school to chant that one. Especially the popular crowd she hung around with; Jane's refusal to wear a ton of make-up or give up her studies to fit in with them had gone down very, very badly.

'So you're a nerd? Nerdy's good,' George said with a smile. 'My sisters are all nerds. Have you met the girls yet?'

'No.'

'You'll like them. They boss Ed around, and he...' George grinned. 'Well, he just lets them. He's putty in their hands.'

She could just imagine it. And she'd just bet that the girls adored both their brothers. 'Do they boss you about?'

'They try—but, until one of them can beat me down a double black diamond ski run, they're not going to get very far.'

She laughed. 'Right now, even I could beat you down a nursery ski slope. You can't ski when you've got a pin in your leg.'

'Tell me about it.' He rolled his eyes, looking disgusted. 'The doctor said I can't ski until the end of the year, at least. Ed says they'll take the pin out when I'm healed, because I'm under forty.'

'Ed's been, how shall I put this?' She gave him a wicked smile. 'Well, he's been boning up on orthopaedics.'

George laughed. 'Oh, I *love* that you do bad puns. So will Charlotte. Actually, the girls will all love you.'

To be part of a big, noisy, warm, close family… Jane would give a lot for that. But she knew she was already presuming far too much. She and Ed had known each other for only a month. Yes, they were getting on well. Really well. But, given her track record in relationships, she'd be foolish to let herself hope for too much.

She pushed the thought away. 'Have you met your physio yet?'

George grimaced. 'Yes. He made me get up and walk about the day after the op.'

'Absolutely. You need to keep you moving so your muscles don't seize up—it's going to drive you mad, but you really need to do what he says, to save yourself a lot of pain and hard work in the future.'

'I can follow directions, you know.'

'Can you?' she asked.

He gave her a rueful smile. 'OK, so I like to run my own life.'

'At a hundred miles an hour.'

He laughed. 'That Queen song was made for me.' He sang a couple of bars from the chorus of 'Don't Stop Me Now'.

'I think you might be right.' She smiled back at him.

'I'm glad Ed's met you. You're definitely more his type than the debutantes who used to throw themselves at him.'

'Debutantes?' What debutantes?

George frowned. 'You mean he hasn't told you?'

'Told me what?'

'Forget I said anything,' he said hastily.

'No. Especially as you're in check. Told me what?'

He ignored the chessboard. 'What do you call him at work?'

'Ed.'

'No, I mean, do you call him Dr Somers?'

'No, he's a qualified surgeon. He's a Mr.'

'Uh-huh.' George paused. 'Did he tell you what I do for a living?'

'He said you're in the family business.' And that his family was well-to-do, though Jane hadn't paid any real attention to that. It was Ed she found attractive, not his bank account.

'I am. But I'm guessing he didn't tell you what the business was.'

She frowned. 'No.'

'I'm learning to run the estate. Which comes with a country pile whose roof just *eats* money.' He paused. 'And, as the eldest son, that makes me heir to the barony as well as being the future custodian of said money-eating roof.'

Barony? Jane felt the colour drain from her face. Their father was a baron. Which meant that Ed, George and their sisters would all be targets for the paparazzi. The kind of people *Celebrity Life* was desperate to run stories about—the magazine that had judged her so very harshly, just recently.

George's eyes widened with dismay. 'Oh, God, I've really messed things up now, haven't I?'

'No.' She dragged in a breath. 'I suppose you get snapped a lot by the paparazzi.'

'Usually doing something dashing, with my arm around a leggy blonde,' George said ruefully. 'I'm afraid I'm a bit of a stereotype. Well, I hope there's more to me than that, but that's how the press sees me. The playboy with a taste for blondes.'

Jane thought of Jenna, and felt sick.

As if he guessed part of what was worrying her, he said softly, 'Jane, they tend to leave the rest of the tribe alone. They're scared Alice will skewer them in court. Bea's learned to turn it round so they end up being wowed by her architecture instead of her private life and give her the right sort of column centimetres. And Charlotte...well, she just speaks Latin to them and they don't understand a thing she says, so they can't get a story out of her. And Ed, they can't work out at all. The only stories they can dig up about him tend to be him as the hero doctor, and he downplays it, so they can't get a quote. Honestly, it's just me they go for, normally.'

'So am I going to get snapped on my way out of here, because I'm visiting you?'

'I very much doubt it,' he said. 'I can hardly do anything scandalous with both wrists in plaster and a pinned leg.'

'Oh, I think you could.'

He smiled. 'Teasing me back—I like that. You'll fit in to the family just fine.'

'Ed and I are just good friends.'

'Are you, hell. I haven't seen him like this about anyone, and that includes Camilla. He moons about you.'

She rolled her eyes. 'No, he doesn't.'

'Yes, he does, when you're not with him. And that's good.' George looked solemn, for once. 'I worry about him being too serious, and he's way too hard on himself.'

'He worries about you going too far.'

'I might have learned my lesson. Almost a week of

being stuck in here has given me an awful lot of time to do nothing but think.'

'So you're going to settle down? Every cloud has a silver lining, hmm?'

'Something like that. He's serious about you, Jane. Don't hurt him. He's a good man—the very best.'

'I know.'

'You're in love with him, aren't you?'

No way was she admitting to her feelings. 'Can we change the subject? And, by the way, you're in check again.'

'Why didn't you warn me how good you are at chess?' George grumbled. But to her relief he changed the subject, and the conversation stayed light for the rest of her visit.

That evening, Ed said, 'You've made a real hit.'

'How do you mean?'

'George. It was your day off, and I gather you spent half of it playing chess with him. And you took him strawberries. Hand-fed them to him, I hear.'

'Well, he can hardly feed himself, given that his fingers are splinted and his wrists are in plaster as well. Wielding a spoon for him isn't a big deal.' She paused. 'Do you mind?'

'No.' Though he didn't meet her eye. 'George talks a lot,' he muttered.

So that was what was bothering him. He was worried that George had told her things he'd left out. Which was pretty much the case, she had to admit. She brought Ed's hand up to her mouth and kissed his palm, then curled his fingers round the kiss. 'He told me a lot about you. Probably things you'd rather I didn't know, and I'm not breaking his confidence. But I can tell you that he really loves you.' And she'd guess it would be the same with his sisters and his parents. How she envied him that. Knowing that he was loved for being himself.

She paused. 'So when were you going to tell me what the family business was?'

Ed grimaced. 'Sorry. I know I should've said something to you myself. But…how do you tell someone that you're the son of a baron, without sounding as if you're a huge show-off?'

'The same way you do when your mother used to be a supermodel thirty years ago.' She shrugged. 'So do I need to start watching out for paparazzi?' That was the one thing that had really worried her. George had said it wouldn't be a problem, but she couldn't imagine George being upset by the press, the way she was. Ed knew her better—not well enough to know about the reasons why, but he'd guess that her childhood had been partly in the spotlight because of her mother. And not always in a good way.

'No, you don't need to worry about them,' Ed confirmed. 'Something you should know,' she said carefully. 'I'm really not good with paparazzi.'

'They must've been so intrusive when you were young, with your mum being a model.'

'Something like that.' She knew she ought to tell him about Jenna, about the article and the full story about what had happened with Shaun—but she just couldn't bear to see the pity in his eyes.

'I'm only the second son. They're not interested in me,' Ed said, kissing her. 'I'm boring Mr Edward Somers, consultant obstetrician, who doesn't even have a private practice delivering babies to the stars and minor royalty. So they leave me alone. George is far more interesting.' He sighed. 'Sometimes I think that George only does what he does to draw their fire away from us. But I could put up with a bit of annoyance from the paparazzi if it meant he'd stay in one piece.'

The following evening saw Ed sitting at George's bedside. 'I gather you ratted me out to Jane.'

'Ah. Sorry about that.' George looked faintly guilty. 'When she said you'd told her about Camilla, I thought you'd told her the lot. Including about the baby.'

Ed blew out a breath. 'Oh, *great*. She didn't mention that.'

'Because she's tactful and I talk too much.'

'Actually, no, you don't talk enough,' Ed said, seizing the opening.

'Why do I get the distinct impression that I'm not going to like this conversation?' George asked.

'Because I want you to tell me what's wrong.'

'Nothing's wrong. I'm just grumpy about having to be more sedate than I usually am.'

'No, I mean before that.' Ed paused. 'I've been thinking. Are you feeling trapped?'

'In this hospital bed, and knowing I can't drive for weeks?' George rolled his eyes. '*Totally.*'

'I mean trapped by all the expectations on you. You've grown up knowing everyone expects you to take over from Dad. But if there's something else you'd rather do—maybe there's something we can work out.'

George shook his head. 'Ed, you don't have to worry about that. It's not the barony stuff. I'm just an adrenalin junkie, that's all. I'm fine with taking over from

Dad. Actually, I'm beginning to see what he likes about managing the estate.'

'Really?'

'Really,' George confirmed.

'And you'd tell me if something was wrong? Even if I couldn't help you fix it, I'm always here to listen. You know that, don't you?'

'Of course I do. Just as I'm here for you, Tarzan.' George raised an eyebrow. 'You're serious about Jane, aren't you?'

'Don't try to change the subject.'

'I like her,' George said. 'She gets what makes you tick. She wouldn't make you miserable, like Camilla did.'

'That's not fair, George. I made Camilla just as miserable as she made me.'

'But you're taking the blame for it. And that's not fair either. She trapped you into marriage. She lied her face off, knowing you'd do the right thing by her.'

Ed waved a dismissive hand, not wanting to talk about it. Or about how much he'd loved the idea of being a father. Or how something in him had broken when Camilla had made it very clear that she didn't want to try making another baby, and he realised he'd married completely the wrong woman for him. 'I still think something's up. Something you're not telling me.'

George just laughed. 'You'll turn into a conspiracy theorist next! I'm fine. Let's set up the chess board.'

He wasn't fine, Ed thought. But clearly his brother wasn't ready to open up yet. Ed had a strong suspicion that it was something to do with their mother and the meeting George had had with her solicitor, but he was just going to have to wait until George was ready to talk. And when he was ready, Ed would make sure he was there.

CHAPTER TEN

'I KNOW it's a big ask, and it's not really a "come and meet the folks" thing,' Ed said on the Friday night. 'George is bored out of his mind, you're the only person who's managed to beat him at chess in five years, and he's desperate for a rematch.'

'And it's going to be easier for us to go and visit him than for you to bundle him into your car and bring him here, especially as he's probably not going to be too comfortable in a car,' Jane finished.

Ed looked relieved that she understood his worries. 'Yes.'

'So is your whole family going to be there?' she asked.

'Um, yes. George is staying with our parents until he's out of plaster. But I'll tell them to back off and keep their questions to themselves. And there won't be any paparazzi. Though I can guarantee that lunch will be good—Frances is a fantastic cook.' He looked beseechingly at her. 'So will you come with me on Sunday?'

To meet the rest of Ed's family. But she'd already met George and liked him; plus the heat would be off her, because everyone's attention would be on George and they'd all be trying their hardest to persuade him not to do anything reckless once he was out of plaster again. 'So am I going as your colleague who just happened to beat George at chess?' she asked carefully.

'Um, no. George has told them all that my new nickname's Tarzan. And why. And I can't even shake him for it because he claims he might still have concussion.'

Ed looked so disgusted that Jane couldn't help laughing. 'Poor George. He really is bored, isn't he? Of course I'll come.' She paused. 'Um, what do I wear?' Fashion had never been her strength. What did you wear when you met a baron? Was she going to have to grab Sorcha for an emergency clothes-shopping trip?

'Wear anything you like. It's the country pile, so I'd suggest something dogproof. If it helps, I'm wearing jeans.'

On Sunday morning, Ed drove them to his family home in Suffolk. It didn't take as long as Jane had expected before Ed turned into a long tree-lined drive. Finally, the house came into view and Ed parked on the gravel in front of it. The hall was a huge redbrick building with stone mullioned windows; at each corner there was a narrow tower, each capped with a leaded domed roof.

'Wow, it's gorgeous,' she said. 'And I take it that's the money-eating roof George was telling me about?'

'It certainly is,' Ed said with a rueful smile.

'Has your family lived here very long?' She grimaced. 'Sorry, I'm being nosey. I didn't look you up on the Internet because—well, it felt a bit too much like spying.'

'Ask whatever you like. And it's not spying.' Ed took her hand and squeezed it. 'Yes, the Somers family has lived here ever since the house was built, nearly five centuries ago. Dad's the fifteenth baron. There is a little bit of family money left, but back in Victorian times there was a baron who dabbled in scientific experiments and rather neglected everything else, and my great-grandfather lost a small fortune in the Wall Street Crash. So I guess we're like a lot of old families—land-rich and a bit cash-poor, because the maintenance is crippling and everything's entailed.'

'Meaning you can't sell because it has to go to the next generation?'

'Exactly. Dad says we're custodians and we're privileged to have grown up here. And he's right. We are.' He stole a kiss. 'We have a maze. I am *so* showing you that.'

'A maze. Like Hampton Court?' she asked.

'Sort of, but on a much smaller scale. And the rose garden. Dad's got a thing about roses. But it's fabulous—at this time of year, you walk through and you just breathe in the scent and it's like drinking roses.'

'So it's a big garden?'

He nodded. 'It's open to the public on Wednesdays and Saturdays, and whatever national garden open days Dad wants to do. The estate has to support itself. Frances got the hall licensed for weddings five years ago, so we can offer packages; and there's a minstrel's gallery in the Great Hall, so we sometimes hold concerts here.' He shrugged. 'Most summer weekends, there's something on; we're lucky that this weekend it's just us. Come on. Dad and Frances are expecting us.'

She followed him over to the front door, feeling ever so slightly out of her depth. As soon as Ed opened the front door, three dogs bounded down the hallway, barking madly and their tails a wagging blur. Jane crouched down to greet them and had her face thoroughly licked by the chocolate Labrador.

'That's Pepper,' he said. 'The Westie's called Wolfgang, and the setter's Hattie, short for "Hatter" because she's as mad as one.'

'They're lovely.' She continued making a fuss of them. How lucky Ed had been, growing up in a sprawling place like this. She'd just bet that the children had all been encouraged to run around the garden, with no shouting if they got grubby because it would all come out in the wash. Her own family had lived in a smart London apartment with too much glass and all-white furniture you didn't dare touch in case you left fingermarks. Which was fine for Jenna, who'd perfected elegance at a very early age, but Jane had always been in trouble for breaking things and making a mess. Even in her parents' new home in Cornwall, the furniture was so carefully arranged that the rooms felt ready for a photo shoot; you didn't dare relax in case you moved a cushion out of place.

'Ed, we're so glad you could make it.' A tall, elegant woman hugged him.

Jane got to her feet, aware that she was already covered in dog hair and slightly dishevelled. Not exactly the best impression she could make on Ed's family, but never mind.

'And you must be Jane. I'm Frances.' The older woman looked at her for a moment, as if considering shaking her hand, and Jane felt even more intimidated; and then she was enveloped in as huge a hug as Ed had received. 'It's so lovely to meet you. Come into the kitchen. It's a bit manic around here—but, then, George is home, so of course it's going to be manic.'

All her nervousness vanished instantly. Everything was going to be just fine. Ed's parents weren't in the slightest bit snobby; they were warm and welcoming, like Ed himself. As she followed Ed and Frances into the kitchen, Jane was shocked to realise that she already felt at home here—far more so than she did in her own parents' home. Here, she knew she'd be accepted exactly for who she was; and she didn't feel like a disappointment, the second-best child.

The man sitting at the table with the Sunday papers spread out before him looked up. Even before they were introduced, Jane could see that this was George and Ed's father; he had the same colouring and strong features.

Ed's father stood up and hugged him. 'Ed, my boy.' Jane received the same warm greeting. 'It's so nice to meet you, Jane. Welcome.'

'Um, shouldn't I be curtseying or something?' she asked.

'Good God, no!' David smiled at her. 'Don't even think of standing on ceremony. We're perfectly normal. Well, possibly except George, and you've already met him—and you're just as he described you.' He gave Ed a speaking look. 'At least *one* of our sons tells us things, Tarzan.'

'Oh, no—he's got you at it as well,' Ed groaned, but he was laughing. 'And may I remind you that one of your sons doesn't also spend his time narrowly avoiding avalanches or paragliding into cliffs? You can't have it both ways, Dad. Sensible and silent, or mad and gossipy. Your choice.'

'Oh, stop it, you two.' Frances flapped a tea towel at them, laughing. 'Jane, you've just come all the way from London, so you must be gasping for some coffee.'

'I'd love some, but I can see you're up to your eyes.' Jane gestured to the pile of broad beans that Frances had clearly been podding. 'Shall I make the coffee for everyone, or would you prefer me to help you with the beans?'

Frances gave her an approving smile. 'Making the coffee would be lovely. Thank you.'

'So where's George?' Ed asked.

'In the library, plotting,' David said. 'He's thinking about setting up some ghost walks for the winter. And just talk him out of this fireworks idea, would you? It terrifies me that he's going to take a course, get qualified and start blowing things up.'

'Since when does George listen to me?' Ed asked.

'You'd be surprised. And he's set up the chess board, Jane; he's desperate for that rematch with you.'

'So Ed told me.' She smiled back at him.

'Are the girls here yet?' Ed asked.

'Bea's got a meeting but she'll be down just after lunch. Alice is bringing Charlotte with her from the ivory tower,' Frances said. 'They'll be here any time now.'

Jane made the coffee, and Ed added milk and sugar to various cups. 'We'd better take one of these to George.'

'With a straw,' Frances added. 'He's not coping very well with losing his independence.'

'I did warn you he'd be a terrible patient,' Ed said dryly. 'If he gets too fed up, he can always stay at my place.'

'In your flat, he'd be too cooped up. At least here

he can limp around the garden with the dogs and mutter that he's never going paragliding again,' David said with a smile.

Ed ushered Jane through narrow corridors to the library—a light, airy room with more bookshelves than Jane had ever seen in her life, with several battered leather sofas scattered about, a grand piano and a huge, huge fireplace.

George was reclining on one of the sofas with a pair of crutches propped next to him, and a small table on his other side with a chessboard set out on it.

'Janey. Lovely to see you. Excuse me for not standing up; I hurt a bit, today. And, yes, Ed, I have done my physio today, before you ask.'

'I didn't say a word.' Ed spread his hands. 'I know better than to nag.'

Pepper had sneaked in beside them, and curled up on the sofa between George and his crutches.

And Jane was happy to curl up on one end of the other sofa next to Ed and play chess with George, with Hattie's head resting on her knee. This was the most perfect Sunday ever, she thought. In a place where she felt as if she belonged.

She beat George again, much to his chagrin; but before he could ask for another rematch, the library door burst open.

'Georgie-boy. You have—'

'—done my physio, yes, Alice.' He rolled his eyes. 'It's Sunday. That means no nagging, OK?'

'You wish,' Alice said with a grin.

Ed introduced his sisters to Jane. She liked them on sight; Alice was as brisk as she'd expected and Charlotte looked like a scatty academic, but Jane already knew not to be fooled by that.

'Lovely to meet you, Jane. George tells us you're a doctor, too,' Alice said. 'Please tell me Ed didn't tell you about the red-faced squeaky business.'

Jane smiled at her. 'No comment.'

George gave a crack of laughter. 'Well, he's right. You were red-faced and squeaky. You still are.'

'I might be eight years younger than you, Georgie-boy,' Alice said crisply, 'but I at least have the sense not to fly into a cliff.'

'Yes, m'lud,' George teased.

'Milady,' Alice corrected. 'Except I'm not a judge. Yet.'

Jane could see exactly why the paparazzi were scared of Alice. Though she also had a feeling that Alice had as big a heart as her brothers.

Lunch was in the dining room. The table was set with porcelain, solid silver cutlery and what looked like ancient Venetian glassware; Jane was terrified she'd drop something priceless and break it.

Ed moved his foot against hers so she glanced at him, then gave her a reassuring wink as if he understood what she was worrying about and wanted to put her at her ease.

The meal turned out to be full of laughter and noise and teasing—good-natured teasing, not the stuff with a nasty edge that she was used to from Jenna—and Jane was most definitely included as part of the family. The food was fantastic, too; Ed hadn't been exaggerating when he'd said that Frances was a great cook. 'Thank you. This is the best roast beef I've ever had,' she said, meaning it.

'It's from one of our farms. And all the vegetables are from our kitchen garden—I'm making a proper potager,' Frances said, 'before David takes up the whole of the garden with his roses.'

She and David shared an affectionate glance, and Jane realised that was another thing missing from her own childhood. Her father had always been tiptoeing round her mother, careful not to upset her, but there had never been that look of affection or adoration between them.

Alice was taking full advantage of the fact that George still couldn't manage cutlery and was making a big deal of spoon-feeding him.

'That's it—Frances, from now on I'm living on soup, custard, and anything else you can stick through a blender and I can drink through a straw,' George said with a pained look.

'No, you're not. This is such sweet revenge for all the times you spoon-fed me when I was a toddler and deliberately got yoghurt up my nose,' Alice said.

'Behave, children,' Frances said, laughing.

Alice gave George a hug. 'You can't get Mum to stick roast beef through a blender. It'd be disgusting. And you know I love you, really.'

'Love you, too, even though you're the bossiest woman I've ever met. Ruffle your hair for me, will you? I can't do it with these mitts. Not without cracking your skull, anyway,' he said wryly.

Jane was aware of a rush of envy as well as wistfulness. How wonderful it must've been, growing up in this kind of atmosphere, laughing and joking and secure in the knowledge that you were really, really loved.

After lunch, Ed took her for a stroll round the gardens. They were utterly beautiful and she could see why the public flocked there. The rose garden in particular was fantastic. 'Wow. You were right about the incredible scent,' she said, inhaling appreciatively.

'Do tell Dad. He'll be pleased. These are his babies, now we've all left home,' Ed said with a smile.

The promised maze was small, but big enough to be very private, and Ed kissed her at every corner before finally taking her back in to join the family.

Bea arrived mid-afternoon. 'Sorry I'm late. I'm up to my eyes in meetings, right now—but it's going to be *such* a good commission. I think it's going to be the one that'll make my name,' she said. And then she proceeded to grill Jane over coffee at the kitchen table, abetted by Alice and Charlotte.

'Charlotte, do you want me to fetch the spot-lamp from Dad's office so you can really make this an interrogation?' Ed asked in exasperation.

But Jane didn't mind at all. 'It's great that you look out for Ed.' She smiled at them. 'Anyway, my best friend did exactly the same thing to him, the first time she met him.'

'Don't you have any brothers and sisters to look out for you?' Alice asked.

'No.' Technically, she had a twin sister; but Jenna had never looked out for her. It had always been the other way round.

'Hmm. In that case, you can borrow us,' Charlotte said.

Looking at her, Jane realised that she meant it. And there was a huge lump in her throat as she hugged Ed's sisters.

'Your family's just *lovely*,' she said on the way back to London that evening.

'I know. And I told you they'd love you,' Ed said.

She could see the question on his face: when was she going to let him meet her family?

'Mine aren't like yours,' she said carefully. 'I'm not close to them.' She made regular duty phone calls home, but she hadn't actually seen her parents since Shaun had cheated on her with Jenna. And she most definitely hadn't seen her twin. She'd needed to take a step back and put some distance between them.

Ed reached across to squeeze her hand briefly. 'I can't imagine you not being close to anyone. My family loved you straight away.'

She dragged in a breath. 'You know I told you my mum was a model? Well, she didn't plan to have children. Pregnancy was hard for her.' Especially as she was carrying twins. Not that she could bring herself to tell Ed that, because then she knew he'd ask her about Jenna. 'She wasn't able to work during her pregnancy. Then she had really bad post-natal depression. And she couldn't go back to her career.'

'Why not?'

'Cover shoots and stretch marks don't mix,' she said dryly. It had been one of her mother's mantras. Though at least one of her daughters had been able to get her back into that charmed world. Going on photo shoots with Jenna had brought a small measure of happiness back to Sophia. Whereas Jane's world was alien to her. Disgusting. Particularly as it involved working with babies...the things that had ruined Sophia's life. She sighed. 'Appearances are really important to my mother.

I'm never going to be tall, thin and elegant—and I'm clumsy. I drop things.'

'No, you don't.'

She coughed. 'If you remember, the very second I met you I spilled a whole glass of champagne over you.'

'Which wasn't your fault—someone knocked into you.' He paused. 'So your mother blames you for the end of her career?'

'If she hadn't been pregnant, she wouldn't have had stretch marks. Or had PND. She could've carried on doing what she loved.' Jane shrugged. 'And I can understand that. I know how I'd feel if I had to give up my job. It's who I am—just as modelling was who she was. She's fragile.'

'Fragile?'

'She has depression,' Jane said. 'On bad days, she doesn't get out of bed. Bad days can last for weeks. And, yes, she's seen doctors about it. Depression's tricky. It doesn't always respond to treatment.' She sighed. 'It's a matter of keeping her on as an even keel as we can. I guess seeing me upsets her, reminds her too much of what she's lost.'

Ed pulled off at the next layby.

'Ed? Why have we stopped?'

'Come here.' He pulled her into his arms. 'I'm sorry that your mum can't see you for who you are. And blaming you for losing her career—that's really not fair. You didn't ask to be born. What about your dad? Can't he help her see things differently?'

'He…' How could she put this? 'He's a bit like Mike Duffield. He likes a quiet life. Which is ironic, considering he used to be in advertising—that's how he met Mum. She was a model on one of his campaigns.'

Ed stroked her hair. 'I'm sorry. I wish I could fix this for you.'

'I don't think even a superhero could fix it. But it's fine. I'm used to it.'

The expression on his face said that he didn't think it was something you got used to. But he kissed the tip of her nose. 'Come on. Let's go home.'

CHAPTER ELEVEN

OVER the next couple of weeks, Ed and Jane grew closer still.

On the Friday night, Ed told Jane to dress up. 'A prom-type dress,' he said, 'seeing as you always ask me about dress codes. But I'm not telling you where we're going—it's a surprise.'

The first surprise was that he picked her up in a vintage sports car.

'It's George's. I'm taking full advantage,' Ed told her with a grin. 'He says he's going to inspect it minutely when I take it back on Sunday, and if there's a single speck of dust on it, I'm toast.'

She laughed. 'We'd better get a chamois leather and beat him to it.'

He opened the door for her and helped her inside.

It was the first time she'd ever sat in a low-slung sports car. 'Wow. I feel like a princess,' she said.

'Good. You look like one.'

'Thank you.' She felt colour seeping into her cheeks.

He stole a kiss. 'You're so sweet.'

'I haven't missed your birthday or anything, have I?' she asked.

'No. I just wanted to make you feel a bit special and have some fun.' He squeezed her hand, then drove her to a very swish hotel, handed the keys to the valet, and ushered her inside.

'Doesn't this place have three Michelin stars and you have to book up months in advance?' she asked.

'Yes to the first, usually to the second, but they had a last-minute cancellation. I had to book the tasting menu in advance. I hope that's OK?'

She smiled. 'That's more than OK. I've always wanted to do something like this. Ed, this is such a treat.'

'Good.' He looked pleased that she liked his surprise.

Ed stuck to mineral water because he was driving, but he ordered her a glass of champagne.

'One's definitely enough,' she said softly. She smiled at him. 'And I'll try not to spill this one over you.'

He laughed. 'Good. But I'm still taking you dancing, afterwards.' His eyes glittered. 'And I have plans after that.'

Repeating the night they'd first met. Except this time they really knew each other. A thrill of pure desire skittered through her. 'That,' she said, her voice husky, 'sounds just about perfect.'

The food was amazing; she savoured every mouthful.

And the dancing turned out to be very similar to that of the night of the hospital ball. Just like before, Ed made her feel as if she were floating when she danced with him.

'That was the perfect evening,' she said when he'd driven her home. 'Thank you. You made me feel really special.'

'That,' Ed told her, 'is because you are.'

And then he proceeded to show her exactly how.

* * *

At work, too, Jane found that she and Ed were completely in tune. When Pippa Duffield started bleeding in the shower and Iris came to fetch them from the patient they were seeing, they spoke in unison: 'We're going to need the anaesthetist and the neonatologist, and we need Pippa in Theatre now.'

Jane got one of the nurses to call Mike Duffield and put him on speaker phone for her while she scrubbed in. 'Mike, it's Jane Cooper from the hospital. Unfortunately, Pippa's started bleeding again, so we need to deliver the twins now.'

'Are they going to be all right?' he asked anxiously.

'I'm sure they will be,' Jane said, 'but the bad news is that we have to give Pippa a general anaesthetic, so you won't be able to come in with us and see the twins being born as we'd planned. But you can see them as soon as they've been checked over.'

'Tell Pip I love her,' Mike said, 'and I'm on my way now.'

Pippa was in tears. 'I didn't do anything out of the ordinary. I've been taking it so easy ever since I've been here. I can't understand why I started bleeding like that. And there was so much of it!'

'I know, and it's not your fault,' Jane soothed. 'We did say this might happen, and you're in exactly the right place for us to help you.'

'Two days before the babies were going to be delivered anyway. Why couldn't I have hung on for just two more days?' Pippa asked despairingly.

'That's just the way it goes sometimes,' Ed told her gently. 'Pippa, there's something else we need to talk about. If we can't stop the bleeding, we might have to give you a hysterectomy. We'll only do that if there's no other way, but may we have your consent?'

'So…then I won't ever be able to have another baby? Even with IVF?'

'No,' he confirmed quietly. 'I know this is a lot to take in, and it's unfair of us to dump this on you right now when you're worried sick about the babies, but we do have to think about you as well.'

Pippa swallowed hard. 'And if I don't have a hysterectomy, would that mean you can't stop the bleeding and I'll…?'

Jane squeezed her hand, realising that Pippa knew exactly what the consequences were but just couldn't say it. If they couldn't stop the bleeding, she would die. 'Yes.'

Pippa dragged in a breath. 'If it's the only way, then do what you have to. Just make sure the babies are safe.'

'Thank you,' Ed said.

She bit her lip. 'I so wanted Mike to cut the cords.'

'I know,' Jane said.

'Nothing's gone to plan.'

'But the babies will be here safely soon, and Mike's on his way. He told me to tell you that he loves you,' Jane said, and held Pippa's hand while the anaesthetist counted her down.

In Theatre, Ed swiftly made the incision; he delivered the first twin into Iris's waiting hands, ready to be wrapped in a towel and checked over by the neonatologist.

Just after he'd delivered the second twin, the anaesthetist said, 'Blood pressure's still dropping.'

Just what they'd wanted to avoid: Pippa was haemorrhaging.

Although they were prepared for it and had ordered cross-matched blood, the transfusion didn't seem to be helping. Jane went cold. Please don't let Pippa go into DIC. Disseminated intravascular coagulation meant that the clotting factors in the blood were activated throughout the body instead of being localised to the site of the injury, so small blood clots developed through the body, using up the blood's clotting factors so it couldn't clot where it was really needed.

If they couldn't get her blood to start clotting, there was a very good chance they were going to lose her, and she'd never get to meet the twin girls she'd wanted so desperately.

They continued pumping blood into her.

Please, please, let her start clotting, Jane prayed silently.

After what felt like a lifetime, the anaesthetist said softly, 'We're there. Blood pressure rising nicely.'

'Thank God,' Ed said softly.

Finally they managed to close the incision ready to take Pippa through to the recovery room.

'How are the babies doing?' Ed asked.

'I'm going to take them to the special care unit for a while; I want them on oxygen for a bit. But they're fighters, like their mum. They'll be fine,' the neonatologist said.

'We need to take pictures of the babies for her, for when she wakes up,' Jane said.

Iris grabbed the camera they kept for this kind of situation and took pictures of the twins. While Ed sat with Jane as she started to wake up, Jane went out into the corridor. Mike was there, pacing.

'What's happened?' he asked desperately.

'You have two beautiful girls, and Pippa's waking up now,' she said, smiling.

'Can I see them?' he asked.

'The babies are going down to Special Care—not because there's a major problem but at this age they often need a little bit of help breathing.' There would be time enough to let him know that they'd been close to losing Pippa; for now, she wanted him to enjoy the first few minutes of being a dad.

She took him through to the recovery room; he held Pippa tightly. 'I was so worried.'

'I'm fine. But the babies...they're in the special care unit.' A tear trickled down her face.

'We've taken pictures for you for now, until you're ready to go and see them,' Iris said, and handed over the photographs.

Mike and Pippa were both crying. 'They're so tiny.'

'They're good weights for thirty-five weeks,' Ed said. 'I know it's easy for me to say, but try not to worry. They're doing just fine.'

Back at Jane's flat that night, they collapsed into bed.

'What a day,' Jane said.

'Mmm. I had a few bad moments,' Ed admitted. 'If she'd gone into DIC...'

'But she didn't. It was a good outcome. Twin girls, both doing well, and with luck they'll be out of Special Care within the week.'

'We did well today,' he said with a smile. 'Great teamwork.'

'Absolutely.' Jane curled into his arms. Funny, she'd never thought she could ever be this happy. Neither of them had actually declared their feelings, but she knew.

She'd fallen in love with Ed, and she was pretty sure that Ed loved her all the way back. Just the way she was.

Life couldn't get any better than this. She just hoped it could stay this way.

The next morning, Jane called in to see how Pippa was doing, to find her in floods of tears.

'I'm just so tired—and I'm dreading Mike's mum coming in to see the babies and taking over,' Pippa confessed.

Jane sat next to her and took her hands. 'You've been through an awful lot, Pip. And, the thing is, Mike's mum doesn't know the half of it. I reckon if you tell her what's been happening, she'll be a lot gentler with you than you expect. She'll realise that you need support and help, not someone taking over and telling you what to do.

'But we've never been close. She always made it clear she felt I took her son away.'

'Maybe,' Jane said softly, 'that's a defence mechanism. Mike's her only child, is he?'

Pippa nodded.

'Maybe she always wanted a daughter as well—and, now she's got one, she's scared she's going to get it wrong because she's used to just having a son, and she's too proud to tell you. Just like you're too proud to tell her that you went through IVF,' Jane said, 'Right now, I think you could do with a mum to lean on, so why don't you talk to her? Tell her how you feel.'

Pippa bit her lip. 'It's hard.'

'But it'll be worth it if it lets you build that bridge.'

'Do you think so?'

'I know so,' Jane said confidently.

* * *

Later that afternoon, she dropped in to see Pippa again, and was surprised to see an older woman sitting on the side of the bed, cuddling one of the twins and talking animatedly to Pippa.

'Jane, this is my mother-in-law,' Pippa said, introducing them almost shyly.

'Pip's told me so much about you,' Mrs Duffield said. 'She says you've been so supportive, right from the moment she had the pregnancy test after her IVF.'

So Pippa had taken her advice, Jane thought. And clearly that bridge had been built from the other side, too. She smiled. 'That's what I'm here for. And it's lovely to see the babies getting stronger and stronger every day.'

Mrs Duffield beamed. 'I'm so looking forward to being a hands-on granny. But things have changed a lot since my day, so I'm taking my lead from Pip.'

Jane looked at Pippa, who mouthed, 'Thank you. You were absolutely right.'

Jane had to blink back the tears. 'Well, if there's anything you need, any questions you have, just ask. And congratulations on being a granny of twins.'

'They're beautiful. Just like their mother,' Mrs Duffield said. 'Though I think they both have Mike's smile.'

'Yeah.' If only she could find a way to build a bridge like this with her own mother, Jane thought. But she pushed it aside. Brooding wasn't going to help anyone. 'I'll see you later,' she said with a smile.

CHAPTER TWELVE

A COUPLE of weeks later, Ed dropped in at his brother's flat on his way home.

'How are you managing, now the plaster's off?' he asked.

'Fine.' But George's smile didn't reach his eyes.

'What's up?'

George sighed. 'Nothing.'

'Come off it. Fed up with being stuck in the slow lane?'

'I guess.' George shrugged.

'OK. Let's take your car,' Ed suggested. 'I'm not breaking the speed limit for you, but a quick drive up the motorway with the top down might make you feel a bit better.'

George dragged in a breath. 'Sometimes I wish you weren't so nice. It'd be easier.'

'What would?'

'Nothing.'

Ed took his brother's hands. 'Is this about the fertility stuff? Look, they said it takes time. Don't write yourself off just yet. You took a hard knock when you hit the cliff. Wait until the next test. And even if the motility of your sperm doesn't get much better than it is now, it doesn't mean you can't ever have kids. There's a special form of IVF called ICSI that could work for you—they pick out the best sperm and use them.'

'It's not that.' George looked bleak. 'Forget it.'

'No. George, I can see that something's wrong.' He'd been sure of it when George had been in hospital, too. 'You're my brother. You've always been there for me. Let me be there for you.'

George's face was full of anguish. 'What if I'm not your brother?'

Ed frowned. 'Of course you're my brother.'

'I might not be.'

'How do you work that out? We have the same parents.'

'Not necessarily. Supposing Dad isn't my father?'

'Of course he is.' Ed frowned, too. 'George, you and I look alike. We've got the same colouring, the same cleft in our chin—exactly the same as Dad's.'

'We're not *that* alike,' George said.

'Where's this all coming from?' Ed asked, mystified.

'I've read her diaries.'

Ed didn't have to ask whose. Because something was becoming nastily clear. He'd been right about the unfinished business. 'Is that the package you had to collect from the solicitor's, earlier this year?' The meeting that only George had been invited to after their mother's death; Ed had pushed aside the hurt at the time. Of course it would be George. He was the eldest of her two children.

'Her diaries, letters and photographs.' George gave a mirthless laugh. 'I knew Dad used to send her photographs of us on our birthday. Stupidly, I thought she might've kept them. She didn't—the photos were of the men in her life. But I started reading the letters and the diaries.' He shook his head. 'I really don't know how to tell Dad. Ed, I know it for sure. I'm not his.'

'But *how* do you know?'

'She had an affair. Well, more than one, while she was married to Dad. And...Dad just isn't my biological father.'

'No way. You look like Dad. You look like me,' Ed said again.

'Maybe the guy looked a bit like Dad—maybe he had the same colouring and build and what have you.' George blew out a breath. 'I hate to think the girls aren't really my sisters.'

'They're your sisters, all right. The same as I'm your brother. Nothing's going to change that.' Ed paused. 'Is this why you've been taking more risks than usual, the last few months? Since you first read her papers and came to that completely crazy conclusion?'

'It's not crazy. It's the truth.' George sighed. 'Yes.'

'And this was what was distracting you when you crashed?'

George nodded.

'And you've kept this to yourself for months? You *idiot*. Why didn't you tell me?'

'Apart from the fact that you were in beating yourself up over your divorce and I didn't want to dump yet more burdens on you, I guess I didn't know how. And I kept hoping that maybe I'd got the wrong end of the stick. When I woke up after the crash, I thought maybe I'd got it all wrong and I was being an idiot. But I've read the diaries again, since I've been back home. And the letters.' He limped over to the dresser, pulled out a thick envelope, rummaged through it and brought out a diary and a handful of letters. He dumped them on Ed's lap. 'Read them and tell me if I've got it wrong.'

He'd marked the pages with a sticky note. Ed read through them, and went cold.

'She doesn't say you're definitely not Dad's. She says she's not sure.'

'Which is the same thing.'

'No, it's not. Look, we can do a DNA test. That'll prove it for sure.'

'But what if,' George whispered, 'what if a DNA test proves I'm not who I always thought I am?'

Ed could see the demons haunting his brother. He was afraid of being the cuckoo in the nest, unwanted by their family. Just as they'd both been unwanted by their mother. 'It won't matter at all,' he said softly. 'I don't give a damn about genetics. You're my brother and I love you. I know the girls will feel the same. And Dad and Frances.'

'Maybe.'

'No, *definitely*. You're ours, and you always will be.' He gave George a hug. 'I love you.'

'And I love you, too.' George looked bleak as Ed put the papers on the table and came back to sit beside him. 'But if I'm not Dad's, that means legally we're talking about a whole new kettle of fish. It means I'm not the heir. *You* are, Ed,' he said softly.

Ed was glad he was sitting down. If he was the heir... It meant he'd have to give up the job he loved to run the estate. He couldn't be selfish; he'd have to put his duty first. Of course he'd do it.

But this didn't just impact on him. How would Jane react to the idea of such a change in his life—and what it would mean for her, if their future was together?

'Oh, hell,' Ed said.

'You get it now?' George asked dryly.

'I get it.' Ed ran a hand through his hair. 'So how are we going to deal with this?'

'I don't know. I've got to think of a way of breaking it to Dad. Without hurting him.'

'We need to do the DNA test first.'

'Right, and I can really say to him that I need a sample of his DNA for a quick paternity test. Not.' George rolled his eyes.

'Maybe they can test you and me, to see if we have parents in common.'

'And what if we both have different fathers, and neither of them's Dad? Or if we do have the same father, and he isn't Dad?'

Ed hadn't thought about that. 'This is one hell of a mess.'

'You're telling me.' George swallowed hard. 'All these years, I've tried to tell myself that it doesn't matter. That I have Dad and Frances and you and the girls, and it doesn't matter that she left us. I tried to feel sorry for her, because I knew she was unhappy. But now...' He shook his head and grimaced. 'I just wish I'd never seen those bloody papers.'

'So do I,' Ed said. 'Not just for me, but because you've been going through hell ever since you read them. I hate to think you've been brooding when I could've been there for you. I *knew* there was something wrong. I even asked you about it. And you still didn't tell me.'

'You know what they say about a problem shared being a problem halved? It's completely untrue. I just told you and it's double the misery.' George looked bleak. 'I have no idea how we're going to sort this.'

'We need DNA testing. You, me and Dad. There isn't any other way.' Ed thought about it. 'I know people in the lab at work, but they don't do DNA testing. We'll need a specialist lab. Maybe Alice knows a reliable, discreet one?'

'I don't want Alice involved,' George said immediately.

'Then we're going to have to tell Dad and get the test done. There's no other way round it, George.'

'How long does testing take?' George asked.

'I have no idea. And it'll depend on the workload of the lab as well as the physical time it takes for the test to run,' Ed warned.

'This feels like all the exams I've ever taken, rolled into one,' George said. 'Except this time I don't have a clue what the results are going to be. And I don't know if I'm going to pass.'

'Whatever the results say, you're my brother and that's never going to change. Dad, Frances and the girls won't stop loving you, either.'

'Damn, I'm so bloody wet,' George said, closing his eyes and rubbing his forehead.

'No, I'd feel the same.' Ed gave him a wry smile. 'Actually, now I think about it, it's the same for me, too. How do I know that Dad's my biological father? And if he's not…then who the hell am I?'

'This weekend,' George said, 'is going to be one of the worst of my life. And yours.' He limped over to the table to collect his laptop. 'Right. Let's find ourselves a lab.'

'You start looking them and I'll make us some coffee,' Ed said. 'We'll sort this out. Together.'

'Yeah.' George gave a deep sigh. 'Thanks.'

'Well, what did you think I was going to do? Make you the worst breakfast in the universe and make you drink tea with too much sugar in it?'

'It worked for you,' George said. 'But please don't do it to me. Coffee's fine.'

Ed laughed, then sobered slightly. 'I know we're keeping this quiet for now, but I do need to let Jane know what's going on.'

'Because it's going to affect her as well. If it gets messy, she'll end up under the spotlight because she's your girl,' George said.

'She won't leak it.'

George rolled his eyes. 'State the obvious, why don't you?'

'Yeah.' Ed was heartened that his brother could see it, too.

In the kitchen, he texted Jane swiftly. *Running a bit late. Don't wait dinner for me. Still OK to call in later?*

Her reply was almost instant. *Course it is. Is everything OK? George?* she texted.

I'll explain later, Ed replied. *Don't worry.*

Though not worrying was a lot easier said than done.

When Ed left George's flat, he headed straight for Jane's flat.

'You look like hell,' Jane said when she opened the door, and wrapped her arms round him.

He leaned his cheek against her hair, breathing in the comforting, familiar scent of her shampoo. 'Sometimes life really sucks.'

She shepherded him inside. 'Come and sit down. Have you eaten?'

'I'm not hungry. But I wouldn't say no to a mug of tea with about ten sugars in it.'

'That bad?' She stroked his face. 'Tell me about it.'

'It's a long and very messy story,' he warned.

'I'm not going anywhere. And whatever you tell me won't go any further than me.'

'I know that.' He trusted her. He knew she wouldn't lie to him.

He let her lead him into the kitchen and sat down. When she'd switched the kettle on, he scooped her onto his lap. Just holding her made things feel a bit better.

'So what's happened?' she asked softly.

He sighed. 'You know Frances is my stepmother.'

She nodded.

'My biological mother left Dad for someone else when I was four and George was six. She never said goodbye, and she never sent either of us so much as a Christmas card or a birthday card after she left.' The fact that she hadn't wanted them: Ed was pretty sure it was half the reason why George wouldn't settle down with anyone. His brother didn't want to risk being abandoned again.

He'd made that mistake himself, with Camilla. He'd thought he was doing the right thing by her. That together they'd make a family, a strong one like his father and Frances had. But when he'd turned out to be completely wrong and Camilla had left, it had brought back some of the old hurt, the stuff he'd thought buried and forgotten about.

He sighed. 'I know Dad would never have done anything underhand like not giving us her cards. George said he used to send her photographs of us every Christmas, trying to build bridges that she just knocked down every time. And I once overheard him ranting about her to my godfather. He said he could forgive her for leaving him, but he couldn't forgive her for how she'd behaved to me and George.'

'Oh, Ed. How could she possibly…?' She swallowed hard. 'I just can't imagine walking away from my children. Not that I have any, obviously, but… How could she do it?'

'Because she was damaged,' Ed said softly. 'Dad's love wasn't enough for her. Her children weren't enough for her. And all the men she flitted between—they were never enough for her, either. Sometimes I think that maybe she did love us really—that she realised Dad would be able to give us a happy, loving childhood more than she could, and she stayed away because she didn't want to wreck that.'

And now for the biggie. 'George thinks he's not Dad's.'

'Why?'

'She died earlier this year, and her solicitor gave George her diaries and some old letters. He read them, and he's convinced himself that all the evidence says he isn't Dad's.'

'Could he be right?'

Ed sighed. 'I don't know. But that's why he's been so reckless, these last few months. He was thinking about it when he had the accident. And he's been brooding about it ever since.'

'Poor George. But he does have you.'

'That's what I told him.' Ed sighed again. The only

way to be sure of the truth is to take a DNA test. We're telling Dad this weekend and taking the test kits with us.'

'What can I do to help?'

He'd known Jane would say that. She had the biggest heart of anyone he'd met. He held her tighter. 'Nothing.'

'Even if all I can do is listen or give you a bit of moral support, I want you to know I'm here.' She kissed him lightly. 'Anything you want me to do, just say. If you want me there with you at the weekend, that's fine. Though it's pretty sensitive. So if you'd rather leave it as just you, your dad and George, that's also fine—I won't go huffy on you.'

'Thank you.' He gave a tired smile. 'I have to be honest with you. I don't have a clue what's going to happen next. If the test proves that George and I really are Dad's, then that's brilliant and we can stop worrying. But we have to be prepared for it not to go our way. If we're *not* Dad's, then the papers are going to drag up some truly horrible stuff. Things about my mother flitting from man to man, things about George never dating anyone more than three times because he's a chip off the old block.' He paused. 'I hate to think of you being dragged through what could end up being a real mess. So if you'd rather walk away now, I understand.'

She shook her head. 'No chance. I don't care what the papers say and I don't care what the DNA test says. I know *you*, and that's all that matters.'

She was standing by him. Regardless. Ed's chest felt tight. 'Thank you. But if you do change your mind, then I'll understand that, too.'

'I'm not going to change my mind.' Jane held his gaze. 'I'm not Camilla. Just as you're not Shaun.'

Camilla might have sat it out until the DNA test results came through, especially if there was a chance that Ed could be the heir to the barony. But if the tests had shown him not to be David Somers's son, he knew how she would've reacted. The complete opposite from Jane.

And there was a subject he'd been avoiding. Since they were talking about difficult stuff already, they might as well add this to the whole mess, he thought. 'I know George told you about the baby. And he probably told you his theory.'

'That she lied to you about being pregnant in the first place.' She nodded. 'Is he right?'

Ed shrugged. 'Maybe. But you know as well as I do how many pregnancies end up in an early miscarriage. And, once you're in the middle of wedding preparations, it's not that easy to say you've changed your mind and call a halt to everything. Especially when it's a society wedding and there'd be so much talk.'

She could understand that; and for Ed to give his ex the benefit of the doubt like that just showed what a huge heart he had. 'Did Camilla know about your mum?'

'Her family have known mine for years.' He shrugged. 'I guess they must have talked about it at some point.'

'So she knew you wouldn't walk away from her if she was accidentally pregnant,' Jane said softly. 'Because you're a good man and you do what's right.'

'I tried. But I wasn't what she really wanted. And I *was* selfish, Janey. It wasn't all her fault. I didn't give her the choice about moving to Glasgow,' he reminded her.

'She didn't give you a choice about getting married,'

Jane pointed out. 'Or about the baby.' She paused. 'I'm not going to ask you if you wanted a family. I've seen you with your sisters, and I've seen you with the babies on the ward. You never miss a chance to chat to a mum and cuddle a baby.'

'Busted,' Ed said with a wry smile. 'Yes. I wanted a family. But later, when I suggested we try again, she made it clear that the baby had been a mistake and she didn't want to try again.'

Jane swallowed. 'You don't think she...?'

'Had a termination?' He shook his head. 'She wasn't that hard-bitten.' He stole a kiss. 'I've seen you with the babies on the ward too, Dr Cooper. Is that what you wanted with Shaun?'

'A family. Like the one I didn't grow up in,' she said. 'But I don't think that was what he wanted.'

'More fool him.' Ed stole another kiss. 'Jane—I know we only met a couple of months ago. It's probably way too soon for me to say anything. And I shouldn't be saying anything at all when my family's in such a mess. But I know how I feel about you, and I just...' He swallowed hard. 'I love you. Ever since I've met you, I've felt so in tune with you. I told myself I'd be sensible and I wouldn't repeat my mistakes with Camilla, that I wouldn't let anyone get close to me again. But I can't help myself; with you, I feel complete.'

'Oh, Ed.' Her eyes filled with tears. 'I...I never thought I'd let myself feel like that about anyone, either. That I'd learn to trust again. But you—you're different. And I love you, too.'

'Thank God,' Ed whispered, and kissed her.

CHAPTER THIRTEEN

ON Saturday morning, Ed felt as if he was driving the condemned man to the gallows—except George might not be the only one who was condemned.

He half wished he'd asked Jane to come with him. Her calm, quiet support would have helped. Then again, given the bombshell that he and George were about to drop on their father, maybe it did need to be just the three of them and Frances.

He drove on through the rain with a heavy heart.

Jane reached for the entryphone. Had Ed changed his mind and wanted her to go with him to Suffolk after all? 'Hello?'

'It's me.'

Jenna. Jane recognised the voice instantly, and ice slid down her spine. What did her twin want? Given the radio silence since that article had hit the news stands, she guessed it wouldn't be to apologise.

'Are you going to let me in, or what?' Jenna asked. 'It's peeing down out here and my hair's getting wet.'

For a moment, Jane wondered what would happen if she said no. Then she remembered what she'd said to Pippa Duffield about building bridges. It had worked for Pippa. Maybe this time it would work for her. 'Come up,' she said, suppressing a sigh and pressing the button to let Jenna in through the building's front door.

The kettle had boiled and Jane was infusing peppermint tea by the time there was a knock on the door.

Jenna looked cross. 'You kept me waiting for *ages*.'

Oh, great. It looked as if her twin was spoiling for a fight. Jane tried to defuse the atmosphere. 'I made you some peppermint tea.' She didn't drink it herself, but she knew Jenna did, and she kept a stock in for her sister. 'I'll put some honey in the cup in a second.' She nodded at Jenna's luggage. 'Have you just come back from a shoot?'

Jenna rolled her eyes. 'Why else do you think I'm here?'

To get a convenient bed for the night. Not to see how her twin was and spend some quality time together. Jane suppressed the hurt. 'Where was the shoot?'

'The Big Apple.'

'A night flight home, then. You must be tired.' Jane tried to be conciliatory. 'Can I get you a late breakfast or something?'

Jenna rolled her eyes again. 'Little Dr Perfect.'

What? Jane frowned. 'What's this all about, Jenna?' OK, she could understand that her twin was tired and grumpy after travelling, but why did Jenna have to take it out on her?

'You always have to *nag*, don't you?'

Normally, Jane let it go and tried to avoid a full-on fight. But today she was keyed up, worried about Ed, and the question just burst out. 'Why do you hate me so much?'

'Why do you think? You and your perfect job and

your perfect life.' Jenna scowled at her. 'You have no idea what it's like to struggle.'

Jane couldn't believe she was hearing this, from Jenna of all people. Her childhood had been a lot tougher than Jenna's. The only time she'd ever really felt loved had been at Great-Aunt Sadie's. 'That's unfair. I've always tried to look after you. When we were kids and Mum was too ill, I used to cook dinner for us.'

'Exactly. Dr Perfect,' Jenna sneered. 'Always doing everything right. So *perfect*.'

'Perfect? Give me strength. You made my life a misery all the way through school. You and your friends laughed at me because I'm clumsy and I was always picked last for sports. You sneered because I studied instead of partying, and you made sure the whole school called me that horrible name.'

'Oh, you *studied*.' Jenna made exaggerated quote marks with her fingers. 'And don't we all know that you always got straight As? You're the clever one. I had it rammed down my throat all the time by the teachers—why couldn't I be more like you? The good twin, not the bad one.'

Said the girl who'd made her feel bad for not being like her. And now she was complaining? Jane saw red. 'If you'd made the slightest bit of effort in class instead of spending all your time fiddling with your hair and make-up, you could've done well in your exams, so don't you dare throw that at me. You made your choices and I accept that, so why do you have a problem that my choices were different? Why can't you just accept that we're different? I don't whine all the time that I'm not as tall and skinny as you. I accept myself for who I am. Why can't you do that?'

Jenna curled her lip. 'You're just jealous because I take after Mum.'

'No. I'm fine with who I am. But I'm tired of you putting me down all the time. Like having that horrible article printed.'

'It's not my fault the journo wrote it up like that.'

Jane doubted that. Jenna's publicist would've insisted on approving the copy.

'It's not just the article, it's been my entire life. Even my first boyfriend—I'd had a crush on him for months and I could hardly believe he wanted to go out with me. The day after our date, it was all round the school that he'd lost a bet with you and his forfeit was to date me. That's the only reason he asked me out.'

Jenna shrugged. 'It never seemed to bother you.'

No, because Jane had been determined not to let Jenna see how much it hurt. Or how it had felt when she'd discovered during her teens that half of her boyfriends were only dating her in the hope they'd meet Jenna, and the other half saw what they were missing as soon as they met her twin and dumped her. Before Ed, she'd had lousy taste in men.

'And Shaun.' Jenna had never apologised for that. 'I could've understood it if you'd fallen for him, if you really loved him—but you dumped him as soon as I left him.'

Jenna shrugged again. 'I didn't want him. It wasn't my fault. He came on to me.'

Jane had no idea if Jenna was telling the truth or twisting it. 'Couldn't you have said no?'

'He wasn't right for you—so, really, I did you a favour. If you'd bought a flat together or even got married, it would've been harder for you to walk away, with all the legal mess and expense.'

Jane blinked. 'You slept with *my* fiancé, in *my* bed, and you're telling me you did me a *favour*?'

Jenna lifted her chin. 'You know I did.'

'What kind of weird planet do you live on?' Jane shook her head. She'd had enough. 'Jenna, I've tried and tried and tried to be a good sister to you. But I just can't do this any more. I'm tired of you pulling me down all the time and making me feel bad when I've done nothing wrong. I'm sure you have plenty of other people you can stay with in London. I'm going out now, and I'd prefer you not to be here when I get back.' Jane grabbed her coat and bag, and walked out of the flat before she said anything she'd *really* regret.

Jenna stared after her twin, absolutely furious. Little Doctor Perfect was throwing her out?

She wasn't in the mood for dragging down to Cornwall to stay with the parents. And now it looked as if she was going to have to find somewhere to stay.

She used Jane's landline to ring round her friends. Half of them were away on shoots, but she finally found someone who could put her up for the night. She was about to leave when the phone rang and the answering machine clicked in.

'Janey, it's Ed. I said I'd ring you when I got to the Hall. You're obviously out. I wish I was with you instead of here in Suffolk.' There was a sigh. 'George and I are going to talk to Dad about the paternity test stuff now. I'll ring you later, OK?' A pause. 'I love you.' And then the beep as he ended the message.

I love you? Jenna frowned. As far as she knew, Jane wasn't even seeing anyone. Who was this Ed person?

Whoever he was, he lived in Suffolk, he'd gone to some hall or other, and there was someone called George.

Intrigued, she flicked into the search engine on her mobile phone and typed in *Ed, Suffolk, Hall, George*. Just to see what would come up.

Right at the top of the list there was a link to 'Visitor Information, Somers Hall'.

Jenna skimmed through it. Interesting. David Somers, fifteenth baron, and his sons Edward and George. Hmm. It looked as if Jane was dating the younger son of a baron.

But why would Ed Somers be talking to his father about a paternity test?

Jenna thought about it a bit more, then smiled. Her contact at *Celebrity Life* would just *love* this story. And it would serve Jane right for being such a bitch and refusing to give her a bed for the night.

'What's all this about, Ed? You both look as if you haven't slept in days.' David frowned.

'You need to sit down, Dad. And you're going to need tea with about ten sugars,' Ed said.

'You're both here, so it's not as if George has finally managed to break his neck,' David said. 'What else could be that bad?'

'This.' George tossed the packet of letters and the diary onto the kitchen table. 'And I'm sorry, Dad, there's no way of softening it.'

'That's your mother's handwriting,' David said as he saw the open diary.

'Tea with ten sugars coming up,' Frances said with a sigh.

George told his father what he and Ed had worked out.

David looked in shock by the time George finished.

'I knew about the affairs, but it never occurred to me that you might be another man's child. Either of you.' His eyes narrowed. 'This doesn't change anything, you know. You're *mine*. Both of you.'

'And mine,' Frances chipped in. 'I know I'm not your biological mother, but you've both been my sons for more than a quarter of a century. I hope you two haven't been worrying about that.'

George and Ed exchanged a guilty glance.

'Idiots, the pair of you,' David said, rolling his eyes.

'Dad, there's the legal side to consider,' George said. 'I'm sorry, this is going to sound horrible and I'm certainly not wishing your life away, but we have to face it. If neither of us is yours, then the hall, the title and everything else reverts to another branch of the family when you die. Which means Frances loses her home and we all lose our childhood. Given this evidence...' He gestured to the papers.

'Which is all circumstantial, as Alice will no doubt tell you,' David cut in.

'No. It sheds enough doubt on the matter to mean that we need to do a DNA test,' Ed said gently. 'We've found a lab.'

'And paid for the kits. They came to my place yesterday,' George added.

'All you do is swab the inside of your mouth so you get cells and saliva, let it dry out, send the samples off in labelled envelopes and their machines do the rest,' Ed explained.

David sighed. 'Right. Let's get it over with.'

'We can't eat or drink for half an hour beforehand,' Ed said.

'Then tea is on hold,' Frances said, removing the pot from the middle of the table.

'There's a set procedure to follow,' Ed continued. 'We need to use gloves to make sure that none of the samples are contaminated, and the samples all have to dry out in separate glasses.'

'This is where it's really useful to have a scientist in the family,' George said, patting Ed's shoulder.

'How long does it take before we get the results?' David asked.

'About five working days. So that means we have a week to wait,' Ed said. 'And, no, they can't do it any faster. George already asked.'

'Whatever the results, *nothing* is going to change the fact that you're my sons and I love you,' David said softly.

'I love you, too,' George and Ed echoed.

Ed left George in Suffolk, knowing that his brother could get a lift back to London with one of their sisters the next day, and drove back to London late that afternoon. Back at his flat, he rang Jane. 'I'm home.'

'How was it?' she asked.

He sighed. 'Difficult.'

'Do you want me to come over? Or do you want to come here?'

'Can I come to you? I could do with your warmth.' And his flat didn't feel like home, the way hers did.

'Come over now,' she said. 'I've been baking. The choc-chip cookies are fresh out of the oven.'

'Now there's an offer I can't refuse.' He smiled despite himself. 'See you in a bit.'

She buzzed him up as soon as he rang the entryphone. He took the stairs three at a time, and wrapped his arms round her. 'That's better,' he said softly.

'How are George and your dad bearing up?' she asked.

We're a united front,' he said. 'In private as well as in public. Dad says that whatever the results show, he doesn't give a damn about the barony or the hall. We're his, and nothing's going to change that. Frances said the same.'

'And so will your sisters. I could've told you that,' she said. 'It's so obvious in your family, the love and affection—the way you talk to each other, the way you look at each other.' She swallowed hard. 'A million miles away from the way my family is.'

He held her closer. 'Oh, Janey. I'm sorry they give you such a hard time.'

'Some things you can't fix, and you have to learn not to beat yourself up about it,' she said. 'Remember that. And love…love can fix an awful lot of things. I'm not giving up on them quite yet.'

Monday morning started in a rush, with a breech birth where they needed to try turning the baby into a better position for delivery; and then a patient with all the symptoms of pre-eclampsia but with the addition of jaundice, meaning that it was more likely to be acute fatty liver of pregnancy. The only treatment was to deliver the baby; though, at thirty-five weeks, it was better for the baby to stay where he was for a while longer, until his lungs had matured properly.

Although the mum was on a drip to maintain her glucose levels and stop hypoglycaemia, routine monitoring of the baby showed that the foetus was in distress, and they ended up needing to take her straight into Theatre for an emergency section.

'We can't risk an epidural in case there's a bleed at the anaesthesia site. It'll have to be a general anaesthetic,' Ed said grimly.

Luckily the delivery was fine, without the mum having any of the clotting problems Jane and Ed had worried about. And he caught her eye at the end of the operation, mouthing, 'Well done.'

They worked so well as a team. So in tune.

Jane was writing up the notes at her desk when the phone rang.

'Janey? It's Sorcha. I've just seen the papers on the ward and it's not good. There's a story about Ed and his family. About how there's a paternity test going on.'

Jane went cold. How could the press possibly have got hold of the story?

'And it's worse than that, Jane. The source—they say it's close to Ed Somers. His girlfriend.'

'No. That's not true. I don't understand.' Jane blew out a breath. 'Thanks for the heads-up, Sorcha. I'd better take a look online and find out just what they're saying.'

The story was all over the place. *Somers: who's the real heir?*

Oh, hell. She needed to talk to Ed. Right now.

He was in his own office, talking on the phone; he acknowledged her with a gesture, then finished his conversation and replaced the receiver.

'Ed, do you have minute? There's something you really need to see,' she said urgently.

He looked grim. 'If it's what I think you're going to say, I already know the story's leaked. George just called me. He's been trying to get hold of me all morning, except we were in Theatre.'

'I haven't talked to anyone about this, Ed. Nobody at all. But the one I read—' she felt sick '—it says the source is me.'

'Maybe someone overheard you talking to me about it.'

She shook her head. 'I don't see how. And if they had, then surely they would've said that you were the source, not me.' Then a seriously nasty thought hit her. 'Your phone message.' She closed her eyes. 'Oh, my God. Saturday, when you and George went to see your dad. When you called me and left a message. Jenna must've still been in my flat. On her own.'

He looked mystified. 'Who's Jenna?'

Her throat felt dry. 'Oh, God. Can I close your door?'

'Sure.' He looked concerned.

She did so, and sat on the edge of his desk. 'I'm sorry, Ed. I should've told you about her before. You know I said my mum couldn't model any more once she was pregnant? It's because she was having twins.'

'You have a *twin*?' Ed looked at her in seeming disbelief. 'But you said you were an only child.'

'No,' she corrected, 'I told Charlotte I didn't have a brother or sister to look out for me.'

His expression went hard. 'That's semantics.'

She knew what he must be thinking—she'd lied to him, just as much as Camilla had. 'Ed, it's complicated. My family's not like yours. And you have no idea how much I envy you having George and the girls. They love you. I've never had that.' Her eyes pleaded for him to understand. 'The thing is, Jenna's like Mum. She's a supermodel. And she takes after Mum emotionally as well as physically. She's fragile. Any cold or virus, she always gets it. She had glandular fever the other year, and couldn't work for six months. Whereas I've got the constitution of an ox and I'm almost never ill.' She sighed. 'I tried to look after her. When we were kids and Mum was ill, I'd cook dinner for us. Jenna can't so much as boil an egg. But she told me at the weekend that she's always hated me for it. She called me Little Dr Perfect.' She dragged in a breath. 'I thought I was being caring and kind and nurturing, looking after her, and she thought I was just showing off.'

Ed stood up and put his arms round her. 'Oh, honey. You're very far from being a show-off. If anything, you hide your light under a bushel.'

'She wanted to stay at my place on Saturday—she lives out of a suitcase most of the time, so she normally expects to stay with me if she's in London—but she was spoiling for a fight, the second she walked through the door. I shouldn't have risen to it, but...' Well, she wasn't going to blame Ed for the fact that she'd been worried about him. 'I just snapped. I told I was going out and I didn't want her there when I got back. She must've heard your message and worked everything out.' She swallowed hard. 'I haven't told her or my parents that I'm even seeing you and I'm so sorry. I never wanted you to get mixed up in all this. I'll understand if you don't want to see me again, and I'll write an apology to your family.'

'Jane, you don't have to do that. And no way am I dumping you. It's not your fault that the story leaked.' He sighed. 'But I wish you'd told me about her before.'

'My relationship with my entire family is rubbish,

and I'm not very good at being a failure. I guess she's right about me wanting to think I'm perfect.'

He stroked her hair. 'Nothing of the sort. It isn't you.'

'I'm the one who doesn't fit into my family. So it feels like it's me.'

'What does Sorcha say?' he asked.

She rolled her eyes. 'You don't want to know what she calls Jenna. Especially after...' She stopped.

'After what?'

Given that her sister had hurt his family like this, she owed him the truth. 'Shaun.'

He blinked. 'Your *twin* was the one you caught him with?'

'Yes. '

Ed shook his head, looking stunned. 'Wow. That's seriously... I'm not sure I could forgive George if he'd done that to me.'

'George would never do that to you. He loves you.' She shrugged. 'Jenna hates me.'

Ed looked her straight in the eye. 'Please tell me you weren't worrying that the same thing would happen with me? That I'd meet her and go off with her?'

'No, of course not. Jenna might have tried it on with you, but you're not Shaun. You have integrity. I know you would've turned her down if she'd come on to you. I didn't tell you about her because...because no matter what I do, I can't get close to her, and she makes me feel bad. And I hate that.'

'What a mess.' Ed leaned his forehead against hers. 'And I hate that you're feeling bad when none of it's your fault.'

'It is. Because if I hadn't blown up at Jenna and

walked out, I would've been there to answer your call and she wouldn't have overheard the message. And she wouldn't have been mad at me for telling her to leave, and…' She shook her head. 'I need to talk to her and find out what the hell she was playing at. And then maybe I can call Dad and find out the number of Mum's old publicist, see if she can help with some damage limitation.'

'George is bound to know someone. So will Alice. Don't worry about it.'

Jenna wasn't answering her mobile, and her parents didn't answer their landline. Jane sighed. 'I'll try again later.'

'Janey. It's really not your fault.' Ed took her hand and kissed the back of her fingers. 'I know it wasn't you who leaked it. When I said to George I wanted to tell you, he said immediately that he trusted you, too.'

But, thanks to her family, she'd let him down. Broken their trust in her.

'You know, before all this blew up, I'd been thinking,' he said. 'You know I love you.'

'Even after this?'

'It's only talk. We can just ignore it. I'm sure worse things have been said about my family over the centuries.' He took a paperclip from his desk and began fiddling with it, then dropped to one knee in front of her. 'This is quite possibly the worst timing in the universe. I have no idea what the DNA results are going to show. If it's the wrong result, a lot of sticky stuff's going to hit the fan. All that "for richer, for poorer" stuff—I could be asking you to take an awful lot more of the rough than the smooth. And I know you've had a bad experience before, being engaged to someone who let you down badly. But I love you, Jane. I want to be with you, and life's a million times better with you than without you. And you're the one who's taught me I can put the past behind me and believe in the future. So will you do me the honour of marrying me, Jane?'

She caught her breath. 'Are you sure about this? I mean, with my mum and Jenna the way they are, it's never going to be easy with my family.'

He shrugged. 'They're difficult and they don't appreciate you. That's their problem. I'm not asking them to marry me—I'm asking you.' He reached up to stroke her face. 'For what it's worth, my family's got enough love to support us both through anything that happens in the future. But at the end of the day it's you and me. And I'll be right by your side, through the bad times as well as the good. So will you marry me, Jane?'

He was asking her to take a chance on him and join her future with his. To risk having a lot more rough times than smooth times.

She'd been here before, full of hopes and listening to a speech that turned out to be a piecrust promise, empty and easily broken.

But Ed wasn't Shaun. He wasn't saying that life would be a perfect paradise and offering her the moon and the stars. He was offering her something better: something realistic and solid. A life that wasn't always going to be easy, but he'd always be by her side.

She bent down to kiss him. 'I'd be honoured. Yes.'

'Good.' He slid the makeshift ring onto the ring finger of her left hand and kissed her. 'Let's go shopping after work tonight and choose the real ring together.'

He smiled. 'And it really doesn't matter if the paps follow us. It just means they'll have a nice story to print about my family instead of a pile of spite. And we're going to celebrate.'

CHAPTER FOURTEEN

JANE tried ringing Jenna's mobile and her parents' land-line several times more before the end of her shift, and at last her father answered.

'Dad, is Jenna there?' she asked.

'Yes. She's in bed.'

Which meant that Jenna could be feeling guilty enough about what she'd done to push her into depression. Normally, Jane would be sympathetic about her twin's depression, but not after what she'd just done. This time, Jenna had gone way, way too far.

'I need to talk to her.'

'Is something wrong?'

You could say that again. But Jane also knew that Martin Cooper would go into protective father mode and make excuses for Jenna. He always did. And this time her twin had to face up to what she'd done. Jane made her voice sound as light as she could. 'I just need to talk to her about something, Dad.'

'She's resting. Can't it wait?'

'It's important.'

His voice hardened. 'She told me you threw her out.'

Jane sighed. Of course Jenna had got her story in first. And she wouldn't have said *why* Jane asked her to leave; she only ever told the bit of the story that made her look a victim. 'Dad, there are two sides to every story, OK? Please. I really need to talk to her.'

'To apologise?'

If that was what it took to get Jenna on the phone... 'Yes,' she fibbed.

Jenna took her time coming to the phone. 'What do you want?'

'The story in the press.'

'What story?'

'The one about Ed. I know you were the leak. You must've heard his message and worked it out for yourself.' Jane sighed. 'Look, I get that you hate me, but this time it isn't just me you hurt, Jenna—you've hurt some really nice people, none of whom deserved this.'

'I was trying to help,' Jenna said defensively.

'Help? By spreading scandal in the tabloids? How do you work out *that's* helping?'

Jenna said nothing.

'You have to stop hurting people, Jenna. Or you're going to end up destroying yourself.'

Jenna's response was to hang up.

Two minutes later, Martin was on the phone to Jane. 'What the hell did you just say to her?' he demanded. 'She's breaking her heart down here.'

'Nothing like what I wanted to say, believe you me.' She put her father in the picture about exactly what Jenna had done, the people she'd hurt.

'It's a pity you don't think more about your *own* family,' Martin commented. 'You haven't even bothered seeing us this year.'

And they'd bothered coming to London to see her? Not. Jane finally saw red and everything she'd never said before came pouring out. 'Actually, Dad, have you ever considered things from *my* point of view? That Jenna expects and demands and takes all the time? And you let her get away with it. You never, ever tell her no. She can put the vilest stuff in the press about me, and it's fine, because it all boosts her career and that's far more important than not hurting me.'

'Jane! How can you say that?' He sounded shocked.

'Because it's true, Dad. You and Mum value looks above everything else. You've always made it clear that I'm the disappointment—the one who can't strut down a catwalk and be like Mum. But I'm doing just fine in my own field. You're the ones missing out. And in future you can just count me out. I'm tired of bending over backwards, being nice and saying nothing, no matter how badly Jenna behaves or how nasty she is.'

His silence gave her the courage to continue. 'And do you want to know why I've backed off from you all, why I haven't visited you this year? Then let me tell you why I gave Shaun his ring back last year. It's because I came home early and found him in bed with Jenna. My fiancé. In my bed. With my sister.'

'I had no idea.' He sounded stunned.

'Well, you do now. And this week she's leaked that story to the press—a private message that was on my answering machine—and claimed she was trying to help. If you can work out how the hell hurting people she doesn't know—nice, genuine, kind people—is helping, then do let me know. Have a nice day.' Gritting her teeth, she replaced the receiver.

She'd well and truly burned her bridges, now, so she might as well make it complete. She sent her father an email with a link to the *Celebrity Life* interview. *When the journalist wanted to do the interview and photo shoot, I was doing my exams. I said I couldn't do it and explained why. This is the result. Perhaps now you'll understand why I've had enough. I just can't do this any more. And if you can't accept that, then perhaps I'm better off without all of you.*

She was brushing the tears away when Ed walked in. 'Janey? What's happened?'

She told him about her conversations with her father and Jenna. 'I think I've well and truly done it now. I've as good as given him an ultimatum.' She sighed. 'I guess it's been a long time coming.'

'Maybe it'll make a difference, now you've told them how you feel. Sometimes it takes a crisis and some hard words to make things work properly,' he said. 'Look at Pippa Duffield and her mother-in-law. You're the one who persuaded her to try building bridges, and her mother-in-law responded brilliantly.'

'I know, but I don't think this is going to work out for me,' Jane said.

He wrapped his arms round her. 'I'm so sorry, Janey. If it helps, you're most definitely part of my family, and they all love you to bits.' He kissed her. 'And we're going to make it official tonight.'

After work, Ed took Jane to choose the ring: a single diamond in a pretty platinum setting.

'Now you're officially mine,' he said, and kissed the back of her ring finger before sliding the diamond on to it. 'Do you mind if we call in to see George and share the good news?'

'No, I'd like that.'

Except when they got to George's flat, the whole of Ed's family was there; so were Sorcha and Jake, and champagne was chilling in the fridge.

'Ed? Did you organise all this, just this afternoon?' she asked.

'After you said yes?' He smiled. 'Yup. I thought we could all do with some good news to celebrate. Do you mind?'

'No—I'm just…' She swallowed hard. He'd done this to surprise her, to make her see that his family would drop everything at incredibly short notice to come and celebrate their engagement, because they considered her one of them.

He kissed the single tear away. 'I know. Your family should be here, too,' he said softly, guessing her thoughts accurately. 'That's why I asked Sorcha.'

Her best friend. 'The sister I wish I had.' And who would never, ever hurt her the way her biological sister had. 'Thank you.'

'I love you, and you love me. And whatever lies ahead, we're going to cope with it,' Ed said, holding her close. 'Together.'

The next morning, a huge hand-tied bouquet arrived for Jane at the hospital.

'How lovely. Your family works fast,' she said to Ed. Then she opened the card. 'Oh.'

'Who are they from?'

'Jenna.' Jane sat down. 'She's never apologised to me before. Ever.' She paused. 'Then again, they might not actually be from her.'

'How do you mean? Isn't her name on the card?'

'Dad likes a quiet life. I know the way his mind works.' She sighed. 'He thinks that if I believe Jenna's apologised, I'll let it go and things can carry on as they were.'

Ed looked surprised. 'You think your father sent them?'

She nodded. 'With the best of intentions. But it somehow makes everything feel worse.' She put the card back in the envelope and left it on her desk next to the flowers. 'We have rounds to do.'

'OK.'

It was a busy morning on the ward; halfway through their rounds, Rosie called them to come and look at a mum whose labour wasn't progressing.

'Why it's taking so long is that the baby's turned round and his back is against yours,' Jane explained.

'You've done a wonderful job, but you've been in labour all yesterday afternoon and all last night, you're tired now, and the baby's starting to get a little bit distressed. I think it's time to say enough,' Ed said gently. 'I'd recommend a section.'

'I'd so wanted a natural birth,' the mum said, looking miserable. 'I was going to do this with just gas and air. But I might as well make my birth plan into a paper plane.'

Ed squeezed her hand. 'Babies don't read birth plans. They have their own ideas,' he said with a smile. 'Come on. You've done brilliantly. If you really want to keep going for another half an hour, then I'll go with that, but if you haven't progressed any further then it's time to call it a day, for the baby's sake. Then we'll ask you to sign the consent form for a section.'

She sighed. 'It's not going to work, is it?'

Jane squeezed her other hand. 'I'm sorry, I don't think it will.'

'OK. I'll sign the form now.'

Half an hour later, she was cuddling her baby, and Jane was wiping away her usual tears of joy at helping a new life enter the world. She went to her desk to write up her notes, and realised that there was a registered post envelope on her desk. And she recognised the handwriting: Jenna's.

Warily, she opened the envelope.

Jane,

I'm sorry. I've always been jealous of you—you're the clever one, the strong one, and I'm as flaky and hopeless as Mum. You always make me feel as if I'm not good enough.

Jane stared at the words, barely taking them in. She'd made Jenna feel useless? But—that wasn't at all what she'd intended. She'd tried to make Jenna feel cherished, looked after.

I'm sorry I gave you a hard time when we were growing up. And I'm sorry for what I did to Ed and his family. I hope he doesn't dump you because of me. I'll apologise to him in person, if you want me to.

Jenna was actually apologising. Sincerely.

I hope you like the flowers. I sent them, not Dad.

So Jenna, too, knew how their father's mind worked.

I've had time to think about it. I know it's a lot to ask and I haven't been good to you, but can we start again? This time, as equals?
Love, Jenna.

Ed came over. 'Janey, are you OK?'

Wordlessly, she handed him the card.

He read it swiftly. 'Wow. I would never have expected that.'

'Me neither. I don't...' She shook her head. 'I don't know what to think, how to react. I mean, it's the first time she's ever offered me any kind of olive branch.'

And then Gwen, one of the junior nurses, came over with another huge bouquet of flowers. 'Janey, is there something you're not telling us? Like it's your birthday or something?'

Jane exchanged a glance with Ed. There was something they weren't telling, yet, but they were waiting until the DNA results came back before they told the rest of the world. 'No, it's not my birthday. I had a fight with my sister.'

Gwen rolled her eyes. 'Tell me about it. I have those all the time—my sister never sends me flowers, though.'

'This is a first for her,' Jane said dryly. She opened the card and read it.

I'm sorry. Jenna's fragile, like your mother. You're like me, the one who gets on with things. I never meant you to feel second-best. You're not, and it won't happen again. I'm so proud of you, Jane. And I love you.
Dad.

* * *

'They're from my dad,' she said.

'Did you have a fight with him, too?' Gwen looked surprised. 'You've never fallen out with anyone since I've known you. And then you had two fights in one night?'

Jane gave her a wry smile. 'I guess it's a bit like buses. You wait for ages, then two come along at once.'

'Well, they're lovely flowers,' Gwen said with a smile. 'Enjoy them, you lucky thing.'

When Gwen left, Jane handed the card to Ed.

'Judging by that card and all those flowers,' he said when he'd finished reading it, 'I think your family's finally started to see you for who you are—and realised your worth.'

'Maybe.' There was a huge lump in her throat. 'I'd better ring them. I have some making up to do.'

'Go for it. And come and grab me if you need me,' he said, and kissed her.

CHAPTER FIFTEEN

THE results of the test were due back on the Monday. Jane and Ed had both managed to swap shifts so they had a day off to wait in for the post; David and Frances had come up from Suffolk to stay with George; and the girls were all on standby to come straight over to Ed's flat as soon as the post arrived and he called them.

Ed couldn't settle to anything and was pacing the flat. There were lines of tension on his face, and he glanced at the clock every couple of seconds and then looked shocked that so little time had passed since he'd last looked.

'Oh, honey.' Jane kissed him lightly. 'There's not much longer to wait.' If only she could take this strain from him.

'This is worse than waiting for exam results to come. George said the same thing. You've always got a good idea how you did in your exams. This...this is completely out of my control.' He shook his head in obvious frustration. 'I know who I am right now, but that envelope could tell me I'm someone completely different.'

Jane squeezed his hand. 'Ed, whatever the results are, you know they won't change how I feel about you.

I love you for who you are, not for who your biological father is. And David will always, always see you as his son, regardless of what the test says.'

'I know. And thank you. Sorry. I'm being difficult.' He sighed. 'This waiting is killing me. I can't *breathe*, Jane. My chest feels tight and my head hurts, and it feels as if someone swapped my blood for ice.'

There was nothing she could say, nothing she could do, to make things better. Only hold him.

When the intercom buzzed, he froze. 'Oh, my God— the results are coming by registered post. That must be the postman now.' He rushed over to the intercom. 'Yes?'

'Can you *please* let us in before I start threatening the paps with my crutches and Alice has to bail me out in court?' George asked plaintively.

Ed buzzed him up and went to open his front door. Jane switched the kettle on and busied herself making coffee.

'The results aren't here yet,' she could hear Ed say. 'I said I'd call you the minute they came.'

'I just couldn't stand the wait any longer.'

'Even when they do turn up, you know we can't open them until the girls are here,' Ed warned. 'We promised.'

'True, but I'd still rather wait here with you.' George limped into the kitchen and hugged Jane. 'Hello, Janey. How's my favourite sister-in-law-to-be?'

'As nervous as you lot are,' she said. 'Ed can't settle to anything.'

'Me neither. I'm not good at waiting at the best of times, and this is driving me crazy,' George said.

'Especially as he had to put up with me driving us

here from his flat,' David said wryly as he walked into the kitchen. 'Trust me, we're all desperate for his leg to be good enough for him to drive himself again, so we don't have to put up with all the instructions and comments.'

Frances ruffled George's hair. 'Don't listen to your dad, love. He's a worse passenger than you are—which is why I never drive him anywhere!'

Jane handed round mugs of coffee. Although she'd put cookies on a plate, nobody was hungry and they just sat there in the middle of the table.

'I wish there was a way you could just wind time forward,' George said.

'Me, too,' Ed agreed.

'We need to talk about something else. *Anything* else,' David said.

'The wedding?' George suggested. 'We can plan it all now. I mean, we have the bride here, the groom, the best man...'

'Do you seriously think we'd let you loose on the planning?' Jane asked. 'You'd have us getting married in mid-air on one of your paragliding things!'

'What a great idea, Janey.' George dimpled at her. 'Maybe we could offer that as one of the wedding packages in Suffolk.' Then he frowned. 'Well. Maybe not. It might not be my place to suggest that any more.'

'Of course it will be.' David rolled his eyes. 'I already told you. I don't give a damn what the genetic specialists say; you're both my sons.'

'And mine,' Frances added. 'You don't have to be biologically related to be someone's parent.'

'Frances, you've been a much better mother to us than ours could ever have been,' Ed said quietly.

'Actually, George and I have thought of you as our mum for years.'

Jane could see Frances' eyes mist over with tears. 'Oh, Ed.'

'It's true,' George said. 'And, Dad—we couldn't have asked for anyone better than you.'

'I couldn't have asked for better sons. Even though you give me grey hairs with those damned extreme sports, George.' David patted his shoulder. 'Ed, how does this DNA thing work exactly?'

'They look at genetic markers. With every pair of genes, you inherit one from each parent. Obviously we couldn't give the lab a maternal sample, but if your DNA profile matches one of each pair of alleles in our DNA profile, then it proves you're our father.'

David was white-faced as he asked, 'And if it doesn't match?'

Ed took a deep breath. 'Then the results will say that they exclude you from the possibility of being our father.'

The minutes ticked by, slower and slower; none of them felt like making small talk, and the kitchen was filled with a silence so heavy that it weighed down on all of them. Ed resumed pacing, George drummed his fingers on his crutches, and David turned his cup round and round in his hands.

Finally, the intercom went again; this time, it really was the postman.

Ed buzzed him up, then said, 'George, ring the girls while I sign for the letters.'

When he came back, George said, 'They're all getting taxis. They'll be here in twenty minutes, tops.' He blew out a breath. '*Twenty more minutes*. Do we really have to wait for them?'

'Yes, we do—this is a family thing, and we're all in it together. Right, Jane?' Frances said.

It warmed Jane that Frances had included her. 'Right,' she agreed.

Finally the girls arrived; they all refused coffee and just leaned against the worktops in the kitchen, looking grim.

'OK. This is it,' Ed said, and swallowed hard. He ripped the first envelope open and unfolded the sheets of paper.

'And?' George asked impatiently.

Ed scanned the paper. 'Yours and Dad's markers match—it says there's a 99.9 per cent probability that Dad's your father. Which is as good as it gets.' He looked up and met his brother's gaze. 'Thank God.'

'And you?' David asked.

Ed took a deep breath and opened the other envelope. He looked at the sheet swiftly, and sagged in apparent relief. 'Me, too.'

'So all that stuff in her diaries and those letters… She was completely wrong,' George said.

'Your mother was completely wrong about an awful lot of things,' David said. 'I'm sorry that you both had to go through this.' He hugged both his sons. 'And now we tell the press the truth, and they'll can go and find someone else to write their stories about.'

'If this is an official statement, Dad, do you need it written down?' Alice asked.

'It'll be short and sweet,' David said. 'And, no, I don't need to write it down. What I'm saying comes straight from the heart.'

The whole family, united, went down to the entrance to the flats. David stood between his sons. Flashes started popping, and there was a barrage of questions until it became very obvious that David had something to say and he wasn't going to answer a single question until they'd given him a chance to speak.

Eventually the hubbub died down.

'Thank you,' David said. 'I'm aware that you've all been interested in the paternity of my sons, George and Edward. So I'm delighted to announce that the DNA testing has conclusively...' His voice cracked, and he stopped.

George put his hand on his father's shoulder to bolster him.

'Conclusively proved that my sons are...' David stopped again.

Clearly their father had been bottling up his feelings all week. Despite his assertion that he hadn't needed to write anything down, emotion had robbed David of his voice and he couldn't make the announcement.

George widened his eyes at Ed and gave the tiniest nod.

Ed decoded the message: *you're the scientist—it's better coming from you.*

He lifted his chin. 'The DNA testing proves without a shadow of a doubt that George and I are our father's biological sons.'

There was murmuring from the press pack. Obviously this was robbing them of the scandal story they'd been hoping for.

Maybe it was time to give them something else instead. Something much, much more positive. He held out his hand to Jane.

She gave him a tiny nod, and stepped forward to take his hand.

'We also have some other news,' Ed said. 'I've found the love of my life and she's agreed to marry me. I know she'll mean every word of those vows, because she agreed to marry me before we knew the results of the testing, and she didn't care whether they'd make me a prince or a pauper. Dr Jane Cooper and I are going to get married as soon as possible.'

'So is there a third bit of news, Ed?' one of the journalists called out.

Ed laughed. 'You mean, are we getting married because we have to?' But this would be nothing like his marriage to Camilla. 'No.'

'We're getting married quickly,' Jane said, 'simply because we don't want to have to wait for the rest of our lives to start.'

'Exactly.' Ed pulled her into his arms, bent her back over one arm and kissed her. Thoroughly. And the flashing lightbulbs felt like stars exploding in his head.

The headlines the next morning ran, *George is the boy*.

And Jane smiled at the caption beneath the photograph of Ed kissing her speechless: *Ed with Dr Cinderella*.

The following Sunday afternoon, she and Ed headed down to Suffolk, with Sorcha and Jake following them; Alice had the task of driving George, and had threatened to ask Bea to bring gaffer tape to shut him up if he said a word out of place.

'We could've had a big party, you know,' Ed said.

'A marquee, a band, a chocolate fountain and lots of champagne.'

'I just wanted the important people there,' she said softly. 'A small, intimate family lunch to celebrate our engagement.'

Ed reached over to squeeze her hand. 'I spoke to your dad on Friday night. If they don't come, *don't* take it personally. It's at least a seven-hour drive from Cornwall to Suffolk, and that's assuming they don't get stuck in traffic.'

Which meant that they would've needed to drive up the day before and stay nearby. Jane was pretty sure that Frances would've offered to put the Coopers up, but she was equally sure that her mother would've refused the invitation.

Her father and Jenna had wished them well. Jenna had even said the photos in the press of Ed kissing Jane were gorgeous, like a fairy-tale. But there had been a resounding silence from Sophia.

Well, OK. Maybe her mother would thaw out by the wedding, next month.

Though Jane wasn't going to hold out much hope.

When they finally arrived at the hall, Frances greeted them warmly. 'Come through to the rose garden. David's spent all morning putting a gazebo up.' She glanced up at the skies. 'And it looks as if the weather's going to be kind, so we won't have to make a run for the house.'

George and the girls were already there, Sorcha and Jake were only a couple of minutes behind, and Jane was very, very aware of the empty places that would be at the end of the beautifully laid table. Where her family should've been.

'I thought a cold buffet might be best,' Frances said. 'Though I have hot new potatoes in the Aga, and the bread's still warm.'

Jane's eyes widened as she saw the spread. 'Wow. That's fabulous. Frances, you've gone to so much trouble. That's an awful lot of work.'

'It was a labour of love,' Frances assured her. 'We're so pleased you're going to be part of our family.'

If only her own family felt the same way. But she damped down the disappointment and forced herself to smile.

It was only when Ed nudged her and said softly, 'More guests to greet,' that she turned round and saw her parents walking across the lawn towards them, along with Jenna.

'Jane.' Sophia, as always, greeted her daughter with an air kiss. Jane tried very hard not to mind.

But Jenna surprised her with a warm hug. 'You look beautiful,' she said. 'My little sister.'

Jane blinked the tears back. 'Only by five minutes.'

And Martin surprised her further by holding her really, really tightly. 'Janey. My clever, special girl,' he whispered. 'I think your mother and I have got a lot of making-up to do to you.'

She swallowed hard. 'It doesn't matter, Dad. Not any more.'

'No, because you and Ed have each other. This one's going to do right by you.' He smiled at her. 'I never liked the other one in any case. He wasn't right for you. But Ed…he's the one.'

'He certainly is.'

She caught Ed's eye, and he mouthed, 'I love you.'

David tapped a wine glass with a fork. 'Now we're

all here, I think we should have the official business before lunch.'

'Absolutely.' Ed took Jane's hand and led her to the middle of the gazebo. 'We already know Jane agreed to marry me when everything was going wrong and it looked as if she was going to have a lot more of the rough than the smooth. But that's all behind us now, and I think it's made all of us stronger. So today I want to do this properly and get engaged officially, with the people we love most in the world around us, and in a place that's special to both of us.' He dropped to one knee and opened the velvet-covered box, just as he'd done in her kitchen. 'Jane Cooper, I love you with my whole heart. Will you do me the honour of being my wife?'

There was only one answer she could possibly give. 'I love you, too. Yes.'

And as Ed slid the ring back on her finger, everyone cheered and George opened the champagne with a very, very loud pop.

* * * * *

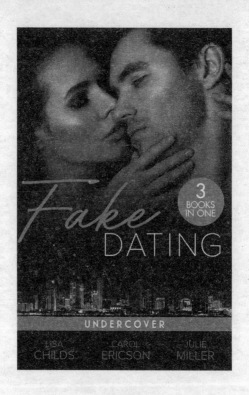

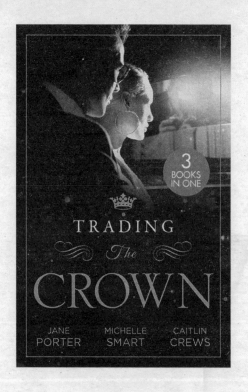